monsoonbooks

THE SHALLOW SEAS

Dawn Farnham was born in Portsmouth, England in 1949. Her parents emigrated to Perth, Western Australia, when she was two. She grew up a sandgroper, barefoot and free, roaming the bushy suburbs and beaches with her friends. In the 1960s she, like so many other young Aussies, left on a ship for London, aged seventeen. In the Swinging Sixties she met and married her journalist husband, moved to Paris, learned French and travelled round Europe in a Volkswagen Beetle.

As a foreign correspondent, her husband was posted to exotic locations and they lived in China, Hong Kong, Korea and Japan in the 1980s and 1990s. During this time she raised two daughters and taught English. Back in London she returned to school, doing a BA in Japanese at The School of Oriental and African Studies (SOAS) and a Master's Degree at Kings College.

She and her husband now live in Singapore where she is a volunteer guide at the Peranakan Museum and the Asian Civilisations Museum. It is in this thriving port city-state that she found her muse and began to write, finding particular pleasure in Singapore's colourful and often wild past. This is her second novel and continues the story of Charlotte Macleod, who first appeared in *The Red Thread*.

For more information about Dawn Farnham and her books, visit www.dawnfarnham.com.

The Shallow Seas

A tale of two towns: Singapore and Batavia

DAWN FARNHAM

monsoon

monsoonbooks

Published in 2008
by Monsoon Books Pte Ltd
52 Telok Blangah Road
#03-05 Telok Blangah House
Singapore 098829
www.monsoonbooks.com.sg

ISBN: 978-981-08-1079-5

Cover photograph copyright©National Museum of Singapore,
National Heritage Board

National Library Board Singapore Cataloguing in Publication Data
Farnham, Dawn, 1949-
The shallow seas / Dawn Farnham. – Singapore : Monsoon Books, 2008.
p. cm.
ISBN-13 : 978-981-08-1079-5 (pbk.)
1. Singapore – Fiction. 2. Java (Indonesia) – Fiction. I. Title.
PR6106
823.92 -- dc22   OCN255893252

Printed in Singapore
12 11 10 09 08   1 2 3 4 5 6 7 8 9

For Roger

Glossary

Alus: Javanese word meaning "graceful and refined".

Ang moh: A racial epithet that originates from Hokkien (Min Nan) and is used to refer to white people in Malaysia and Singapore. Literally meaning "red-haired", the term implies that the person referred to is a devil, a concept explicitly used in the Cantonese term *gweilo* ("foreign devil").

Armenia: Landlocked, mountainous country between the Black Sea and the Caspian Sea surrounding Mount Ararat. In 301, it became the first country in the world to adopt Christianity. Located between Europe and Asia, Armenia was invaded countless times and its people spread all over the earth. Part of the Soviet Union until its collapse, it is now an independent country.

Boreh: A fragrant yellow paste made from spices and used as an unguent.

Borobodor: Ninth-century Mahayana Buddhist monument in central Java.

Brieswijk: The place of breezes.

Bugis: The people of southern Sulawesi. They are still outstanding shipbuilders, sailors and navigators who have traded legitimately in the region for thousands of years. When the colonial powers displaced traditional trading relations of the region, the Bugis turned to piracy and slave trading.

Claddagh ring: Traditional Irish ring, given in friendship or worn as a wedding ring. The design and customs associated with it originated in the Irish fishing village of Claddagh, located just outside the city of Galway. The Claddagh's distinctive design features two hands clasping a heart, usually surmounted by a crown. The elements of this symbol are often said to correspond to the qualities of love (the heart), friendship (the hands), and loyalty (the crown). The way that a Claddagh ring is worn on the hand is usually intended to convey the wearer's availability, or lack thereof. Traditionally, if the ring is on the right hand with the heart facing outward and away from the body, this indicates that the person wearing the ring is not in any serious relationship: "their heart is open". When worn on the right hand but with the heart facing inward, this indicates the person wearing the ring is in a relationship, or that "someone has captured their heart". A Claddagh worn on the left hand ring finger, facing outward away from the body, generally indicates that the wearer is engaged. When worn on the left hand ring finger and facing inward toward the body, it generally means that the person wearing the ring is married.

Danjang desa: The spirit of the village.

Dukun: Medicine man, healer in Java.

Eling: Pronounced "ailing", it means "remember". When a person is overcome with sorrow or anger, the Javanese advise that it is necessary to *eling*, to regain self-control. Self-control is the highest Javanese value. In this context, *eling* refers to a high level of self-awareness that enables the individual to observe and control all movements of the self, both inner and outer—its actions, words, and thoughts.

Factories: The name for trading stations where goods were imported, stored and exported for sale in Europe.

Gamelan: A *gamelan* is a musical ensemble of Indonesia typically featuring a variety of instruments such as metallophones, xylophones, drums and gongs; bamboo flutes, bowed and plucked strings, and vocalists may also be included. The term refers more to the set of instruments than the players of those instruments. A *gamelan* as a set of instruments is a distinct entity, built and tuned to stay together—instruments from different gamelan are not interchangeable. The word "*gamelan*" comes from the Javanese word "*gamel*", meaning to strike or hammer, and the suffix "an", which makes the root a collective noun.

Guanxi: A network of contacts which an individual can call upon when something needs to be done, and through which he or she can exert influence on behalf of another. In addition, *guanxi* can describe a state of general understanding between two people.

Isin: *Isin* is a powerful concept in Javanese thought. *Isin* is what happens when you cannot bear what you are seeing and feeling, when you are watching but no longer controlling your reactions, when your energy mounts in a vain attempt to deny what is here. *Isin* in particular, together with all extreme emotions in general, produces imbalance; love, hate, euphoria, despair and fury are all subject to the "law of balance".

Jamu: Traditional herbal medicine in Java.

Kajang Mats: Mats made of the leaves of palm trees, used for roof coverings on boats and as seating.

Kala: The Kala is a monster that devours itself, representing the relentless passage of time. It is usually shown without its lower jaw, which it has already eaten. Originally a Hindu god, it is often seen above windows and doors.

Kampong: Malay word for village.

Kapitan Cina: The leader of the Chinese community in colonial cities. The Kapitan and his Council ensured a good relationship between the European and Chinese members of the town, dealt with disputes and crime amongst the Chinese community, and registered births, marriages and deaths.

Kemiri: Candlenuts. The oil of mashed candlenuts made hair glossy and was said to keep grey hair at bay.

Kraton: Javanese word for royal palace.

Kris: The *kris* or *keris* is a distinctive, asymmetrical dagger indigenous to Indonesia, Malaysia, Brunei, Southern Thailand and the southern Philippines. Both a weapon and spiritual object, the *kris* is often considered to have an essence or presence, with some blades possessing good luck and others possessing bad.

La seraille: The seraglio, the luxurious women's harem quarters in a Sultan's palace.

Laudanum: An opium tincture, sometimes sweetened with sugar and also called wine of opium, used widely during the Victorian era.

Loro Kidul: Queen of the South Sea, a fierce goddess to whom all the kings of Java are still wed on ascending to power, their power and legitimacy being vested in her. Myth says she was the daughter of the last king of the Western Javanese Hindu Pajajaran kingdom, which was overthrown by the Muslim invasions.

Merang: A dye made from the burnt stalks of rice to conceal greying hair. Used throughout tropical Asia for centuries, the soaked stalks form an inky liquid which foams like a shampoo and acts, in addition, as a cleansing agent and a tonic.

Mestizo: Spanish term meaning "to mix", the term spread quickly and became generic and synonymous for "mixed race".

Nyai: A native woman, consort, or concubine of a European man in the Dutch East Indies. The status and the fate of the *nyai* varied widely, depending entirely on the actions of the man. After Christian baptism, she could become his wife or he could legitimise her and her children as a secondary "wife". Once legitimised and recognised in law, she was entitled to upkeep by the man and to inherit part of the man's estate. In theory, and often in fact, a legitimised native *nyai* could quickly pass from being a slave to being a wealthy widow of a Dutch official or merchant. On the other hand, many *nyai* could simply be abandoned and, up to 1782, if they were still slaves at the death of the man, both the *nyai* and her offspring could be separated and sold to other owners. After 1782, this practice was prohibited.

Pempek: *Pempek* or *empek-empek* is a delicacy from Palembang which is made of fish and sago.

Pinisi: Double masted gaff-ketch rig boat built by the sailors of South Sulawesi. It was the ubiquitous commercial trading vessel of the Southeast Asian islands.

Prahu: Literally, the Malay word meaning boat. There are many types of *prahu* throughout the islands of the archipelago.

Prambanan: Largest Hindu temple compound in Indonesia, located near Yogyakarta. Built in the 9th century, a temple to the glory of the Hindu gods, Shiva, Vishnu and Brahma.

Qi: Also commonly spelled *ch'i*, this is a fundamental concept of traditional Chinese culture. *Qi* is believed to be part of every living thing that exists, as a kind of "life force" or "spiritual energy". It is frequently translated as "energy flow", or literally as "air" or "breath".

Revenue Farm: A revenue farm is a franchise with a license to collect state revenue and with a monopoly right to practice a certain business. Such a monopoly was granted by the state government to a "farmer" for a limited period of time in a strictly defined location in a city, district or province. In return, the farmers/bidders had to pay the government in advance to be guaranteed monopoly status. In Java, the revenue farms were almost exclusively licensed to the Chinese and included monopolies on gambling establishments, liquor distribution, entertainment, transport, road toll gates, markets, money lending and opium.

Ronggeng: A type of social dance in which couples exchange poetic verses as they dance to the music of a violin or gong. By the 19th century, *ronggeng* dancers were popular entertainers, singers and dancers in Java, usually assumed also to be prostitutes.

Sambal: A condiment or side dish used in Indonesia, Malaysia, Singapore, the southern Philippines and Sri Lanka, as well as the Netherlands, made from a variety of peppers, although chilli peppers are the most common.

Saman tree: The rain tree, a tall, wide-spreading tree used for shade. Its leaves close when the weather is overcast, allowing rain to penetrate the canopy and nourish the plants beneath, one of the few tropical jungle trees to do so.

Sireh: Malay word for betel. The leaves of the betel tree are used as a wrapping for the slices of the areca nut, lime paste and other ingredients and chewed as a stimulant.

Slametan: Communal feast symbolising the unity of those participating in it. The ceremony is taken from the Javanese word slamet which means a peaceful state of equanimity, in which nothing happens. A Slametan takes place at marriages, births and deaths, major events in the Islamic calendar, and to mark unusual events: moving house, going on a long trip, illness, sorcery, etc.

Slendang: Long cloth used to carry a young child around the shoulders

Sultan: The royal appellation of the kings of the court of Yogyakarta. By definition they are secondary to the Susunan, for their court was created out of the division of the lands of Mataram by the Dutch in 1830.

Susunan or *Susuhunan*: The Emperor of the Royal Court of Surakarta, sometimes called *Solo*. The *Susunan* is recognised as the legitimate descendant of the court of the second Mataram dynasty, the Muslim dynasty which displaced the previous Hindu Sailendra dynasty. Its name was taken from an older Hindu/Buddhist dynasty called Mataram which ruled Java from the 8th to the 10th century.

Tuaru: Hibiscus bush. The crushed leaves were commonly used for hair washing in Indonesia before the advent of manufactured shampoo.

Tempeh: Referred to as the "Javanese meat", *tempeh* is made by a natural culturing and controlled fermentation process that binds soybean particles into a cake form. Invented by the Javanese, it is now common in other parts of Southeast Asia as well. It is still especially popular on the island of Java, where it is a staple source of protein.

VOC: Or the Vereenigde Oostindische Compagnie in Dutch, literally "United East Indian Company", it was established in 1602, when the States-General of the Netherlands granted it a 21-year monopoly to carry out colonial activities in Asia. The first multinational corporation in the world, it was also the first company to issue stock. It remained an important trading concern for almost two centuries until it went bankrupt and was formally dissolved in 1800, its possessions and debts being taken over by the government of the Batavian Republic. The VOC's territories became the Dutch East Indies and were expanded over the course of the 19th century to include the whole of the Indonesian archipelago.

Waringan tree: Indonesian name for the banyan tree.

Wayang: *Wayang* is an Indonesian word for theatre, but comes from the Javanese word for shadow or imagination and also connotes "spirit". Famous stories of the *wayang* are the Javanese adaptation of tales from the *Mahabharata*, of which the most famous character is Arjuna. *Wayang kulit* shadow puppets, prevalent in Java and Bali, are the best known of the Indonesian *wayang*. *Kulit* means skin and refers to the leather construction of the puppets that are carefully chiseled with very fine tools and supported with carefully shaped buffalo horn handles and control rods.

Wei qi: Classical board game known in the West by its Japanese name, *Go*, and believed to have originated at least 4-5,000 years ago. Some say that the board, with ten points out from the centre in all directions, may have originally served as a forerunner to the abacus. Others think it may have been a fortune-telling device, with black and white stones representing yin and yang. By the time of Confucius, *wei qi* had already become one of the "Four Accomplishments" (along with brush painting, poetry and music) that must be mastered by the Chinese gentleman.

Zhen Jiu: Acupuncture

Zhi Ya: Acupressure

"The shallow sea that foams and murmurs on the shores of the thousand islands, big and little, which make up the Malay Archipelago has been for centuries the scene of adventurous undertakings."

Joseph Conrad, *The Rescue*

Foreword

Water links Singapore and Jakarta, which once was Batavia. Long ago, during the ice ages, they were part of the Asian continent and shared one vast shore called Sundaland. When the ice melted and water crept over it, the land below became the Sunda Shelf and the lands above became the Malay Peninsula and the Malay Archipelago. The big islands of Sumatra, Java and Borneo were born and so, too, the myriad smaller ones.

The warm waves that whisper on the shores
of the thousand islands
have a thousand tales.
This is one.

Prologue

Et in Arcadia ego. Once I, too, lived in paradise.

The words came into her mind as she stood, still and silent as stone. Her eyes followed the waves that curled and glinted in the long trail of the ship's wake leading back to the cliffs of Singapore. The island with the red earth—*tanah merah*; the cliffs now mere ruddy smudges on the horizon. Her sojourn in Arcadia had been brief. For the second time in her short life, a ship was carrying her away from joy and into misery. Suffering the grief of absence, condemned to remember joy and then remember absence, an endless circle. Grim-visaged comfortless Despair, and Sorrow's piercing dart. Until this moment she had not thought beyond the parting, the heart-stopping moment of leaving. The black brig rose on the dark swell, and she felt sick.

A cloud drifted across the morning sun, smothering the light, plunging the vista into obscurity, and the brig sank into the valley of the wave. The land vanished and the world became water. Charlotte leaned against the rail and began to vomit violently, coughing, retching, tears coursing down her face. She had left him. She felt the power of her body ebb from her so quickly that she slumped to the deck. She would not see him again. She could still feel the strength of his arms, the imprint of his body against hers, could hear, in the roar of the wind, his deep voice, bitter and hurt. It would never relent, she thought, this grief. She felt a vice, like fingers, around her heart, as if his hands had sped over the waves to pull her back to him. Taking no care for the mess on her clothes she rose, stumbled to a low chest and began to climb.

As she grasped the rail, strong hands gripped her waist, carrying her back down to the deck. She turned in fury to the man who had stopped her and struck him as hard as she could. She began to struggle with a grim determination, gasping for breath. She had to go back to Singapore, to Zhen.

Tigran held her firmly until her desperation lessened and she let him support her. She looked up, and he saw that in the distraction of her mind she did not recognise him.

I have to go back, you see," she said shakily, in her most reasonable voice. She shook her head. "It's a mistake. Can you take me back please?"

"Yes, I will take you back, but now rest a little and take some refreshment."

As he felt her legs fail, Tigran took her in his arms and signalled a man to fetch the Javanese maid who had been brought on this voyage to care for Charlotte. In the cabin, he laid her gently on the bed. She did not stir, and he saw she was asleep, overcome with sickness and emotion. He left the maid to care for her, changed his clothes, felt briefly the place on his cheek where her blow, surprisingly strong, had landed, and went back to the deck.

Tigran Manouk was the master of this brig, *Queen of the South*, and a fleet of merchant ships, part of his vast empire in the Dutch East Indies which included coffee, tea, sugar plantations and factories, indigo farms, ship-building, banking. His father, Gevork, an Armenian merchant, had become one of the richest men in Java—so rich that, on occasion, he had bailed out the impoverished Dutch government in Batavia as it struggled to take over administration of the former VOC possessions.

Charlotte Macleod had been just eighteen when Tigran met her in Singapore. He had been visiting his sister Takouhi and his niece Meda, a lovely, sweet-hearted girl, daughter of the new settlement's master architect, George Coleman. George had fallen in love with Takouhi years before in Batavia, where, as a young man, he had built sugar factories and embankments for Tigran's father. George and Takouhi had been together for eighteen years, until Meda fell dangerously ill.

Grief tightened its fingers around Tigran's chest, and he took a deep breath of windy, salty air. Takouhi had been sure that a return to the cool hills of Java, the *jamu* and the magic of the *dukun* would cure her child, but they had not. Meda had died only a few months ago. It was a blow so shattering that no one had yet recovered. George, crushed, had resigned his government position as Superintendent of Public Works and disappeared to Europe. No word had been heard from him since.

Takouhi and Charlotte had become close friends in Singapore. When George left, Charlotte had written to Takouhi, and Takhoui dispatched Tigran to fetch her friend and bring her to Batavia. This Tigran did gladly, for he had, the very night he had met Charlotte, and to his own vast surprise, floated like a powerless moth inexorably and dangerously into her flame. Love had taken possession of him, and try though he had for a brief moment to reason her from his heart, he had realised, with a strange and joyful acceptance, that he would not be able to forget this woman. She was like an exquisite melody, a haunting tune which inhabited his mind.

Now he could hardly believe his good fortune in having her here. He frowned. There was a man—Takouhi had mentioned a man in Singapore. A love affair. It would cause a great scandal, for Charlotte's brother, Robert, was the Chief of Police of Singapore, and such a storm would have doubtless meant the end of his position. That was all Tigran had known when he set out on this voyage.

But he knew more now. Charlotte's reaction to this departure told him of the violence of her feelings. Love is the devil's weapon, he thought, for it forces reason and all the natural instincts of self-care from the mind, like a damnable battering ram. His own feelings for Charlotte were of an intensity he had not believed possible at his age. Tigran was forty years old, toughened and shielded by experience—so he had believed—from life's jolts. His looks belied his years, for his eyes were full of a restless energy, and his body retained its youthful vigour. Dark-eyed, he wore his long black hair pirate fashion, half-braided and beaded. Although the Manouks were Armenian Christians, brother and sister had been raised by native women, and many of Java's ancient customs clung to them.

Tigran reflected on his desire for Charlotte, so vulnerable now, so beautiful though that every moment he was with her he wanted to bury his face and hands in her hair, kiss her lips until she could hardly breathe. He subdued the effect these thoughts invariably brought upon his body, gripped the shroud rigging and stared into the moiling waves.

He had intended to ask Charlotte to marry him on his last visit to Singapore, but Meda's illness had forced his rapid return to Batavia. Now he was angry at himself for not coming back immediately, though it had been impossible whilst Meda was so deathly sick. That was forgotten now in his ardour, and he cursed and punched the wood of the rail hard, wincing as his skin broke from the blow. He would have taken her to Java, and this damn mess with the other man would not have happened.

He watched the blood well from his skinned knuckles and hung his hand over the rail, gazing as a stream of scarlet coursed down his fingers, feeling the sting of the salt spray. Regret, regret! Well, he would not regret again. He was determined to have her promise before they landed. This enforced departure of hers would be his good fortune. Time would heal her, she would forget the other man, and he would make her the happiest woman in the world.

He ordered the wind sail to be rigged to send fresh air to the cabins under deck and went below.

1

Charlotte's first impression of Batavia was of a ghost town. It was not just the oppressive thoughts in her mind at leaving Singapore, Zhen and Robert. Nothing could have stood in starker contrast to the harbour at Singapore, with its low red-roofed buildings, its wide and busy harbour of sapphire blue, the gentleness of its island sands and the low green hills beyond. The *Queen of the South* had threaded its way through the thousand islands which lay before the port of Batavia and dropped anchor near the mouth of the Haven Kanaal, the stone-walled channel which projected far out into the shallow sea like a long grey tongue. The sky, overcast and hazy, turned the water of the roadstead to slate.

It had been two hundred years since ships had sailed up this canal to the shipyards and docks beyond, Tigran explained. A combination of bigger ships, the narrowness of the channel and the constant sand banks which built up at the mouth meant that ships must anchor far from shore and await the arrival of the slow, flat-bottomed lighters. If the waters were choppy, this could be treacherous. The weather that day was calm, however, and while she waited for the boat, Charlotte took a long look at this place which was to be her home.

The approach was deceptively pretty: islets scattered amongst the diamond glints of the blue sea like jewels from a broken necklace; a hundred white-rimmed emeralds, distant amethysts, hued agate, rugged grey quartz and far-flung, filmy amber. But as the ship drew closer to the mainland, the illusion dropped away. As far as the eye could see, there was nothing but a low, muddy morass dotted with palms. The high mountains beyond the city, of which she had been told, were invisible, veiled in dense cloud. Of the city itself, she could see nothing but a chalky white lighthouse on the end of the canal wall, a few grey stone houses and a small, low fort. Charlotte's heart sank. It was as if all colour had been sucked out of this joyless day. The night of her arrival in Singapore flooded her memory. The moonlight, the forest of masts, the swaying lanterns on the ships like dancing fireflies, the Chinese junk and the man who had called to her. Her heart swelled, and an unbidden tear slid down her cheek.

Tigran stood by her side, wishing to pull her close into him, not daring. He wanted her happiness more than he could express. For two days she had been ill, sick to her soul, caught in a web of misery. Then, on the third day, exhausted, with the wind beating her face, staring at the white-tipped waves swirling remorselessly beneath the hull, she had found a certain calm and made a decision.

She had not deceived Tigran. When he confessed his feelings to her, she told him of her love for another man and the baby to come. Tigran had blinked slowly but thought for no more than a second. He realised that he did not care. Nothing about Charlotte's past mattered. To lose her was unthinkable, to be her protector his highest thought.

He had sunk to his knees, put her hands against his forehead and asked her to marry him. Now he was grateful beyond words that she had agreed, had let him kiss her cheek, even that fleeting touch inflaming. He had dreamed of touching her for too long. He knew it was dangerous, this rapture he felt. He smiled at the word. His English tutor would have chided him for such a grandiloquent term, but he could think of no other which described his condition. Old man's folly is what his friends called it. How often had he seen it in others and laughed? Never mind. Did not even the great Erasmus write that "folly seasons man's life with pleasure"? Something like that, he felt sure.

Now he wanted to divert her from thoughts he saw crowding her mind. He pointed to the rowboat approaching the ship. The *equippagemeester* came up to Tigran. He had sailed over from Onrust Island, where he supervised the extensive ship repair docks and warehouses. Part of his duties was to board ships to inspect the list of passengers and crew, as well as any cargo, and to check for sickness. Satisfied, he saluted Charlotte with a lingering look. He had not seen a fair-skinned European woman in the ten years he had lived in Batavia. Certainly not one as lovely as this: long, jet- black hair and violet eyes, full, pink lips, her figure slender as the Indische-Chinese women he liked to visit in Glodok, the Chinese quarter. His wife, a daughter of a former councillor, had assured his lucrative position but was regrettably short and dumpy, and six children had not improved her figure.

As the rowboat pulled up to the channel there was a sudden jolt, and Tigran threw out his arm to prevent Charlotte from falling from the seat. Despite its shallow draft, the boat had run aground. The canal, Tigran explained—attempting to keep his temper—was constructed to narrow the current so that it had sufficient force to keep the channel clear of silt. Tigran would rather have used his own cutter, but the Dutch authorities had sold the three-year licence for this transport to the Kapitan Cina, the leader of the Chinese in Batavia. With volleys of shouts and wild gesticulations, the crew pushed the craft off the sandbank, several boatmen floundering as it shifted suddenly to the deep channel. The crew burst into laughter, joshing and pulling the bedraggled men back onboard. Charlotte could not help but share in the good-natured amusement, and Tigran, relieved that she was unhurt, joined in.

As they entered between the channel piers, three of the crew jumped quickly up to the side with a rope fixed to the boat, and began to track it upriver. The other boatmen rowed, but the current was too great to permit an ascent by oars alone. Charlotte could see the men straining as the boat moved slowly along. Their boat passed another, laden with sick-looking European men heading, Tigran told her, to the hospital ship lying offshore. Convicts in leg chains squatted sullenly on a lighter anchored to one side of the canal wall, covered from head to toe in brown sticky mud. Their task was to clear the silt from the river, and Charlotte could hardly begin to imagine the exhaustion of such dispiriting, endless labours. Here and there lamp-eyed crocodiles floated along devouring garbage, unmoved and unafraid of the boats which passed around them and ignoring the men who laboured in the river and even the small children playing around the boats. They are tame and fat, Tigran told her, because they are protected from injury by the authorities. They fulfill the useful purpose of eating the refuse of the slaughter-houses. Charlotte wrinkled her nose.

The grim aspect of the canal was redeemed by the crowds of brightly painted double-masted *pinisi* and the single-masted *prahu*, the elegant small craft of the islands, moored to one side. When the *prahu* was under sail, the low shiny hull all but disappeared under the white sail flung back like a bird's wing. Men squatted lazily on the decks watching the extraordinary sight of this *hantu*, ghost woman, with such white skin. Cooking smells and human stenches floated faintly on the breezes of the salty air. The craft moving on the canal were rowed by Javanese "sea dogs", Tigran told her, so named by the Malays for the shrill and incoherent songs with which they beat time with their oars, each verse ending with a lengthy, loud and vigorous howl. Thus, accompanied by curdling wails and pungent odours, they arrived finally at the pier at Kleine Boom.

Tigran was anxious to be away from the lower town well before dusk and the onset of the night winds. Its reputation for miasma and death had not diminished since the time of the VOC, when it killed scores of men a day and was known as the Graveyard of the Dutch. Europeans might be obliged to work in the port's godowns and offices alongside the sluggish and infested waters, but, by three o'clock, they left rapidly for the healthier southern reaches of the city.

Sensing Tigran's urgency, she recalled, with a small shiver, the words of John Crawfurd in his *Dictionary of the Indian Islands*, which she had read in the Institution library at Singapore. "The Dutch, unmindful of a difference of some 45 degrees of latitude, determined on having a town after the model of those in the Netherlands, within six degrees of the equator and on the level of the sea. The river spread over the town in many handsome canals, lost its current, deposited its copious sediment and generated pestilential malaria, which was transported by the land-wind even to the roads."

Helping Charlotte from the boat, Tigran accompanied her to the small whitewashed inn near the landing stage. The journey to their house in Weltevreden would be quite long, he told her, for the city was sprawling. The entry formalities were slow, the niggardly *mestizo* clerk fussing over Charlotte's British papers, for the English were suspect in Dutch water— even this young girl it seemed. Tigran concealed his annoyance. This was the only power this little despot possessed and he would not be hurried. But it was done with finally, and the luggage arranged to follow, and, relieved, he settled Charlotte into his town coach and the four horses pulled away from the port, along Kanaal Weg and over the bridge. Tigran did not tell her that this bridge, owing to the state of the river, was commonly known as Schijtbrug. They moved onto Kasteelplein Weg and through the Amsterdam Gate, formerly the southern entrance of the original fort of Batavia.

From Prinsenstraat, Tigran pointed out the old Town Hall in the distance; then the carriage turned towards the Kali Besar, as this part of the Ciliwung River was known. They crossed Middelpunt Brug, with its backdrop of lofty sails. This bridge was the furthest south on the Kali Besar that sailing boats could go, and they massed together like flocks of white-winged birds peering at the rowboats beyond. Tigran showed Charlotte the long two-storey building which housed the offices of Manouk & Co., its open godowns bordering the bank, before going back over the river and onto Binnen Nieuwpoort Straat.

Charlotte was astounded at the decayed appearance of the city. It seemed almost deserted, the canals dilapidated and the buildings broken-down. Barefoot native soldiers kept a slouching watch at the portals of red-tiled, low merchant houses. The occasional European man they passed seemed pale and emaciated. The atmosphere of degeneration was relieved only barely by the large-leafed plantains and the tall stems of coconut and betel nut trees spreading their feathery leaves far into the sky. The horses' hooves sent up fingers of ash-white dust which touched eerily against the glass of the coach windows. A fetid, cloacal stench rose from the canal. The humidity was a damp cloak, dense and oppressive. She did not know whether to laugh or cry at this introduction to Java, a land she had heard of as the fabled home of Ptolemy's Golden Chersonese, of Solomon's Ophir, of gold, perfume and spices.

Within a few minutes, the architecture changed and Charlotte saw houses like those in Singapore: white two-storied buildings with curved red-tiled roofs. Long-tail-haired Chinese sat crouched in the street or were busy sculling *kajang*-roofed boats on the river. Only twenty minutes more and they would be home. As he said this, Tigran glanced at Charlotte, unsure of her feelings. Batavia, he felt sure, was a confusing and disconcerting city for a European woman.

Charlotte said nothing, the sight of the Chinese men with their tailed hair arresting her, wrenching her thoughts away from these streets, back to Singapore. She closed her eyes, not wanting to see any more, and rested her head against the back of the seat.

The Chinese town faded in the dust behind them, and the carriage entered a broad, perfectly straight avenue running alongside a wide canal. The air felt cooler here. Tigran lowered the glass to let in the breeze. "Molenvliet," Tigran said. Mill Way, the road linking the old city to the new. The canal was over a hundred years old, built by the Kapitan Cina to bring wood from the forests to the old walled city for ships and houses and to carry sugar from his mills to the port. The wealthy of every race built their houses out here. It was healthier than the low-lying coast. The road was firm, and in the late-afternoon light Charlotte saw large, elegant mansions of both Chinese and European appearance, with ornate wrought-iron fences and gates. Pretty bridges spanned the canal to a similar avenue on other side, lined with the dusky shapes of tall trees. Birds kept up an incessant high-pitched twittering among the leaves; every now and again a fragrance of invisible flowers came floating on the windless air. Lights appeared, and Tigran pointed out a large hotel and, just beyond it, elaborate gates which stood open between lantern-topped columns. Flames flickered, and a waft of coconut oil drifted over the carriage.

"We are here," said Tigran and took Charlotte's hand in his.

The carriage passed the columns and began to describe an arc around the dense mass of trees beyond. The path was firm and mossy, and the dust died away. Firebrands on either side stretched into the distance. Despite her previous forebodings, she felt a flurry of tingling excitement at the prospect of seeing this house which Takouhi had described to her in Singapore.

"Brieswijk is Tigran's estate. Was built by VOC man long time ago, and our father buy this place. Is very nice place, very big house, maybe best house in Batavia. I grow up there."

Charlotte suddenly remembered. Takouhi would be waiting for her. She squeezed Tigran's hand lightly for, no matter what else she felt for him, she trusted him absolutely. He felt a constricting emotion for this woman rise in his chest. *Learn to love me, please*, he thought. *Let me love you*.

Between the trees, Charlotte saw lights flickering. Tantalised, she almost held her breath, listening to the horses' hooves beat dully on the earth, watching the shadows of their bodies dance past the firebrands. Then the carriage rounded the last tree, and light flooded the ground, so bright after darkness that she threw up a hand before her eyes. A great mansion came into view in a blaze of light. High windows occupied the floors of the facade, and long lower extensions stood to either side, with French doors of intricate wrought iron and glass from ceiling to floor. The panes cast glints of fire on the ground. Marble steps and columns marked the main entrance to the house, illuminated by a hundred dark-skinned, white-saronged servants holding swaying lanterns. As the dusk stole rapidly across the sky, the impression of aerial flame and brilliance was overwhelming.

"Oh," she said and looked at Tigran, lost for words. He had sent a servant on a fast horse ahead to create this moment for her.

"It's yours, ours," he said and kissed her hand. "Welcome home."

2

In the next days Charlotte barely had time to brood. There was so much to discover.

The banns had been posted and the wedding day set for four weeks hence. It would take this long to settle the legal affairs of the marriage settlement and inheritance. By the laws of the government of the Dutch East Indies, a widow was entitled to at least half of her husband's estate. Legalised minor children, by any woman the man recognised, were left strictly defined percentages of the estate. If there were no legitimised minor children, the totality of the husband's estate would pass to the widow. The liberality of this law took Charlotte's breath away.

In English law, a wife had no rights at all. Upon marriage, she ceased, legally, to exist. She and all her goods became the property of her husband to dispose of as he wished, and, after he died, his wealth would automatically pass to his eldest son or away to the first male in line. Unless a husband had made specific provisions for his wife, an English widow, no matter how wealthy she might have been before her marriage, could find herself destitute and thrown on the charity of her family or the church.

Charlotte and Takouhi sat on the balcony overlooking the great lawn. Off to the right, at the edge of a grove of waringan trees covered in a blaze of red berries, construction was underway on the big square *pendopo* hall which would be used for a wedding reception. Lines of small, dark workmen passed to and fro, lifting, sorting, sawing and planting the squat, thick beams into the carved stone plinths. To the feast would come special guests, including the Governor-General, the Resident of Batavia and the Kapitan Cina, friends of the Manouk family and all the village people from the estate. There would be *ronggeng* dancing and a *wayang* play. After the wedding at the chapel, a reception for the European town would take place at the Harmonie Club. Takouhi was explaining this to Charlotte.

"Tigran has made bequests to me and Miriam and to his *nyai* and his legitimised children. All the rest, including this estate, will come to you," Takouhi said.

Charlotte looked out over these vast grounds of lawn and forest stretching down to the silver line of the river and beyond. What she could see was not even one tenth of the land which Tigran owned in Batavia. In addition, Takouhi went on, there was the tea plantation in the hills at Buitenzorg, coffee in the Preangar, the sugar lands and factories near Semarang, the fleet of ships and other business interests and properties too numerous to mention.

On top of this breathtaking wealth, to her amazement Charlotte discovered a good many things she did not know about both Tigran and Takouhi and the whole Manouk family.

The first was that Takouhi had been married! Charlotte was filled with an almost indecent sense of curiosity, but to her annoyance Takouhi did not elaborate. She merely said that she had been widowed and inherited half of her late husband's estate, with which she had bought the house she owned in Nordwijk, Batavia's most fashionable street. It was currently rented out to a Captain Palmer, an American who had set up in business with a long-time Resident of Batavia, Gillean Maclaine. In a few days, Takouhi said, she would take her on a long visit to this street and its fashionable shops and they would pay a visit to Captain Palmer and look at the house. Listening to Takouhi discuss legal arrangements and property rental, Charlotte discovered a very different side to her friend, one which was quite hard-headed and down to earth. Perhaps, Charlotte thought, I had just not seen this before. In Singapore, Takouhi had been a mother and loving companion, revelling in George's adoration of her and their daughter, happy and carefree in love and security. Here in Batavia, she had a different role. Here she was an older widowed sister of a wealthy merchant, no man by her side, her child lost. And, too, Charlotte found that Takouhi had another sister, Miriam, who was the wife of Josef Arathoun, another wealthy Armenian merchant. She was Tigran and Takouhi's younger half sister, by a concubine of his father's, whom he had legitimised.

This discovery of an extended family certainly surprised Charlotte, but the greater shock was this news about Tigran. For it transpired that, though Tigran had no wife, he had, for many years, had a *nyai*, a native woman, by whom he had two sons and a daughter. There were two grandchildren. He had legalised their relationship. In this society, that meant he had papers of legitimacy for the children who had been baptised into the Christian faith. He had recognised his *nyai* as their legal mother and had given her, as was the custom, a Christian first name and his own surname spelt backwards. Her name was Mariana Kuonam, therefore, though the family still used her native name, Mia. She was an Ambonese slave woman who had been given to him as a companion when he turned fifteen.

Mia was older than Tigran, of course, by some ten years, Takouhi told her. Since the birth of Nicolaus, the first son, she had always lived in her own household. Nicolaus and his younger brother, Samuel, worked for Tigran's merchant house, and his daughter, Valentijna, was married to the Assistant Resident in Semarang. Charlotte calculated that the two eldest children were older than her! And grandchildren! She had given little thought to Tigran's life during the years before he met her, but somehow she had not imagined this encompassing and practical domesticity.

Takouhi, seemingly finding nothing odd in the proposal, spoke of taking her to meet Nyai Kuonam.

Charlotte did not know what to say, but Takouhi read on her face a certain shock. No, no, she reassured her, it was all perfectly normal here. For a mature man, the situation was only to be expected. Most men had a wife, several *nyai* and dozens of slave-concubines. Tigran had never had slave-concubines. His head had been turned when he was much younger by a woman who had been his willing concubine, but that was years ago. Girls still came here from the *kampong*, Takouhi added, matter of factly, wanting to be with him. Certainly, though, such goings-on would cease once Tigran was married to Charlotte.

Takouhi smiled at her friend but was horrified to see two large tears sliding down Charlotte's cheeks.

"*Alamak*! So sorry, Charlotte. Too much for you. I am just silly-billy, I think better to know everything, but still hard for you."

Charlotte took out her handkerchief and wiped her eyes, annoyed at herself.

"It's just so strange. I thought I knew you, but you have had a life I know nothing about. And Tigran ..." She stopped and took a deep breath. "I'm pregnant, Takouhi, by the Chinese man. Tigran knows, says he does not care. Now, this whole family of Tigran's and concubines, for heaven's sake. It's just so... not what I expected, I suppose."

Takouhi took her hand. "I know about this baby. Is great blessing. Change is hard, nobody like change. When I bring Meda here, I miss George so much, and all my life in Singapore. Then Meda pass away. I sorry now I take Meda from George, he not there to hold her when she die. So sudden, no time for him to come. She like angel to him. Sorry he go far away. He give you no letter for me. He hurt I know. Maybe cannot forgive me. I not know where he is now. Cannot write to him. I love him Charlotte. Still I try not to be empty."

Takouhi looked down, falling silent, turning the Claddagh ring on her left hand. Charlotte knew something of this pretty gold band with two hands holding a heart surmounted by a crown. Worn on the left hand, with the heart facing the body, it signified marriage. George had given it to her. Charlotte clutched her friend's hand, felt a flush of shame and a constriction in her throat. She swallowed and took a deep breath.

"Forgive me, Takouhi. Just feeling a bit sorry for myself. Feeling sick and missing Zhen, just like you miss George. I miss George too. He loves you, I know it. He will come back. He built the cupolas on the hill in Singapore for you and Meda, you know, filled with love for you both."

Charlotte rose and put an arm around her shoulders.

"I am the silly billy, eh? Scared about marrying Tigran, about being with him, you know. Scared about the baby, scared of everything."

Charlotte gave a tight little laugh. Admitting all this fear was a relief. She was not sure where it all came from. She was not unused to feeling out of place. Her own life had made her stoical. She thought of Robert, how she missed him, this brother who had been everything to her for so long. What a strange life had led them both to these tropical climes. She recalled the happiness of their childhood in Madagascar, the devotion of their French-Mauritian mother and Scottish missionary father. How hideously it had all ended when they had been dispatched for their safety to Aberdeen's grey, cold stones and the keeping of a dour grandmother, their parents lost to them forever. Robert had gone off to school, and Charlotte had found herself alone. Lessons in the morning had been all that constrained her, and she had roamed the hills and sailed the waters of Scotland with her cousin Duncan and found solace in the care of her maiden aunt, Jeanne. Only Duncan and Jeanne had loved her, and fortunately that had been enough. Jeanne had been a perfect aunt, Charlotte and Robert the children she never had. Jeanne had lost her officer fiancé young, in the war with Napoleon, and Charlotte had learned, like her aunt, to build her defences out of good sense, good humour and Macleod grit. She had sailed with Duncan on the chilly waters around Aberdeen and developed a tough sailor's hide, an ability to look danger in the eye. Robert's unexpected appointment as police chief to Singapore had saved her from an unwanted marriage to some lecherous old squire.

She had loved Singapore immediately, all the more completely for meeting Zhen. Her mind strayed to his silken-skinned body, his dark almond eyes, his full lips, the curve of his jaw and the long, lustrous black queue which fell to his waist. She could still feel her fingers entwined in his hair, the touch of his lips on her skin. He had invaded her whole being. There was never going to be anything but trouble with him, though, for not only was he Chinese but she knew he was promised to another woman. But after an ineffectual and pointless struggle with Pallas Athena, the Goddess of Reason, she had simply fallen into the whirlwind. Even now, though, she could find not an ounce of regret. He had "subdued her heart" as ever Othello did Desdemona's and "to his honours and his valiant parts did she her soul and fortunes consecrate." Not entirely, of course, for her fortunes and his were not in their hands. She had had to leave: nothing but scandal could have ensued. It would have ruined Robert, and eventually Zhen, especially with the child on the way. Love had made her vulnerable; thoughts of motherhood, separation from Robert and the familiarity of Singapore had made her anxious. There were little rents and tears in her nature which allowed doubt and fear to enter, and she was having trouble rebuilding the edifice.

Takouhi patted her friend's hand.

"We make a life here, different life maybe, but not unhappy. We wait for this baby, and wait for Meda's *slametan*, and feel better."

Takouhi rose and called a servant to serve tea outside on the terrace.

Together they left Takouhi's sitting room and went down a wide marble staircase into the hall and out through the French doors onto the great basalt and teakwood terrace which ran the length of the house. A deep roof sheltered them from the sun. A dining table and chairs stood to one side, for the family took all their meals here. Charlotte saw three long *punkahs* standing idle now over the table. In the evening, the *punkah wallahs* pulled them to and fro, creating the semblance of a cooling breeze. Several rattan and bamboo easy chairs and tables were set about the terrace, and they sat and looked over the vast lawn where spotted deer grazed silently.

"Tigran have love for you, Charlotte. He can be hard in business, hard with other man, but with woman is kind and gentle. Like Robert for you, Tigran is for me. Best brother in whole world."

Takouhi poured some tea, and looked at her friend. She so much wanted Charlotte to care for Tigran, to be happy, to make him happy, and she knew that meant Charlotte must learn something about him, about them, for there was so little time before the wedding. Takouhi knew Tigran was passionate about Charlotte. She had never seen him so filled with emotion about any other woman. Surya, yes, he had adored her. Perhaps Petra Couperus for a brief time? But not quite like this. She debated whether to take Charlotte into her confidence. She loved Charlotte; this woman had become her closest friend, would be her sister, Tigran's wife. The baby and others to come would be Tigran's children. She wanted Charlotte to feel a connection to them all, a connection to Batavia, to Java. She wanted her to forget the Chinese man.

Takouhi took a sip of tea and placed her cup gently on its saucer.

"I will tell you a story. This story between you and me. Only Tigran and George know this story."

Charlotte looked at her. After all the other revelations, she had no idea what to expect.

"My mother die when I am seven years old. Her story also very sad. I tell you this another time."

Takouhi ran a hand lightly over her hair, which had blown across her face in the breeze, and looked out over the lawn. Charlotte was again struck by her beauty. She was almost fifty-six years old, but her appearance belied every year. Slender as a reed, she was a graceful, tawny cat, black shining hair to her waist, dark eyes turned up at the corners. Her age was revealed only in the tiniest lines at the corner of her eyes and on her hands. Usually she dressed in a sarong and *kebaya*, like all the mixed-blood Indische women, but today, surprisingly, she was dressed in a former European fashion, in a soft, pale yellow lawn, the dress falling Empire-style from beneath her bust. It suited her, but Charlotte thought it was unlike Takouhi not to dress in the latest fashion. In Singapore she had always been vastly interested in any new books that came from London, Boston or Paris.

"Father marry again. Marry Tigran's mother who become like my mother. She very good woman. Widow of Dutchman. Her name is Valentijna, so beautiful woman. Why she marry Father then not understand. He cruel man. Now understand, she no choose anything, like me, like my mother. She lose many babies. Now I know Father never leave her alone, always greedy for her. Before she can think of losing baby, she pregnant again but he not leave her alone. Never give her peace."

Takouhi shook her head slightly, frowning, her eyes misty.

"Really I love her. She and Jawa maids care for me, love me. She teach me letters, show books, speak Dutch. This not usual in Dutch house. Girls not read or write, only talk Malay or Javanese, do nothing, learn nothing. But one day, nothing she can do. When I am fourteen, my father give me to old Dutchman for wife. His name Pieter Laurens, old friend of father in government. He maybe fifty years old. Very fat, very ugly ... very cruel."

Charlotte frowned. Takouhi's voice had changed.

"I married at church in Batavia. I never forget that day. I scared so much. When pastor say he and me husband and wife, he pull me to him and put his hand hard between my legs. In the church in front of priest, Father and all people. Then put his mouth and tongue on my mouth, how you say, lick me. His breath smell bad, his mouth like old tobacco and betel. I never forget that smell."

Charlotte was transfixed, filled with shame for her friend. Fourteen years old. It was unimaginable.

"He not wait. Before even wedding party finish, he take me to his room, rip my dress. When I cry out, he hit me. Hit so hard I think he break my face. Then he put me on bed, take down his pants. He do this to me hard, hurting, fat belly on my chest. I cannot breathe, so much pain I think I die. He finish, thank the gods, finish quickly, big groan in my ears. Then he go, tell me to shut up and sleep. I have blood on my legs, blood everywhere."

Takouhi's tone had changed again. Now she was just telling a story as if it was about someone else.

Charlotte put out her hand to her friend's, but Takouhi curled her hands into her lap.

"He hurt me a lot inside, I very small, must call doctor. When I am sick he don't touch, but as soon as I well, he come again. I fight, but he beat me. One time he tie me to bed and leave me, two days, no food, no water. When he come he lie on me, heavy, put hand inside me, beat me, have sex with me. Blood everywhere. I think I die that time, really. Maids save me, give water, clean mess. When he go out, they free me, care for me though very dangerous for them. They are slave girl, he can kill them, anything, and no one care. When he see I no fight anymore, he let me go. I live like slave. Cannot go out, live with his other women in house. When Valentijna try to see me, he say no. I am pregnant, get very sick. Then he let her come. She see my arms and face, cry for me. He beat a lot, all the women. I think he hate women. She tell father but he do nothing. Doctor tell Pieter don't touch me, but he don't care. Thank all gods, I lose this baby. Pieter want sex too much, beat too much. Then I understand, just survive. Other women help me, all slave women, I never forget them. But I lucky, after six months he lose interest in me. Always he want new girl. So I stay very quiet, away from him, far away."

Charlotte was listening, horrified. Takouhi rose and, taking Charlotte's hand, led her off the terrace and they began to walk to a thick grove of tamarind trees, beyond which lay the small chapel and the graveyard.

"When Tigran born, Valentijna ask father please let me come back

37

to help with him. Father want son, so happy to have son that he agree. Pieter don't care then. He forget about me. Go to be Resident in Makassar. We all hope he die there, of drink, of fever, of anything, but somehow bad man always live. When I am eighteen, Pieter come back. He see me. I pretty—how you say—grow up. He want me come back. My father order this. But I not fourteen anymore. I clever girl. Think about this moment long, long time. Learn many things. I go back and first night he come to me, I smile and give him drink of Madeira wine."

They had entered the deep shadow of the tamarind trees, with their feathery, lime-coloured leaves and thick clutches of long, brown pods. Takouhi stopped and turned to face Charlotte.

"Listen, Charlotte. I kill Pieter. Give *upas*, poison, understand. I put a little in drink every time he come to me. He get little sick and soon cannot come anymore. But I give poison to him, little bit every week. Sometimes I stop, then start again. He take long time, have pain. Everybody very sad for me, poor young wife. When I am twenty, he die. I am widow, I have his money. That day I decide never marry again."

Charlotte looked into Takouhi's eyes. She gazed steadily back at her friend. So many things fell into place: Takouhi's refusal to marry George, though he asked her many times, even after the birth of Meda. Her separate residence at Tir Uaidhne, the mansion George had built for her in Singapore, her independence.

With a soft swish, a sudden breeze swept through the leaves of the fecund trees around them, rattling the pods and moving the supple branches like long, tender arms. Charlotte nodded and put her arm through her friend's. They walked on through the dark grove and out into the sunshine. In front of them was the chapel. They sat on the grass by Meda's grave.

3

Charlotte began to discover the immense beauty of Brieswijk.

The house had been built over seventy years before by a Cornelius van Riejmsdijk, a senior merchant in the VOC. His initials and coat of arms adorned several of the inner doors. Over the main portal stood the great open fanlight, with the carved initials of the VOC, the V huge, overlapping the smaller O and C. On either side were fanlights depicting Asia and Europe, surrounded by garlands and fruits. Tigran had explained a little about the Vereenigde Oostindische Compagnie which had established the town of Batavia over two centuries ago.

From its trading origins, the United East India Company had grown to be a mighty force, controlling the agriculture and all trade between these Spice Islands and Holland. Establishing the tiny fort at Batavia, the VOC had not sought territory. With territory came responsibility, and responsibility was expensive. Java was merely a great storehouse waiting to be sacked, to the profit of their investors. Gradually, though, the Company had acquired territory, and the armies of the VOC were called on to wage battle for and against the ever-feuding local kings and princes, ceding rights and land to the Company each time. Slowly and inexorably, the royal families gave away all of Java to the VOC, whether the Company wanted it or not. For two hundred years, to belong to the Company was to be part of the greatest enterprise on earth.

Since the 1760s, though, the Company had been in financial difficulties due in part to abuses, corruption and smuggling by its senior servants, including the Governor-General himself. The initials became known everywhere as *Vergaan Onder Corruptie*, "ruined by corruption". When war between Holland and England broke out in 1780 over support for the American Revolution, it sounded the death knell of "Jan Company", as it was commonly known. The English blockaded the Channel, bringing VOC ships to Amsterdam, destroyed the Dutch fleet and ruled the seas. By 1790, the Company had debts amounting to 85 million florins. The VOC colonies in Guinea and Bengal, Ceylon, the Coramandel coast, Malacca and the Cape were lost to English domination. The Dutch state was obliged to step in to prevent the total collapse of the VOC and the loss of the India trade. Finally, the Company was disbanded in 1800, but not before Holland itself had fallen to the French emperor Napoleon, through the army of Marshal Herman Daendels, amongst others. When Louis Napoleon was made king of Holland by his mighty brother, Daendels was named Governor-General of the Dutch East Indies, and the French flag flew over Batavia.

Tigran showed Charlotte a pair of golden candelabra which stood on a long sideboard to one side of the formal dining room. Winged victories, in Greek dress, held aloft a long floral wreath, from which ten candle sockets sprang, decorated with fluting, acanthus leaves and spirals.

"My father bought these from the effects of Marshal Daendels after he left. They are said to have been a gift from Napoleon himself, although no one knows for sure. He paid a hefty price for them, so I am certain he believed it to be so. In those days, like him or loathe him, anything touched by the great Frenchman was like gold."

Tigran smiled wryly. He was taking her on a tour of the house. It was a veritable repository of the recent history of the Dutch East Indies and Batavia. Tigran had begun the tour in the downstairs study, where a portrait of Riejmsdijk and his family hung on one of the walls. The grand merchant stood, thin and rather humourless, in his embroidered velvet coat, ruffled shirt and buckled shoes.

Next to him was a small woman also dressed, Charlotte presumed, in the Dutch style of the 1760s, covered in pearls. She was Javanese, Charlotte supposed, but, just as the thought came into her head, Tigran said, "Riejmsdijk's wife was Japanese. He brought her and his children when he left Deshima, the VOC's trading station in Japan. Smuggled them out, actually. All Japan trade is still Dutch and still comes through Batavia. Two vessels per year go for copper, and we sometimes trade in lacquer wares and fine porcelain."

Charlotte examined the portrait more carefully. She was not sure where Japan was, had had no idea that the Dutch traded there. Now she could see, emerging from its darkened paint, the figures of a boy and two little girls.

"When we ride down to the river you will see a bridge over the Kali Krukut which leads to the villages on the other side. It is a Japanese-style bridge. It, and some of the trees around the bank, are all that remains of a Japanese garden he built for his wife. I understand she and the children all died before him."

When Riejmsdijk himself had died suddenly, Tigran told her, the estate was put up for auction by the Orphan's Chamber to find funds to support his vast number of illegitimate children. Riejmsdijk had kept over fifty concubines. Charlotte marvelled at this Eastern profligacy. The Dutch in Holland were Calvinist. Something happened to the men, she thought, when they arrived on Asia's shores. They forgot their upbringing and in short measure fell into Asia's sensual and tempting arms and became sometimes more immoderate than even the Asian princes and potentates who surrounded them. There was, thought Charlotte, a bizarre contradiction between the almost prudish seemliness of the selected or legitimised wife and the base attitude to other native women, who could be abandoned at will; the white man's own progeny by them callously sold and forgotten.

Charlotte looked at Reijmsdijk. He must have loved his wife and children, for he had risked smuggling them out of Japan. He had built her a garden that she might feel, in some measure, less homesick. He must have suffered at their loss. Yet he had been able to abuse and discard other women in equal measure. Charlotte shook her head.

Tigran was explaining something about the Orphan Chamber, and Charlotte abandoned her musings. The Orphan Chamber had been set up long ago to address the problem of the vast number of children born out of wedlock to native women and abandoned to their *kampong* lives when the men either died or returned to Holland. The VOC had early on decided to bring these light-skinned *kampong* children into the church, baptise them and support them. Thus, the girls could serve in the houses of Dutch men, and become acceptable half-white wives or companions.

Dutch women had been forbidden to come to Batavia since 1659, for they rarely flourished in the climate and simply caused rank discontent among the men. Even the wife of the present Governor-General, Tigran explained, had her origins in this manner. She was a legitimised daughter of a Balinese slave girl. The boys were groomed to be soldiers for the VOC's ever-needful army or minor clerks in the government. Where the girls might, through judicious marriages to white men, rise to the highest rungs of this closed society, the boys of low-ranking officers and officials were forever locked into low status and poorly paid jobs. For boys to succeed, they had to be raised and sent to school in Holland. Only the wealthiest men in the land could afford it.

Tigran looked at Charlotte. He knew Takouhi had mentioned his family with Mia and was not sure how she felt about it.

"I, too, was supposed to go to Amsterdam. I did not go, my father told me, for when I was of the age the seas were terribly dangerous for Dutch ships. England was at war with Napoleon, you know, and Holland had been annexed and become simply a French province. Batavia flew the French flag, and invasion was inevitable—the more so as the exiled Dutch prince placed the colonies under English protection. I had Dutch tutors and, after Raffles came, an English one. For my sons, a Dutch education was no longer useful. Everything had changed. When Napoleon was defeated and the English returned Java to the Dutch, the new Netherlands government appointed only men born in Holland, loyal to Holland, who brought their Dutch wives. People like my sons are *mestizo*, like me: not white, not Dutch. High office is out of their reach. They must make their lives in commerce and on the plantations."

Charlotte was listening to him and looking out of the window. Impulsively she asked,

"Did you love your *nyai*, Tigran?"

Tigran was nonplussed. He had not expected this question. He frowned. Charlotte turned to face him, waiting somewhat nervously. There was a silence. Had she gone too far? Did she really want to talk about love to Tigran?

"Love her? I cared—care—for her. She was the first woman I ever had, for a long time the only woman. She was sent to change me from a boy to a man. That was her role. Possibly I thought I loved her when I was very young."

He took Charlotte's hands in his and looked directly into her eyes.

"We always love in some measure the woman, or man, who awakens powerful feelings. Don't we? Is that real love? I don't know."

As he said this, he felt again a deep regret at not having been Charlotte's first man—truthfully, her only man. Now he would always stand in comparison to this other who had awakened such feelings in her. But never mind, he thought, time will pass. She will forget, as those feelings have faded for me. I will make her forget. I will seduce her as this man did, but I will give her everything he could not.

He gripped her wrists and pulled her towards him, putting her hands under his coat, against his chest, holding them there. She could feel his heart beating. It was the second time today she had found herself so close to him.

"Do you want to talk about love, Charlotte, and passion? I know you know these things. I too. Do you want me to tell you how I feel about you, or shall I show you?"

Charlotte could not hold his gaze. She wished she had not asked him this question. She looked down. Tigran smiled and released her hands, glad he had made her heart beat faster, glad to see the confusion on her face.

After a moment he said, "Come and let me show you treasures."

He walked over to a large carved wood cabinet and unlocked the doors.

"Reijmsdijk brought many things from Japan."

Charlotte was grateful for the change of subject and peered inside. On one shelf lay four boxes. Tigran took one out. It was a double-layered box of black lacquer, with gold images of clouds and mountains. In between pictures of trees and elegant halls were little figures carrying boxes on their backs and staves in their hands. It was delightful. Tigran saw the look of pleasure on Charlotte's face and brought all the boxes down from the shelf. He himself had never really looked at these things; they had simply been left for years in this cupboard. Charlotte tried to analyse their appeal; perhaps it was their perfect detail, their orderliness. A chaotic world made simple through art.

As she ran her finger over their shiny and intricate designs, Charlotte remembered other oriental things: Zhen's wedding clothes with dragons, phoenixes and peonies. She closed her eyes. Tigran, not sensing her mood, went to another shelf where a quantity of cloth of exquisite colours lay folded neatly along the shelves. Eager to please her, he took out a bundle of the clothes and put them on a table. On top lay a folded fan. Charlotte shook herself from her thoughts and picked it up. It felt as fragile as gossamer in her hand. She opened it carefully, and there lay before her eyes a scene in gold and blue: a crooked bridge over a river and along the bridge, ladies and children looking down over the rail into the water. On the water floated fans exactly like the one she was holding; it was a fan race. Charlotte was transported to the place, so far from her own imaginings, and felt the peculiar pull of this exquisite art. Then Tigran opened the top cloth and laid it out. It was a large coat, a kimono, he said, from the Japanese court. It was exactly the garment the ladies on the fan were wearing.

The silk was pale gold and covered with many-coloured pictures of little children frolicking amongst willow trees and cherry blossom, small dogs running at their feet. Others were playing hide-and-seek around flowing skirts. The whole was a picture so charming that Charlotte looked up at Tigran and laughed with pleasure. Tigran lifted the coat to turn it, but then it suddenly seemed to melt before their eyes. Rents appeared like rivulets of black in this paysage of colour. Charlotte watched, horrified, as the entire garment disintegrated, destroyed by insects and humidity.

"Oh," said Tigran, looking at Charlotte, worried that she might be upset. Charlotte ran her fingers over the now shattered garment, its gold turned to silken shards and slivers.

She met Tigran's eyes.

"*Golden lads and girls all must,*
As chimney-sweepers, come to dust."

As she said this, she laid a hand on her waist.

Tigran's father had bought Brieswijk at great advantage to himself, for it included a vast estate in the surrounding countryside. The central house was two storeys, with a large, Dutch-style ornate gable adorning the roof. Here was the huge hallway, a dining room and the sitting rooms

44

of the family, a library, a study, one huge bathroom with low porcelain bathtubs and several commode closets. The ten bedrooms, sitting rooms and four other bathrooms were all on the second floor overlooking the lawn and down to the river or out over the entrance and its screen of jungle trees and plants. The side additions were set back, the ballroom to one side and the formal dining room on the other. Kitchens and storerooms adjoined them. Down paths on either side of the house, screened by great bamboo groves, were stables for the horses and for Tigran's carriages. Servants' quarters lay beyond.

Charlotte's bedroom occupied a corner of the main house, with four tall windows at the side and a sweep of French doors towards the river. A wide terrace with a wrought-iron balustrade ran the full length of the house at the back, looking down over the shingled roof of the verandah and beyond to the park. It was a beautiful room. Takouhi had brought her here the night she had arrived, after supper on the terrace below. The lamps had cast a low warm glow; a breeze rilled and billowed the muslin curtains at the open windows. The polished wooden floor gleamed in the lamplight, and the bed stood near the window, veiled in gauze netting. A faint odour of sandalwood from the burning oils along the balcony wafted on the air. She was so tired that after the maid left, she climbed into bed and fell immediately into a deep sleep.

In the morning, though, she had examined the room. The carved teakwood four-poster bed was covered in fine, soft Indian cotton sheets and a pale green satin bedspread. When she looked closely, she saw, to her astonishment, that the initials CM had been embroidered in the middle, in the exact same shade as the coverlet. This must mean Tigran had intended her to come, to visit perhaps. Or had he always held out hope of marrying her? Charlotte was not sure. Now, though, the initials would not need to be changed. She would pass from Charlotte Macleod to Charlotte Manouk. If she had ever doubted, it told her much about his feelings for her.

A maid had brought her coffee that morning, shyly, curious at this white-skinned woman, placing the tray on the table before the French windows that were open to the lawn. A bowl of white jasmine flowers lay on the tray, with a small note. It was from Tigran.

"Good morning, Charlotte. I hope you slept well. *Saya cintamu.*"

Charlotte knew what the last phrase meant. It said "I love you" in Malay. She frowned a little. How could he love her? He did not know her. Then she remembered how quickly she had fallen under Zhen's spell, and suddenly, achingly, missed him.

Do not dwell, she thought, *hold fast*, the devize of the Macleod clan. She looked up and took in the view from the balcony, down over the vast grounds to the silver line of the Kali Krukut, which flowed through the estate down to Chinatown. She found a shawl on the back of a chair, casually thrown—a shawl of exquisite gold and brown batik with a long, silky fringe. She knew he had left it for her and touched its watery softness, putting it over her nightdress and looking in the mirror, admiring the loveliness of the garment and the way her hair looked lying on it. If I'm not careful, she thought, he will turn me into a vain peacock! But she smiled at the thought. She went out onto the terrace and looked into the distance, contemplating the extraordinary events of the last few days which meant that she would now be mistress of this beautiful estate.

She turned her head as she heard a door opening, and Tigran came out onto the terrace. She had not realised that his room was next to hers, and she blushed slightly—all the more since Tigran was naked to the waist, his lower body wrapped in a black sarong. He turned, unembarrassed apparently, and came towards her. Charlotte's heart gave a small thump. He was strong, not big like Zhen, but muscled and lean, the sarong falling loosely around his hips. As he came to her side, Charlotte was acutely aware that she was naked under the thin cotton nightdress and pulled the shawl around her. Tigran stood, silent, looking at her in this gift he had made her, ridiculously glad she was wearing it. He could see her body outlined against the cloth. Slowly he put out his hand, laying it on her waist, gently pulling her against him.

Charlotte was unable to react, her breath shortened. She had not expected this. Tigran looked down at her and turned her face to his, holding his hand on her cheek. The feel of her body against his was exquisite. He brought his face down to hers, his lips close but not quite touching, the dark plaits of his hair brushing against her face. He looked into her eyes, then closed his own, felt her breath on his lips. It took every ounce of his willpower to go no further. But he would go no further. To have her loving and willing, he must tempt her. And he wanted her to be his wife first, his wife before man and God.

"*Saya cintamu*," he whispered. He released her and took her hand, kissing it.

"After breakfast, we will see the house and go to the *kampong*, visit the estate." He smiled, then turned and went back into the house.

Charlotte regained her breath. She had expected his kiss and had gone back into her room embarrassed at these feelings and his professions of love.

Now, though, she had recovered her poise.

Tigran opened the sideboard and took out a blue and white dinner plate from the large service which lay inside. She recognised again the arms of the VOC adorning, in blue, the centre of the plate.

"These were Reijmsdijk's also. Father bought the estate and everything in it, including Reijmsdijk's portrait. I have never bothered to change anything in the house. Since my mother, no woman has really lived here as mistress. Should you wish to do anything, make it over to your taste, change everything, you have only to say, and all will be as you wish."

Tigran looked at her, and Charlotte found again, to her annoyance, that she felt like blushing.

They went into the great hall. The floor was tiled in white, surrounded at the outer edges with a frame of Dutch Delft blue tiles.

"These tiles tell a story, the story of Holland," said Tigran.

He pointed to the many images of fish in a variety of numbers and dispositions swimming around the floor; other tiles showed fish piled in baskets, some sold by sturdy women, some in boats.

"Herring," he said and smiled at her frown. "A humble fish to be sure. But without the humble herring, Holland would never have become the greatest trading nation on earth."

He pointed to a tile that showed a fat-bottomed ship heaped with herring. Elsewhere, merchants stood proudly displaying their wealth, their houses, their cities. The square-rigged, wind-filled sails of 17th- and 18th-century ships sailed around the edge of the hall floor.

"A Dutchman, Jan-Willem Beukelszoon, you see, discovered a method for curing the herring at sea so that it would not spoil. In a stroke, the Dutch had a long-lasting and delicious commodity they could trade all over Europe. They became sailors, traders and merchants of repute, began to build great new types of ships and invented a country which was built and governed not by some war-mongering and greedy king but by sensible and clever burghers. When they outgrew Europe, they looked to the rest of the world. It was inevitable that when the power of Portugal and Spain waned, the Dutch with their ships and knowledge would take over world trade, especially here in the Spice Islands. The VOC was their means of conquest, the first joint stock company every formed. In 1602, it raised six and a half million guilders. Can you imagine such a sum!"

Tigran pointed out other tiles showing coats-of-arms of the countries which had flown the VOC flag, including the fan-shaped man-made island of Deshima and its bridge in Nagasaki harbour, which the Japanese had built to prevent their enterprising trading partners from encroaching on their country. The VOC had ruled over Amboyna, Banda, Ternate, Macassar, Malacca, Ceylon, Java and the Cape of Good Hope. They had had factories in Bengal, on the Coramandel Coast, in Siam and on the Persian Gulf. Their trade routes connected the whole of the Orient, Africa and Europe with Amsterdam. In the Persian Gulf the Company traded spices for salt, in Zanzibar salt for cloves, in India cloves for gold, in China gold for tea and silk, in Japan silk for copper and in the islands of Southeast Asia, copper for spices. The inner Asian trade had been as profitable as that with Europe.

"My Dutch tutor used this floor as a history lesson," Tigran said as he wandered around the hall. "He was always somewhat annoyed that VOC had traded New Amsterdam in exchange for the English leaving the Spice Islands, but it must have seemed a good proposition at the time. It is ironic that Holland has lost all these places because of their support of America, a colony they traded away over a hundred years ago."

He looked over the hall.

"They created the first stock exchange, the first exchange bank. By the middle of the 17th century, they controlled half the world trade. Holland was a tiny nation, but what enterprise, what vision! Fifty fleets a year, 150 trading ships, 40 warships, 20,000 seamen, 10,000 soldiers, 50,000 employees from all over Europe. With all this it still managed to pay a dividend of 40 percent. Remarkable."

Charlotte felt the admiration in Tigran's voice and smiled at this enthusiasm. He noticed and laughed, embarrassed.

"My apologies," he said and bowed slightly. "I confess to an admiration for such a people. The Dutch then had a great intellectual curiosity, and the VOC profits paid for arts and inventions. Their religious tolerance allowed my Armenian family to find refuge and a new life in Amsterdam. My father taught me to admire Holland, and I was sorry not to have gone to Amsterdam for my education."

From the hall the doors led to the terrace and, on either side, the white marble staircase curved to the upper landing. Charlotte could see it needed care, for in parts the white limewash was dingy, and some of the tiling was chipped. It needed attention, a woman's attention. She would have liked to know more about the original Japanese mistress of this house, about the extraordinary circumstances that had led her, much like Charlotte, to become the first lady of such a place. Before she could carry these reflections further, however, Tigran took her hand and led her to the main door.

4

A wide-bodied, big-wheeled carriage with a white calico sunroof stood waiting. The two ponies were pretty black-and-white *kumingans*, ubiquitous in Java. They appeared slight and fine-boned, yet they were strong and resilient, capable, Charlotte knew, of pulling heavy loads. The shafts of the carriage were shining black and bore at the heads finely wrought silver *garuda* birds, their wings flung back imperiously in flight. Tigran held on to Charlotte's hand to help her in. Then he took the reins, and they turned onto the road around the house and out onto a broad avenue of monumental *saman* trees which formed a shady canopy over their heads and cast a dappled light on the road which would take them down to the river. As they clipped along in the morning breeze, a faint sound came to her ears. It was a *gamelan* orchestra playing somewhere out of sight, the sound of gongs and bells carried on the air. It was almost magical, as if the music were being played by invisible nymphs or carried down from the spheres. Then Tigran astonished her as he began to recite a poem.

> "*Thus spoke the Genius, as He stept along,*
> *And bade these lawns to Peace and Truth belong;*
> *Down the steep slopes He led with modest skill*
> *The willing pathway, and the truant rill,*
> *Stretch'd o'er the marshy vale yon willowy mound,*
> *Where shines the lake amid the tufted ground ...*"

Charlotte looked at him and laughed, and he grinned broadly.

"You see, Madame, not just an ignorant dull Indiesman. My English tutor put poetry into my head. I'm sure you cannot name it? Eh? Eh?"

Charlotte laughed out loud. She could not.

"Erasmus Darwin, 1731 to 1802, *The Botanic Garden*. Very long and very difficult for a poor half-Dutch boy. I have forgotten much, but some just stays. I learned words like *effulgent* and *adamantine*, though I am still not sure what they mean. Are you not impressed?"

Charlotte bowed her admiration.

At the end of the avenue, the view of the river opened out. Charlotte saw the Japanese bridge, and Tigran stopped briefly. It was unusual but incredibly lovely, she thought, with its faded red wooden balustrade. Its curved shape was mirrored below in a constantly changing and intricate shadowy distortion of itself as the river ran over the stones, forming small waterfalls and pools. The sound was like bells, and the windrush in leaves. Here on the river she understood why the estate had been named Brieswijk. She could see the gnarled shapes of trees and old bushes, quite unlike jungle flora. The Kali Krukut was a swift flowing river. Tigran pointed out a hut amidst giant trees which extended out over the water. He often held bathing parties here, with picnics on the park. It was quite a common custom in Java, where the villagers used the river for washing and bathing.

Tigran jigged the horses into movement and turned the carriage along the bank. They passed a boathouse, with boats pulled up on the side: little sharp-prowed, blunt-sterned, gaily painted craft with palm-leaf roofs to shelter from the sun and one large oar to row and punt.

As they rode along the river's edge, Charlotte saw that on the far bank, where the jungle relented or had been removed, there was a series of villages surrounded by sun-glinting paddy fields of rice. She heard a clear whistling sound, as plaintive as a wind-harp, and she saw floating high above three brightly painted kites, shaped like birds and winged dragons. She had seen fighting kites in Singapore, but these were new to her, and she shaded eyes and watched as they swooped and soared, sending their music floating on the air. Their owners were lost in the undergrowth, and their lines so slender as to be invisible. They seemed to hang and swoop of their own volition, and Charlotte smiled.

Here, Tigran told her, the villagers grew rice for themselves and for the estate. He took one-fifth of the rice as a tax, and the villagers were obliged to supply labour for repairs of roads, riverbanks, canals and other works on the estate and to grow and process indigo. Otherwise he levied no taxes. On the fringes of the estate, towards the west, he had opened a free market to combat what he saw as the pointless and invidious habit of charging taxes to transport and trade at the market places which existed in other parts of the city. Here the villagers could sell their surplus produce for money, for *doits*, the small copper coins of the Dutch Indies.

They rode on, and Charlotte found that she was very interested in everything Tigran told her. She realised with a small jolt that she had already accepted that she would now be mistress of this place. It was a seductive and unsettling thought. He stopped the carriage, and they looked back over the park to the house standing on the knoll. From here, it looked quite small.

"I want you to love this place, feel it is your home, Charlotte," Tigran told her. He would have liked her to say, with ardent and passionate avowals, that home was in his arms only, but it was too soon, he knew, and he smiled at the thought of these boyish wishes. When he smiled like that, his mouth rose to one side and made his eyes crinkle. She looked into those eyes now, and for the first time she noticed that they were a deep brown flecked with gold. Like his sister's, they turned up very slightly and were framed in long, black lashes. His face was etched with lines at the eyes and a slight furrow above his nose, which deepened when he frowned. These were the only reminders of his age, but they were not unattractive. She found herself smiling back, knowing his meaning.

The road gradually moved away from the river and became a jungle path. The shade was deep and cool. Great groves of thick bamboo spread feathery green leaves along the length of the path and whispered and rustled, though Charlotte could feel no breath of air. It was as if they spoke a secret language known only to themselves. Tigran looked straight ahead.

"I do not keep concubines, Charlotte, though it is common practice. I do not oblige women to occupy my bed."

"But you did, Tigran. You had concubines. Takouhi told me." Oh, dear Charlotte thought, why do I blurt out these things? What is the matter with me? But she wanted an answer. If she was to marry this man, at least she must know about this.

Tigran slowed the carriage. Charlotte sensed in the tightening of his jaw a certain discomfiture. He spoke softly.

"There were two women. One was a Balinese girl who was in Takouhi's house. Her name was Surya. I was a young man, just nineteen. Takouhi always freed her slaves immediately they came into her house. Actually, when I inherited this estate she obliged me to free every person on Brieswijk too. She cannot abide slavery, particularly women in slavery. Of course, I did so. Not to have agreed would have chased her from my life, something that was impossible to imagine. So this girl was a free girl. I thought about nothing but her for months. She was so lovely. So young, only seventeen. Near my age. I admit I was a little crazed."

Charlotte, listening to him, found herself wishing she had not asked. She felt a strange annoyance at these professions. Was she jealous? As the thought entered her head, she dismissed it. It was twenty years ago, and she was the one filled with rather uncivil curiosity.

"I was nineteen and already a father of two children. I had not known real love, I think. I asked Takouhi to see if Surya would want to be with me, and she was so happy." He smiled at the thought, and Charlotte could see that in some ways it was still fresh in his mind. "We had two girls, but they died, you know ... of fever, on the same day." He stopped speaking, and Charlotte could sense his thoughts flying back to that time.

"The same day ... God bless them." His voice had grown very quiet. "It was a bad time and she got ... low and very sick."

Charlotte now utterly regretted prying into past wounds. She put out her hand to his.

"I'm sorry, Tigran, I should not have asked."

He turned to look at her.

"No, I'm glad to tell you. I want everything to be clear between us. These things are in the past, old wounds. If we live, and especially if we love, we must have wounds. But when we are young they heal, Charlotte, though it seems they never will."

She said nothing, looking down.

"The second girl was Ambonese, like Mia. After Surya, I needed someone. I couldn't bear being alone. I didn't want Mia. It was a strange time, a bit like I was dead. I can't remember the days. I needed a woman with me all the time at night. If I was alone, ghosts would come. I couldn't get rid of them. She wanted to come to me. When Surya died, she went to Takouhi and asked. She was so good to me, for she must have known I did not love her at all. There were no children. It would have been too much.'

Tigran smiled and looked at Charlotte.

"The ending is happier. When I was healed, I lost all need, all feeling for her. There was nothing I could do. So I proposed to find her a husband, gave her a dowry. She is respectably married to a trader in Surabaya and has three children with him. She has become a Dutch housewife; it is far better than being my concubine."

Tigran jigged the horses into movement.

"Now you know my whole life. I gave my heart a rest and thought it would be peaceful, but now here you are, unsettling it again. Are you satisfied, Madam?"

Charlotte looked straight ahead.

"For now, sir. Just so long as when you are done with me, you do not send me off to a trader in Surabaya."

Tigran laughed. He had a nice, throaty laugh, she thought.

"Impossible. You shall be mistress of all you see, the unassailable queen of Brieswijk."

They emerged into the sunshine, and Charlotte saw a village ahead. An old man was driving a pair of buffalo down the track with two little boys mounted on their backs. Their long horns curved from their heads like crescent moons. Two baby buffalo, fluffy and gangling, came behind. It was a charming scene, like a painting, almost unreal. In the distance lay the village, clean and swept, the stilt houses of wood and thatch surrounded by the greens of the jungle and the lime-coloured rice stalks. A narrow, three-tiered, thatch-roofed mosque occupied one side. On the other was another small temple of unusual design, it too, three-tiered with a manicured thatch roof but much smaller, a shrine made of carved stone and wood, dressed in a wide skirt of black-and-white checked cloth. A Balinese temple, Tigran told her.

Five hundred people, husbands, wives and children, occupied this *kampong* on the river bank. The rice, the herds of animals, the vegetables and fruits supplied the house and the *kampong* first, and any surplus was sold in the market. Charlotte realised quickly that thousands of people lived on Brieswijk alone.

Charlotte had been somewhat startled at the number of domestic servants. At least a hundred gardeners worked tirelessly to confine the ever encroaching jungle, tend the fruit and spice trees and grow the lowland vegetables. Cows, sheep and goats grazed on the low slopes by the river. Cotton, kapok, java jute and a myriad of other grasses and plants were harvested, and in the *kampong* the women wove, dyed and printed the cloth for the house and for the town. In the big house, there was an individual servant for every chore, and each jealously guarded his or her preserve. Keeping squabbling at bay was one of the senior housekeeper's most onerous duties. The fire servants would not gather the wood, which was the wood servant's job, nor the oil for the lamps. The cooks would not cut the food; the bath maid would not wash the floor. The maid who ironed the sheets would not touch the tablecloths. Charlotte had four personal maids, each with her appointed task, and she transcended their duties and privileges at her peril. She reflected that the Javanese domestic enjoyed a life of ease which her sisters in Scotland would have envied. All of this Tigran related to her as they moved along the path, the little horses' tails waving gently from side to side, flicking at the occasional insect which annoyed their flanks.

She was glad no one here was a slave. Her Scottish family had been vehemently against slavery; her grandfather had been, she knew, a vocal and heartfelt supporter of Wilberforce and the abolitionists.

She questioned Tigran on the Dutch Indies attitude towards slavery. Where did the slaves come from?

They were sold to Bugis and Macassarese slavers by the local kings themselves, he said. The chiefs rounded up their own people, the poor, the destitute and the criminals of their islands and sold them to the markets in Batavia.

Charlotte looked at Tigran. He knew what she was thinking. The English ideas on this matter were common knowledge.

Raffles, Tigran said, during his command of Java, had tried to convince them all of the benefits of getting rid of the practice, but, apart from his own sister and a few others, no one had been receptive to these ideas. Raffles had imposed a tax on slave keeping and the *official* numbers had dropped dramatically, Tigran said with a wry smile. Raffles had officially prohibited the trade, but many, even in his own entourage, kept slaves and concubines, which caused no end of trouble. It was well known, for when they left, they advertised their sale quite openly in the *Java Gazette*.

The Sundanese people of West Java, this area, and the Javanese of the east had never been enslaved, not by their own kings, not by the Dutch; it was strictly forbidden. Mohammedans did not enslave those of their faith, and the Dutch were careful not to antagonise the Mohammedan population. The slaves came from the other islands, from Sumatra, Bali, Makassar, Ambon, Kalimantan, the eastern islands. In the VOC days, they came from everywhere: Africa, India, wherever the Dutch had colonies. Tigran admitted that during his father's time he had thought nothing of keeping slaves. The slaves at Brieswijk were treated with kindness; many of their domestic slaves more like old friends. The worst abuses, he had heard, were generally at the hands of some of the *nyai* wives, who, being too much surrounded and spoiled, grew petulant and cruel. They were often jealous of the pretty slave girls who might catch the master's eye and would resort to beatings and even poison. But slavery was, he assured her, on the wane. The English presence had had at least one effect on the Batavian attitudes. The English officers and officials brought their own free servants, who were quite cheap and worked hard and showed the old Batavians that one could do without slaves. The costs of slaves had risen dramatically, and they died too frequently. The whole business had come to be seen as uncouth and unsophisticated.

"So you see, the worm has turned. When we freed all the slaves on Brieswijk we were the laughingstock of the town, but now we are thought of as the most sophisticated and avant garde of enlightened citizens."

Tigran laughed, stopped the carriage and helped her down. He was glad now that Brieswijk had only freemen, for this, he could see, pleased Charlotte, and at this moment he had no higher aim than pleasing her in every possible way. He silently thanked Takouhi for her actions so long ago, which at the time had been something of a *cause célèbre*, arousing enormous gossip and great consternation amongst his neighbours.

The Governor-General had called him to account, but his lands were not government lands. Batavia was surrounded by private estates; the government had no say here.

A throng of villagers gathered, staring curiously at Charlotte. Tigran said something she did not understand, and there was a ripple of smiles and low murmurs. They bowed their heads slightly and put their right palms to their hearts. Tigran did the same. Then the crowd parted, and an old man came through the women and children and greeted Tigran. He was wizened and tiny, with sinewy tendons standing out on his arms and neck. His mouth was stained a bright red from betel chewing, and what teeth remained to him were quite black.

Tigran explained that this was the headman, grandfather of his childhood friend, who was nicknamed Petruk after one of Arjuna's wise and loyal servants in the *wayang* stories. Petruk's great-great grandmother had been brought from Bali, they thought, but this history was lost in the mists of time. They were not Mohammedans, Tigran added; they still kept to the Balinese ways. Petruk and Tigran had grown up together at Brieswijk. His mother had been Tigran's wet nurse and had taken care of him. Petruk was out now, he said, probably in the fields.

Actually, Tigran was relatively sure that his friend was engaged in a cockfight somewhere out of sight. Petruk loved his pretty brown-and-white fighting cock more than he loved his wife. Cockfighting was farmed out to the Chinese as part of their monopoly on gambling taxes, but Tigran closed his eyes to the practice on his lands. Petruk and his family, he added, had been freed long ago and chose to stay and live here. Petruk's father was long dead, and when his grandfather passed on, Petruk would be the headman.

Charlotte was rather lost in all these explanations, but she could not ask questions as the headman ushered them to a highly ornate pavillion built out over the river on fat teak stilts. The headman appeared flustered. Tigran was calming him; he explained to Charlotte that their visit had been unexpected. It was quite naughty of him, for the headman was unprepared.

Charlotte tried hurriedly to inspect this lovely building, but before she could take a long look, Tigran touched her arm and whispered for her to take off her shoes. As they stepped onto the highly polished floor,

Charlotte saw a large number of instruments gathered on a raised dais to one side. This, she knew from Takouhi's instructions, was the *gamelan*, the Javanese orchestra. Today it was silent, but she knew now that she had heard the strains of the *gamelan* from here as they had set out from the house.

Chairs were rushed in from somewhere in the village—heaven knew where, Charlotte thought—and placed in the verandah. Two tiny young women, pretty and gaily dressed in tight-fitting bodices and batik sarongs, brought tea and a silver and brass *sireh* set. Kneeling, they deftly took the leaf of the betel tree in their long, supple fingers, cut a slice of areca nut, added lime paste and condiments from the little containers on the tray, rolled the quids expertly and handed one, first to Tigran, then to Charlotte. Both girls wore hibiscus flowers in their hair and cast deep, coquettish glances at Tigran. Charlotte, remembering Takouhi's words about the village girls' liking for the white master, could not quite dismiss this as fancy.

Tigran hardly appeared to notice them. Their lips were stained a pinkish red, from the *sireh*, Charlotte knew, with a mounting apprehension. Tigran took the quid of *sireh* and placed it in his cheek, holding it there and nodded to Charlotte to do the same. She had seen the Indian money-lenders in Singapore chew on this *sireh*, noticed the reddened lips and teeth of the Chinese Nonyas and the Malays but had never thought of trying it herself. Truthfully, she thought it quite disgusting: the red mouth, the red spittle. Now she was expected to put it in her mouth! Tigran saw her hesitation and murmured to her,

"Put it inside the cheek only, do not chew. After the visit we can get rid of it, but not to accept is an insult. Sorry, Charlotte; I should have warned you."

Tigran looked so crestfallen that Charlotte screwed up her courage and quickly, without allowing another thought to enter her head, put the quid inside her cheek.

The headman was squatting in front of them, chewing his own wad with obvious pleasure. A period of silence ensued as tea was offered. Charlotte thought she might choke. The taste was everything at once; bitter and sweet, fizzingly hot, peppery and yet tangy with tinges of chocolate mixed with what she could only imagine would be the taste of soil after rain. Even though she was not chewing, she could feel the wad become a grainy mash, sticking to her teeth and gums. She had begun to salivate and swallow, breaking out into a sweat. As Tigran and the headman chatted amiably, she thought she might gag and put her hand on his arm. He turned and saw her face, rose and brought a brass spittoon to her. She looked at him, distressed, and spat out the mixture as delicately as was possible under the circumstances, wiping her mouth with her handkerchief. He, seeing her embarrassment, shielded her from the prying eyes of the villagers who were seated on the ground in front of the pavilion. Then, turning back to the headman, he spat out his wad, noisily, distracting the attention from her.

Tigran handed Charlotte the tea and she drank, clearing her mouth. When he saw her relief, he sighed and rose, taking his leave quickly.

Regaining their shoes, Tigran looked so serious that Charlotte said, "I am well, Tigran, but perhaps I should not try that again."

"I am sorry, Charlotte. I don't enjoy this *makan sireh*, either, but I am used to it. If you live here, it cannot be avoided. But there is no need for you to do it again. We have done our duty to the *kampong*. I have invited them to our wedding celebrations. They have had a look at this white madam who I intend to marry and now can gossip for weeks. The headman will inform all the other villages on the estate."

He looked shyly down.

"I hope you do not mind me showing you off."

Charlotte took his hand as she climbed back into the carriage. "Tigran, I do not mind anything you do, other than offer me another betel quid! I, too, want to feel at home here."

Her words affected him like a heady wine, and he repaid her with a smile of delight. Tigran climbed into the carriage and took the reins. He hesitated slightly, then turned to her.

"Can you drive, Charlotte?" he asked.

She was taken aback. Actually she had never driven a carriage, was somewhat afraid of the horses. Tigran put the reins in her hands and covered them with his.

"Together, yes?"

He clucked softly and shook the reins. The ponies moved gently away, and Charlotte drew a nervous breath. Within a few minutes he had taught her how to guide them, slow them, urge them on. She had not thought it so easy and laughed with delight. Tigran withdrew his hands from hers, and with an increasing confidence Charlotte drove the ponies on the path to the chapel, which led along the edge of the forest and ascended gently in a long sweep to the white building which gradually came into sight over the rise. Though she laughingly begged him to help her pull the ponies to a halt, he refused, smiling, and when she mastered this little skill and the ponies stopped, she gave a little cry of triumph and turned to him. The sight of her face flushed with delight pulled at Tigran's heart, and he itched to take her into his arms, but he quickly leapt down from the carriage.

The chapel was a perfect jewel of simplicity and elegance: a white building with a Dutch gable and two stout teak doors. On one door was carved the image of the Virgin and Child, Mary's cloak wrapping the baby Jesus. On the other stood St. Gregory the Illuminator, first Primate of Armenia, bedecked in flowing robes and wearing his mitre of office. Charlotte could see that these images had been carved by Javanese craftsmen, for they had the elongated features of the elegant heroes of the *wayang*. This merely added to their charm.

Seeing her run her fingers lightly over the carvings, he said, "The Javanese carvers, as Mohammedans, are forbidden to create the human image. It is an offence against Tuan Allah, who created man in perfection. I understand little of the subject, but have been told that when the Mohammedan faith came to Java it found stubborn resistance from ancient Hindoo traditions. With time and a little wisdom, the religion was subtly altered to allow the Javanese their traditional arts, the music of the *gamelan* and the shadow world of the *wayang* in particular. Thus were created the elongated, grotesque features of the *wayang*, which resemble but little the true features of humans but which stand as their shadowy spirits. I cannot speak to the truth of this, but that is what I have been told."

They entered the church. Through the windows of lead and clear glass in the chancel and the nave shone a soft light on the teak wood pews and the cool tiled floor. On the altar stood a cross inlaid with gold and lapis lazuli, on the wall a painting of the Ark sitting atop a mountain.

"We are the descendants of Noah," Tigran said. "This picture reminds us that Mount Ararat lies at the heart of our country, that we were the first Christian nation on earth."

Charlotte recalled the Armenian church in Singapore and wondered aloud if George had visited here.

"Yes, of course," said Tigran, "but I think George's building is much finer than this. He had more authoritative guides among the priests in Singapore. My father built this simple chapel when he moved here, for the Armenian community. He kept to the Dutch style of the house, for he was, in almost everything but religion, a Dutchman. We are few, no more than fifty in Batavia. But the Armenians are a people used to hardship. *A small tribe whose wars are fought and lost, whose structures have crumbled and whose prayers are no more answered.* My father used to say that nothing can destroy them utterly, however, for when two of them meet anywhere in the world, they create a new Armenia. This chapel was a centre for this 'new Armenia'. There is another church south of Koningsplein now, built by Miriam's husband, but we shall be married here."

Charlotte was touched by this poetic articulation of his people's troubles, their stoical survival against all odds. She viewed with renewed eyes the church and the motives behind its construction. It was a tiny bulwark against annihilation standing in the distant East, so far from the mother land, keeping a candle burning in this dark history.

Tigran led her to the graves of his father and mother, of three babies lost to them very young and of his father's concubine, Miriam's mother, who had been baptised and laid to rest here. Charlotte was curious why Takouhi's mother was not buried there. Tigran explained that Takouhi's mother had been Javanese, of the Mohammedan faith. Really their father should not have married her, for she never converted. He finished and began to turn away, but Charlotte put her hand on his arm, silently requesting to know more. Tigran smiled at her curiosity, glad that she was showing an interest in his family.

"She was a Javanese princess from the Kraton in Surakarta in the eastern part of the island who was given to my father. As I understand, this should not have happened. Takouhi knows the whole story. You will have to ask her. In any case, when she died, the court took her back to be buried in the royal cemetery."

He led Charlotte to a corner of the graveyard where thick gardenia bushes grew in profusion and filled the air with a heady scent. He showed her a little carved stone shrine which stood on a plinth just outside the fence, wound about with a faded, chequered black–and-white cloth. Flowers and woven grasses adorned it. Charlotte looked up at him.

"This is for Surya and the children," he said. "They are not buried here," he told her, reading her mind. "Surya was Balinese; it is not Java, it is an island, an island unlike any other in the archipelago. It has kept to its ancient traditions of the Hindoo and the Boodha, driven there by the spread of the Mohammedan faith which moved slowly through Java hundreds of years ago. Every week, someone from the *kampong* comes to put flowers," he said. "Many former slaves are Balinese. A great number of slaves in Batavia have always been Balinese. I think they like this little piece of Bali. My father would not have allowed it, but I am happy it is here."

Tigran plucked a gardenia bloom and placed it gently on the little shrine.

"Everything I loved about her was in her Balinese ways, her looks, her grace. I didn't want to change any of that. The Hindoo burial is by fire. So she was cremated together with the babies in her arms, and I put their ashes into the sea."

Charlotte felt a sob rise and controlled herself with difficulty. The way he had said this, so simply, the way he had silently placed the flower on the shrine, spoke of the deepness of his feelings for this young girl, dead at twenty, the same age as herself.

Tigran moved quickly away. He did not want Charlotte to grieve over this. He had spent three years doing that, filled with desolation and quiet madness. As he watched their funeral pyre, he had thought he might lose his mind, and when he had placed their ashes on the ocean he had wanted to slip over the side with them, quietly sink down into that deep dark watery place, forget Surya's flowing hair and dark eyes, forget the gurgling laughter of his little girls, drown love. Only restraining hands had prevented him, the hands of Petruk, his friend and Takouhi's Balinese manservant. Takouhi had come, but he had not wanted to share this moment with anyone else. When the grief had finally, slowly, lessened, and he could breathe, he had sworn never to feel like that again. But here was Charlotte, so like Surya, though he would never say it: light-skinned, dark-haired, lovely and young, filled with promise and light.

They moved to the stone of Miriam's daughter, Maria, who had lived but three short years, next to Meda's grave. Fresh leaves and flowers adorned all the graves, but the greatest number had been spread over these. Charlotte saw, half covered by grass and earth, a rope chain connecting all the children's gravestones, joining them, it seemed, so that they would have companions in the afterlife. Charlotte knew that Takouhi came here almost every day. They stood looking down at these little mounds, and Charlotte felt her heart in her throat, remembering Meda, her pretty face, her lovely voice. It wasn't fair. This lovely child. Her thoughts fled to George, alone, lonely, travelling in Europe, missing Takouhi and grieving for Meda, wanting desperately for him to come home. Tigran moved behind Charlotte and put his arms around her, laying his hand on her waist.

"We all lost these children, but a new one awaits. It is God's will. I promise I will love this baby as I love all my children, as I loved Maria and Meda, as I love you, Charlotte."

Charlotte felt tears rise in her throat and turned in his arms, burying her head in his shoulder. Tigran held her tight against him, putting his cheek gently against her hair, filled with emotion, feeling her sense of loss and pain—relief, too, he hoped, at his assurances. He knew she would think of this Chinaman as the baby grew, but after the birth, gradually, day by day, he would fade in her memory. In the meantime, Tigran would surround her with luxury and love. He would make this child a Manouk, his own child, endow it with privilege. He did not care what other blood ran in its veins. Half the blood was Charlotte's. It was enough. He would be the true father of her child. Not a Chinaman's bastard, but heir to a fortune and enviable social status. Charlotte could not remember this Chinese man forever. Tigran would teach her to love him more through kindness and affection and wealth and position. He was certain of it.

The following evening, by the candlelight of the terrace, blessed by the holy water of the priest, they exchanged promise rings. His was a gold band, hers a circle of silver and white diamonds. He put it on her right hand. On their wedding day the rings would pass through the hands of the priest, to their left hands. As he put it on her finger, Charlotte tried to feel something for this man who knelt at her feet, kissed her hands. Gratitude surfaced; she understood him better now, liked him more. But her other thoughts were fragmented.

From then on, almost every day, Tigran brought her something new. Silks, lace *kebaya* and exquisite batik sarongs, velvet and feathered hats, jewels of every colour.

Yet every night, before she slept, she opened the little box and gazed at the single white pearl on the necklace of woven red silk threads. The necklace *he* had given her the day she left him. What did anything else matter? She thought of Tigran's words. We all love in some measure the one who awakens powerful feelings. Is it true love? She shook her head. It was not like that with her and Zhen. Poverty had locked him into a marriage with a woman he did not love. Her situation was so like his that she was drawn even closer to him. Like him, now, she was forced by convention and self-preservation to marry someone else. In the day she lived entangled in her European life in Java; in the day he lived entangled in his Chinese life in Singapore; but at night, she knew, was certain, they lived in each other's dreams.

5

A gold embossed invitation to dinner at the Governor-General's palace stood against her mirror. It was clear everyone wanted to inspect Tigran's new fiancée. This was no small thing, Takouhi had told her, a beautiful white-skinned European woman. The last ones seen in Java had been Olivia Raffles and the wives of the British soldiers and officials who had run Java briefly for six years or the few, often plain, aristocratic wives of the Governors-General and officials who came out from Holland.

This extraordinary period of British rule was of enormous interest to Charlotte, who would have liked to hear more, but Takouhi put her off.

"I will let Wilhelmina tell you. She is wife of Pieter Merkus, the Governor-General. My English not good but Wilhelmina speak very good."

Takouhi had selected their clothes with extraordinary care. They were to be dressed up-to-the-minute from head to toe in the latest European fashions. This was to be pure theatre, a statement of the Manouk power, wealth and "chic." The old Dutch biddies and their dowdy daughters must be made to swoon with envy. In particular, Petra Couperus, who had been dying to marry Tigran for at least three years.

"We meet her tonight. She is rich widow like me and wait and wait for him. Since her last marriage she say no to every man who come to marry her. But she also has nasty tongue. Talk, talk about everyone. But he meet you, and now Petra lose hope. You remember poor Lilian Aratoun, who also swoon—is word, no?—swoon for Tigran in Singapore. Here in Jawa, Tigran is Arjuna, you know Arjuna? The lover of the *wayang*.

Later I tell you why we call him like that."

Charlotte smiled ironically. She knew who Arjuna was. Takouhi and Meda had told her the stories, loved them, of Arjuna's amorous and heroic exploits. He was the gallant and handsome Galahad of the Indian world, the peerless archer, the compassionate seeker of meaning, full of love and bravery and honour, the Javanese knightly ideal. Women everywhere it seemed longed to be where she was today: on the threshold of marriage to Arjuna.

As they finished their toilette, Tigran entered. Charlotte rose from her chair, and he felt his heart thump. She was so beautiful he could hardly breathe. He stood unmoving as she came towards him and offered him her hand, with its diamond ring. She was dressed entirely in white—virginal white, Takouhi had insisted—and wearing the blue diamond flower spray he had given her in Singapore. The bodice was just immodest enough to reveal her bosom, creamy white, and the silky beauty of her neck and shoulders, against which rested the long low coiffure of her blue-black hair. Her violet blue eyes had been made up with *kohl*—he could see it—imparting a smoky sensuality. He kissed her hand and calmed himself, chiding himself silently for being a fool. From his pocket he drew a flat box and opened it towards her. Inside lay a necklace, a chain of diamonds of exactly the same cut and colour as the brooch, almost the blue of her eyes, which Tigran sought to match. Charlotte had not quite ceased to be amazed at these gifts and smiled her thanks up at him. She had some inkling of the trouble he had gone to in order to find these rare blue stones. She invited him to put it around her neck, and as he fastened the clasp he could not help but drop his lips to her naked shoulder. She smelled faintly of roses.

Charlotte moved away as if she had been stung, and Takouhi, who had taken it all in, moved quickly to her friend's side and frowned at Tigran. Charlotte realised that her error, utterly involuntary, stemmed from other memories, and quickly moved to Tigran's side and put her arm through his.

"Thank you for your beautiful gift. You look most handsome tonight, Tigran. We shall be the finest couple in the room, shall we not?"

Tigran put his hand on hers and smiled, thanking her for forgiving him. In fact, Charlotte thought, Tigran did look handsome, dressed in black and white, his hair long and shining, the jet beads she liked so much glinting, his eyes with their gold flecks filled with a love which shone on her like sunlight. She was annoyed with herself. She had not disliked the feel of his lips on her shoulder; she should not have shied away like a nervous virgin. She had to make it up to him.

Turning, she touched his face and lightly kissed his cheek. She felt his intake of breath, the movement of his arm curling round her waist, and withdrew quickly. His face was flush, the golden flecks in his eyes darkened. Takouhi took Charlotte's hand and led her out of the room quickly.

"Charlotte, be careful. Tigran love you, I told you. He control himself, but very hard. Don't forget."

They went slowly down the staircase, and as they arrived at the door, Tigran took Charlotte's arm to help her into the carriage.

"You ride with Takouhi; it is safer for you. I will take her carriage."

He smiled, and Charlotte realised that he was making light of the incident and was grateful to him and, somehow, slightly disappointed they would not be riding together. She was not absolutely certain anymore that she did not want to kiss Tigran, but before a dinner at the Governor-General's palace was probably not the time to experiment with this idea. She settled back with Takouhi as they set off down the flame-lit path. This was the first time since her arrival that she had left Brieswijk, and a feeling of pleasant and exciting anticipation suffused her.

The carriage entered the broad avenue of Molenvleit. Takouhi pointed out the white walls of the Harmonie Club as they crossed the canal and turned onto Rijswick.

"Daendels order this building for European people to meet, but no money, so Raffles finish it. All of Rijswick and Nordwick is Raffles's work. Before him there were some big VOC estates, but also *kampong* and Chinese shops. When he come, he order all pull down, move out. Only European can build here, make shop here. Raffles house next to Governor-General's, other side. Is hotel now."

As she finished speaking, the coach passed through gates and, by the light of lanterns and firebrands, a rather plain, two-storey white house appeared. In Charlotte's view, it hardly, from here, earned the name "palace", looking no better, she thought, than a colossal horse station. Tigran's stables, indeed, were more grandly constructed.

Tigran was waiting and, taking a lady on each arm, climbed the marble steps and walked into the brilliant light of the hall. He was not ordinarily a boastful man, but tonight he brimmed with a proud desire to show Charlotte, this fair and lovely woman that he had won, to his acquaintance.

A band was playing Viennese tunes, and the room was already full of men and woman in conversation, divided, Indies style, into two. To her alarm, as Charlotte entered the conversation fell to a murmur and every eye turned to her. Suddenly the music seemed unnaturally loud. Then, just as abruptly, it stopped, as if their arrival was a signal, and began again with a gentle and lilting version of *Wilhelmus van Nassouwe*, the anthem of the Netherlands. Doors at the far end of the room opened, and a couple emerged. The man, the Governor-General, for this was he she could tell from the almost reverential hush that fell on the crowd, was older, tall and spare with a thinning pate and sharp black eyes. On his arm was a woman of about thirty-five, small boned and pretty, with brown hair. Tigran left Charlotte and his sister and instantly gained the men's side of the room. Takouhi and Charlotte joined the women. Pieter Merkus, the Governor-General of the Netherlands East Indies and his wife, Wilhelmina, made their way slowly down the aisle, talking now and then to their guests. When they arrived at Charlotte, she curtsied deeply and was introduced. Pieter bowed graciously over Charlotte's hand and Wilhelmina kissed her cheek warmly.

"Welcome, my dear, to Batavia, and congratulations on your illustrious marriage to one of our favourite men. I fear you have broken many hearts this week."

Her English was absolutely correct, with a slightly odd intonation now and again, as if she had learned much of it from a book.

As Pieter went up to Tigran, the band struck up a popular tune and the buzz of conversation resumed, but Charlotte felt as if every eye were drinking her in. Takouhi led her to a group of women seated in the corner of the room, some hugely fat, some rake-thin and pale, most simply dull and remarkably plain. As they ogled her, out of the corner of her eye she saw a striking woman, dressed in dark red silk, go up to Tigran and lay her hand on his arm. Takouhi gazed at her, in fact almost all the women in the room had swivelled their eyes to her, for this breaching of the line was an extraordinarily daring break in protocol.

"Petra," Takouhi whispered.

Tigran turned to Petra and bowed. She had moved in very close, keeping her hand on his arm and whispering something against his cheek. Charlotte felt a sudden, unexpected flush of annoyance at this intimacy. She could not see his face. All the ladies were now watching Charlotte intently. She opened her fan, waved it gently and waited, curious now to see what Tigran would do.

At that moment, a group of men approached Tigran, and he removed Petra's hand from his arm and bowed over it, taking his leave. Petra made her way slowly over to Takouhi.

As they curtsied, Charlotte could see there was no love lost between the two women. Petra looked Charlotte up and down in the most insolent manner. Charlotte felt the blood rush to her cheeks.

"Con-gra-tu-la-tions," Petra said slowly and deliberately in accented English, then turned on her heel. Charlotte could see that Petra was very beautiful. Thick, black curly hair which fell about her face and shoulders in a most alluring manner, full rouged lips, dark almond eyes with long lashes, a voluptuous figure, fine brown skin. She could also see the woman was angry and jealous, and Charlotte wondered why Tigran had not married such a belle years ago.

"Takouhi, why did Tigran not marry her? She is beautiful and rich."

Takouhi contemplated the swaying figure. "Yes, lovely. She is Mardyjker blood somewhere. She married already three times. There was a time he care for her, she have chance, but she make big mistake with Tigran."

Charlotte waited to hear more. "Mardyjker?" she asked quizzically. It crossed her mind that she had developed an unseemly interest in Tigran's former relationships, especially this one.

"Mardyjker is child of free black slave." Takouhi sneered as she said it, and Charlotte was astonished, for such gracelessness in Takouhi was unusual. "They always clever and proud." Seeing Charlotte's face, she continued. "Before Dutch come to Java, Portuguese have big power in Asia. Like Dutch men, Portuguese men make million half-blood child which they baptise, make Christian."

Charlotte smiled at this surely exaggerated number, which Takouhi used for anything over ten.

"When Dutch come, they take many prisoners in old Portuguese towns like Ambon, Malacca and Coromandel. They make slave and bring here. Those people Catholic, but Dutch not allow this, so Dutch say if slave join Dutch church, they be free. So Mardyjker mean "free man." They speak Portuguese. Even in my father time here, many speak mix Bengal and Portuguese. Now no one speak Portuguese, but here is still Portuguese church in the Kota. So, anyway, long ago, maybe, but Petra's blood like that."

Charlotte looked at Petra with renewed interest. A truly scarlet woman with a colourful lineage. How wonderful! Perhaps Tigran was the only one she could not have. Charlotte looked over at Tigran, standing, dark and handsome, in the group of ordinary- looking men. She could see that his long-haired piratical demeanour gave him an undeniable air of romance and danger. Petra, too, was gazing at him.

As if sensing Charlotte's eyes, he turned and looked at her; it was a long look, of such smouldering intensity that she looked down in embarrassment. But she smiled nevertheless. Petra too saw this look and turned away, fanning herself violently. This was becoming most enjoyable.

A white-liveried servant came up with drinks, and Charlotte chose French wine in a fine crystal glass. Several introductions passed; then the Reverend Walter Medhurst, the Anglican pastor of All Saints, introduced himself. His wife, Eliza, a small, frail-looking woman was with him. They found they had a mutual interest in the London Missionary Society and a common acquaintance in Benjamin Keaseberry in Singapore, who had studied printing with him. Medhurst had arrived in the East to spread the word of Christ to China. China being closed to foreigners, however, it was decided to minister to the Chinese outside who might, if they returned home, take Christianity with them. Java had been chosen. That had been eighteen years ago, he added with a wry smile, but now things had changed. He and others were preparing to depart. The Treaty of Nanking had ended that country's isolation. His own son, educated at

Macau, had been Chinese secretary to the expeditionary leader Charles Elliot during the war. He and his wife would be joining their boy in this new town of Hong Kong before proceeding to Shanghai. It was a double blessing.

"Now we shall all begin this glorious enterprise." His colour had heightened, and Charlotte could see his enthusiasm. She talked a little of her father's life in Madagascar for the Society. As ever, she was impressed by the quiet, unrelenting faith of these missionaries, but was somehow also confounded by their attitudes to the violence and horror of war, the invasion of other lands. She thought of her father. For the first time she asked herself why on earth he had gone to Madagascar. The Chinese in Singapore seemed happy with their ordered and peaceful religion. She could not think how Zhen's deep soul would be improved by Christianity.

"Do the Chinese need Christianity, Reverend Medhurst?" she asked, now suddenly curious, for surely his reasons must have been those of her own father.

"My dear child, oh yes." He looked shocked. "They worship idols. It is our duty to bring the grace and love of the true Lord to the heathen and to the poor downtrodden masses. And the enormous advantages of an advanced and benevolent civilisation.

Before she could ask more, other Englishmen and their wives joined them. Charlotte found herself relaxing in their easygoing company. John Price was a plantation owner, and his wife was Dutch Chinese. Gillean Maclaine was a trader with a Javanese wife who spoke good English. His sons were by his side with their Indische wives. As she looked round the room, Charlotte realised what Takouhi had said was true: there were few white European woman in the palace. Clearly these English guests had been invited to set her at her ease, and she was grateful to Wilhelmina for her thoughtfulness. The only bachelor present was Nathanial Fox, a naturalist and archaeologist who had been in Java for many years; a slim, pleasant-faced man with blue eyes and curly sandy hair, some ten years older than herself. He reminded her immensely of Robert.

As the others wandered away to pay their compliments elsewhere, Nathanial, seemingly unconcerned about the proprieties of sitting amongst the women, began an exposé of the various guests. The Reverend

Medhurst, he said, dear old fellow, was a worthy soul and an excellent scholar.

"He has made a first translation of the Bible into Chinese. He works tirelessly in Batavia. All Saints opens its doors to all the Christian faiths. He has a printing press. There is a native school and an orphanage. He petitions the government for aid in diffusing Christian knowledge amongst the people of Java, but his pleas fall, I assure you, on very deaf ears. The government dreads any such actions and will not brook interference with the religions of the country for fear of stirring up rebellion. Doubtless they are correct."

Over there, the wild-looking one was Baron van Hoevell, president of the Batavian Society for the Arts and Sciences, an institution which Raffles had revived and encouraged. The Society met at the Harmonie Club, where there was an excellent English library. He himself would be presenting his findings to the Society in due course.

The group in a huddle around Tigran, he said, were all Freemasons, for it was strong in Batavia.

"De Ster in het Oosten," he said with a strong, mock-Dutch accent. "The Star of the East. You should probably know that your fiancé is doubtless adept in its black arts. You are warned, Mademoiselle."

They shared a smile.

The grumpy group of old men dressed like figures in a seventeenth-century Dutch painting were members of the Raad van Indie, the council which ran the Indies and met here in the palace. The Governor-General and his wife, like Raffles and all others before them for a hundred years, spent almost all their time in Buitenzorg.

The most grotesque man in the room, but one of the most entertaining and pleasant, was old Leendert Miero, Nathanial confided.

Charlotte looked at this little old man, wizened and bald, with a prominent and hairy chin which contrived to meet his nose. No mouth was discernible, and Charlotte realised that the old fellow clearly had no teeth. He was dressed in an ancient blue velvet coat and a frilled cravat and attended by what were clearly, by their looks, his children.

"He has a wonderful story. There is a house, not far from Brieswijk on Molienvliet West. It was built around 1760 by a former Governor-General, Reinier de Klerk, and passed through various hands to those of John Siberg, who was acting Governor-General before Daendels. Anyway, it happened that Siberg returned home one hot day and found a Polish Jewish soldier sleeping at the entrance whilst on duty. The furious Siburg ordered the man to take fifty lashes. On the day of the lashing, so the story goes, he swore by his forefathers Abraham, Isaac and Jacob, that one day he would own the house. After he finished his military service, the soldier became a goldsmith and made a fortune. He purchased the house and still to this day he invites all Batavia to celebrate the anniversary of the day he was given fifty lashes."

Before Nathanial could continue, Wilhelmina Merkus came up to them, fanning herself rapidly. Nathanial bowed and departed to the correct side of the room.

"Are you admiring us all? Will you join me on the terrace before dinner? I am so hot, and I should be glad to talk a little alone."

6

The terrace of the palace overlooked a vast park, dark now, with candles and flames flickering here and there. Night-blooming flowers—tuberose, gardenia, jasmine and moonflower—exhaled their invisible scent. Charlotte was grateful to escape the heat and the pressing attentions of the ballroom. They sat in the semi-darkness. A servant boy stood to one side with a large fan.

"You have caused quite a little stir in our town. you know," said Wilhemina.

Charlotte smiled.

"That was certainly not my intention, Madame," she replied.

"Call me Willi, please, for I feel we shall be *amies*. You are English, I think, and, though it is not fashionable for a Dutch Governor-General's wife to say so, I love everything English and spend a great deal too much time with the English citizens of our city. I am sometimes reprimanded for it, but *Merde!* I say. Officially, of course, we do not care for you all very much, though we are grateful to your Wellington for ridding Holland of that *connard* Napoleon and restoring these islands, at least, to us intact."

Charlotte was not sure how she should react to these frank expressions nor what to think of what her grandmother would have called the "*leid ay a huir.*" Fearing to offend, she sat absolutely still.

"When the British came, you know, I have heard they were not at all impressed with us. Lord Minto, the British Governor-General of India, considered us lacking in all beauty—no difference between us except in varieties of ugliness and ordinariness of dress and manners. Another officer, Lieutenant Fielding, was known to remark that amongst us all there were no more than three tolerable—a collection of 'queer-looking quizzes', as he put it. Doubtless he was right at the time, for the old women dressed in rather dull Indische style and the old men in very long embroidered velvet coats down to the heels.

"To the old Batavians, the English were an intrusive horror. But to the young they were a breath of fresh air. We couldn't change fast enough. I was a thoroughly ignorant child when they arrived, but my father, who was Raffles's principal councillor, got an English tutor and encouraged us in all things English. I was taught to read. This would not have happened if the English had not come. All sorts of books in English were available: spellers, grammars and geography texts. New novels, essays and prayer books arrived all the time. My favourite was Aesop's Fables."

Charlotte set down her glass. She had not bothered to correct Wilhelmina's idea of her being English, for though she was, ostensibly, Scottish, sometimes Charlotte hardly knew what she was. She was cooler now and more at her ease, caught up in Wilhelmina's memories and her zest.

"Was it not a strange time for you all, with the arrival of so many foreigners?" she asked.

"Oh yes, *mon dieu*, indeed, but there was a good deal of excitement too. In the beginning all we women were terrified, for the men were ordered into the cantonment and we were left on our own. Not gallant, eh? But after five days it was over, and the English soldiers were very decent. They did not loot or touch the women. We were surprised. Looting was all by the slaves. There was little resistance. The French, Dutch and Javanese soldiers, who did not much care to lose their lives for Napoleon, so I believe, just gave up. Janssens, who was the Governor at the time, was humiliated of course, but frankly relieved. He told my father that he would not have known how to continue with the colony if the English had not succeeded! Holland was cut off, and Batavia was virtually bankrupt. We accepted it all rather quickly. Then of course, it brought so many more interesting and eligible bachelors into town. Officers in the army, officials in the government. We were suddenly outnumbered and awash with young men."

She looked over at Charlotte in the penumbra.

"Takouhi was a beautiful, rich widow of twenty-six. I can assure you the interest in her from the English gentlemen was considerable. I imagine she was one of the 'three tolerable beauties' who Lieutenant Fielding spoke about, for he most definitely was enamoured of her, but she might have had her pick from many."

This last was something Charlotte had not considered. Takouhi had met George Coleman when she was almost thirty-seven. There was a good deal of her life that was very mysterious.

"For the old boys, they were at least pleased that the English blockade was finally lifted. Ships had not arrived from Holland for four years, and, besides no young men, we had no beer, no wine, brandy or rum, good oil, no salted bacon, pickled meats or butter. Daendels stopped almost all the light in houses: no parties or balls. All that changed in a moment. Raffles and Olivia dragged the wives into society by all means possible. Can you imagine, these women who had lived in virtual *purdah* their whole lives had suddenly to dress in European fashions and dance at balls in the arms of English men. The English were horrified to discover the ignorance of the women here, whom they considered lazy and helpless through the constant attendance of slaves. We were untutored and lacking social graces, chewing betel, which they disliked more than anything. In England, women participated in the lives of their husbands.

They were determined to change us. My own mother was a native woman, my father's *nyai*, so she was spared. But for Maria, my father's wife, it was fearful, I imagine. She was not allowed to go abroad with her slave attendants and her umbrellas of rank. She had to go out and dance, eat with a knife and fork, sit on chairs and mix with men she did not know. *Madre de dios!* It caused a great fuss."

Wilhelmina stopped briefly. "Awful for them, now I think about it. But for the young, truly it was wonderful."

She called to a waiting servant, and he placed two fresh glasses of wine on the table which separated them.

"There was an English newspaper, so lively and interesting, and how we were scolded to give up our Indies ways. The English considered that we lived in our underwear—the sarong a petticoat and the *kebaya* a chemise, as if we had, somehow, got our clothes on the wrong way round. The innocent *kebaya* became a battleground. You were either pro-*kebaya* or anti-*kebaya*. To this day, I still remember one stout Batavian who leapt to our defense.

"*De Vrouwen al te zaam op eene leest te schoeien. C'est incroyable*, but I memorised it in English. We children used to chant it.

To condemn all women together, in a fashion most uncouth,
To place the customs of a country in the worst of light;
Is it a goose who does this, or just a callow youth,
Who has never in his life learned how to be polite?
Let an Indian teach you a lesson short and sweet:
Never without reason scoff at other folk you meet.
Just stick to your roast beef, your Madeira, port or beer,
For after all that's the only joy Life holds for you out here."

Wilhelmina let out a loud guffaw, and Charlotte, too, laughed.

"So fashion plates of the latest London and Paris styles always found a place, though the fashion at the time was quite horrid, I recall. We were not sure why they were so critical of us when it was rather the English ladies who appeared to be wearing a nightdress. Our shawls, though, became quite popular with the English ladies—the more ornate and expensive the better.

"We were to be *improved* by literature and poetry. The wives who were obliged to wait on Olivia found the betel banned, cuspidors removed and local dress frowned upon. Raffles and his officers arranged meetings and dances at the Harmonie Club; the Military Bachelors' Theatre and the Shouwburg put on musicals and English plays to which the ladies were encouraged to come. I still remember going to a theatre for the first time. I do not remember the play, but it was thrilling. We went to many plays after. We always knew the stories because they were printed in Dutch in the newspaper, which Father read to us. Plays, dances, music, *madre de dios*! It was wonderful."

She drank a draught of wine and fanned herself, recalling those heady days.

"Most of the regulations which Raffles put in place remained: the land tax, for instance, the justice system, even driving carriages on the left side of the road. Of course, Batavia had an effect on the English, too.

Many men who had come as bachelors very rapidly began their own little harems of slave women. In Borneo, the Resident of Banjamarsin, Alexander Hare, was notorious, my dear, for his slave plantation and his vast harem. Even Gillespie, the military commandant, had slaves in his households. For all the sermonising and official edicts, nothing ever really changed in that area until much later."

Charlotte remembered Tigran's words on the subject.

"Ah, but many of us admired you English a great deal. So avant-garde, so enlightened, so lively. Raffles's comptroller christened his daughter Olivia Mariamne Stamford Raffles Villeneuve." Wilhelmina gave a short laugh. "It was *de trop*, my dear, don't you agree? And my uncle Petrus Couperus, one of Raffles's councillors, called his son, Willem Jacob Thomas Raffles Couperus. He was Petra's brother, my nephew. Petra is my niece through the marriage of my half-sister Catharina. Poor Willem died very young, bless his soul."

Wilhelmina looked over at Charlotte and detected a heightened interest at the mention of Petra. Actually, Charlotte was thinking what dull days they must have been indeed, when the *English government*, of all groups, should have had a lightening, gay effect upon society anywhere.

"And now you will marry Tigran Manouk, the Arjuna of Batavia, the great catch. So many maidens, and widows, will cry in their beds tonight, now they have seen your beauty and how hopeless is their position."

Wilhelmina laughed.

"Yes," said Charlotte, "I am only discovering what it is that I have done. I had no idea."

"Oh dear, Charlotte, even worse. All achieved without guile or intent. They shall be vexed indeed."

The deep sound of a gong resounded around the garden. Wilhelmina finished her wine and rose.

"Come, we must return. Tigran will be looking for you to take you into dinner, and my Pieter hates it when I disappear off in the darkness." As they returned to the ballroom, Charlotte could not help a feeling of warmth towards Wilhelmina, the highest woman in the land, who often disappeared off into the darkness, to her husband's chagrin.

Dinner, Charlotte discovered, was a vastly different affair to those in Singapore. Before they sat down, the table had already been covered thickly with open dishes of vegetables and viands. These were, she discovered, to be eaten cold. The soup however, came boiling to the table, so hot as to be a danger to the palate. The desserts and fruit were all present, and thus the whole meal was displayed at once. Charlotte was somewhat disconcerted to find that some of the older diners, both men and women, used their knives for purposes which most English would perform with a spoon or fork. After the soup was dispatched, there was a general mêlée, with desserts preceding meats or interspersed with them, vegetables and fruits taken together, beer and wine drunk as the diner chose. The diners were attended by an array of quiet servants, leaping forward to fill a glass, pass a dish and generally assist in the Rabelaisian fray. It was certainly lively, Charlotte thought, whilst resisting all attempts by others to combine on her plate a piece of roast fowl with the sago pudding. Tigran was seated near Wilhelmina and occasionally smiled over at her and raised an ironic eyebrow. Charlotte, fortunately, was seated between John Price and Reverend Medhurst and was thus afforded a measure of protection.

The dancing stood in direct contrast to the frenzy of dining. Slow waltzes were the order of the evening. Everyone seemed to know how to dance most gracefully. Tigran took her in his arms. She remembered an evening in Singapore when there had been dancing, but he had not waltzed. Now she wondered why; he was an excellent dancer. She thought it scandalous—he kept no space between her body and his, holding her tightly against him. Though all eyes were upon them, this seemed to excite no general stirrings around the hall, and she could see from the other dancers that this was, in Batavia, the mode of the dance. What her acquaintance might have thought of this in Singapore and certainly in Scotland she could only imagine.

Tigran smiled down at her, and she blushed, unused to such full-blooded attentions and realising too the rather unforeseen enjoyment at feeling the movements of his body against hers, the sureness of his guiding touch. He held her for two dances, and she was breathless and hot as he released her to a chair and kissed her hand.

Pieter Merkus came up and claimed her as a new dance began, and she saw, out of the corner of her eye, Petra Couperus go up to Tigran and, taking him by the hand, lead him out onto the terrace. He put up little resistance, Charlotte thought, and could not wait for the dance to end. She curtsied to the Governor-General as Pieter took her back to sit with Takouhi. He called for wine and began to converse with her friend. Charlotte paid no attention at all, her eyes riveted to the terrace. She could see nothing but blackness, with a flickering of lamps. She drank down her wine in one gulp and rose, excusing herself with a need for air. The dances were in full flow, and she moved nearer to the door, then, seeing no one, dared to go out into the darkness. She heard a murmur of voices, and, advancing quietly, she leant against a pillar.

Tigran was talking low, but Petra's voice had risen slightly. They were talking in a mixture of Malay and Dutch, which Charlotte could not understand. She looked around the pillar and saw them standing by a low wall, in the flickering light. Petra had her hand on Tigran's arm. He said something to her, and suddenly she dropped her hand and turned away from him. He stood behind her. It was clear he took no pleasure in seeing her upset. He murmured, and she turned again and put her arms around his neck, pulling his face towards hers. He took her arms from his neck and moved her firmly away. When he made to leave, she dragged at his arm, stumbling as he pulled away. It was obvious she was abject, and Charlotte wished to see no more. She ran quickly back to the ballroom and walked to her seat.

Tigran returned with two glasses of wine. He handed one to Charlotte and chatted amiably with Pieter. When the music began again, he pulled Charlotte gently into his arms and into a waltz. She was dying to ask him about Petra but sensed that he would most certainly not welcome such inquiries.

When the evening finally ended, Tigran helped Charlotte into the coach. She was utterly exhausted and befuddled from the wine. The lamplight cast a gentle glow inside the carriage. As Tigran settled in beside her, she kicked off her shoes. He took off his coat and cravat, loosed his thin, soft cotton shirt, threw his head back and closed his eyes. Within a few minutes, as the coach set off swaying, she realised he was asleep. She looked at him, liking the way his hair fell down his neck and onto his cheek. She could see the outline of his chest and waist against the cotton. She let her eyes go down his body. What did she feel for this man? Tonight he had been wonderful. Handsome, gallant, a wonderful dancer, an attentive companion. Tonight he had been Arjuna. She had been the envy of almost every woman in the room.

What did she want? She closed her eyes and saw Zhen. Tired and befuddled, she let her mind rove over his face and body, remembered the feel of his hands on her and let out a low moan. She opened her eyes, but Tigran was still asleep.

Inside the coach it was close and hot. She dropped the glass on the window and put her head outside, watched the swaying horses, heard their snuffling breath and the beat of their hooves on the ground. It had rained, and the path was still slightly wet. The quarter-moon flitted between the branches like a scythe cutting the dark masses of the trees, racing ahead of the coach. The sky was clear and high, washed fresh by the rain. A smell of smoke came from the tall palm leaf torches which the two red-coated footmen held aloft from the back of the carriage.

Footmen, thought Charlotte in a muddled way. I am in a carriage with footmen, like Queen Victoria. The thought was suddenly comical, and she began to giggle.

Charlotte's hard embroidered bodice was hooked in the front, and it felt hot and tight. Takouhi had forbidden any corset wearing, which she herself loathed and which she deemed unhealthy and unsafe for a pregnant woman. Takouhi could not understand these contraptions with which white women bound themselves. Charlotte undid three hooks and allowed her chest to breath against the light camisole underneath. The wind flowed around her body, and this felt so good she undid all the hooks, allowing it to swing open and feel the coolness against the cotton. She looked quickly at Tigran. Did she want him to awake and find her like this? Did she want him to make love to her inside this dark swaying carriage? She released the camisole from her skirt and allowed the air to circulate around her breasts, over her hot skin. It felt wonderful.

She looked again at Tigran. She had only to reach out and take his hand, put it against her skin and he would awake, she knew.

Charlotte was completely overtaken with feeling, her blood beating like the hooves of the horses against the path. She threw off her bodice, undid the skirt and let it drop to the floor. She dropped the petticoat also, leaving only her pantaloons. Under this she was naked. The blue diamonds lay against her throat. She liked the feel of the necklace on her naked body.

She knelt next to Tigran and put her hand tentatively to his face. He did not awake but merely moved his head slightly. Somewhere in her brain came the thought that this was wrong, but it was far away. Charlotte frowned, annoyed at his lack of reaction. She put her face to his, her lips on his, and pressed them. He awoke surprised and pulled his face away. He took in Charlotte's dress thrown on the floor, the outline of her breasts against the camisole, the heavy-lidded gaze. He saw what she wanted, but was it with him or someone inside her head? He had expected this moment to come, but not so soon, not here in the darkness, where it would be so easy to succumb to his own desire for her.

Charlotte moved into his arms, putting her lips against his throat, touching his hair, running her fingers into the plaits and beads which she found so arousing, willing him to touch her. She had taken a surfeit of wine, he knew. The movement of the coach swayed her body against him.

A sudden jolt over rough ground caused her almost to fall from the seat, and he pulled her to him. He lowered his window to the night air and called to the coachman. "Slow down, no hurry. Go carefully."

The pace immediately slowed to a gentle trot.

By the lamp's dim light, Tigran looked at her. She locked her fingers into his braids and pulled his lips to hers. She sighed a shuddering sigh, and he could not resist deepening the kiss, their first kiss. He pulled her more tightly into his arms, wanting to rip off her clothes, do what she was begging him for.

But, tomorrow what would she feel? Revulsion? Invaded, shamed? He couldn't bear any strain between them. These first weeks of their life together were too important, and she was too vulnerable. For the first time in his life, he was glad to be forty and full of sense. If he had been a younger man, he would not have had the will to stop.

He pulled away.

"Zhen," she groaned. "Please."

Tigran stiffened. Before he could think, he felt her suddenly go completely limp and her head fall against his shoulder.

He let her fall back gently to the seat. Her camisole had risen, half revealing her breasts, the smooth curve of her waist. Her hair was mussed around her face and neck. The blue diamond necklace lay slung back loosely against her skin, and he put out a hand to pull it, bring her up to him with it. He was tempted, his blood pounding. He was furious at her, too, for saying that man's name. Was she dreaming of this damn Chinaman?

As he had this thought, he pulled his hand back and flung himself into the corner of the carriage. What was he thinking? He hated this man more than he had imagined possible. He wanted to reach down inside Charlotte and rip this Chinaman out.

His head resting against the side of the carriage, he turned the ring on his finger and breathed in the night air. Once he was calm, he arranged her clothes and moved her gently until her head rested on his lap. He would not wake her when they arrived. He would call for a cover and have her carried to her bedroom. What the servants would make of their half-dressed mistress he did not care. But he had made up his mind. Whilst this baby and this man lived inside her, he would not make love to her, even after the wedding. She must come to him, *must* come to him. Patience, Tigran, he thought, then called to the coachman to speed up.

7

When Charlotte awoke she felt wretched. As she opened her eyes, Takouhi rose from the chair next to the bed and came to her, wiping her sweating face with a cool cloth. Charlotte tried to get up but felt waves of nausea sweep over her, and Takouhi, seeing the whiteness of her face and lips, called the maid for a bowl. Charlotte leaned over the edge of the bed and vomited again and again until nothing was left. Yet still the waves of nausea came, engulfing and shaking her body. When at last they subsided, she fell back, exhausted.

"*Alamak*, Charlotte. Too much excitement last night. No more wine for a while," Takouhi said, smiling, for she knew Charlotte would be well now that her body had cleared itself. She and Tigran had worried, though, and a watch had been set over her all night.

"You pregnant, must be careful."

As she said this, the maid raised Charlotte from the pillows and put a cup of warm liquid to her mouth. It tasted of honey and ginger, but there was a bitterness and sourness in it, too. It was not unpleasant, and Charlotte, her throat parched, drank it down willingly. Within a few minutes she began to feel better.

"Today you rest. We go to the river. Drink tea, ginger, lemon, nettle. Eat little bit, fish and vegetables. This evening you be fit as fiddle."

Charlotte smiled at this English expression, which Takouhi had clearly learned from George. Then her mind suddenly turned to the night before. It had been an exhilarating evening, and then in the coach, something had happened. She had vague memories of the wind, of her body next to Tigran's, then nothing.

"Takouhi, did I do something silly last night at the dinner or ... later? Where is Tigran?"

Takouhi handed her another drink and helped her sit up. "Tigran has gone to Buitenzorg. It is tea plantation up in the hills. He has business there. We go there later, after the wedding. Soon hot season begin. Cool in the hills."

Charlotte felt an irrational disappointment. She would not see Tigran today. Gone? For how long? Until the wedding, which was two weeks away? It felt like a long time.

Takouhi opened the windows wide on both sides of the bedroom. A breeze billowed the gauzy curtains. Tigran had told Takouhi about last night, her calling of the Chinese man's name. He wanted to get away for a while, leave Charlotte to her thoughts; perhaps she would begin to miss him.

Takouhi could see in Charlotte's face that in some measure she missed him already. Charlotte had grown used to weeks of constant and affectionate attention from him; now it was time for her to feel its loss. Tigran was a wise man, and she smiled to herself. She knew he had a village girl in the hills, though she had no intention of mentioning this. He needed to relieve the tension. Also, Charlotte needed less upheaval and violent emotion. A period of calm was good for her and the baby. She was, Takouhi calculated, just over two months pregnant. An important time for rest.

"Tigran come back before wedding. We take visit to town. I show you my house. We go to Harmonie Club and go to theatre. You like this. French company always do good play at the Shouwberg. Forget about man for little while."

Charlotte lay back, slightly uneasy. She knew something had happened last night in the coach but could not quite think what. What had she done to make Tigran leave? She felt sure that was why he had disappeared without even a good-bye.

A thought had wormed its way into her mind. She did not want to lose Tigran; she needed this marriage. Did she want him or need the marriage? Which one mattered more? A week before, she would not have cared, but now she had a sudden realisation of what she would lose if she lost him. He had not left her a note. *Saya cintamu*, she remembered, but he had not left her a word.

"Takouhi, have I hurt him? Is he angry with me?"

Takouhi took her friend's hand. "Not angry, cannot be angry with you. Look at time, afternoon. You sleep very late, and he go early. Long ride to Buitenzorg, No worry. He come back."

Takouhi was now concerned that Charlotte would be anxious, fall back on her old memories. Perhaps Tigran should not have gone after all. She sighed.

"*Alamak*, all well. We go to river and bathe, feel much better."

Charlotte relaxed as Takouhi left to make preparations. She drank the honey drink and revived.

Within the hour, they had taken the pony trap down to the river. The bathing pavilion was set among tall trees with deeply buttressed trunks of whitish bark. The drooping branches of long, delicate leaves swept down in a cascade, throwing the river into deep shade. The wooden path from the road to the river ran between and around these giant trees.

"Arjuna trees," said Takouhi as they looked up into their great height. "Tigran's mother, Valentijna, was born in Jaffnapatnum, in Ceylon. Her mother half-Indian woman. First husband was VOC man, bring her here. She love this tree, which she say is Sita's favourite tree. You know, Sita suffer a lot, like many women. So she plant many tree here and pray to gods for son. When Tigran come, she call him Arjuna, the white prince. This is our name for him when he is little boy. This place is Tigran's special place. Everybody in Batavia know this story. Many children come here to play with Tigran when he is boy."

Takouhi pulled a little of the fibrous bark from the trunk.

"This make medicine for fever. Good for heart when heart is sick."

As she said this she smiled and passed the bark to Charlotte. Charlotte understood Takouhi's meaning.

The bathing pavilion turned out to be the ideal proposition for improving spirits. Takouhi knew that in the steamy heat of the day a stream of cold water healed a thousand things. It washed away not merely the dust and heat but weariness too, and vexatious thought. A wooden verandah stood over the riverbank, with steps which led to the small, sandy beach. Here were bamboo and rattan chairs, small tables and divans covered in cloths and cushions.

With the Javanese maids surrounding them, they stepped into the river in their sarongs. The water was shallow, but there were deeper pools in which it was possible to sit and feel the cool water moving gently around them. From here they could gaze down the river towards the Japanese bridge, watching the water grow stronger, rushing and spilling in foamy waves down to the town. The maids had brought some baskets to the small beach, and Charlotte watched from her watery seat as they cut open long, spiky plants and squeezed the sap into a dish. Takouhi let her hair down, and the maids began to massage this sap into her scalp.

"Charlotte, this is aloe vera. George told me name of this plant. We call *lidah buaya*, 'crocodile tongue'. Please, you rest and let maids take care of hair. Feel very good."

The maids rinsed her hair and massaged her scalp, bringing a sudden feeling of relaxation. The sap was cooling and tingling. Her mind drifted to Zhen's hands, running through her hair, massaging the herbs into it, combing it. She closed her eyes, willing tears not to come. Would every single thing always remind her of him?

When the maid had finished, she took a pin and deftly tied up Charlotte's hair into a roll. Charlotte looked at Takouhi.

"Now leave little bit. Then wash with *kemiri* oil and *tuaru* leaves. Rinse with lime water. I use ginseng and *merang* also, but you no need. Use to stop white hair. I use but still have some. *Alamak*, big problem."

Charlotte smiled at Takouhi's annoyed expression, as if grey hair had been sent to aggravate her good temper.

Charlotte watched the sunlight play a melody on the shifting rills and the eddying sands of the river bottom. When the heat began to leave the air, Takouhi called the maids, for she liked to leave the riverside long before dusk.

In her room later, Charlotte felt as fresh as a naiad in a shimmering stream. River bathing was a ridiculous proposition in Singapore, even more so in Scotland. But here it seemed so natural. All the villagers used the river to bathe.

She looked in the mirror. The maid had brushed her hair and it shone. She now understood why Tigran and Takouhi had such youthful appearances. She was dressed in a loose silk gold-and-black batik robe which Tigran had given her. It felt like liquid on her skin. She had never worn so much silk as here, for Tigran spoiled her with shawls and exquisite garments.

The sun was setting on the rim of the trees, casting long shadows into the golden light across the lawn and into her room. In half an hour, the maid would come and help her dress. This evening she had chosen to dress Java style: a plain, dull blue bodice and an exquisite sarong, her favourite of all those she had. It featured a muted blue background covered in dark blue and rust-red flowers—large peonies and small blooms—surrounding spread-winged phoenixes. It was a Chinese motif, she knew, so different to the austere Javanese batiks, which had their own restrained beauty. Cirebon batiks were exuberant.

Charlotte smiled, thinking of how quickly she had become the Indies maiden, how much some ladies in Singapore would have disapproved. But in the indolent heat it was so easy to relax into this undemanding way of life. She went to the balcony to watch the rapid fall of darkness. No sooner had the sun dropped below the horizon and dusk begun its dominion of the sky than, in an instant, it was gone. The shade of night was drawn, and the streaming jewels of the Milky Way flooded the sky. In this starry canopy, the brilliance of the great cross of the South appeared. The beauty and elegance of this constellation, the *crux australis*, that sailors steered by in the vast darkness of the southern ocean, had an aura of mystery and romance. For the Christian sailor, it was a symbol of faith in the sky, the divine manifest in the stars.

Charlotte recalled reading something about how these stars had been known to the ancient Greeks. The gradual procession of the equinoxes had lowered them below the skyline so that they were lost to Northern eyes and knowledge for a thousand years. The thought was, somehow, very moving.

Bowls of sandalwood and lemon-grass incense swirled smoke on the air to chase insects. A booming, croaking orchestra of frogs performed in the gloom. She looked along the verandah to Tigran's door.

She took a candle and went into his room. She was curious to see his things, his bed. It was very dark, and she could see no lamp to light. His bed stood, like hers, near the windows, surrounded by a gauzy net. It felt stuffy and hot. She felt her skin pearl with sweat. She could see almost nothing and went back to her room. She had not felt him in there. She looked around her own room. This was the room he had slept in, she was sure of it. It was here he would make love to her, on their wedding night, with the breeze billowing the curtains.

Charlotte sat at her mirror. She was in a turmoil, uncertain of what she felt. Loyalty, love, curiosity, obligation were all mingled into a vast web of uncertainty. She looked into her reflected eyes. What was she doing? She shook her head and sighed. What choice did she have?

The following day, she felt better than she had for a long time. Today Takouhi had planned a visit to the town, a little shopping in the French "quartier", lunch at Raffles's old home, now the Hotel Royale, and a tour of Koningsplein.

They alighted first at the bakery and pâtisserie of Leroux & Fils on Rijswijkstraat. As they pulled up, Jacques Leroux himself opened the door of his emporium and rushed out to welcome them. Takouhi said a few words in French. M. Leroux beamed with pleasure and ushered them inside.

The smell of fresh bread and cakes assailed them. As they sat, Charlotte asked M. Leroux about his life in Batavia. He was delighted to chat with this lovely lady who spoke French. He told her he had arrived on a ship as a cook's assistant in the fleet which brought Marshal Daendels to Batavia. "So long ago!" he exclaimed. He had served in Daendels's household and later in Raffles's, for excellent bakers were hard to find. When Raffles left, he decided to set up on his own account, for he had saved a great deal of money. Raffles had encouraged him to buy this piece of land, for he had been told the street would become one of the most fashionable in Batavia. And so it had turned out to be.

His two sons worked with him, and he had many other staff. Everyone came to buy here, for he was the finest pâtissier in all Java. He said this with a Gallic flourish, and Charlotte could not help but like this short, corpulent man with his beaming smile and obvious *joie-de-vivre*.

The two sons came from the back of the shop to bow. Then Takouhi, sipping the coffee and seated like a memsahib, whispered something to M. Leroux, and he clapped his hands.

Two young men came forward bearing large platters, which they presented to Charlotte and Takouhi. On each tray lay eight miniature, beautifully decorated cakes.

"Voilà, mademoiselle. A vous de choisir, s'il vous plait," said M. Leroux.

Charlotte looked at Takouhi, who smiled with delight at her friend's expression. "These are small cakes for you to choose the one you want. This will be your bride cake."

Charlotte looked at the small masterpieces in flour and eggs, each a miniature marvel. Some were layered, and some were single, but all were decorated with a profusion of white icing roses or piped flowers, trailing leaves, small hearts. She had never seen such elaborate confectionery. It was impossible to choose, and Charlotte was having trouble keeping her emotions in check. She was getting married. Here were the arrangements before her eyes. Marrying, but not the man she wanted. She swallowed and gazed at the cakes.

The silence lengthened, and M. Leroux frowned. Did she like none of the designs? "Mademoiselle," he said gently in English. "If you do not like these, I make others for you."

Charlotte came to her senses. "No, no, monsieur. Every one is so lovely it is difficult to choose."

She examined the cakes carefully. One simple design caught her eye. The cake itself was a deep square covered in plain white icing, unadorned except for a wide ribbon of intricate Dutch lace tied around the cake into an elaborate raised bow. She put out her hand and was astonished to see that the ribbon was itself made of spun sugar. It looked incredibly real.

"This is lovely," she said and looked at M. Leroux. Takouhi smiled, and M. Leroux himself beamed broadly.

"My son has made this design." He called out, and a young man with his father's prominent nose and, she guessed, his mother's tawny skin, came forward to bow over Charlotte's hand.

"Quelle artiste, monsieur; merci beaucoup," she said. He bowed again and retreated somewhat awkwardly to the kitchen.

"Well, Mr Leroux," said Takouhi rising. "This is the cake. I will send detail about guest number later today."

As Charlotte and Takouhi climbed into the barouche, he bowed extravagantly.

Next they made a stop at Lapeyroux et Dudogne, the jewellers, where Takouhi urged Charlotte to look at some stones for a comb to hold her veil. Charlotte realised that she had no idea what she was to wear on her own wedding day. After a short examination of some pearls she said in a low voice, "Takouhi, What on earth shall I wear? Have you chosen a dress? Should I not see it?"

Takouhi was pleased. Her little ruse had worked. Charlotte was finally taking an interest in the details of the wedding.

Leaving the shop, they called next at the Maison de Rouffignac, who Takouhi assured her was the best tailor in Batavia. For men, Oger Frères, but for ladies Rouffignac. He showed the ladies some silks and satins, some plain, some figured. From a pattern book Charlotte selected a dress with a tight-fitting bodice and a deep V into the skirt, which was gathered and fell in smooth sweeps to her feet. She could not decide on the material and wondered aloud if M. de Rouffignac had oriental silks. Unexpectedly, he rose with a "*Oui, oui*" and presented a bolt of white silk crêpe, which carried the faintest design of waves. Japanese silk, he told her, and she felt its heavy delicacy. How fitting, she thought as her mind went to Reimsdijk's wife. Seed pearls, he suggested, to be sewn along the neckline and into the waist.

"Now," Takouhi said when measurements had been completed, "Tomorrow we shall choose the pearls for your hair, a string arranged Grecian style, à la Josephine, so nice I think. And for the shoes we go to Maison Seuffert."

Charlotte said nothing. I shall be covered in pearls, she thought, but not the one I truly want to wear.

As they drew up at the Hotel Place Royale, Charlotte recalled that this had been Raffles's own property, his residence when he was in Batavia. She knew that most of the time he stayed at the Palace at Buitenzorg in the cool hills, south of the city. Her thoughts strayed momentarily to Tigran.

Now it was an elegant hotel. As they crossed the threshold into the tiled inner hall, she imagined Olivia Raffles here, perhaps feeling as out of place as herself, though this house had been hers. It seemed odd to be walking through the halls of Olivia's home. After proceeding down a long corridor, they emerged onto a verandah giving onto a vast garden, which Charlotte knew ran down to Koningsplein.

Charlotte had never before experienced such an elegant hotel. The mere idea was somewhat intriguing. In Singapore the only hotel she had entered was on Commercial Square; it was a rather plain and practical place, meant for the sailors who passed through the town. Here, Takouhi had told her, the chef was French, a student of Beauvilliers, the famous gastronome. Takouhi lowered her voice and confided to Charlotte the rumour that he had come to Batavia because of some scandal. He had been in service with Van der Cappellen and Du Bus de Gisignies, but, so the story went, quickly got tired of the Dutch palate of his employers and had been engaged by the Hotel Place Royale with the understanding that he would be in charge of the restaurant. Here food was served *à la russe*, one dish after the other. Charlotte had not heard of this man, but marvelled somewhat at the number of the French who seemed to so thoroughly dominate the couture, cuisine and arts of Batavia.

They were shown to a table at the edge of the terrace by the maître d'hotel, a middle-aged Javanese dressed in a dark-patterned sarong, a white jacket and batik cap. Charlotte was somewhat amused to note that his feet were bare. The owner of the hotel, knowing that Charlotte would soon be married to one of the wealthiest men in Batavia, had immediately paid his respects to both ladies. He was a small man with an impeccable moustache and slightly yellowing teeth. He smelled of lavender water and had the disconcerting habit of sniffing at the end of every sentence. He offered to bring them some wine, with his compliments, but they declined. Charlotte did not wish to see a glass of wine for a long time to come.

The menu arrived, they made their choices, and Charlotte looked around her at this house of Olivia and Thomas Raffles. The other diners threw glances in their direction, and some of the men made no effort at all to contain their stares.

"Takouhi, did you know Olivia Raffles at all?" Charlotte asked as a basket of small hot rolls arrived, followed rapidly by their first course, a soupe à la purée de pois.

"Yes, not well. She spend most time at Buitenzorg or travelling with Thomas. Often sick. Sometimes she come here to this house and wives have to come to see her. I come too because Indies women scared of her.

Thomas very kind man to me, very, umm, how to say, gracious."

"What was she like?"

Takouhi finished her soup. "Quite beautiful, lovely skin, white and pink, like that. Eyes very lovely. Dark, thick hair. Good figure. She like to wear colourful clothes. She speak good Malay, clever. Kind, not bad person I think. We have, how you say, no same experience."

"Nothing in common?" Charlotte offered.

"Yes, nothing in common, right. English want to change us. I not mind, I think some changes nice, but many hate this. She often with friend, Flora Nightingall, wife of second military commander. When she talk with Flora, very easy. My English not good like now but I see that."

A grilled white fish arrived with a delicate sauce, and a dish of asparagus. A second waiter spread a quantity of small side dishes around the table. *Sambal*, chilli, fish sauce, small raw vegetables with peanut sauce, *pembek*, *tempeh*, tall cones of rice arranged in fresh green banana leaves, preserved fruit. The Indies table, it seemed, could never be abandoned, even in a French restaurant.

As they finished their meal, a man walked over and bowed.

Takouhi looked up and smiled. "Oh, Captain Palmer, hello." she said.

Captain Palmer took her hand gallantly and raised it to his lips. "Miss Manouk, how lovely to see you."

He turned his gaze to Charlotte. He was entirely charmed. There was no doubt, he thought to himself, the dusky maidens served their purpose, but the skin of a lovely young white woman was heaven to behold. Her creamy bosom was exposed just enough to excite admiration, and her hair was as black as midnight. But her eyes were her feature, blue as Boston skies. Sometimes he missed America, but not, of course, enough to go back. Besides, this creature was beyond anything he had ever seen in America or anywhere else. He felt a dangerous pull, even as she was introduced as Tigran Manouk's fiancée.

After the presentations were made and the exchange of civilities completed, he took his leave with obvious reluctance. Takouhi watched him depart.

Palmer was a ruggedly good-looking man, tall with broad shoulders and grey eyes. Takouhi sensed something dangerous in him that she could not put her finger on. She knew little about him. He had been recommended to her as a tenant for her house in Nordwijk by Gillean Maclaine, with whom he was in business, provisioning the American ships which were often in port.

They departed, with compliments to the chef. He was one of a number, Takouhi told her, French, Chinese and Malay, who would prepare the food for the European reception at the Harmonie Club. Charlotte had begun to realise the stir that this wedding was having on the town.

The heat was now oppressive, and the skies growing heavy. Rain was in the air, and they turned for home, abandoning other plans. As they alighted from the barouche, a wind whipped up quickly. Within seconds, the trees were tossing their heads, and servants rushed around the house, closing windows and doors with rapid clacks. Charlotte knew that once the wind got up, it could whirl vegetation into the air and whisk papers in the house into a dance. Lashing rain would follow in minutes.

8

Tigran caressed the girl's face, motioned her to dress and go. She was pretty and pliant, as the hill girls were, but he had been unable to arouse a single ounce of passion for her. She was probably amazed— disappointed perhaps—but it was not important. For as long as he wanted her, she would stay in the house. He would send her home tomorrow. She was not a slave; she was Sundanese, and she had asked to come to him. They always asked to come to him. To be with the white master was a mark of prestige over all the other girls in the village. But any child of these village girls he would not legitimise. He would see them cared for but nothing more.

He examined his conscience. Charlotte had awakened thoughts he would rather not examine. How many children of his or even his father's were in the villages on the plantation? He had once wondered if he were sometimes sleeping with a half sister and made sure to choose only the darkest girls. It was kinder to leave the children to the *kampong* life than rip them from their mother's arms to a bizarre life in limbo. Everyone accepted this. Most men were happy to marry the women, for they came with dowries from him and could never go back. Village women in Java were not subservient or restricted. Divorce and multiple husbands were not unusual. The women understood before they came to him. And in the villages he was known as a kind man. The women were curious about him. He discouraged pregnancy, made sure Madi, the woman who had helped give birth to him and all his children, always instructed them. If they became pregnant, they told her. If they wished to keep the child he did not argue, and sometimes they stayed with him until they gave birth.

Tigran was aroused by pregnancy, the rounding of the belly, the aura a woman had when she was carrying her child, and was happy for them to stay. But he never took them back. Once they had a child with him, they could not return, they knew that. Mia had never come here, nor Surya. When he was here, he was always alone. How many had there been?

With Surya he had been utterly faithful. Surya ... his mind fell softly on her. Charlotte was like the very reincarnation of her that the Hindoos believed in. The same slenderness and grace. Only their eyes differed: hers violet blue, Surya's deep black.

He shook his head. He had returned to Mia, briefly, out of loyalty, and there had been no other women. But he had quickly grown tired of her. In the years he had stayed away, her looks had suffered, and he now found repugnant the breath she exhaled from continuous chewing of the betel and the greasy oiliness of her hair. When she became pregnant with their last son, he never went to her again, turning instead to these casual liaisons with the village girls. After Surya, he didn't want another constant in his life to care about, fall in love with, grieve for. Since then there had been dozens of women. And, for a while, there had been Petra.

He thought about her, their words at the ball. They had come together after her old, third husband had died. Two of her husbands had married her virtually on their deathbeds.

He had thought theirs was a love affair, and it had been for him, for a while. He had courted her. She was as lovely as dusk on a river, but elegant, too, and clever. She was one of the many women who had benefited from the brief English rule. Educated and sociable, she was so different to the older Indies women or the native women, with whom he could not share a conversation. They rode together; she was a wonderful horsewoman, full of adventure and fire. He had never met a woman like her. She had cast a spell over him, he saw it now. He had been warned that she was too dangerous, but he had liked her danger. He had not touched her other than to kiss her, and that was enough. She had kisses of fire, full of endless promise. She had the same feelings for him, he had been sure. He had contemplated marriage—the idea of her companionship in his house was a pleasure, and the prospect of her in his bed every night filled him with lust.

Then he had called on her one day, unexpectedly. The maid had gone off, and he had wandered out into her garden. He had heard sounds and gone down one of the alleyways where a pavilion stood in a grove of trees. Two big black men, former African soldiers of the Dutch Army, now her guards, were with her. Her dress lay in wild folds about her waist. One was holding her legs as the other ... even now he could not put the words in his mind. Her head was flung back in abandon, her eyes half closed. Her voice was making animal grunts. As the men saw a white man, they froze, and she turned her head momentarily and saw him. He had left immediately. He would not see her, and for months she stayed away. Then gradually, he knew, she had begun to have regrets. When they met finally, she accused him of hypocrisy; she was only doing what every man in Java did with native women. She was sorry he had seen it, but it meant as much to her as Tigran's own liaisons.

But he could not forgive her. A woman did not act like a man. The image stayed with him, and the spell was broken. Now, even as he announced his marriage, she wanted him back, in her bed, she said. She would be his mistress. But everything had changed, he had told her. I love Charlotte; I will never want another woman. Not you Petra, not any more.

And everything *had* changed. Love changed everything; it was as simple as that. He had submitted to its power as a knight submits to his queen. He would wait for Charlotte to be his wife. He looked at the ring on his hand. His vows in the church would be sacred. He could hardly wait to make them.

His thoughts flew to her. He felt her absence as a shadowy space, a physical void which she filled with light. But he knew he had to be out of her life for a while, especially whilst the wedding preparations were underway. He had left everything in Takouhi's hands.

He went to the window. How much should he tell her? Would she think him a monster? It had all seemed so normal, so natural before he had thought of taking a wife. Every man in the Indies had the same life. Now he saw how it might look in her eyes. She was European. She had accepted Mia and his concubines in Batavia. What would she think of this? But why should she know? It was over.

He dressed, for the room was growing cold. He threw some logs onto the pile of glowing embers, moving it with the iron until it blazed into life, crackling and throwing starry sparks into the air.

Charlotte would surely grow to love life in the hills. As soon as they were married he would bring her here, to the cool air, away from the sweltering plains. After the baby was born, he would teach her to ride. He had just the pony for her, gentle and sweet-natured. They would walk on the high slopes where the flowers were like stars. And the views over the volcanoes, wreathed in threads of cloud, would bewitch her. A sentiment of the utmost tenderness flooded him, occupied his entire body, and he suddenly felt a moment of weakness, as if love could melt bones, and threw out his hand to grip the bedpost.

He walked, shakily, to the desk in the corner of the room and took out the letter.

It had come to his warehouse in the Kota a week before. A letter addressed to Charlotte at the Manouk offices. He would not have known; the writing was in Chinese. It had come via one of the Chinese sugar trading houses with her name and his written in alphabet on the front. He had no idea what it said or who had passed it to him. He had looked at it for a long time. Then he had put it away for two days. Then he had called his office chief and asked him to find a man who could translate from Chinese to Dutch or English or Malay and who was discreet. Two days after that a translation had arrived in excellent Dutch. He felt absolutely no guilt at reading the letter. Charlotte was betrothed to him, and it was his duty to protect her from harm.

Now he opened it again. *You are my heart. I am dying every day from missing you.*

Tigran looked up and out of the window. The evening was drawing in rapidly, and the hills had become indistinct, lying like dark, hump-backed giants against the violet sky.

You are my heart. I am dying every day from missing you. These were his own feelings. He had known instantly who had written the letter and looked down to the end, but there was no name. She would know, this man knew very well, she would know who the letter was from. This was the man whose name she had called, but he had forgotten it. He searched his memory, but it would not come. Chinese names were all so alike and unmemorable.

He looked down.

Lao Tzu said, "to be loved deeply gives you strength, to love deeply gives you courage." We have strength and courage. Our love is deep. You live in my skin."

Tigran frowned and stared at the letter. His first thought was how on earth this man had imagined it would ever reach Charlotte. Then he realised the man did not know Charlotte would be married, knew only she was alone and far away. He felt the truth of the words trying to reach out over the dark ocean, through the mist of unshared language to a woman he loved, wanted to reassure, give peace in separation. He was certain the Chinese man did not know she was pregnant.

You live in my skin. He curled the letter in his hand into a tiny ball and threw it into the fire, watching, eyes narrowed, as flames consumed it.

He sat at the desk and began to write to Robert, Charlotte's brother. Tigran knew that Charlotte had written to her brother when she arrived in Batavia. He had made sure he read the letter before it was sent. He had felt a momentary hesitation, but his need to know had overcome everything. It contained nothing more than reassurances of her safe arrival, her affection for him. She had not mentioned his proposal.

Now he gave Robert news of their forthcoming marriage, inviting him to the wedding if at all possible, though he knew Robert would not be able to come. He sent news of her health, of her well-being, of the inheritance he had settled on her. He was not sure if Robert knew she was pregnant and did not mention this. It would be better if everybody thought this child was his. He intended the birth to be here in the hills. The society of Batavia might do their sums on their fingers, but they would imagine only that he had been unable to resist the temptation of sleeping with his beautiful wife before the wedding. Then he added a final sentence.

Charlotte is much improved and slowly forgetting her past experiences in Singapore. I think you understand my meaning. However, should she seek news of the person she has left it might be best not to lend encouragement to her enquiries. I leave it up to you, of course, but we both have her best interest in our hearts. I'm sure Charlotte joins me in sending good wishes and news of our coming nuptials to all her acquaintance in Singapore.

He sealed the letter. He was annoyed he had not written when he was in Batavia, but she distracted him there. He would send it by the first ship to Singapore. At the same time he would make an announcement in the newspaper.

He dropped into a chair before the fire and contemplated the flames.

At the same moment in Brieswijk, Charlotte, too, sat composing a letter to her brother. The time had come, she realised, to announce her wedding. She sent news of her health, Takouhi and Tigran, the splendid house he owned, of which she would soon be mistress. She asked for news of her acquaintance. She described the society of Batavia, told him of the ball with the Governor-General, the French shops and the prospect of visiting the French Opera. Now she sat, contemplating the page, wondering if she dared ask about Zhen. On a separate page she began a few lines: *it would ease my heart to have news … to know he is well. Robert, I should be happy to have news … Please, Robert, when you see Zhen give him my fondest regards.* This last she crossed out vehemently. Perhaps later she would dare to raise this subject. At the moment, it made her head whirl. And to ask for news of him in a letter announcing her marriage … She shook her head and finished the letter with words of affection.

From the drawer of her bedside table, she took out the simple box. The necklace from Zhen lay on a bed of old wizened nutmegs, and she inhaled the odour of the sweet spice. It took her back to the old orchard where he had first kissed her, that kiss like an alchemist's potion, altering her in an unknown and profound way. She fastened it around her neck. A small white pearl, round like the moon, in a silver mount of filigree shaped like the upturned eaves of a Chinese temple, on intricately braided and thickly entwined red silk threads. It was not expensive like the diamonds that Tigran offered her, but Zhen had given it to her when she knew he had nothing. It was as if it had some magical power, for as it lay on her skin she saw him, in the mirror, behind her, so real she gasped and turned. But no one was there. She put her head in her hands. She wanted so desperately to see him. Surely they would meet again. When would this subside?

Charlotte took up a book of poetry. Her eyes stopped on Byron.

Still Hope, breathing peace through the grief-swollen breast,
Will whisper, Our meeting we yet may renew:
With this dream of deceit, half our sorrow's represt,
Nor taste we the poison, of Love's last adieu!

She threw the book onto the bed. A dream of deceit. Love's last adieu. She took the pearl in her hand. Would they never meet again? Was it impossible even to have news of him, to know he was well? She crawled onto the bed and began to cry.

9

Charlotte put the finishing touches to her toilette. The maid had overfussed with her hair, and she pulled it out, tying it more loosely. Charlotte was a little afraid of the maids and rarely dared complain or change anything they did. She was not used to servants and she found herself altered. Somehow she had lost a certain confidence in herself. She recognised it but could do little about it. When she talked of this to Takouhi, her friend just waved her hand and told her to do as she liked with the maids. With Tigran away and Takouhi so engrossed in the wedding plans and other business of her own, Charlotte found herself alone and lonely.

She had wandered down to the river in the early morning. It took half an hour to reach the bank, but the heat was not yet up. She enjoyed meandering along the road lined with the spreading crowns and nomadic roots of these mighty *saman* trees. She knew this type of tree as a "rain tree" and had discovered it was the goddess Liberalitas of the jungle. It shaded man, beast and plants from the burning sun, but on cloudy days and from dusk to dawn its leaves curled into tight little wads, allowing rain to fall to the ground below and nourish the earth. Birds, small lizards and tiny creatures nested in its capacious nooks and harvested its bounty. In every cranny its body was benevolent host to dozens of sprouting thick green leaves living off the watery bark. Orchids and spidery ferns lovingly hugged its every limb. It oozed a sweet honeydew for sap-loving insects, made into nectar honey by the villagers. In flower it was covered in thousands of fragrant pink and scarlet blooms like small fan-shaped feather dusters standing up from the leaves in a crown, beauteous to the eye and nose, food for monkeys which ran about its height and nectar for moths and bees. The fruit, in long black lumpy pods, was bursting with sticky pulp which was sweet and edible and tasted like licorice. The children sucked the pods, and the villagers made a tea from them. From the infused bark they brewed a medicine for the stomach. The beautiful wood was used for boats, furniture and carvings. Small rodents and the deer in the park feasted on its fallen pods, and its green leaves and seeds were nutritious fodder for the other domestic animals. To walk beneath these trees was to know in some small way the infinite gift of the forest to all creatures who dwelt within its life-giving compass.

They seemed to give her succour too, and the sickness Charlotte felt when she rose had abated. At the river bank she turned to look for the orchard which Riejmsdijk had laid out for his wife. The bathing pavilion was much further up the bank, surrounded by the Arjuna trees. Near the Japanese bridge, however, she found signs of the garden. A grove of gnarled trees stood back from the river, and underneath them a broken and tumble-down wooden hut, its thatch gone, only clinging in places to the corners of the roof, like whispery hairs on an old man's head. The trees must have tried to flower, for though now full of leaves, the ground was covered in a mat of fading white blossom. Bamboo poles supported the leaning branches of these trees, now straggling and parched. Charlotte presumed that these were trees from Japan which had not grown well, so far from their native soil.

Like them, Charlotte thought, reflecting on the early deaths of Riejmsdijk's wife and children. A stone lantern covered in creepers and moss stood, just visible, to one side of the hut. She cleared it a little and saw its distinctive roof shape, like the Chinese temples in Singapore, like the silver mount on her pearl necklace. She saw a stone bench and sat down, overcome with momentary sorrow: for herself, for Zhen, for this Japanese girl who had been transplanted to another soil and failed to thrive. She felt tears welling, and shook her head angrily.

"Stop crying, Kitt," she said to herself. "I am so sick of this endless crying, so tired of feeling sick."

Charlotte knew that this sickness should go away in a few weeks, but at the moment it seemed interminable.

She looked into the mirror. She was pale, and there were dark circles under her eyes. She applied a little whitening, a touch of rouge, then rose and made her way downstairs to where the carriage was waiting. This evening she and Takouhi were going to the Shouwberg to see the French theatre troupe perform *Hernani, ou L'honneur Castillan*, the famous play by Victor Hugo which had caused riots in Paris.

As they drew up at the theatre, Charlotte peered at this building, with its Empire architecture, a sense of excitement building. She had never been to a theatre before. It was thrilling; the sight of ladies and gentlemen dressed in their finery climbing the marble steps, the buzz of conversation about this play which had become notorious, the faint sounds of an orchestra tuning instruments. Exuberant baroque mirrors lined the walls of the entrance hall, reflecting the crowd endlessly around the room. Nathanial Fox hailed them and picked his way through the throng. They left the crush and made their way to the red-velvet-lined seats to one side, set away and slightly above the rest. Wilhelmina Merkus had lent them the Governor-General's booth for the evening.

The room was hot, and every fan was in motion, like the incessant wings of hovering moths. Oil lights at the foot and to the sides of the stage threw brightness onto the dark blue curtain, but the rest of the room was in semi-darkness. Ushers with lamps showed couples to their seats. Charlotte was impatient for the play to begin, fanning herself rapidly. She watched the audience buzzing with conversation and then, suddenly, the orchestra fell silent. Three loud raps resounded from the stage. A hush fell on the crowd.

The curtain rose, and Charlotte held her breath. A room appeared, a bedroom. Near the bed, in the middle of the room stood a table with a lamp. An ancient crone dressed in black had risen from a chair and begun to pull crimson curtains across a window when a knock was heard at a concealed door. It sounded loud in the hushed theatre, and Charlotte jumped. The crone stopped and listened.

A second knock, louder than the first.

"*Serait-ce déjà lui,*" the old crone muttered, surprised

A third knock, then a fourth,

"*Vite, ouvrons.*

She went to the door, opened it and a tall man entered, a hat shading his eyes, his coat collar masking his face. He threw off his coat and hat and stood revealed in a rich Castillian costume of velvet and silk.

The old woman gasped and took a step back. "*Quoi, seigneur Hernani, ce n'est pas vous? Au feu!* "

Charlotte was spellbound. This was Don Carlos, the King, who had come to seduce Doña Sol, though she was betrothed to Ruy Gomez, her old uncle. She was expecting not Don Carlos but the man she truly loved, the bandit Hernani. The king bribed the crone to hide him in a cupboard, and as the door closed a young woman entered from the left of the stage, dressed in white. Charlotte gasped; she was incredibly beautiful, her voice plaintive.

> "*Ah je crains quelque malheur*
> *Hernani devrait être ici.*"

Then a knock came at the door, and Hernani entered, wearing a great hat and coat, a cuirasse of leather, a sword and a knife in his broad belt. He was a figure of romance, young and vigorous, though Charlotte thought him not nearly handsome enough.

Doña Sol ran to him, her love evident in the way she said his name. His love obvious in the poetry he whispered to her

From that moment Charlotte was utterly caught up in the play. Star-crossed lovers: Romeo and Juliet, Charlotte and Zhen. Hernani came into the power of Ruy Gomez, who spared his life but extracted a pledge that Hernani must take his own life on hearing the sound of Ruy Gomez's hunting horn. Hernani was found to be a noble, and his rank restored by the king, who had abandoned his ardour for Doña Sol and given her to her beloved. The audience breathed a sigh of relief. The lovers were married and came into each other's arms. Joy was all around, when suddenly the fatal hunting horn sounded. Ruy Gomez, thwarted, was implacable and demanded Hernani's death, placed before him a poisoned cup. The audience gasped, and tears sprang to Charlotte's eyes. Her thoughts flew to Zhen. Surely he would not obey. But honour was at stake, and he took up the fatal chalice. Doña Sol threw herself at his feet.

> "*Non, non, rien ne te lie,*
> *Cela ne se peut pas! Crime! Attentat! Folie!*"

But honour demanded it, and he drank, and she, pulling it from his hands, drank too. Ruy Gomez watched now, horrified at his act of villainy.

As the lovers died in each other's arms in an ecstasy of devotion, Ruy Gomez killed himself. The tragedy was total; the orchestra boomed its doom-laden salute. Charlotte watched, her handkerchief in her mouth, tears streaming down her face. Takouhi too, and even Nathanial, were caught up in the drama, and when the curtain fell, they all breathed a sigh of relief. The audience erupted, standing, clapping and calling. A triumph!

The curtain rose, and the actors and actresses appeared. When Doña Sol came forward, the audience gave her a long, standing ovation. The performance had been a revelation. Charlotte clapped until her hands stung. Nathanial, smiling, said he knew the main actress. Would she and Takouhi care to meet her? Charlotte eagerly agreed, and Takouhi, happy for her friend, accepted. They went backstage.

The actress they had so admired was seated at the mirror, her black curly locks flowing over her shoulders to her tiny waist. She turned as she saw shapes on the mirror and rose in one fluid movement, the flow of her gown a swish on the floor. She gazed at Charlotte and smiled, a smile of such feminine sweetness that Charlotte was utterly charmed.

Then, unexpectedly, she put her hand to her hair as if to stroke it, but with a gesture polished, evidently, by long practice, the hair was removed from her head with a flourish and a cloud of powder, and she bowed low. "Louis Isidor de Montaillou, Madame, a votre service," he said courteously in a low masculine voice.

The hair was a wig, the actress was a man! Charlette gasped, and Takouhi made a low sound of surprise.

It was exactly the effect Louis had desired, and he let out a long peal of delighted laughter. Nathanial was pleased at his little ruse, and Charlotte too began to laugh, though Takouhi continued to stare silently at this apparition, his hair flattened by a net, the face rouged rose, the lips a scarlet red, the bosoms, so seemingly real, perfumed and powdered.

Over the next days, Louis and Nathanial would call for Charlotte, for they had discovered a profound pleasure in each other's company. When she was with them she forgot about sorrow, forgot about Tigran, forgot about the wedding and almost forgot about Zhen. Nathanial had a wicked and wry sense of humour and Louis was simply and charmingly reckless. They gossiped about everyone in town, and she did not stop laughing.

With Nathanial, she spent afternoons at the reading rooms of the Harmonie Club. The library of the Batavian Society was extensive and gratifying, supplied with journals, manuscripts in the strange writing of the archipelago, and books in English, French and Dutch. There were several encyclopaedias in English, a rather dog-eared *Rees's* and the 7th edition of the *Britannica*. It also had an extensive oriental collection. She had taken from the shelves Reverend Medhurst's recent book on China, Karl Gutzlaff's *Sketch of Chinese History* and several copies of *The Chinese Repository*, through which she was currently flipping, regretting the absence of anything so unworthy as a novel. Nathanial was particularly partial to reading the old Dutch writers on Batavia and Java. When he found a particularly pithy passage he would stop with a small pleased laugh and translate.

"Listen, this is the splendid Doctor Nicolaas de Graaff writing about the ladies last century. It is beyond everything."

"All the women are so garrulous, so proud, so wanton and lascivious that from sheer wantonness they scarcely know what to do with themselves. They are like princesses and have a great many slaves of both sexes at their beck and call, waiting on them like watchdogs, day and night, and watching their eyes closely in order to catch their slightest whim; and they are themselves so lazy that one will not stretch out her hand for a thing, not even to pick up a straw from the floor, but will call a slave to do it. And if they do not come quickly enough the woman will scold them for a lousy whore, negress whore; son-of-a-whore and worse. For the very least fault, they have slaves tied to a stake and mercilessly flogged with a cat-o-nine-tails until the blood pours down and the flesh hangs in tattered stripes, which they then rub with salt and pickle to prevent the wounds rotting."

Charlotte put up her hand, frowning. "Nathanial, really."

"No, Charlotte, listen." Nathanial looked up, met her blue eyes with his, grinned and pushed his sandy curls back off his face. He was older than her, Charlotte knew, by ten years, but his face had a cheeky boyishness which always made her smile.

"These women are too lazy to walk and cannot rear their own children, but leave their upbringing to a slave nurse, who are brought up with their slaves' ideas and speak as good Malabar, Bengali and bastard-Portuguese as the slaves themselves and can hardly speak a word of Dutch.

"The worst are the Liplap women, the half-castes who know nothing, are fit for nothing except to scratch their arse ..."

Charlotte half-choked on scandalised laughter. Nathanial was smiling broadly.

"Scratch their arse, chew betel, smoke cigarettes, drink tea or lie on a mat; in this wise they sit the whole day, idle and bored, squatting for the most part on their heels like an ape on its arse."

Nathanial looked up as Charlotte again objected. "Look, this is scientific work. That is what is written here."

"Their usual topic of conversation is their slaves—how many they have bought, sold, lost, etc., or of a tasty curry or rice dish. They eat only with each other, seldom with their husbands, their table conversation being limited to such remarks as, 'A good chicken soup is not so tasty as an appetizing curry sauce.' They mix their chicken or fish with their rice and gurgle and suck it up through their fingers like pigs from a trough, and then stick their hands and fingers in the mouth so that the juice runs down between and slops over them.

"If these Liplap women should chance to be invited to a gentleman's table or a wedding, they have no idea how to behave or say a word lest they make fools of themselves. It happened, on a certain occasion that one of these ladies, sitting at a table with a number of other ladies, was served by one of the gentlemen present, as a compliment, with a piece of roast chicken. Upon which she took the meat very ungraciously from her plate and put it back on the dish saying, "I don't want to eat a bit of hen's arse."

Nathanial could not continue for laughing and was seized with a fit of coughing. Their merriment died away, until they saw the alarmed face of the old Indies man peeping around the door, at which point they both went off again in gales, and he departed in alarm.

From enjoyment she regained confidence. One day when Nathanial was busy, Louis came early, and they rode down to the boathouse. Louis had told her they could go down the Kali Krukut to the Chinese village at Glodok. This was an adventure she could not resist, and she sent for a boatman. A thin, wiry, copper-skinned man arrived, pushed out the boat expertly and took the long oar in his hands.

They both sat back and watched the banks of the river move by. Here the current was fast and the jungle went by in a blur. Louis had barely time to point out the grounds of the Hotel de Provence before they had arrived suddenly at an arched bridge. Gang Chaulon, he said, the street named for the pompous Frenchie who owned the hotel. "I am waiting for a Gang montaillou," he said, and his laughter boomed as the boatman swept them under the bridge. Beyond, the river slowed, and the boatman could guide it more easily. Watching him was like watching a dance, so delicately and easily did he manoeuvre the craft. It was like looking back into time, through hundreds, perhaps thousands of years, as the ancient people of Java had travelled this river in exactly the same way. Nathanial had spoken to her of discoveries which showed very old civilisations in this land. Charlotte felt like a dewdrop suddenly, a drop of water in this river, where bodies no more consequential than herself had bathed and roamed and lived and died. Through the trees, sunlight fell on the water like blossom.

They flowed down to Glodok through banks of overhanging trees, rice fields and villages. Then gradually the scene changed, and houses began to appear, clinging to the riverside or back on the embankment. Chinese houses. The boatman rowed them to Toko Tiga, beneath a crooked bridge, and moved over to the bank. Louis helped Charlotte out of the boat, and they stood for a moment looking around them. The boatman had turned and was now on his way back to the estate. How he was to negotiate the full-flowing river she did not know. Louis shook his head. Never mind, he said.

Louis took her hand, and they walked along the street. They had been there barely a few minutes, but in that time, it seemed, every inhabitant of the shops and houses had heard and was now hanging out of the windows staring at them. Charlotte felt that she had landed on alien shores. Suddenly she had begun to think differently about this adventure, and it occurred to her that Tigran would not have approved. She had come in some measure to feel closer to Zhen, to the people who formed part of his life, his soul, but it was not turning out like that. "How were they to get back?" she thought.

They followed a muddy and winding lane, and Charlotte began to feel thoroughly lost and apprehensive. Then Louis ducked his head and pulled her into a shop. She realised it was an opium shop, for she recognised the smell from Singapore. The interior was so dark and dingy she could barely make out the back wall. He motioned her to sit, and a young woman brought some tea. The table looked clean but Charlotte had no wish to touch anything in the store. She felt the strangeness of this place. She loved a Chinese man and was carrying his child, yet she had nothing to do with, nothing in common with these people at all.

Shadows of incomprehension and mistrust clung to the walls and streets and invaded her mind. She wanted to go home. This did not feel like the Chinese town in Singapore, where a white woman could walk with ease. There the town was small, a few streets at most, fitting neatly between river and sea, the salty winds blowing freshly, the European and Chinese merchants mingling on Commercial Square and Boat Quay. This felt dangerous. Here the town sprawled miles along rivers and dirty canals, sinuous, treacherous, or so it felt to her, like a many-tentacled creature ready to swallow up unwary travellers who stumbled into its lair. She had not the slightest doubt that the Dutch citizens rarely penetrated its shadowy regions except for the Pancoran pleasure quarter which Louis had told her about.

Louis dragged a young man from a back room. "Voici Tong," he said delightedly.

Tong, it transpired, was Louis's friend. This was his father's shop, and Tong worked as a translator in the Chinese Bureau at the offices of the Resident of Batavia. His Dutch, Louis said proudly, was most excellent. His mother was Malay, and he spoke the language fluently and as they started to use this language, the tension evaporated and Charlotte relaxed. As news of their arrival spread, two other young Chinese men came into the shop. It was clear to Charlotte that they were curious about her, but equally anxious to be with Louis. One good-looking young man sat next to Louis, who was lounging on a long bench, and began openly to caress his hair. Charlotte was amazed and blushed. Louis laughed.

"*Eh oui, ma petite Charlotte, une tante, un pédéraste.* There are

110

many names. Are you shocked?"

Charlotte *was* shocked and suddenly very uncomfortable. She knew such men existed, for the sermons from the pulpit in Aberdeen had thundered against "unnatural affections", but it had not occurred to her that Louis ... She rose, and as she turned towards the door, she saw it was crowded with people staring in.

Now thoroughly afraid, she turned angrily to Louis. "Why bring me here, Louis? I do not care what you do, but why involve me?"

Louis shook his head. "I want you to know about me. That's all. Honesty."

Charlotte looked at him, her fury increasing. "Well, now I know. It would have been easier just to tell me. Now take me home."

Tong shouted and moved the crowd apart, and even Louis, seeing the faces of the people and their hands touching Charlotte's dress, sensed his mistake. The crowd followed, like a seething, chattering wake, as they walked towards the Glodok market at Pancoran. Here there were *sado*, the back-to-back pony traps, and Tong spoke to the driver very seriously. Tong turned to Charlotte and bowed deeply.

"Sorry, Louis made a mistake. Sometimes he's very stupid, likes to shock people. Perhaps we will meet again." He reminded Charlotte suddenly of Zhen's friend in Singapore, and she felt a small rush of affection for him.

As they pulled away, she saw the crowd had not dissipated, many men turning to interrogate Tong. All the way back to Brieswijk in the bone-shaking and dusty contraption, Charlotte said nothing, reflecting on how she felt about this news. As she stepped down from the *sado*, she took Louis's hand.

"Louis, don't do that again. I do not understand about you and Tong, but that is your affair. If you want to be friends, we can be honest with each other without shocks."

Louis kissed her hand, and she knew he was contrite. This desire to *épater les bourgeois* was part of his nature.

Louis looked over her shoulder, and she turned. Tigran stood in the doorway. He took in Louis, her hand in his, the pony trap, the mud and dust on her skirts, and she saw his eyes narrow. He turned and went inside, and she told Louis to go.

10

Dinner that night was strained. Takouhi was absent. Charlotte saw how it must look to Tigran, but she did not know how to tell him. As the silence between them lengthened, she plucked up her courage. After all, he had been away, and she was not his slave.

"Tigran, Louis is a friend from the French Opera troupe and he … he does not … how can I tell you … care for women in the way …" Charlotte stopped, thoroughly embarrassed. She did not dare tell him where they had been.

He looked up. His hand gripped his knife a little tighter.

"Yes, I understand. I did not imagine he was your lover, for your heart lies elsewhere, as we both know."

She heard the bitterness in his voice. Then he calmed down.

"Louis de Montaillou is well known amongst some people in this town. He is not alone, there are others. Well. His way of life is not appreciated in Batavia, as I'm sure you can understand, but as an artist with the French company he is tolerated. As long as there is no scandal, there is no cause for the Resident to act. Everyone knows what the French are like."

Charlotte looked down. "I did not know, Tigran. I met Louis only a week ago."

Tigran's heart softened, for he wanted to forgive her everything. "Never mind. Louis is a silly fellow but sometimes good company, I gather. But you must not go about the town with him, you understand, Charlotte. It would be hard on you and me. There would be difficulties. This is not a strictly conventional household, as you may have seen. My wealth gives me … dispensations. However, there is a line. And please, if you want a carriage, I have many. Do not use those terrible things. What does it look like if you go about in such contraptions?"

Charlotte looked up and smiled. He really was an understanding man. She was glad he was back, sorry she had made him angry. Louis had been rash today, taking her to Chinatown, and she had been equally foolish. It had opened her eyes, though, again, to the impossible prospect of a life with Zhen. A life with a Chinese man. A married Chinese man. The wishes of her heart needed continual reminders of this reality, for she forgot it as quickly as the memory of him flooded her thoughts.

"Our wedding is in three days, Charlotte. Are you ready? Are you sure?"

Charlotte was unable to say if she was ready or sure, but she had begun to like Tigran very much, and above all, *above all*, in this vulnerable state, to feel the web of protection and affection which he spun around her in an alien land. She had read and re-read Miss Ferrier's novel *Marriage*, and though she could not agree with the Earl that love was only for the *canaille* of the countryside—what woman could?—still, perhaps love in marriage was not such an exigent necessity as she had first thought.

"Yes," she said.

Five days went by in a blur. Fittings for her dress, selection of jewels, talk of food and guests. The evening under the stars watching the *wayang*. Even the marriage ceremony, with all its pomp, the guests, the church and the vows flew by. The reception at the Harmonie Club seemed like a dream. She recalled the white and gold coach, the *diligence à l'anglaise*, bedecked with floating ribbons; someone made a long speech, perhaps Pieter; the banquet was lavish. She remembered waltzing in Tigran's arms, the first dance as a married woman; cutting the enormous and exquisite cake. It was like a fantasy, and she could not quite see herself. Only later, when the maid had left her and she stood in her room, looking at the circle of diamonds on the third finger of her left hand—the *vena amoris* which was supposed to run directly to the heart—did the realisation of what had happened sink in.

Then her door opened and Tigran came in. He, like she, was still dressed in his wedding clothes.

He approached her, and she suddenly realised that the thought of a physical encounter with Tigran filled her with dread. A man she did not love. Her ideas on the matter, of tremulous and brief duration, fled. Could anything be more abhorrent! Perhaps if she had been raised differently, in a more confined way, with less freedom to use her imagination. Perhaps if she had not already known one man, the perfect man. The human mind has wondrous abilities, she discovered yet again, as once more she realised that the impossibility of a life with the perfect man did not make her want him less.

But Tigran did something utterly unexpected. Taking her hand he led her to the balcony, and as they looked out over the moonlit grounds, a scene so inalterably romantic that it seemed conjured by a playwright's pen, he said quietly, "Charlotte, I understand your feelings. We hardly know each other. You remember the words of the marriage ceremony: 'Marriage is honourable, and the bridal bed is holy.' Until you are ready, I will not touch you."

Charlotte burst into tears. The relief was so obvious on her face that Tigran felt a powerful wave of annoyance. She might have had the goodness to conceal her feelings a little. But he had made this promise to himself, and in fact these tears only strengthened his resolve. No man, after all, wishes to be found disgusting, particularly on his wedding night.

He kissed the wedding band on her hand coolly and left her.

Within a few days they departed for the house in Buitenzorg, and Charlotte discovered a wonderland. A vertiginous and verdurous wonderland, she thought, the exaggerated adjectives necessary to describe such a place. An impossibly high, deep-red roof dominated the big two-storey stone house, covering a verandah which encompassed the whole building. It stood embedded into the hillside like a citadel. The grasses and trees of the lower slopes of the garden fell away at the edge of the mossy stone parapet into tiers of tea plants, green waves sweeping down into the valley like sculpted carpets and rising on the surrounding peaks.

This plantation was recent, Tigran told her as they gazed down. Tea had been introduced to Batavia in 1686 by Andreas Cleyer, the

Opperhoofd of the factory at Deshima, as a decorative plant. In 1728, the VOC began to bring in tea seeds in large quantities from China to be cultivated in Java, but without success. Only those seeds smuggled from Japan to Java almost a hundred years later, in 1824, by Von Siebold had flourished. The first tea plantation had been started in 1828, and Tigran's father had begun this plantation a few years after that. It had recently begun to make a good profit. Europe's thirst for tea was phenomenal.

In amongst the rows of stumpy bushes, workers in flat straw hats moved like golden bees, some weeding and trenching, some gathering the top leaves of the plant. In the distance rose the violet shapes of the volcanoes. It rained three hundred days a year, wrapping the mountains in a vaporous mist, a constantly changing pattern of shapes and nebulous light. In the late afternoon, rays of gold pierced the shifting clouds, illuminating the green slopes and the valley far below. The air was crisp, transparent, invigorating. It imparted a jewel-like sparkle to the lush colouring of the landscape. She loved it immediately.

She met Madi, the *dukun bayi*, who would care for her through the growth and birth of her child. Tigran showed her the place where the baby would be born.

La seraille. That's what Charlotte named it when she saw it. Thick teakwood columns supported a deeply eaved, manicured thatched roof. A small rill from the hillside contained by stone canals spilled into geometric ponds on either side of a stone bridge before continuing its fall. When she sat by these deep dark pools, watching the splash of the rill, Charlotte knew that from here the water would join the swift-flowing rivers until they slowed to meander through Batavia to the wide low sea. She felt this long, silvery thread as if she could see through miles of jungle space and over the Java Sea, connecting her to him.

Beyond the bridge, a carved Javanese stone gate mounted by the half-head of the Kala and guarded by two stone creatures concealed the pavilion. When the weather was fine and warm, perfumed incense filled the curtains floating on the breezes, for the pavilion was on a ledge giving onto the long valley below. Here the female *dukun* had tended to Meda; the masseuses had oiled and gently kneaded her skin and bathed her in the flower waters of the bath. Then she and her mother would lie on the silky cushions and talk and eat fresh fruits and drink the herbal tonics and gaze at the rainbow of butterflies which flitted below the lacy parapet. Beauty would heal her, Takouhi was sure. But it had not.

Visitors came frequently to Buitenzorg, and Tigran included Louis and Nathanial. She was grateful to him, for Louis also brought some of the French troupe, who sang and put on little plays in which everyone took part.

Nathanial took her to look at the Batu Tulis, a field covered in stone slabs, some prone, some upright, etched with figures and inscriptions in bas relief. They were adorned with garlands of jasmine blossoms, and smoking incense stood at their bases. They celebrated the virtues and victories of Hindu kings, he said. This was the capital of the ancient Hindu realm of Pajajaran, destroyed by a Muslim conqueror. These stones were still venerated as relics of a glorious past. The Javanese, he told her, as they wandered amongst the stones, were a gentle and thoughtful people. They embraced the Tuan Allah but did not forget the grace and valour of ancient times, the monuments to which stood everywhere on the island. On the contrary, they drew power from them. The *gamelan* and *wayang*, the love of Indian tales, of Siva and Krishna, of Sita and Rama, which were transformed into Javanese tales, were part of their souls, impossible to eradicate. They honoured those who had trod the land before they came, before the creed of Mohammed came, before even the Hindoos came, those hidden in the mists of time.

At the riverside, a massive round boulder stood in the riverbed covered in inscriptions and marked with two large, distinct footprints. The writing was in Sanskrit, he told her, an ancient language of India. It said, *This is the print of the foot soles of the very honourable Purnawarnam, who is brave and controls the world, like the God Vishnu.*

"He was king of the Taruma kingdom. You see, we are walking in the footsteps of Vishnu, the all-pervading essence of beings, the master of past, present and future, he who sustains and supports the universe and from whom all its elements emanate. Is it any wonder that these stones continue to wield power over the country folk? Yet they honour these stones as monuments to the faith of Mohammed, too. According to the villagers, they are the transformed shapes of Siliwangi, the last King of Pajajaran, and his followers, who were turned to stone by Tuan Allah as punishment for their refusal to embrace the faith."

Nathanial gathered water into a bottle from a swift-flowing stream, and they returned to the field. Charlotte put up her parasol. The day had grown warm, but here in the hills only pleasantly so. A profusion of wildflowers—violets, primulas, ranunculas—spread like a carpet. Nathanial led Charlotte through the field to a stone which lay sheltered amongst the canopy and ropey pillars of an ancient banyan tree. This tree was a forest in itself, new branches reaching down to take root to strengthen the old trunk, an affectionate emblem of parent and children supporting each other through earthquakes, storms and tempests. The banyan, Charlotte now knew, was holy, a home of gods and spirits, a noble place of worship.

A small footprint was visible on the surface of a stone which was sheltered with palm leaves, garlanded with flowers and smeared with golden *boreh* unguent. On either side were gifts to Dewi Sri, the rice princess, and to the *danjang desa*, the village spirit. Further round in the columns of roots were offerings to djinns, spirits of evil who could bring pestilence and flood, as powerful for harm as the *danjang* was for good. It was wise to keep on terms of amity with them. Further along, placed in a niche, was a small statue of the Boodha, crudely made, and one of Gajah, the elephant-faced god who was Ganesh in India, a son of Siva, who was the compassionate bestower of all wishes. In some parts the tree was festooned with coloured threads. They were tied, said Nathanial, by women, to secure long lives for their husbands. In this one place, it was possible to see all the golden mix of Javanese belief, tumbling down the centuries, seared into the land.

"There is a tale, a love tale, which the villagers told me. Remember, this story is six hundred years old, but it was told to me only a year ago."

Nathanial took off his coat and spread it on the ground, and they sat in the shade. He took two cups and poured the cold water, handing one to Charlotte. She leant back against the buttressed root of the banyan tree and drank.

"This footprint, I was told, is that of a beautiful princess. Of all those who fled with Siliwangi, she alone, the consort of his son, escaped their fate, through the help of an Arab priest, who had converted her. She could not, however, save her husband, her beloved one, whom she saw turned to stone before her eyes. The victor, overcome by her beauty, wooed her, but it was in vain, for she would not be separated from this stone which was him, which was love. She built a little hut under the banyan tree and came each day to sit and gaze upon the stone which bore her husband's semblance. Filled with love and grief, she would hold this stone in her gentle arms and murmur into its deaf ear soft words and vows of love. Day by day, month by month, year by year, her tears would fall on the stone which now lay felled by time until at last it became as soft as clay and received the impress of her tender foot, which had known no other peaceful resting place for so long."

Charlotte smiled at Nathanial for this pretty tale.

"Do you think it is possible to love someone forever, even when they are gone, when you can never see them again?" she asked, gently tracing the footprint with her fingers.

Nathanial looked at her. He knew he was already half in love with Charlotte. "I think it is possible to be unable to relinquish the idea of love, the memory of passion, the ideal, no matter how impractical, of the loved one who is gone. Or," he added, "the one you can never possess."

Charlotte looked up, but Nathanial had risen and held out his hand. They walked through the field to the river and over the curved bamboo bridge into the village, where their carriage was waiting.

11

Life at Buitenzorg flowed at a comforting and steady pace. Tigran was sometimes away, and she was always glad when he came back. Gradually she grew used to his kiss on her cheek in the morning, his hand in hers when they walked on the estate, his arm on her waist when he helped her from the carriage. When they returned to Brieswijk, she had grown comfortable in his undemanding and attentive presence.

Despite her longings for Zhen, as time went by and she assumed the mantle of the mistress of Brieswijk, a gradual change came over her.

But there had been a time when she thought she would never recover.

No word ever came from Zhen. Irrationally, she thought he might find a way to send her a message.

Art thou gone so? love, lord, ay, husband, friend!
I must hear from thee every day in the hour,
For in a minute there are many days ...

How she felt them, those days in the minutes. She finally asked Robert to give her news, but he simply replied that he rarely saw Zhen, had merely heard that a child was to be born, a first grandchild to Baba Tan. Doubtless, Robert said, Zhen knew of her marriage, for it was in the newspaper and had been the talk of Singapore for some time. This news, so casually announced, broke her heart, and she took to her bed and, when she was alone, cried until she was exhausted. She had hideous dreams of dark woods and seeking him. She thought she might as well be dead for all the pleasure she could derive from life. Only the life inside her kept her from the darkest thoughts.

The doctor thought it was fever. He gave her sleeping draughts. But Tigran could see she was heartsick. She refused to see him or Takouhi, refused to eat. Tigran grew anxious; he had burned the other letters he received. The most recent one was in English, translated somehow, and he kept it. He took it out and read it, examining his choices. The man knew of Charlotte's marriage, loved her still, understood. There was a poem. Even Tigran felt its power and this man's enduring and infuriating love for Charlotte.

No flocks of geese thither fly
And she ... ah, she is far away
Yet all my thoughts behold her stay
As in the golden hours gone by
The clouds scarce dim the water's sheen
The moon-bathed islands wanly show
And sweet words falter to and fro ...
Though the River rolls between

If he gave it to her, her spirits would rise, of that he had no doubt, but then it would all begin again. And would she ask then to communicate with the man in Singapore? How could he agree to such a thing?

Finally, at his wit's end, he had sent for Louis. In these dark hours, Louis came every day to make her drink soup and cheer her. Louis was dark-haired like her, with limpid brown eyes, slight figured with long-fingered, perfectly groomed hands. He had an actor's grace, an actor's voice, which he could alter at will. His family, he said, had not approved of his life; he had joined the acting troupe and, like most of the flotsam and jetsam of the Old World, had eventually washed up on colonial shores. He was entertaining, honest and charming. It was easy to open her heart to him.

She told Louis everything, in a long, exhaustive tale. Zhen had arrived in Singapore, the poorest coolie, and, because he was pure-blood Chinese and had an education, was selected by one of the richest Chinese merchants in Singapore to be the husband of his eldest daughter. He had had no choice for his, and his family's, entire survival depended on the match. Charlotte told Louis how she had been Zhen's teacher of English; he had saved her life and virtue from an attack in the jungle, and they had fallen in love. Their meetings, their love, had been doomed in advance.

Louis had understood, and she, overcome, had turned her heart to him as he told her of his passion for a handsome Danish soldier in the Dutch army, now married to a rich widow, for whom he had become an occasional amusement and usually a nuisance. The visits to Tong and Chinatown, the liaisons with Javanese boys: simply a search for oblivion. Charlotte held his hand and thought no more of this love as natural or unnatural. It was simply love, and Louis suffered as she did.

Louis adored Byron and had learned English expressly to revel in his poems. He quietly voiced his own emotion through Byron's words.

> " ... he lov'st me not, and never wilt,
> Love dwells not in our will.
> Nor can I blame him, though it be my lot,
> To strongly, wrongly, vainly love him still."

Love dwells not in our will. "What a wonderful line," they murmured, and wept, their dark heads together. She ate to please Louis, and gradually she grew well.

Nathanial came, too, with old copies of the *Java Gazette* from Raffles's time, which he could always plunder for titbits to confirm his disdain for the Dutch.

"As you lie on your couch in this lovely room with the breeze wafting through the window, consider how the Dutchman lived in times gone by," he said and began to read.

"The beds of Batavia were large and spacious and provided with as many as ten cushions and pillows including the "stomach pillow" which was used to protect the lower body against cold. There was such a general horror of catching cold, partly because of the fantastic notion that this originated noxious fevers, that the sleeper not only surrounded himself with a mass of pillows but often wore a night neckerchief and a woolen nightcap. When to that is added that the bed curtains were not usually made of gauze or muslin but of cotton, linen or costly thick

textiles, *and that the bedroom was on the ground floor and stuffy from absence of ventilation, then one begins to get some idea of the ambrosial nights passed by the well-to-do in Old Batavia.*

"*The Dutchmen at Batavia disdained rice and always preferred their costly, difficult-to-get, half-sour or rancid, ill-preserved European foods. From Holland came pickled meats and salted bacon, cheese, ham, smoked salmon, sausages, herrings, smoked tongue and meat. Jan Pieterszoon Coen wrote, "Our nation must drink or die," and for hundreds of years his nation seems to have done its earnest best. Everybody drank a bottle of wine a day as a matter of course, quite apart from beer, sake and spirits.*

"*When one considers the mode of living, it seems that Batavia might well have been built to show exactly how not to live in the tropics. The city was built on marshy land—what Stavorinus called one of the most unwholesome spots upon the face of the globe—with the houses built close together on the edges of ditches and canals. The doors and windows were kept closed, and light and air excluded as far as possible. Curtains were hung to keep the sun out, and even then one often sat behind a screen. Exercise was almost never taken, and baths only occasionally, whilst it was de rigeur to overeat grossly of heavy foods and to regard spiritous liquors as a splendid and indispensable medicine against fever. Morning, noon and evening, the Hollander drank gin, rum and cognac. Only too common were pale, wan and bloated faces, shaking hands, red and watery eyes, a foul breath. In the evenings it was customary to sit smoking and drinking gin by the side of a stinking ditch or canal, after which a heavy supper was taken, after which one passed out, half seas over, behind the thick curtains of the heretofore mentioned beds.*"

"How perfectly delightful! It is no surprise," Nathanial concluded with something approaching a macabre glee, "that, in no other country did people hear of the death of a friend with more nonchalance or less surprise and concern. Batavia could boast of screeds of widows of the best kind—young, pretty, ignorant and rich."

To draw her out of Brieswijk and herself, Nathanial took her on long carriage rides around the city. One day they set out north on Molenvleit and turned into the Sawah Besar, which ran, as its name revealed, between vast wet rice fields. They turned south onto the Groote Zuider Weg, which would take them eventually to Buitenzorg, Nathanial explained, but which, here, ran along the canal of Gunung Sahari to the market at Pasir Senen. Today was not a market day, so they did not stop but carried on, going west into Perapatan, over the Ciliwung River. Bamboo rafts laden with bricks were negotiating the long curve of the water. With their high, pointed bows, fat bodies and curled tails, they looked like scorpions. The water in Batavia was omnipresent and adorned by a seemingly infinite array of native craft.

They called for tea with Reverend Medhurst and his wife, for hidden behind a thick forest of palms was the English church, white columned and cool. The road from here ran along Kebun Sireh, a large plantation of betel trees, crossed the little Menteng stream and emerged at another large country residence at the southern end of Tanah Abang.

"Much of the land we have just traversed," Nathanial said, "was once the most famous private estate in Batavia, from which this part of the city takes its name, Weltevreden. The man was Justinus Vinck, and he owned, incredible as it may seem today, all of Weltevreden, had a house bigger and finer even than Brieswijk, established both the market at Pasir Senen and that at Tanah Abang and made the Kebun Sireh road to join the two. The estate was home to three Governors-General and finally passed into government hands when Daendels purchased it; it was gradually broken up."

They turned along the wide, red-earthed, rural path of Tanah Abang, where the trees threw shadows into the quiet waters of the canal and they could peer at the goods and curiosities of the ramshackle Chinese shops and *warungs* which dotted the road. The sound of small boys' voices chanting could be heard from a red-roofed mosque which stood behind a low hedge. The mosque was like many in Batavia, a mix of different styles and cultures. Nathanial, whose encyclopaedic interests included mosque architecture, had shown her the Angke mosque at Kampong Bali. The rectangular shape, the small windows with their wooden slats and the two-storey roof were Javanese. The five front steps, the pillars, the double-winged door, the carved fanlight and door frame were Dutch. The roof ends curved like a Chinese house.

Before Tanah Abang joined Riswijkstraat, they turned into Kerkhoflaan to visit the European cemetery. This quickly became a favourite place for Charlotte. The only sound throughout its vast grounds was birdsong. When the day was new, she took the carriage to the gates of the cemetery, where, in the shade of a banyan tree, a flower market sprang up every day. The ground under the tree was set with ancient gravestones, like the floor of an old village church. The blue-grey slabs were emblazoned with worn-out crests and coats-of-arms. Heraldic shapes and long Latin epitaphs were engraved in the curving script of the 17th and 18th century, recording for fleeting posterity the honours and titles bestowed on the deceased by the Lords Seventeen, the rulers of the United East India Company. Nathanial had told her that when the old churches were closed, the gravestones of the first Dutchmen had been moved here. Some had been stolen, some sold to Chinese for their own tombs; some found their way here, now to be daily festooned with heaps of creamy jasmine, stems of lotus buds, bouquets of orchids of every hue, baskets of soft, fragrant petals with tints of ivory and purple mixed with gold. Their customers, village women, their slender figures dressed in bright-hued garments, arrived chattering, bargaining, moving from one flower seller to another. Purchase made, they and their friends sat and twisted orange blossom or jasmine into their coils of glistening black hair. Charlotte always filled a basket with flowers when she came, happy to pay these women for their charming display and happy, too, to adorn whatever headstone took her fancy.

She never tired of exploring the shady lanes of these peaceful grounds. Nathanial had taken her to the white grave and cupola of Olivia Raffles, which lay next to her friend and her most ardent admirer, John Leyden. Leyden, Charlotte knew now, was the very closest friend of Thomas and Olivia. He had died of fever at the conquest of Java. Leyden was one of the most famous of Scottish poets, a friend and colleague of Sir Walter Scott. Though he did not say so, Nathanial felt a little like Leyden, who had clearly fallen hopelessly in love with the wife of his friend. He read Charlotte a poem he had found, written for Olivia:

When far beyond Malaya's sea,
I trace dark Sunda's forests drear,
Olivia! I shall think of thee—
And bless thy steps, departed year

Each morn or evening spent with thee
Fancy shall mid the wilds restore
In all their charms, and they shall be
Sweet days that shall return no more ...

Throughout the grounds, in a disordered profusion, lay all the different tastes and feelings one would find in any graveyard of such antiquity, visible in the writing, styles and sculpture of the tombs. Here a winged marble angel, dazzling white in the sun, a gothic turret, pillars, obelisks; there, sleeping children, mossy marble crosses, baroque coats-of-arms. All the faith and worldly glory which had flitted briefly on the stage of this capital found a quiet remembrance here.

Throughout this time of sadness and recovery, Tigran stayed as patient and attentive as he could. Seeing Charlotte's spirits revived, he walked on the grounds with her and read to her from a book of poetry he had been given by his English tutor long ago, for he understood more than ever her feeling for poetry. He chose carefully, poems of nature and beauty. She recovered her wits and accepted her new place.

12

Charlotte watched her body change and her belly become taut, rounded, uncomfortable ... ugly. Sleep was elusive. Up until this night she had not had the slightest inclination to go near the closet and had kept her own door locked. She was far advanced in the pregnancy. The baby was turbulent now. The first movement had been months ago, and she and Takouhi had laughed and hugged each other. Since the loss of Meda, Takouhi awaited the arrival of this baby with a joy which seemed to invigorate her. Somehow Charlotte felt reluctant to share this time with Tigran, despite all his kindness; this was not his child.

Now she turned and turned, her belly uncomfortable. The constant need to relieve herself was a vast nuisance. The night was hot and close. Finally, as the light began to slip into the room, she rose.

The notion of seeing him had taken root in her mind.

"Oh, Kitt Macleod, for heaven's sake." she said to herself.

Charlotte lit a candle, went to the closet and opened his door. She could hear the bird sounds stirring in the jungly reaches of the grounds. She could make out the four-poster bed and some furniture but little else. What was she doing? If she entered that room he would expect ... would suppose ... Did she want this? She wasn't in the least sure, but the wish to see Tigran had become irresistible.

She moved forward. Tigran lay naked on the bed, one hand thrown back around his face. She took in the form of his body, the way his hair fell about his arm and her eyes went, as if pulled, to the dark indistinct space between his legs. She shook her head, annoyed at this awful peeping. He was asleep. She contemplated him, would have liked to touch him.

Then he turned, and her heart made a violent thump. She put her hand to her mouth. His hair had fallen half across his face, and she stretched forward to move it. Tigran started and opened his eyes, gripping her wrist without thinking, half asleep. Then he sat up abruptly, alarmed. "Charlotte?"

She looked at him, silent, unsure of what to say. He rose, taking up a sarong and tying it around his limbs. "Are you hurt? Is it the baby?"

She heard the concern in his voice. She shook her head. "I can't sleep. I wanted to see you."

Tigran took her hand and led her along the balcony back to her room, which was cooler. He helped her back onto the bed. Then he saw the baby give a great kick and smiled. He put out his hand. She looked at him for a moment, then took his hand and put it on her belly. He could feel the baby moving under the skin. It was time to go to Buitenzorg for the birth, while she could still travel.

He leaned forward and, through her nightgown, very gently kissed her belly where the baby had kicked. Charlotte was moved and suddenly felt a longing to feel his skin on hers. She felt so ugly, deformed by this pregnancy, heavy and stupid. Yet he did not seem to mind; on the contrary. He showed her how desirable she was every day. She ran her fingers into his silky hair, and he looked up and saw the softness in her eyes.

"Can I hold you, Charlotte? Just hold you, kiss you? Nothing more. You need this. It has been too long."

Charlotte saw that he meant it. And his words were true. She desperately needed to be caressed. She wanted to feel his lips on her skin, his hands on her belly, his reassuring presence. He had seen the birth of five children, and she had begun to be fearful of the unknown pain which lay so soon ahead of her.

Charlotte feared childbirth. In Scotland she had once, unknown to her aunt, who was in attendance, seen a woman die in labour, her agonies appalling, her face contorted with pain beyond endurance and a wild-eyed, violent and hideous desperation, like a half-slain animal seeking life. The memory of it had never left her mind, as it could have never left the mind of any woman. She shuddered, and he saw it.

"I am afraid."

He moved on to the bed instantly and lay behind her, the length of his body against hers. He took her in his arms, pulling her against him, his lips on her neck, his hands moving gently on her swollen breasts, her swollen belly, until she released the tension of this encounter and relaxed against him. This feeling was exquisite, and she moved slightly in his arms, facing him, putting her hands in his hair. As their lips met, she sighed and he gave a small groan and deepened the kiss. He undid the ribbons of her gown and slid it down her body, lifting her legs to support her back against the weight of the belly, turning her into him. She did not think of Zhen; she thought of nothing but this feel of his skin, his lips, on her, his hands caressing her.

As she touched him, she wondered briefly why she had waited so long for this. She was married to him, and this seemed the most natural thing in the world. His body was hard, but his skin was soft. Eastern men had skin like silk, smooth and hairless. She felt him grow hard against her under his sarong, but she knew he would do nothing. She liked this hardness, affirming, physically, his desire and her own desirability, which she had begun to doubt. She drifted into sleep.

In the morning he was gone, and she felt the place where he had been. When she went to breakfast, she saw him, sitting at the table, looking out over the lawn. As she arrived he rose, smiling, and kissed her hand. Charlotte smiled too, and went close to him, putting her lips to his, her hand to his cheek. Her belly got in the way, and they both laughed.

"Tonight I will come to you. Like last night. Yes?"

"Yes," she said and looked down. She suddenly felt inexplicably shy.

When Takouhi arrived, she saw that something new had happened. She could see it in the way Charlotte looked at Tigran. Despite the pregnancy, which was almost at term, she seemed lighter. They made plans to go to the hills.

At Buitenzorg, she began to feel a happiness and a surge of feeling for Tigran, especially when he joined her in *la seraille*, sending the women away chattering and giggling, taking her in his arms, feeling the movement of the baby and running his hands over her, pouring water through her hair, massaging her, kissing her. When he came to her she pulled him to her unashamedly. She liked watching him as she touched him, exploring his body, enjoying this power. He warned her, smiling, of his revenge when she was over her confinement. Against his expectations, he enjoyed this delay, this quiet exploration of each other. He had never kissed any woman as much as he kissed Charlotte. She sought his constant touch now when they were together, wanted his lips all over her. This newfound sensuality in her he found surprising and gratifying. Apart from the most intimate place, there could not be one inch of her skin that his lips had not touched, and he found it as heady and potent as any aphrodisiac. He discovered you could get drunk on kisses. For two weeks, he found himself practically abandoning his business; all other claims on his time annoyed him. They shared the big bed in the long room, sinking into the soft cotton kapok mattress, drinking wine, watching the fire, talking of the day, planning the morrow. She lay in his arms as content as a kitten, and he stroked her hair and kissed her, filled with gratitude and joy at her quiet trust in him. He was almost sorry when her time came.

Takouhi had told Charlotte about the Javanese ways of birth, the *jamu*, the ceremonies. To Charlotte's astonishment, the father was always present. Tigran had attended the birth of all his children, Takouhi told her; he was very experienced.

It was not like the horrible English way. When it had been time for her to give birth to Meda, George had been banished. She had been attended only by Dr Montgomerie, a man she hardly knew! Only one of her own Javanese maids was allowed to help her, wipe her sweating body. There was no singing and soothing incense, no water and loving words. It was hideous and embarrassing, utterly cold, a dreadful, fearful experience, especially at her age, over forty. She was amazed to have survived.

Charlotte knew that both Takouhi and George had been surprised by this late conception of their only child, their delight greater for its unexpectedness. But their life together had died with Meda; neither had been able to get over this loss.

The Javanese way of birthing was much better, said Takouhi. And so it was. Though Tigran had brought the Dutch civil surgeon from Batavia as a precaution, the birth was carried out in a Javanese way. The low, square bath was prepared with pure white cloths and soft cushions. Curtains and bamboo screens were hung around *la seraille* against the cold and in case of rain. Flames from the braziers chased shadows on the walls and warmed the air.

It was early evening, and candleglow and frankincense filled the room. The *dukun* chanted quietly in the corner. Two women fanned her continuously, wafting the fragrant and healing smoke of the frankincense gum around her lower body. Clad in a loose white sarong, Tigran cradled her. More frightened than she had ever been in her life, Charlotte clung to him, and he supported her, his cheek against hers, murmuring words to her: words he had never before said, feeling her pain like a knife in his chest. When the crown of the head appeared, Charlotte was exhausted, but Tigran whispered Madi's instructions to take little breaths so as not to tear as the head passed. Madi eased the baby forward with her hands and when the final contraction came, pulled him out gently. Tigran cut the cord, and the Javanese women chanted quietly in that sing-song way, sending prayers. A healthy boy, they exclaimed, praise be to Allah.

It was over, and Charlotte had never felt such relief, such a release.

One hour after the delivery, Madi bathed her carefully with wild rose and jasmine oil and wrapped her like a mummy from below her breasts to her thighs in a long white cloth. Round and round they went, sealing her up. Cooling aloe lotions were massaged into her breasts to encourage milk and warm oils on her lower body to rid her of the lochia, the postnatal blood. Her table was covered in special foods in dozens of tiny dishes—tonics bitter and sweet. Twice a day she was placed in a billowing skirt over the smoking frankincense bowl to cleanse her birth passages, bathed and wrapped again. After six days, she was permitted to walk in the evening around the park with Tigran and Takouhi. In this way, Takouhi explained, she would heal quickly and regain her figure.

Tigran was forbidden to do anything but hold her hand and kiss her for the forty-day period of confinement. He did not mind, though Madi's strict instructions to sleep apart were galling. Madi knew that, though her master might have some control, in her experience many men would require "comfort", some even within a few days of the birth. This lack of care for the birthing woman made Madi despise men. She was adamant, knowing the master would obey.

Charlotte, despite all that had gone before, perfidious, suddenly desperately missed Zhen as she gazed at his little son, seeking a resemblance in his features, his eyes. She let herself be smoked and fed, wrapped and rubbed like a doll. When it was over, however, she had regained her spirits. And she had to admit, it had all worked. She was as slender as ever, her skin glowed and she felt rejuvenated.

On the forty-first night, Tigran banished everyone from their quarters. Madi, knowing this would happen, treated Charlotte carefully with the essence of Neem and other oils to prevent another pregnancy so soon after the birth. Then the maids dressed her in the white satin nightgown Tigran had sent, infused with the smoke of incense, and brushed her hair down her back. As they pampered her she felt as if she was in a story from *Les Mille et Une Nuits*, which she had read avidly in her grandfather's library. But it did not matter. She was happy to play Scheherezade, and she had nothing to fear from him.

All restraint she had felt was in the past. They had lain together too often, touched each other too much. She wanted this final step now, and more than she had thought she would. The forty days had restored her health and filled her with gratitude for Tigran's strength and generosity at the birth of her son. She felt his sureness, the security he gave her in her new motherhood. As he lifted her onto their bed, she held his head in her arms and sought his lips. At first he simply held her, but so tight she thought he would crush her, and she pulled her head from his shoulder and cried out. When he came into her for the first time, he was all urgent and groaning passion, and she felt a disappointment.

She had been adamant in her wish not to compare him with Zhen, but she could not help but feel the difference, almost the shock of this rapidity. Tigran sensed her feelings, but the waiting for her had taken its toll. When Zan was brought to her to suckle, he watched, touching her breasts, kissing her lips, stroking the baby's head, and when Alexander was taken away, he pulled her again into his arms. This time he determined to show he was not just storm. As Charlotte sensed this she relaxed into his hands. He was glad he had had the wisdom to endure the torment of waiting for her. This night and those to come would make it all worthwhile.

Only when the sun began to rise did they sleep.

Zan was a lusty baby. Very quickly her own milk was not enough, and he went to the wet nurse. Before long, she ceased nursing him at all.

Fourteen months later, Takouhi and Charlotte were bathing, surrounded by petals of jasmine and mountain rose. A fire under the stone baths kept the water warm if the day was cool. The odour of aromatic wood smoke floated on the air. Meda's final mourning period, the one thousand day *slametan*, would be next week. The final details were being settled, and Takouhi was speaking quietly to her *dukun*, who knelt on a gold cushion by the side of the bath. When the old woman left, the maids brought cotton towels and they rose, dripping, and then, dressed in batik gowns, sat on the cushions to pick at the little dishes which lay on the low wooden table.

Jasmine-scented incense glowed in the stone bowls at the four corners of the pavilion. Beyond the parapet, the valley fell away five hundred feet below. Two of the maids were occupied in staining henna patterns on Takouhi and Charlotte's feet and chattering quietly. There was always a little tussle as to who would serve Charlotte, her white skin a canvas they all wanted to paint. When Charlotte was here, she felt like Cleopatra.

She looked over at Alexander playing in the smallest pool with the son of the wet nurse. Alexander was as strong and muscled as his little companion was slight and fine-boned. The Javanese children were small and delicate-featured, pretty. Charlotte was not big, but she felt like a giant next to the graceful, tiny Javanese women. Alexander's wet nurse and her niece, his *babu*, called him Iskandar, sometimes Zandar. Charlotte mostly called him Zan. Tigran refused to call him anything but Alexander. He had very light brown skin, dark almond eyes and thick, jet black hair. He was as handsome as Arjuna; all the maids told her so, and showered him with kisses.

His *babu*, who had nursed him since the day he was born, was sitting next to him, ready to cater to his every whim. She adored him and was his ministering spirit. Until he began to crawl she had carried him all day long against her heart in her long *slendang*. She fed him, bathed him, dressed him, took him everywhere, ready always to lift him up against her heart. She never tired of playing with him. She was very young and a child herself at heart. She suffered Tigran and Charlotte to cuddle and play with him, sure in the knowledge he would return to her. At night, she crooned him to sleep and slept on a mat by his bed.

Charlotte had learned first of Alexander the Great from a book in her grandfather's library: a French translation of an ancient Latin text. Now here was the legend of Alexander, the Persian Iskandar, carried forward in a book in the library at the Harmonie Club. It was John Leyden's translation of the *Malay Annals*, which Raffles had published in honour of his friend.

It happened on a time that Raja Iskandar of Makedonia wished to see the rising of the sun and with this view he reached the confines of the land of Hind.

As she read these opening lines she was caught up. The first Mohammedan sultanate in the Malay world had been founded at Malacca by Parameswara, a Hindu prince who claimed to be a descendant of Alexander the Great through sons brought forth from this land of Hind. When he married a princess of the Arab faith, he converted and took the title Sultan Iskandar Shah, for Iskandar was the Arabic name for Alexander. Charlotte recalled the holy tomb on Bukit Larangan in Singapore, where some said he was supposed to be buried. She was immediately enchanted. The first kiss with Zhen had been in the old spice orchard on that hill. They had met there so many times. This mingling of Eastern and Western legend was perfect. Everything seemed to lead to this name for this child.

The approaching *slametan* had affected Takouhi in unsuspected ways. She began to talk of visiting the grave of her own mother, the Javanese princess first mentioned when Charlotte had met Takouhi in Singapore.

"When she die, family take her back to Surakarta, bury her near old palace."

Suddenly Takouhi took Charlotte's hand. "Let's visit my Jawa family in Kraton, go to mother's grave."

Charlotte gathered Zan's wet little body into a cotton cloth on her knee, handing him pieces of sticky rice cakes, smiling as he squished them between his fingers. A visit to the royal palaces of Surakarta! She had read about the Javanese royal courts both in Raffles's enormous tome on Java and Crawfurd's entertaining book on the archipelago. She went often, with or without Nathanial, to the library in the Harmonie Club. The keeper of the books had grown used to her. She enjoyed spending time poring over these books in these elegant rooms as the rain pounded on the roof. It reminded her of childhood hours spent reading in her grandfather's library in Aberdeen.

She squeezed Takouhi's hand. A trip to the princely eastern provinces. Yes, it would be wonderful!

13

M eda's one-thousand-day *slametan* would take place at Brieswijk.
They travelled away from the plantation high on the hills,
down the steep winding road to the Grote Postweg, the Great Post Road,
which swept across Java linking Anyer in the west to Panarukan in the
east. Here, Daendels's great highway passed through the Puncak Pass
eastwards through the high Priangan plateau and on, and westwards
down to Buitenzorg and the capital. Rumour had it that thousands had
died to construct it, from disease and forced labour; that Daendels had
ordered the Javanese regents to supply labour and keep to a tight schedule.
Failure to do so resulted in the death of the labourers and the regents; their
heads hung on trees along the wayside as a constant reminder to others.
Tigran told Charlotte he was not sure how many had died. His father and
the old men talked of the benefits it had brought, not the costs. Corvée
labour was as traditional as the *wayang* in the Javanese countryside. It
had been built in one year. A thousand miles in one year, through swamp,
jungle and mountains, Tigran said. In his *History of Java*, Raffles claimed
10,000 had died, but he did not care much for Daendels, Tigran added.
He shrugged and left Charlotte to her thoughts.

They were glad of the highway, though, as they made their way to
the palace of the Governor-General at Buitenzorg. One of the glories of
this journey was the sight of hillsides covered with rasamala, the liquid-
amber tree, rising straight as a pole to 130 feet.

The colourful majesty of the jungle was impossible to enjoy from the
ground. Only above it, as if offered exclusively to the exalted eyes of gods
and angels, could one gaze on the blossoming beauty of the vast canopy

of trees. Tigran stopped the coach to look down from their vantage point. Below them spread, in swathes of brilliant scarlet and purple, the tubular flower clusters of the rasamala. Here and there, climbing plants of white and fiery orange had found their way to the tops of the trees, and the combination of blossoms spreading from hillside to hillside was of a staggering beauty.

The staging posts offered refreshments and a change of horses. Stalls sold fried *ikan mas*, fried banana, fruits and vegetables. The scenery was always spectacular. The volcanic mountains of Gede, Salak and Pangrango surrounded the lower foothills, pierced with small, rushing waterfalls and rock-strewn rivulets. As the road wound down the mountainside, the tea plants stopped abruptly and gave way to jungly forest and amphitheatres of terraced fields of yellowing rice.

It enchanted the senses, and no matter how often she made this journey, it was always the same.

The Manouks were guests for several days of Pieter and Wilhelmina Merkus.

This was not the first time Charlotte had seen the Buitenzorg Palace, but the first time they had stayed as guests.

Much of it had been destroyed in the earthquake which followed the eruption of Salak Mountain eight years before. The main house had been remodelled from the original grand three-storey to a single story Palladian-style building. There was still much to be completed in the outer buildings, and the grounds remained to be restored to their former brilliance. They liked to come, Wilhelmina said, for the children, and she enjoyed the cooler weather.

Charlotte was standing with Wilhelmina, admiring a painting of the old palace hung in the dining room. The original, Wilhelmina was telling her, had been a private estate purchased by Baron von Imhoff, the Governor-General, in 1744, as a place of cool repose. Buitenzorg meant "*sans souci*", the place without a care. Since then it had always served as the official country retreat. Daendels had spent a lot of time here, and, of course, Raffles had lived here almost all the time with Olivia during the British interregnum.

Charlotte liked the old Governor-General and his wife, with whom she and Tigran enjoyed a pleasant, easy relationship. They were the epitome of Dutch Indies life. Merkus had arrived in Batavia as an ambitious young man from Holland. He had passed through the ranks of government and was appointed Governor of the Mollucas at Amboyna, the capital of the Spice Islands. He fought the British, who marauded constantly in the region, and brought West Papua into the power of the Dutch.

Wilhelmina was a Cranssen, a daughter of one of the most illustrious families of the Dutch Indies. Her father had been a chief adviser to Raffles and her mother, a Balinese, he had legitimised as a Nessnarc, reversing the name. The Cranssens' pedigree stretched back into the VOC times, and they were related by marriage to every one of the great families of that era. Wilhemina's grandmother, Catharina, incredibly old, lived at Buitenzorg. Her grandfather, Abraham Couperus, had been the unfortunate Dutch Governor of Malacca, humiliated and imprisoned when it passed to the British in 1795.

The influence of these Compagnie dynasties had faded with the dissolution of the VOC and the arrival of Herman Daendels. Daendels was a man of the Enlightenment, of revolutionary Europe, and he came determined to make a clean sweep of Javanese feudalism. He abolished hereditary rights and put the princes under his command to build the Great Post Road against an expected British invasion. He completely dismantled the old town of Batavia, ordering the destruction of the ancient fort and the use of its stones to build his new palace at Koningsplein, away from the disease of the old port. He laid out the new town, with its wide streets and vast squares. Charlotte began to understand the broken-down appearance of the lower town. To raise revenue, he took the drastic step of selling public land to private ownership, particularly to rich Chinese to whom the government was already indebted. Three provinces in the far east of Java were swallowed up in these sales.

The lands around Batavia, the *ommelanden*, and in the Preanger, the coffee growing regions, were further sold off under Raffles. Tigran's father, Gevork, made sure he profited from this unforeseen and permanent sale of government lands, and the estates for both the tea and coffee plantations had been purchased during the government of these two men. For this sale of government lands and his perceived profit from it, Raffles was subsequently accused of corruption and had returned to England under a cloud.

Wilhelmina was always most interesting on the recent history of Java. She was well-read and politically clever, a perfect companion to her husband in his high office. From her own family, she had learned a great deal. As well as the most capable Javanese linguists, Raffles had many former Dutch administrators, sympathetic to English ideas, to help him in governing Java. Two of the most important were Herman Muntinghe and Willem Cranssen, Wilhelmina's father, both of whom were able, liberal-minded and spoke excellent English.

"The English and the Dutch, no matter their personal feelings, had to appear united, for the Javanese Regents were constantly on the lookout for a chance of rebellion. However, my father and Muntinghe were close to Raffles, and they admired each other so it was an easy relationship," Wilhelmina said.

Tigran, the Governor-General and the other men retired to the smoking room. Now the ladies were seated in the verandah, where the air was cool. The temperature change from the high hills to here was considerable. The evenings were not cold but merely pleasantly cool. Takouhi had gone to bed, but Charlotte was curious and enjoying, as always, the company of Wilhelmina.

Pieter Merkus was remarkable for having married a divorced woman. This was common knowledge in Batavia. Wilhelmina was unconcerned. Her former husband had been an unpleasant man, stupidly so, since she took away from him a considerable inheritance and influence. Pieter, she had been happy to tell Charlotte, was a man she could respect and love. The divorce had had little effect on his promotion, and she was delighted to acknowledge the fact that she was the first, and perhaps only, divorced woman to be the wife of a Governor-General of the Indies. She took care, with great affection, of his daughter Henrietta born to him by an Ambonese slave woman.

"Raffles governed Java almost entirely from the palace at Buitenzorg. Olivia Raffles died here, you know, and the memorial he built for her is in the grounds of the palace, just beyond the lake. The botanical gardens adjoin the grounds. Would you care to visit it tomorrow and take a turn with the children?"

Charlotte quickly agreed. She very much wanted to learn more.

As the evening broke up, Tigran came out onto the verandah. He put his arms around her, and they gazed out at the jagged moonlit outline of Mount Salak. It looked so peaceful, yet they both knew it contained a heart of fire.

Charlotte leaned against him. "What will you do tomorrow? I am visiting the gardens with Wilhelmina and the children. Takouhi may come. Will you hunt?"

"I'll come with you. Old Teysmann is a good friend. We shall make a picnic on the lakeside, and tomorrow night there is a *wayang* performance. Do you remember the *wayang* play in Brieswijk the night before our marriage?"

The wedding had seemed a dream, but now, in his arms and content, Charlotte remembered that night.

Tigran had asked the puppet master to put on a play in honour of his forthcoming marriage. They had chosen the *Arjunawiwaha*, the Story of Arjuna's Marriage. Everyone understood the conceit. On this occasion, several villainous characters had been added from the pantheon of Dutch VOC Governors, to further merriment. *Wayang* performances could last all night, but Tigran had asked that this one be limited to two hours. In the long, low light of the late afternoon, hundreds of villagers from the *kampongs* made their way to the lawns of the house. Food and drink was laid out on the riverside, which the villagers devoured noisily, chattering, their babes in arms and children running to and fro.

The puppet master was the most famous *dalen* in Batavia. The *gamelan* belonged to the estate and was endowed with the finest musicians Tigran had been able to find. As the last streaks of crimson left the sky and the dusk crept over the grounds, the villagers had gathered. The first star appeared, tremulous as a dewdrop in the heavens, and the groups ceased their chatter.

The *dalen* rose, like a high priest of the shadow world, and spread on a bamboo altar the sacrificial gifts—fruit, yellow rice and flowers— lighting the incense to honour the gods and to keep off evil spirits. As the perfumed smoke rose on the breeze, the *gamelan* began, in a thunderous burst, and the dancers appeared. The village children shrank into their parents' arms at this sound, eyes glued to the stage. Like willowy saplings, the dancers turned and swayed, miming the ballad, the prologue to the play, which a companion was singing. The sound of the *gamelan* was pure and mysterious, like moonlight on flowing water, constantly shifting but always the same. When the dancers disappeared, the shadow play began.

Tigran had told her the story. The king of the demons wished to wed a celestial nymph, but Arjuna would save her through strength and virtue. The puppet of Arjuna was clearly carved to resemble Tigran, with long plaited hair and flowing locks under the huge, curled backsweep of his headdress. Charlotte could see that the celestial nymph was meant to be her. The dress and hair were vaguely European, and she was portrayed with exceptional grace, despite her rather long, thin nose. The demon king was also clearly a European, with a big Dutch hat. He was, Tigran explained, a formidable opponent, for he was invulnerable save in one place—his tongue was his Achilles heel.

The audience all clapped loudly and laughed delightedly at these realistic depictions. The white screen was transformed into a fiery orange courtly world of elegant shadows. Insects buzzed and flapped around the light and onto the screen, increasing its shadowy grip on reality; the *dalen*, the master magician, chanted the story, played every part, the rise and fall of the *gamelan* shadowing him as he made shadows on the screen.

As the battle between Arjuna and the demon king came to a climax, it seemed that Arjuna must die. He fell in a crash of musical frenzy, and the demon, rejoicing, opened his mouth in a shout of victory, but Arjuna, only feigning mortal wounds, rose and hurled his spear into the demon's tongue. The demon faltered, again and again, and finally fell.

Arjuna was victorious, and the audience shouted its appreciation. The wedding to the celestial nymph was a blaze of glory, a symphony of flitting shadow and fire, of bells and gongs, and when the lovers embraced, the villagers rose in a joyous clapping and cheering.

Charlotte had understood not one word of the narrative, but that was unimportant. The fascination was in the constant repetition of the resonant gongs, the hypnotic beat of the drum, the flame and shadows trembling on the screen, the strong, sure and melodious voice of the *dalen*.

Since then she had discovered that the *dalen* and his art were held in the highest reverence. If he travelled, he was welcomed everywhere and at home he was, like a prince, exempt from taxes, his fellows discharging his due in payment for the pleasure he brought them. There was, she thought, something deeply generous and pleasing in the nature of the Javanese that could acquit the artist of all earthly duties because he fulfilled the most supreme one, that of giving joy.

It had been shadows to her then, but she recalled it now with a warm pleasure. She turned in Tigran's arms and pulled his face to hers, thanking him with a kiss.

After breakfast, Wilhelmina took Charlotte by the arm and led the party across the lawn, passing by the descendents of the grazing silver-dotted deer which Raffles had brought here and down towards the lake. A red, Chinese-style bridge spanned a dark, reedy spur of water, and they crossed over to an avenue of ancient, bumpy trees which lined the lake edge. The lake was filled with water lilies of a deep blue and vast pans of bright green leaves, ten feet across. The sun shot rainbows through the water, and wading birds edged away as they approached.

Leaving the children to play with the servants, the four adults penetrated into the palace grounds, long ago converted to botanical gardens. These had been started by Raffles, whose wide-ranging interests included botany. The gardens were developed and now stood unrivalled even by the great gardens at Kew in their scientific and botanical importance. An impenetrable mass of dense, thick-stemmed bamboo lay to both sides of the path, bending its gracious bows and whispering as they passed.

The shade grew deeper. Really, the tropical forest was a perplexing thing, Charlotte thought. In a land with no perceptible seasons, the trees in the forest kept to their own rhythms. Even as one was springing with fresh green leaves, another would be turning brown, each seemingly driven by its own instincts and acting without any regard for its neighbours, yet all in harmony. When the eye failed to separate the mass of this exuberance, the ear drank in the sounds breaking the silence and deepening the solitude. The leaves rustled, and under them, barely perceptible, the breath of the forest, the movement of insects and birds, an invisible and constant pullulation of life which could only be felt, not seen.

They heard rushing water as they approached the stone parapet which guarded the banks of the upper reaches of the Ciliwung River. Here nature had been fashioned by men into embankments, the water deep and clear, coursing over the boulders and rocks of the river bed. They crossed a bridge into a canyon of immense, buttressed banyan trees, the aerial roots forming thick, ropy columns. Tigran waved to a man who was approaching.

Johannes Teysmann, the head of the gardens, joined them. Charlotte was reminded of the bearded face of a Greek philosopher. Teysmann was something of a botanical hero, for he had saved these magnificent gardens from certain obliteration.

He took them to see the Japanese plants brought by Philip von Siebold from Deshima several years ago. Over 2000 specimens had found a home in Java, including the tea plant, which he had smuggled out and which now formed the basis of the recent tea plantations in West Java.

They gazed at the tall *kempas* tree, with its roots spread out like the gnarled fingers of an ancient warlock, and at the stacked roots of the *pandanus*, seemingly ready for bonfire night, supporting the tufty palm. In one alley, the light was all but obscured by the silhouettes of curling creepers, lianas and rattans joining hands across the track. As if unable to grow in the ordinary way, these plants took the shapes of serpents, twining around less pliant neighbours, festooning each tree, some loose and swaying, some stiff as the shrouds which support the mast of a ship.

Wilhelmina was tiring and asked Charlotte to accompany her back to the lake. They left the men to their conversations about Teysmann's experiments in the cultivation of *chinchona* and vanilla and retraced their steps. Her former husband, Karl Blume, she confided to Charlotte, had been the second director of these gardens. He liked the female plant genus, she told Charlotte with a laugh, better than the female human genus.

At the far end of the lake was another small bridge, and on the opposite bank Charlotte could see a white-columned cupola, shaded all around by the soft leaves of overhanging branches.

"Olivia Raffles's memorial," Wilhelmina explained.

Charlotte read the inscription there:

Oh Thou! whom ne'er my constant heart
One moment hath forgot
Tho' fate severe hath bid us part
Yet you forget me not.

Charlotte had read the memoir written by Raffles's second wife, Sophia, a book which, following on Singapore's spectacular commercial success, had served to raise Raffles out of the murky obscurity into which he had fallen in the eyes of the East India Company. The memoir made no mention of Olivia, a woman so prominent in his life and early success, and this absence hinted at Sophia's enduring unease, even dark jealousy, of the other woman. As they walked around the memorial, Charlotte mentioned this, and Wilhelmina shrugged her shoulders.

"Olivia was a lively woman, rather showy, somewhat older than Thomas, of course. I heard from the gossip that she was very fond of a glass of brandy and could be a little wild. But, *après tout*, who is not? To me she was always good-hearted. And she was beautiful. I heard she had Circassian blood, and they are reputed to be of great beauty. Do you recall *Don Juan*? Byron's words about the Circassian beauty in the slave market? *'Beauty's brightest colours. Had decked her out in all the hues of heaven …'*

"He loved her very much, no one who saw them together could ever doubt it. She was his jewel, you know. Her death was the greatest blow of his life. My father told us of it, for immediately after the funeral Raffles travelled in West Java with friends and stayed at my father's estate in Cinere, climbing and walking, exhausting himself. When he returned, he could not, for a long time, come here. When he did, finally, he built this memorial for her. Until he left Java, he worked until he was exhausted. To keep thoughts of her loss from crushing him, I have no doubt at all. Everybody thought it would kill him. I never met his second wife, for they went to live in Sumatra, at Bencoolen, a horrid place by all accounts. I heard that three of his children died there of fever. *Bon dieu*, so much sadness in one life."

They sat on a stone bench carved with vines, which stood to one side of the memorial near thick bushes of soft pink lantana. Here in the dappled sunlight, they could see the children and nursemaids playing on the far side of the lake. She could see Zan tumbling on the grass with Wilhelmina's two little daughters and her son. The water changed constantly with the movement of clouds, as if inhabited by hidden forces. From here, the eye was drawn irresistibly over the water to the sweeping lawn and into the white-columned verandah of the palace.

There was a clear line of sight to the memorial, and Charlotte could suddenly see Raffles standing there, his face like that of the bust in the Singapore Institution, dark and brooding, grieving the loss of this woman, his constant and adored companion, her face in his mind as he stared silently down to this place. The feeling was so powerful that a darkness seemed to veil the sun.

Olivia had died very suddenly, Wilhelmina was saying. She had had occasional long bouts of sickness but always seemed to recover. Of course, it was like that in the tropics. No one was safe. Death came swiftly. Life was merely bubbles on the stream.

Eeerily, Charlotte felt now a presence on the very bench where they sat. Yet she felt intense sympathy for Olivia. Had any woman in all the history of diplomacy inherited such an outlandish society to govern? Olivia had been lonely, surely, with few companions, surrounded by alien and ignorant Indies women with whom she had nothing in common. She'd been vivacious and colourful, where they were slow and dull; often unwell, lacking children. At least, though, she had lived with the man she truly loved.

Charlotte rose quickly, taking Wilhelmina's hand, and walked out into the sunlight to watch the men returning.

14

Charlotte was glad to return to Brieswijk and to the social rounds of dinners and plays which she had come to enjoy. She no longer minded at all the weekly late-afternoon ride around the Waterlooplein. This social "review of the troops" which the wealthy Batavian *beau monde* enjoyed was a chance for each to examine the carriages and costumes of their neighbours with undisguised curiosity. For the benefit of the young women who exhibited their varied charms, the bachelors on horseback showed off unashamedly, displaying, like so many plumed and strutting cocks, the elegance of their dress and, by the movement of their muscled thighs, the superiority of their horsemanship and whatever other activity might suggest itself to the young lady's imagination.

They all enjoyed the game, and she and Takouhi made sure to wear their most expensive and finest jewels and silks. For a fancy-dress ball at the Harmonie Club, Tigran had a copy made of the broad-brimmed black hat worn by Jan Pieterszoon Coen, the founder of Batavia, whose portrait hung on the walls of the Town Hall. This he sometimes wore festooned with the bright feathers of birds of paradise. With his long plaits and loose hair flowing over his shoulders, he looked every inch a 17th-century buccaneer, and both woman adored it. Charlotte always made sure to nod charmingly to Petra Couperus if she appeared and to display the exquisite Japanese fan which Tigran had obtained for her from the latest arrivals from Deshima. Tigran, to her annoyance, however, always removed his hat and bowed respectfully to Petra. Charlotte would have preferred him to make a grand, mocking gesture as he did occasionally to some of their acquaintance, but she recognised in his attitude to Petra an innate kindness and courtesy and could not fault him. Thus they turned around the great parade ground, with its barracks, officers' residences and the Concordia military club.

Before Daendels' enormous palace on the east side, the orchestra played military tunes and old favourites: Strauss, Rossini and Donizetti, songs from the French *opéra comique*, as well as new compositions, particularly a tune from a Signor Verdi's opera—*va, pensiero, sull'ali dorate*: fly, thought, on golden wings—which had lately become immensely popular. In front of the palace, an object of constant derision, stood the towering column which celebrated the victory over Napoleon at Waterloo, adorned with the lion which atop its high plinth unfortunately resembled nothing so much as a large poodle.

As the sun began its slow descent, the horses turned for home. The ride back took them away from Waterlooplein, past the Catholic church, along the broad expanse of Willemslaan, under the towering walls of the citadel and onto the long bridge over the Ciliwung. The river divided around the citadel. It was wide, its banks well kept, and painted boats moved slowly along its expanse. The view of the citadel from the bridge was like that looking up to the ramparts of Edinburgh Castle: so distinctly European that one could be forgiven for a moment for forgetting that it was in Java.

Weltevreden was designated the new "town", for want of a better word, but in truth it was more a picturesque ensemble of villa-studded parks and avenues. The old town, despite the disappearance of its fortifications, retained the atmosphere of the stronghold which the steel-clad, steely-eyed Dutchmen of 1620 built on the ruins of the burnt-down Javanese town of Jayakarta. Here, shadowy paths divided the parks and avenues, with a glimpse everywhere of the rivers which ran between bamboo groves, lined with cool, low-pillared walls and houses in leafy gardens.

Of all the squares of Batavia, the largest and most remarkable was the Koningsplein. In fact it was not a square; it was a field, the mighty brother of the Javanese *alun alun*, vast enough, Charlotte was informed proudly, to contain the city of Utrecht, dotted here and there with pasturing cattle, banyan and betel trees, and bordered on all sides by a triple rampart of branching tamarinds. There was a racecourse fenced off in one part of it, quite large, but reduced to insignificance against the sweeping magnitude of the Koningsplein.

The carriage turned onto Kongingsplein Oost, and Charlotte looked up to the distant mountain tops tipped with gold. The Plein was like a tract of untamed wilderness, savage and lonely, set strangely in the midst of a city. It had a solitary and moody life of its own, prey to the changing seasons. The sunlight on the shady avenues and parks of Weltevreden was muted, even at the blistering height of the east monsoon. Only on the Plein did the tropical sunshine beat down in all its scorching power. Underfoot, the grass was mere hay, the soil cracked and parched.

In the rainy season the old town was a morass of flooded houses and streets; the waters rose to the hubs of the carriage wheels. Houses and stores became virtually afloat, yet the Chinese continued their trades as tailors, tinkers and shoemakers, half a leg deep, their children sailing boats before the door. Canoes traversed the flooded streets. When the rainy season passed, the entire town was exposed to the burning sun on streets and canals oozing with putrescent filth. Charlotte was not surprised to learn that in twenty-two years of the previous century, more than one million souls had perished from the effects of this pestilential miasma.

This, though, was when the Plein came into its glory, the white, cracked soil suddenly bursting with tender shoots. In the morning it was dewy white. At night it was a lake of mist, rising and falling in the moonlight and rolling airy waves against a shore of darkness.

The carriage passed the gardens of several private residences and the imposing and elegant lines of the brand new Willemskerk. Takouhi had told her, with a glint of pleasure, that the old Reformed church of the Kota, where she had been married, had long since been demolished and the Lutheran church too had gone five years ago. The Willemskerk had been built in the south to bring these two bodies together, and the congregations shared the church, holding services on alternate Sundays.

They swung into Koningsplein Zuid and clipped along until they came to the junction with Koningsplein West and into the grounds of the Church of the Holy Resurrection. This simple wooden building was the Armenian Church in Batavia, built by Miriam's husband Jacob some ten years ago, at his own expense. Here they left Takouhi, for she was meeting Miriam for the evening service and later for dinner, to talk about preparations for a remembrance service for Meda, Maria and the all the dead children of the Manouk family.

Miriam came out to greet her sister and brother, bobbing a brief curtsy at Charlotte. Miriam was a plain girl, as unlike Tigran and Takouhi in looks as it was possible to be and share the same blood. She had a severe, thin face, with a mouth that Charlotte thought had doubtless stopped smiling the day she married Jacob Arathoun. Her eyes were her best feature, a deep, soulful brown, but she wore her pretty hair pulled back into an unbecoming bun.

Her husband was very Old Testament and ruled his household with an iron fist. The loss of their only child, Charlotte thought uncharitably, had prevented him from having *two* small female objects to bully, and she felt sorry for Miriam. What he would think if he knew that Alexander was not Tigran's son but a half-caste Chinese did not bear thinking about.

Jacob disliked many things, including the Chinese, whom he considered the pagan Jews of the East: unrelenting and thieving money-makers. He disapproved of these parades on the Waterlooplein and Tigran's play-acting. It obviously made little difference to Tigran, who did not remove his Pieterszoon Coen hat as Jacob came up to his wife.

After a brief exchange of civilities, they left. Tigran took Charlotte into his arms, and they watched in the cooling breeze as the lights began to twinkle in the houses and the street vendors' lanterns came out.

On the riverside at Brieswijk, the *slametan* for Meda's one thousand days was under preparation. Despite the innate sadness of this event, Charlotte felt that Takouhi and Tigran had fallen into the spirit of this particularly Javanese ritual which she did not pretend to fully understand. Neither Miriam nor Jacob would attend. Jacob deeply disapproved of his relatives' participation in what he said was both Mohammedan and a call to spirits. But Takouhi had explained that this ceremony was called a *slametan* because it meant a feast for safety. For her, it had little religious significance.

"The men from the *kampong* and the villages will come, and they will carry out Javanese ritual, speak to all the gods, the *danyang*, the spirit of the place, Hindoo gods, Allah, everyone. I do not mind at all if anything can keep Meda's soul in safe and peaceful place. Do not forget that her grandmother, my mother, was Mohammedan woman. Miriam will hold a service in the church, and we shall have one in the chapel. Then there will be a feast by the river, and everyone is invited."

One morning, a day before the ceremony, Charlotte came down to breakfast alone. Takouhi was away, busy with last-minute preparations. Tigran had left early for the Kota. She smiled as she remembered his embrace before leaving. Half-asleep still, she had let him kiss her neck and lips, lying in his arms like a doll, telling him to go and leave her alone but revelling in his heat, his uncrushable adoration. Whatever her feelings for Tigran had become, she thoroughly enjoyed being loved *by* him.

As she sat at the table on the verandah a servant came up to her and silently placed a letter near her plate. Usually Tigran dealt with the mail. She received few letters. Rarely, a letter from Aunt Jeannie came from Scotland. It took so long, almost a year. Sometimes there were letters from Charlotte Keaseberry, in Singapore, and Evangeline Barbie, from the Catholic Mission, to whom she tried to write regularly. But mostly they came from Robert.

When Takouhi had found that mail was going to her at Tigran's offices, she had tutted and called her a silly-billy. Her mail should come here, to her home. So Charlotte had written to everyone to address letters to Brieswijk. This was the first, which was a small thrill: the first to the house of which she was now fully the mistress. And it was from Robert.

Delighted, she put down her cup and opened it. It was long; she could feel its weight. Good. She had told him off for writing such slender epistles when she wanted news about her acquaintance and about Singapore.

She took the knife and cut the seal.

Kitt my dear,

Your letter arrived today with such good news of the continuing health of my little nephew as well as all the family. How I miss you all so very much. Cannot I tempt you to come and visit me for it is difficult in the extreme for me to leave Singapore? Now you have asked for news and chided me for my lack of detail, and so, dear sister, you shall have it.

Gang crime is worsening in the settlement, organised, as we all know, by the Chinese Brotherhood, to whom the shopkeepers pay protection money in guise of legal dues. A motion has been passed by the Chamber of Commerce for their repression, though what may come of that I cannot say. However, finally I am to have more policemen, a doubling of both European and native. A Water Police is also proposed to prevent escape seaward and the junks ordered to moor well offshore. Pariah dogs are still a plague, and a tax, as usual, proposed. I think I mentioned that the river wall along Boat Quay has been completed and all the little pylons and private piers replaced, presenting an extremely pleasing and neat appearance. Cholera has been bothersome in the more confined localities. The Commander of the China troops has departed and the last of the army and navy will leave within the week, and I am glad of it, for the town will be quieter and my job the easier for it.

Now to a bit of scandal! You will remember that dear old Governor Bonham finally left for Prince of Wales Island in the company steamer and thence home. It was strange to lose Bonham, for he was, as you know, my benefactor, and an easy and pleasant man to work for. He served this town so well these twelve years. The great scandal, though, is that against all expectations a new governor has been appointed, not from among the Straits officials or officers as expected, but directly from Calcutta. We are to expect a military man, a Colonel Butterworth, who has been named by Lord Ellenborough, the current Governor of India. We all know that his Lordship takes special delight in mortifying the civil service, and bestowing the lucrative and honourable posts on the military, but that he should pass over Colonel Murchison who has served here for five years (and who must now take Butterworth's place as head of the 2nd European Regiment) is in keeping with his Lordship's apparently low opinion of the qualities and experience required to govern the Straits and an indication of his increasingly erratic and extraordinary behaviour. The newspaper is all agog and up in arms!

Commerce goes well, though there is some fear that the new port of Hong Kong may threaten Singapore's pre-eminence since the Treaty of Nanking last year, but it is yet too soon to tell.

The first races at the new race course along Serangoon Road took place, and the very first Singapore Cup was won by a newcomer to our shores, a William Read, who has taken over old Johnston's company at Tanjong Tangkap. I almost forgot to tell you the wonderful news about Dr Montgomerie. You may well recall that there was rarely a conversation with William when the subject of his beloved gutta percha did not come up. Well, Kitt, his perseverance has paid off handsomely. He has introduced it to the Royal Society of Arts and has been awarded their coveted Gold Medal for its discovery! There is to be an exhibition at the Society displaying William's collection of Malay gutta percha articles. William thinks it useful for medical instruments, but I am of the opinion it would serve just as well for golf balls! As you can see, we are all a little bit gutta percha mad here at the moment and basking in William's fame. Singapore's first discovery!

The HMS Dido has been in our waters, and Captain Keppel and James Brooke (who is now the Sultan of Brunei's man in Sarawak) are mounting expeditions against the pirates in Borneo. Keppel has become a local favourite and sends his band from the Dido every evening to play upon the Plain when the ship is in harbour. We have a return to cricket, too, with matches between the Dido's officers and we Singaporeans. I am happy to tell you that my bowling arm is still as effective as ever!

Tigers have become a terrible problem, and the fear is that the Chinese coolies, who are attacked with most alarming regularity on the plantations, will give it up and be thrown into more dangerous and dishonest employment, increasing the robberies and attacks on the town. The reward for a tiger has increased, traps are set all over the island and a 'Tiger Club' has been organised to hunt them, but their numbers never seem to decrease.

Now Kitt, I have another special piece of news. I have received information about George.

Charlotte gasped. How like a man to come to the really important news last! All that stuff about governors and race courses. She read on more eagerly.

It seems that he will return to Singapore this year, though it is not known exactly when. It is very good to have news of him, for the last I heard was that he was on a grand tour of the European capitals. That *was last year, and since then, nothing.*

*Tir Uaidhne does well, as far as I can see, and Billy Napier now acts
as agent for Takouhi and seems, tell her, to do a good job. It has been
rented these last six months to a Mr Galsworthy. George's house at No.3,
as you know, has been turned into a hotel, The Hotel London, by Mr
Dutronquoy, the miniaturist—and now apparently master of some new
contraption called a daguerreotype, by which one can have one's image
fixed in two minutes and for which he charges the exorbitant sum of $10!
You may remember him, strange chap, a Frenchman from Jersey.*

*Ah, it is a sorry business, for I remember so many happy times
inside those walls. But it seems George will return to Coleman Street.
Reverend and Mrs White still occupy George's property at No.1, but the
Woods will move out of No. 2 in advance of George's return. It seems
definite, does it not? I for one shall be very glad to see him. The Woods
are building a large new house outside the town. Many of the families
are doing the same, and even old da Souza has a splendid new place in
Tanglin. Dr Oxley has purchased outright 170 acres he calls Killiney
Estate to grow nutmeg, and Carnie has over 4000 trees at his estate
at Carnie Hill. Will Cuppage has bought Emerald Hill, and Scott has
built a new house called Claymore on his plantation. The rich Chinese
merchants are keeping pace. Whampoa grows nutmeg at Tanglin and has
a fine property at Serangoon, and Baba Tan has built a large residence at
River Valley. Which leads me to the next subject.*

*Kitt, you asked for news of Zhen. So much time has passed and I
can tell from your letters that you are happy, which makes my heart very
light. So I shall ignore the strictures suggested to me and give you the
news that I have.*

Charlotte frowned and looked up from the letter. Strictures. What
did he mean? Sometimes Robert made no sense. She resumed reading,
hungry for news of Zhen, more than she had thought possible after all
this time.

*Baba Tan is now the proud grandfather of two girls. As yet no son,
which, as you know, is the paramount matter in Chinese families, for
their ancestors' rites. What other can I tell you? I met him at a dinner*

152

given by Baba Tan recently and at one of Whampoa's. He mixes well with the Europeans now, as his English has become really quite excellent. He has an emporium of Chinese medicines, which I understand is very successful amongst the Celestials. He knows you are married and have a son. What he thinks of this matter is inscrutable of course. I have met his wife only once since the day of their wedding reception, and as I told you, she is quite a shy creature, pretty, I suppose, in that Chinese way, although a little short and tubby for my liking. When he sees me, Zhen always asks about your health and your son's. I must say he has become a perfect gentleman in that regard, quite the urbane Englishman. That is doubtless Tan's influence on him. There, that is all I know.

Bye the bye, I have been thinking about tying the knot myself, but too soon for more on that subject other than that Teresa may be getting impatient with me.

Well, sister, I have answered all your requests in most fulsome manner and expect to be thanked very prettily for it. Write back immediately with your news, and do convince Tigran that you must come, for I long to see you again, my sweet sister.

All my affection,
Robbie

Charlotte felt almost unable to breathe, her heart was beating so fast. She rose. It was necessary to get away from the house, down to the river and read this letter again. Zhen always asked after her! She could not believe the emotion and agitation this news caused.

She walked quickly along the avenue, her mind in disarray. When she reached the river, she sat on the stone bench in the old Japanese garden, took the letter out and re-read the last part slowly.

Her eyes drank his name from the page. He had asked about her, and about Alexander. She could hardly get past this news. He had two children, he was well, his English excellent. She took the page, put his name to her lips and began to cry.

When she felt calmer, she read the whole letter again and could not understand what Robert meant about strictures. He probably meant it was not wise during her pregnancy, perhaps. She could not make it out. She forgot about it, though, when she realised that she had blotted out

153

the news of George. George was coming home! Here was truly occasion for joy. News of Zhen and George in one letter.

She rose and returned to the house, light of step, filled with eagerness to find Takouhi and tell her this news. George was coming home! It was surely a good omen. On the eve of the celebration for dearest Meda, his only child, he had turned his eyes eastward again.

When she arrived back at the house, breathless from the climb, she found still that no one was here. She spent the morning playing with Zan, thinking of his father, re-reading the letter, and the wait seemed interminable until lunchtime, when she heard the coach draw up and rushed downstairs. No sooner had Takouhi stepped from the coach, than Charlotte ran to her taking her hands and dancing round her. Takouhi looked bewildered.

"Takouhi, George is coming back to Singapore!" She almost sang it.

Takouhi stopped and stared at her.

"George is coming home," repeated Charlotte. "Robert has written to me that the Woods are moving out of Number 2 in order for him to take up residence. Oh, Takouhi, this is wonderful news."

Takouhi said nothing but went very slowly up the stairs to her rooms. Charlotte could see she was shocked and regretted her exuberance. She left her friend to take in this news, for Charlotte understood that, like herself, Takouhi needed to be alone.

Takouhi did not appear at lunch, or for several hours afterwards. Charlotte, worried, had questioned her maid, who said she was sleeping. When Tigran returned, she told him the news, falling into his arms.

"Robert wants us to visit Singapore and now, with George coming too, we must go, must we not, Tigran? Please, please," she cajoled.

He was delighted to see Charlotte so gay. Her youth was irresistible, though he had not realised that she was receiving letters now at Brieswijk. His arm round her waist, they went out onto the verandah and he called for drinks.

"So George is returning to Singapore. May I see your letter?"

Charlotte looked at him, and he felt her hesitation.

"It is in my room. Anyway, that is all it says: George is returning, and the house at No. 2 Coleman Street is being prepared for his arrival.

The rest is some personal news of friends in Singapore."

Charlotte felt a sudden guilt at lying to him, but why had he asked to see the letter? He had never made such a request before.

"Oh, and Robert has some vague idea of marrying poor Teresa Crane." She laughed to cover up her sudden confusion, for his eyes seemed to penetrate her mind.

Tigran rose. "Excuse me, Charlotte, I shall change and rejoin you soon. Does Takouhi know?"

"Yes, Tigran, and, oh dear, she has taken to her room. I haven't seen her since I told her the news."

Tigran smiled his crooked smile and took her hand, pulling her gently from the seat. He took her waist in his arm, put his hand to her hair and drew her into a kiss. It was a kiss of an intensity that he usually reserved for the bedroom, and he crushed her in his arms until she could hardly breathe.

Then he turned and went quickly into the house. She sat, unsure what to make of this.

That evening there was a service for Meda in the chapel. Nothing more was said about George. When Takouhi appeared, she seemed composed, and they left for the church together, walking through the tamarind grove preceded by the servants carrying tall torches. Charlotte was silent, knowing her friend was in a deeply sorrowful place: sorrow for her lost daughter, George's lost daughter. As they listened to the priest, Takouhi took Charlotte's hand in hers and they looked at each other. Charlotte nodded. They both remembered sitting like this in the church in Singapore, but then George had been at her side and Meda was a happy and excited flower girl. That night was the night she had taken sick. And, Charlotte remembered, the following day she had given herself to Zhen and he had utterly changed her life. They both had to take this news slowly.

Tigran came to her room late. She was half-asleep when he moved next to her and took her in his arms. She murmured softly, and he kissed her neck, letting his lips linger on her soft skin; then she drifted into sleep, her head cradled in his arm, against his chest. Tigran watched her, beautiful in rest, her full, pink lips parted slightly, her long lashes resting on her perfect cheeks, her bosom rising and falling imperceptibly beneath her white satin gown, wisps of jet black hair escaping from the plait the maid had fashioned for sleep, tied, as always, with a scarlet ribbon. He had bought her a rainbow of silk and satin ribbons, but when she slept she always chose a red one. He loved her little idiosyncrasies, the way her lovely eyes widened when she was curious, the way she bit her lower lip when she was thinking, the way her eyes seemed to change colour when he brought her to the height of passion. When that happened he felt like a king, invincible. How he loved that, how he loved her, to an ache.

He tried not to succumb to the deep anxiety which this news from Singapore had caused in him. But he felt that something had happened. He knew her every nuance. Perhaps it was George, just George, and her desire to see him and Robert. He hoped so. He had thought about looking for the letter but, suddenly weary, he could not muster the energy. She had come so far from sorrow and found pleasure and contentment in his arms, given him so much joy. He had to trust her, for otherwise there was only torment.

15

Tigran was happy to agree to a voyage to Surakarta, although business meant he could not accompany Charlotte and his sister. He was glad that the effect of this news from Singapore had abated slightly. Takouhi had said nothing of George's supposed return. Charlotte thought it wiser to be quiet on the matter too.

This journey had been suggested on the night of the feast for Meda. That night, Brieswijk was turned into a vast park of firelight. From the house to the river, lanterns and firebrands led across the grass to the riverside, where bonfires threw flames and smoky trails into the night. The perfumes of jungle firewood and sandalwood incense filled the air. *Wayang* theatres were thrown up throughout the grounds. *Wayang kulit*, *wayang golek* and a Chinese *wayang* were in progress. The people from the villages and surroundings were invited, and all afternoon boats arrived and vast crowds moved from place to place, watching first one display, then another. An array of food and drink lay on mats along the riverbank: special *slametan* food. Great peaked mountains of rice, one yellow for love, the other white for purity; garlic, red onion and chili to ward off evil; whole chickens for unity, whole eggs for new life; long green beans for long life, and mixed vegetables for diversity, all rested on banana leaves representing strength. Families and groups lounged on the grass, enjoying the festivities.

Louis and Nathanial sat with Charlotte and Takouhi on the verandah. They had shared the food on the banana leaves and drunk tea with the villagers. Takouhi was filled with pleasure for this day. There had been the service in the church and the *slametan* ritual and now the enjoyment of the villagers. It was exactly what Meda would have loved: the throng, the noise, the excitement of the *wayang*, the gongs and drums of the *gamelan*. Takouhi would have liked for one brief moment, just one quiet moment more, to hold her daughter in her arms and feel her tender little body. But this was good-bye, the final *slametan*, the giving of peace to her soul, for the body was gone. She had surrounded Meda's grave with oil lamps and lit double candles in the chapel from herself and George. He was coming back. She could hardly believe it, but she was glad. The end of the festival would be marked by fireworks, but that was still hours away.

Captain Palmer emerged from the garden. The festival had been thrown open to all the Europeans in Batavia, and Takouhi had made an announcement in the newspaper. Wilhelmina and Pieter and many others had come and gone.

Charlotte had seen Palmer occasionally at balls and on Waterlooplein but had rarely spoken to him. Now he bowed over Takouhi's hand.

"What a charming and lovely occasion to remember your daughter. I did not know Meda, but the loss of a child is hard to bear. I, too, have suffered such a loss."

Palmer looked up as Takouhi took his hand in sympathy and asked him to join them.

He looked over at Charlotte and bowed, nodding to the men. Louis and Nathanial eyed him dispassionately.

"Madame Manouk, it has been a long time since we last met. You spend a great deal of time at Buitenzorg."

Charlotte smiled and nodded. Palmer found her more beautiful than ever.

The conversation turned to Nathanial's prospective voyage to East Java, and Captain Palmer mentioned that he too was planning a trip to Surakarta. He told them of some of his voyages in Sumatra, for he had been involved in the pepper trade which the Dutch government had granted to the American merchants from Salem. All at once they were all talking of a large group travelling together. Louis, who would be unable to leave the theatre, pouted.

By the time Tigran joined them, the voyage had virtually been planned. Palmer watched as Tigran went to his wife and sat, taking her hand—proprietorially, Palmer thought—in his and putting it to his lips. Lucky dog, he thought.

Charlotte was excited by the prospect of this voyage, and Takouhi seemed determined. Tigran said they would talk tomorrow. He wanted this trip, if it were to happen, planned to the last detail, with plenty of protection for his wife and sister. Nathanial was a good man and a good companion, but, in many respects, Captain Palmer was a welcome addition. He was older, hardy, had certainly seen battle and sailed the high seas. Six of Tigran's men would accompany them.

"I will write to the Residents of Semarang and Surakarta to ensure that everything is in order for you," he said, and closed the subject.

Captain Palmer rose to take his leave, with a smile, and Tigran accompanied him to the door. The voyage would take several weeks, and he would very much enjoy the company of Mrs Manouk, whom he intended getting to know much more intimately.

"I am not sure about that fellow," Nathanial said.

"Oh, Nathanial."

Takouhi looked over at him. "He has suffered like us the loss of a child."

Nathanial looked down. Tonight was not the time to raise his doubts. He changed the subject, and, as Tigran returned, raised his glass.

"To lovely Meda," he said and they all toasted her.

A week later, the *Queen of the South* stood ready to depart for Semarang. Charlotte had written to Robert, telling of their coming voyage, and her hope that they might return to Singapore when he had more news of George, thanking him for the information about Zhen. She would have liked to write to Zhen, put a note in her letter, but it seemed such a betrayal of Tigran. She asked Robert to send her compliments to Zhen, but dared write no more. He would know, surely. This news was enough for the moment. She felt she could smile when she thought of him now: well, handsome, urbane, a gentleman, speaking excellent English. When she went to Singapore, she was sure that she could meet him with something close to equanimity.

It was with an easy heart, therefore, that she kissed Tigran farewell. He held her tightly, and she embraced him, too, with a strange forcefulness. She wished now he was coming on this voyage but was glad that he would be with Alexander. Tigran loved this little boy like his own, Charlotte could see it when she watched Tigran speaking Dutch with him, playing with the rattan ball, sitting in the river of the bathing pavilion with Zan on his lap, the boy's little fingers wound in Tigran's long plaits.

Now they went up on deck, and she took Alexander in her arms.

"Be a good boy for Papa now," she said gravely and kissed his cheeks. He looked at her with his almond eyes and began to cry, but as soon as Tigran took him in his arms, he stopped, hugging his father's neck.

Tigran held him tight, and he kissed Charlotte again. She felt his emotion at this parting. She hugged them both. Then, quickly, he turned and passed Alexander to his *babu*, and they went down to the waiting lighter. She watched, waving. She felt tears well, but in an instant Nathanial had come to her side.

Within minutes the ship was on its way, heading out to the island of Edam and the open sea. It was swift, the passage from land to sea, and as the breeze caught her hair, she suddenly felt liberated. There was freedom on the sea. Shore cares were left behind, like casting off invisible shackles. She loved the sea, loved to sail; she had forgotten this feeling of pure escape. She looked at the captain, feet planted on the raised poop deck like a king in his dominions, and, as the ship ripped along and the sails roared with wind, she understood why men loved to sail the oceans. The land was immobile; it always belonged to someone. But the water was free, rolling from shore to shore. She liked to think that the waves which now washed the shores of Java would, by the constancy of the moon, tumble up against the sands of Singapore.

She thought, already, of the pleasure of sleeping in the master's cabin below, the row of mullioned windows flung open, listening to the sea slip under the ship, sliding along the black painted sides of the brig; she thought of watching the sea swallow the sun slowly, until only a tiny spark remained floating on the edge of the world before it was, all at once, extinguished. Her last voyage on this ship had been one of deep misery, but now she felt at rest, ready to enjoy this extraordinary voyage. A part of her truly wished Tigran had come so they could share this together, but another was glad to be alone. Now that he was far away, she felt closer to him than she had ever been before. This ship was part of him.

At dinner, they were very merry. There were five of them: Takouhi, Charlotte, Nathanial, Captain Elliott, and Tigran's eldest son, Nicolaus, who was on the voyage for trade. The ship was laden with cloth, iron goods and teak for Semarang, where Nicolaus would also inspect the sugar mills. Tigran was importing new sugar-refining machinery from England. Then Nicolaus would load sugar, tea, rice, cloth and opium to trade for camphor, ironwood, gunpowder, gold dust and diamonds in Pontianak and Bandjermasin. In this island trade, the *Queen of the South* flew the Dutch flag, permitted to trade by government licence.

Charlotte was glad to spend time with Nicolaus. Tigran had put aboard flagons of fine French *vin gris* for this special voyage, and the captain was delighted to have ladies along. He was not one of those superstitious types who thought women on board were bad luck. So particularly eighteenth-century, he said, and they all laughed.

The talk turned to piracy, with Captain Elliott telling some blood-curdling tales and recounting the remarkable exploits of James Brooke, the man who had been created the white Rajah of Sarawak. Charlotte and Takouhi, who had heard only a little of this story, begged for details.

"Well, ladies, he is quite an adventurer, our Brooke, with a dash of luck thrown in. I have met him once or twice, for his yacht, *Royalist*, has plied these waters. Brooke was in Singapore on his way to explore Borneo. As it happened, he arrived in Kuching in time to be of service to the local rajah, who was the Brunei Sultan's relative. The poor fellow was trying, unsuccessfully, to put down a rebellion. The rajah apparently made Brooke some promises in return for the use of his ship and its guns. When it was over, the rajah, so it's told, demurred, and Brooke merely turned them on the rajah's palace and demanded his due—to be the first white rajah in Sarawak! Such audacity! You may imagine the excitement this news created. Every man who sails half-dreams of his own empire on a far-flung island."

Seeing the faces of the women, caught up in this story, Nathanial added, "Good old Brooke. I've heard it remarked that Brooke knows as much about business as a cow a clean ship. Now, the man who is doubtless the silliest of spoilt individuals to sail the China Sea is the toast of the East India Company. They shall be able, through him, to plunder the treasures of Borneo and ply the unsuspecting natives with all the useless manufactures of Manchester."

He raised his glass in mock salute. Captain Elliott did not approve of these sentiments, but his gentlemanly instincts forbade him to challenge his guest in front of the ladies. He changed the subject.

Captain Elliott thought that Mr Manouk was the luckiest man alive. Wealth beyond measure, robust and competent sons, a well-married daughter and vigorous grandsons. And on top of these blessings, an incomparably beautiful young wife and a new, healthy boy. He had seen her when they had brought her from Singapore and was glad she had found happiness. Mr Manouk was an excellent master, and Elliott enjoyed sailing this lovely brig. Tigran had arranged a pension for when he felt ready to retire, as well as a small house in Batavia. Elliott was happy to be able to say flattering things to his master's wife, son and sister. Many Dutch ships employed British-born officers but few employers were as generous as Mr Manouk. Thus, in mutual pleasure, the voyage continued along the coast for four days until they reached the port of Semarang and all too soon had to part.

Nicolaus was fond of Charlotte, who was only a little younger than himself. She in turn saw the young Tigran in him, though he was not so good-looking as his father. He was a good man and had welcomed her into the family from the beginning. Both brothers had done so, but Nicolaus in particular seemed happy for his father.

Charlotte had met Nicolaus's mother, Nyai Kuonam, only once; it had given her a glimpse into a different place, the household of the native woman caught up in the Dutchman's world. She and Takouhi had called on Nyai Kuonam one morning and found her sitting in her sarong on a mat on the floor, her hair hanging down greasily, ringed by women as unkempt as herself, occupied in cleaning vegetables. She was small and wrinkled, with very black teeth, and every now and again spat a stream of blood-red spittle into the cuspidor which stood at her side. She spoke Malay with them but said little. Charlotte could not believe she was younger than Takouhi or that Tigran had ever made love to her, though Takouhi assured her that she had once been very pretty. She was now a wizened old lady. She took little interest in either of her visitors, and they soon departed.

Valentijna, Tigran's daughter, did not care for this marriage of her father's and Nathanial suggested it might have something to do with the instant disappearance of her large inheritance. A new young wife and child were, doubtless, a vast inconvenience to her. Charlotte should have a few more little heirs and heiresses to outrage her. Charlotte had smacked Nathanial lightly when he said this, and laughed.

The thought of children had, however, crossed her mind, for she was late. She frowned and knew exactly when. It could only be the time when Tigran had come unexpectedly to the bathing pavilion and sent the women away. Precautions were impossible, but their imminent separation had visited an urgency upon him, and the look in his eyes was determined. He had thrown off his clothes and come to her side in the river, pulling off her sarong, kissing her mouth and cool dripping breasts, his long hair trailing in the water around her body, like a ravishing river god, then lifting her to the side, to the great pile of cloths and cushions on which she, Takouhi and Alexander lolled in the hot afternoons. He had been forceful and adamant, taken her, protesting, in his arms, and she had succumbed, her resistance turning to excitement at this risqué coupling in the open air.

Now she feared the worst. Charlotte did not want another child. Not now, not ever. She was still terrified of childbirth. Also, unconsciously, she wanted to go to Singapore as slender as *he* remembered her. She shook her head, angry at this half-admission, angry that he could still occupy so easily a part of her mind. She knew Tigran would be delighted at such news, for this time it would be his child, and he had spoken of another child many times. Had he come to her at the pavilion expressly to get her pregnant? He knew her time of the month as well as she did. No, she would not think like that. She would resent him too much. Nothing would dampen her spirits. After all, she had been late before, and a potion from Madi had solved the problem.

While in Semarang, they would stay at a house which Tigran owned in the southern town. Nicolaus would depart after Charlotte and his aunt had left for Surakarta and be back in time for their return in two weeks. Everything had been carefully arranged, and within an hour of their arrival they had received an invitation for dinner at the house of the Resident of Semarang, Martin Eeerens. The wife of the Assistant Resident was Tigran's daughter, Valentijna, and Charlotte was certain she would be present.

The Resident's cutter arrived to take them off the ship and upriver and thence to a carriage to cover the two miles to the house which served as his home. It was a large, columned, double-storey residence set back in a pleasant garden. Much like in Batavia, the European houses lay some way from the port. Charlotte was amused to note that not one of the government residences she had seen so far was as fine as Brieswijk.

The Resident and his wife greeted them effusively. Martin Eerens was a very small man with a very large moustache and a nose which betrayed a fondness for brandy. His wife was his very opposite, at least three times his size, with thinning hair and a long, white nose which supported a pince-nez. Nathanial murmured "Jack Sprat" in Charlotte's ear, and she had to grit her teeth and open her eyes wide to prevent a fit of giggles.

In the drawing room, Valentijna and her husband came up to them. Valentijna embraced her aunt and brother warmly and Charlotte coolly. She was a lovely woman, with beautiful golden skin and Tigran's brown eyes, but Charlotte could not warm to her. There was something haughty and distant in her demeanour. Charlotte had a pleasant relationship with Nicolaus Manouk's half-French wife and through her was well aware that Valentijna thought of Charlotte as a penniless upstart who had brought nothing to the Manouk house and who had somehow bewitched her father. She had said as much to Nathanial. Valentijna's husband was a well-made, very good-looking Dutchman who spoke halting English, and after a perfunctory but very polite greeting he remained silent.

Eerens introduced them to his guest of honour, with many bows. Seated in a corner of the room, dressed in a blue and red serge general's uniform covered in gold braid, stars and crosses, was a portly, red-faced, bald-pated, middle-aged man with a bushy white beard, a smelly meerschaum clasped between his yellow teeth. This was His Serene Highness, the Duke of Saxe-Weimar, a relative, so they were informed, with many condescending looks, of the King of the Netherlands.

The Duke did not rise to greet them, merely looking up and grunting, then downing a full glass of brandy. Nathanial concealed a smile and directed Charlotte's gaze to his feet, which were shod in ancient and worn red velvet slippers, through which a gnarled toenail could be glimpsed.

Charlotte and Nathanial covered their mouths with their hands and Takouhi simply looked scandalised. Other guests emerged—*le tout*-Semarang, Charlotte supposed—and servants brought drinks. Nathanial knew something of this old Duke. He was a distant relative of the King, a military man who, through his profligate stupidity, had lost a fortune and, through his arrogance and ignorance had lost the lives of a regiment of men during the Napoleonic Wars. To get rid of him, he had been sent out to the colonies, given the honorary title of Army Commander, supported by payments from the national treasury. Having been very rich, he was now very mean, and a land where he had never to pay for the labour of his menials suited him very well. He had a house in Weltevreden, where he grew onions and went about under a yellow umbrella carried by a slave.

"Doubtless these visits to the provinces allow him to exercise economies, for I understand he has been in Semarang already for three weeks, living on the hospitality of his hosts, who, I would guess, dare not refuse."

Nathanial shook his head at this folly but before he could continue, Mevrouw Eerens came up to Charlotte to take her off to the ladies' side of the room. This division of the sexes was frequently relaxed in drawing rooms in Batavia, but Charlotte quickly realised that provincial Java adhered to old principles as if they were biblical law; men and women were separated literally like the sheep and goats would be on a certain day. The men had gathered on the verandah, where the gin and brandy flowed, smoking cigars and talking desultorily amongst themselves; Nathanial occasionally threw glances of desperation in Charlotte's direction.

Whilst Takouhi and Valentijna chatted in one corner, the other ladies, led by Mevrouw Eerens, who knew very well how rich the Manouks were, questioned Charlotte closely on her life in Batavia, admiring her dress and jewels, requesting, without the slightest embarrassment it seemed, the price of every garment and object on her person. It did not take Charlotte long to see that as a rich white European woman she found a very high place in her hostess's regard. Mevrouw Eerens's attitude to Takouhi was one of polite deference to her wealth, but it was plain that Valentijna was placed in a much lower position, not only by her husband's inferior status but by her own *mestizo* bloodline. Charlotte understood that Valentijna's marriage had been a match of genuine affection, and, despite her feelings for this young woman, was somewhat sorry for her. It was not easy to succeed in government service without the approval of the ruling class. Her looks, her status in Batavian society, and the wealth Tigran had bestowed on her had been gifted to her husband, a man of ordinary origins, and these had assured his present position. Charlotte hoped that the Assistant Resident would continue to appreciate these advantages.

The clock struck resoundingly throughout the residence. It was eight o'clock, and, in unison, all the men took out their watches and set them right; their countenances brightened and each sought the eyes of his wife. In a moment, the couples had come together and within two they had left. Just as in the court of Louis XIV, *acte de presence* had been made. Dinner was announced. With a resounding *Kreuzmillionen Himmel Donnerwetter!* the Duke rose, mustering a greater animation than Charlotte had thought him capable of, and, grabbing the arm of his hostess, propelled her towards the dining room.

After dinner, the card table appeared. The Duke packed himself off to bed with a large bottle of brandy and without so much as a by-your-leave as soon as the dinner was over, and, in the absence of a higher power, the Resident reigned. The Assistant Resident rushed to his superior's side as soon as the cards were brought out. Mevrouw Eerens told Charlotte that her husband adored card games, and it was fortunate that his assistant shared the same passion and came over three times a week to spend his evenings in this diverting amusement which she herself could not abide. Nathanial made sure they knew *he* did not play. Nicolaus, despite his reluctance, out of feeling for his brother-in-law, allowed himself to be called on to make a third.

"It is most admirable," Nathanial said at Charlotte's side. "Thus, not armed with a sword but with a pack of cards, patience and stoical courage, the low-born but ambitious man must endure his trial until the object of his ambition—preferment, high official honour, a Residency of his own perhaps—shall come his way. Let's hope it shall not be long coming, for the man looks as if his heart grows fainter with every passing month."

Charlotte recognised what Nathanial had told her. The Resident of the Java station was as much a little king as his predecessor, the merchant, had been in the days of the VOC. To his subjects, his gold emblazoned cap was a crown. He travelled with the gilt umbrella raised over his head like a royal canopy, revered by the native chiefs as their "elder brother." The social life of the station was exactly what he chose, for the man lived in an atmosphere of adulation. A lack of humour or an abundance of vanity in his composition would mean that he would certainly take his exalted situation very seriously and exact strict homage.

After several games, Takouhi rescued Nicolaus and the party broke up. As they took their leave of Mevrouw Eeerens, they could see the Resident pouring large glasses of brandy and dealing out cards once more, for the evening was young, he said. Valentijna sat, forlornly staring at her hands.

16

Two days later they left for the interior. The Duke was to accompany them for an extended visit to the Resident of Surakarta. Whilst Charlotte had made a *moue* at this news, Nathanial assured her it was all to the good. The presence of such a personage, a relation of the King of the Netherlands, no matter the distance, would ensure they would be received with the greatest of honours. When she discovered the Duke was to travel separately, accompanied by his own *aide de camp* and guard, the Commander of the Semarang garrison's *aide de camp*, a contingent of soldiers and a swarm of servants, she relaxed.

She had been awakened at four o'clock and risen reluctantly. In the moonlight she saw Nathanial, who had risen even earlier to load the carriage, standing with two servants. There were six horses to pull them, for there had been considerable rain overnight and the road was heavy going. She and Takouhi slumbered fitfully in starts and snatches until the sun began to rise.

The soft light of dawn revealed a vast sweep of countryside, green and peaceful, dotted with villages and rice fields, like so many in Java, neat and clean, on the banks of a sparkling stream. No pen could write, no tongue could utter, Charlotte thought, the sheer beauty of Java. Everywhere the shapes of mountains dominated the landscape, some smoking ominously. To their right lay Mount Merbabu and beyond that Mount Merapi, the sacred mountain of Java, its crown wreathed in ashy smoke and cloud. The road continued to rise.

They stopped to take some refreshment at a post station whilst two buffalo were sought to yoke to the team, for, from here, the climb was very steep and the horses alone could not manage. They could only proceed at walking pace, so Charlotte and Nathanial left Takouhi to sleep for an hour or two. Accompanied by two of Tigran's guardians, they set out.

Nathanial pointed out statues standing by the roadside. One was an image of the Boodha and the other of Siva, doubtless brought from one of the hundreds of temples which lay all around them, covered in long grasses and bushes.

"Indian kingdoms must have dominated this area of central Java for hundreds, perhaps thousands of years," Nathanial said. "We are still not sure how the Hindoo and Boodha faiths are related or indeed if they are related. In my view, one of Raffles's great acts in Java was the discovery and description of the Hindoo temples at Brambanan and the mountain of Boodha at Boro Bodo. Raffles always believed that Java was the home of civilisations as mighty as any in Europe, and these monuments were the proof."

Nathanial stopped at a bridge where some stones provided a way to ford the stream. Helping Charlotte, he scrambled down the bank. Each of the sections of stones was intricately carved and sculpted with figures, plants and arabesque borders. Many depicted girls holding a lotus or other large flower. Charlotte was struck by the elegant proportion of their forms and their exquisite grace. To find such beauty in a pebble-strewn river was an unexpected pleasure, but to think it might soon be gone, erased by the passage of the water and the elements, made her sad. For though the river now was relatively dry, in the rainy monsoon it would be a swift and deep torrent.

Nathanial took out a book and made a quick but expert sketch. Charlotte had not realised that he was so talented.

"A necessity. I have no natural talent, but if one is to record one's observations, it is a useful craft," he explained.

By the time they had made their way back to the road, the coach had caught up with them.

One of the most remarkable things to strike Charlotte as they began their visit to these Eastern provinces was the attitude of the people. Every Javanese peasant, sometimes in groups of hundreds, no matter in what work he was occupied, would, at their approach, drop instantly to his heels as if pulled down by a puppet master. They squatted in the fields and villages and along the roadside, eyes lowered, the farmer quitting his plough and the porter his load at the approach of the great *Tuans'* carriages. Nathanial remarked that this was an ancient custom.

"It is called *dodok*. Whilst it has been virtually discontinued in West Java, where European rule is most strong, here in the native provinces it is still a powerful mark of respect. We English think it a humiliating posture, but the local people submit to it with cheerfulness as a time-honoured custom. They simply sink as we would rise in the presence of important personages. In the courts, you will see, it is most strictly observed, sometimes with comical results."

Nathanial mopped his brow, for the day had grown warm. "In his *History of Java*, Raffles recounts an amusing anecdote when he was at the court of Surakarta holding a private conference with the *Susunan*, the king, at the English Resident's house. It became necessary for one of the *Susunan*'s ministers to go to the palace for the royal seal. The man was, of course, squatting, and, as the *Susunan* happened to be seated with his face towards the door, it was ten minutes before his minister, after repeated ineffectual attempts, could rise sufficiently to reach the latch without being seen by his royal master. The *Susunan* was inconvenienced, of course, but this was an insignificant matter compared with the indecorum of being seen out of the *dodok* posture. I myself have seen the surprising sight of numbers of inferiors, when despatched on some task or other, waddling, like so many ducks, on the hams of their heels until out of their superior's sight."

Charlotte smiled and fanned herself. She was glad to stop thinking, for a moment, that she was over a week late. She had begun to feel the tell-tale signs of pregnancy, a heaviness inside her body and tenderness in the breasts.

They arrived at Fort Salatiga at noon. When they were alone before dinner, Nathanial pointed out, with a tone of rueful smugness, that this fort had the singular distinction of being the place where General Janssens had surrendered to the British in 1811.

"Poor Janssens," he said gleefully. "He replaced Daendels, whom Napoleon recalled, would you believe, because he was considered too autocratic. But luck was against Janssens again. Having previously fought a British invasion and given up the Colony of the Cape, he arrived just in time to once more surrender a Dutch colony to the enemy."

The Duke, they were informed, was to stay overnight with a rich landowner in the region who doubtless, and uselessly, hoped for some advantage by the *hebergement* of such an illustrious personage. In consequence, the evening was quiet, apart from the occasional earth tremor, which the Commander informed them was so common as to be largely ignored. Charlotte was not convinced but was so fatigued and concerned about her condition that she simply decided not to worry about it.

The next day they set out early to avoid the heat, for after Boyolali the road descended sharply. As the sun rose, it revealed the fertile plain of central Java, a sheet of rice fields, a patchwork of ripe green and harvested yellow fields spreading like a vast cloth over the land, tucking into the foothills of the surrounding mountains. All along the route, men and women could be seen carrying goods to market: fruit and vegetables, chickens and capons, turkeys, geese and peacocks.

On the outskirts of Surakarta, they halted at a staging post to change horses, to pay their toll, and to take some refreshment while waiting for the Duke. The day had grown heavy, and a thunderstorm rumbled beyond the horizon. After an hour, a contingent of Javanese troops appeared in the distance. Charlotte and Nathanial had grown rather bad tempered at this waiting and welcomed this new diversion. There was still no sign of the Duke.

To pass the time, Nathanial explained something of the *Susunan* of the Kraton Surakarta Hadiningrat, the "Palace of Surakarta, Finest in the World." Takouhi listened too, for though a granddaughter of the king, Pakubuwono III, she knew almost nothing of the history of these Javanese relatives.

"All I know," she told them, "is that Pakubuwono means something like the 'spike of the cosmos'."

"Yes," said Nathanial. "Mountains are at the centre of Javanese belief. The king is Lord of the Mountain. He stands, like Merapi, at the centre of the universe. He is the pin that keeps the world turning safely on its axis, keeping the harvest plentiful and communing with the gods. The king has a mystical spiritual power which transcends everything,

Hindoo, Boodha and Mohammedan, for he draws power from his marriage to Ratu Kidul, Queen of the South, the spirit goddess of the Southern Ocean. He is the shadow of God on the earth; he possesses supernatural powerful weapons and is heir to sacred powers. The regents emulate the king, and the chiefs emulate the regents, and thus is authority made in Java."

The present king, Nathanial said, was PakubuwonoVII, who came to the throne in 1830. That year marked the beginning of the Dutch annexation of Eastern Java, a growth of a desire, for the first time in hundreds of years, for a Dutch empire throughout the entire archipelago and the beginning of the *cultuurstelsel*, the Cultivation System. The Dutch, who had hitherto not wanted a *real* empire, suddenly needed a source of income to support Holland for they had lost the southern lands when Belgium broke away and the country was virtually bankrupt. The business of the Indies would henceforth be to erase the colonial government and old VOC debts, pay for Dutch expansion into Sumatra and the eastern archipelago and finance the Dutch state. Gone were the momentary dabblings with the liberal policies of earlier times that would give ownership of land to the farmer and open idle land to European cultivation and wage labour. Instead, the colonial government went back to the old monopolistic VOC ways. The Javanese peasant must pay for the comfort of Holland's heedless citizens.

Nathanial had difficulty keeping the contempt and irritation from his voice. He needed the good will of the Dutch authorities to pursue his studies in Java, but he was ashamed and often horrified at their attitudes towards this rich and industrious country and its downtrodden people. This was not the proper forum, though, and he immediately brought the discussion back to the royal courts.

The present king, Nathanial added with a wry smile, seemed content to sit quietly in his palace, reigning over the ritual of the court and remaining the docile client of the Dutch.

"Doubtless," Nathanial said, "he dislikes this subservient position a great deal but conceals it under the refined surface of court affairs. For what can he do? He is a virtual prisoner in his palace, drained of all economic and political power. He and the ruler of Yogyakarta, in the south, have instead taken on the role of guardians of the Javanese soul, its artistic and courtly refinement."

Takouhi and Charlotte began to forget this interminable delay and pressed Nathanial for more information.

Nathanial sought a way to render the wars and intrigues of the Dutch, the Chinese and the Javanese, the battles of royal succession and the countless feuds and rebellions of centuries of Java history, into a simple formula.

"Well," Nathanial said. "I'll try to be brief, for it is devilishly complex. When the Dutch came in 1602, a Mohammedan kingdom, called Mataram, ruled over Java. After over a hundred years of uneasy coexistence, a final rebellion broke the camel's back, and the Dutch, in 1764, divided the kingdom into two courts, one in Surakarta and one in Yogyakarta, to the south. These courts were further split in the years that followed. Thus was the kingdom of Mataram divided into four. In the end, these princes sought only their personal glory. Divide and conquer—the old saying holds true. The Javanese were complicit in their own downfall. From that time, there could be no further royal rebellions to challenge the Dutch."

The rumbling of thunder grew more ominous; the day darkened, rain was certainly on its way. They looked down the road, but there was still no sign of the old Duke.

"We cannot progress without him," Nathanial grumbled. "The Javanese love a procession, and without it we cannot enter in proper fashion into Surakarta. All has been arranged in this way."

How like these pompous aristocrats, Nathanial thought. Really, the French revolution had been entirely justified. Charlotte looked pale and tired, and he was concerned for her. Tigran's manservants sprawled under the coconut palms. Takouhi and Charlotte's maids brought drinks, and two young boys were dragged in from the village to fan the ladies. The boys rested on their haunches, slowly sucking on the betel quids stuck into their cheeks, occasionally emitting a stream of red spittle, staring at Charlotte's white skin and the curious foreign *tuans*.

Finally, as rain began to fall, the Duke's coach appeared in the distance and upon reaching the village, swept through, spraying muddy water, and halted at the contingent of soldiers gathered further down the road. Nathanial helped Charlotte and Takouhi into their carriage hurriedly, and in the storm, they approached the now rain-soaked group of men on horseback gathered in formation by the roadside

The commander of the Javanese troops stood for some time talking, as they discovered, to the Assistant Resident of Surakarta and the Javanese Regent, who had arrived with his large entourage. They greeted the Duke, who did not deign to leave his carriage. The Dutch, Charlotte had read, ruled the vast countryside through the Regents of the districts, who controlled the villages and assured the payment of taxes and carrying out of work duties. In return, they were paid a salary and a percentage of the crops. They also, Nathanial had added, forced their own compulsory labour duties and were heavily involved in black-market trading. Never, however, even in the face of the most wholesale and obvious corruption, was a noble dismissed from office.

As they watched from a distance, Nathanial suddenly, vehemently, spoke his thoughts aloud. "Look at them! It is this greedy collusion between the Dutch and the Javanese nobility which conspires to deprive the peasantry of all freedom and spirit."

Finally, as the rain lessened they were all pulled into strict order of precedence, with Nathanial, Charlotte and Takouhi bringing up the rear. They moved off slowly. Long before they could see Surakarta, each side of the road was lined with spearmen in rich dress, banners streaming, the *gamelan* playing at intervals near gold, three-tiered, silk-fringed royal umbrellas. Amongst this pomp and splendour, the villagers, awed, dropped to their haunches as the procession passed. It was rich and impressive, and Charlotte suspected that had she been a local peasant, she, too, would have done the same.

17

The Resident, Colonel Helvetius Snijthoff, came out to greet His Serene Highness, who, with great difficulty and many curses, was descending from the coach, evidently stiff and grumpy from the journey. The Javanese escort had disappeared. Nathanial presented their passports and letters of accreditation, which the Resident handed to his secretary, and refreshments were immediately served. After luncheon, attended by the garrison commander and other European residents, Charlotte, Takouhi and Nathanial went to the hotel.

The Hotel der Nederlanden was a large, commodious building of brick and shingle, raised from the ground on pillars and surrounded on all sides, for coolness, by a deep verandah and shaded by a banyan. This tree and others in the extensive garden were home to thousands of black and red Java sparrows and the noise of their twitterings, especially at dusk, was deafening. When they rose occasionally, startled, from the trees, they darkened the sky, and the sound of their wings resembled a violent gale.

After a refreshing interval in the cool waters of the hotel bathhouse, all three were glad to retire to their rooms, for the day had grown humid and the heat intolerable. Surakarta stood in a depression, and the natural heat of the day was thereby intensified. Charlotte, exhausted, slumbered to a chorus of cicadas and the croaky cry of the pretty green chick-chack.

When she awoke, it was to a knock at the door and the arrival of tea. She joined Takouhi and Nathanial on the verandah. It was half past four. They were expected at the Residence at seven o'clock for a visit to the palace.

The hotel keeper's wife joined them, and Charlotte thought she might never meet such a creature again. A *mestizo* woman of Portuguese-Malay blood, she was in every respect pleasant, if a little raucous and inclined to chatter, which Charlotte put down to a lack of companionship in this stuffy, class-obsessed outpost. It was not her nature but her appearance which gave, at first look, cause for some alarm. She possessed only one good eye and one good ear. Where the others ought to have been were thick scars, and there was a long gash from forehead to jaw. She had been attacked by a pirate band whilst travelling with her father many years ago, she told them. Marauding pirates were the scourge of the seas, bursting out of the endless bays and rivers hidden by jungle growth to prey upon the ships and boats which constantly ploughed along the north coast of Java or to and fro from the myriad islands of the *Nusantara*, the sprawling archipelago.

Her father, the captain of the ship, his crew and herself had put up a spirited fight against the band of Bugis dogs, she related—for she was handy with a sword. They finally managed to kill the leader, but not before she had received a blow on the face which had left her like this.

She took a large swig of gin and bitters, for tea was not a drink which had found favour with her. One could not help but like her buccaneer spirit, which had seemingly never faded. The married life apparently agreed with her, for she had had seven husbands, all seamen, but had given up the ocean life when she married her present spouse and they moved here. She had had eight children, all born at sea.

The Dutch government needed people to run the inns and staging posts of the interior and paid them well for their labours. This was a subject which exercised Nathanial's opinions as much as the excessive and vexatious use of passports. This circumstance of the State paying the innkeeper instead of the innkeeper paying the State was conclusive proof, to his English mind, that government monopolies do not work.

"The only roads not impassable for half the year are the government roads." he said. "Upon these the ordinary agriculturist is not permitted to travel. Though they built these fine highways, the hard-working Javanese are forced to travel with their heavy buffalo carts over tracks no better than ploughed fields. It is a brutal and incomprehensible tyranny.

"Two Java rupees per mile," he expostulated. "Had the island remained in British possession, how different things would have been. English capital and English enterprise would have destroyed monopolies, and competition would have long since lowered the extravagantly high expense of posting to a rate within the means of all classes, including one so indispensable as the growers of produce. Why the government cannot see that the whole system is rotten is beyond me. There never was a more foolish decision made than to give this country back to the hard, grasping hand of the Dutch."

Nathanial was about to continue when they were interrupted by Captain Palmer and three companions. Nathanial had known the American would be joining them here, but could not repress a scowl.

Captain Palmer went immediately to the ladies and shook Nathanial's hand. Palmer was very happy to see Mrs Manouk, although she looked a little pale. Still, such beauty. It filled a man with lubricious thoughts.

Charlotte knew one of the three men. Owen Roberts, a merchant at Batavia and the current American consul, had attended her wedding reception at the Harmonie Club. He was a quiet-spoken, thoughtful man. He talked of his interest in promoting the import of American ice to Batavia as agent for the Tudor Ice Company. When his English companions, in the oppressive heat of the Surakarta afternoon, laughed gaily at such an outlandish thought, he was rather affronted and told them that ice had been very successfully introduced into Calcutta many years before. He then fell silent.

Palmer introduced Mr Clay, an American merchant involved in the sale of Appalachian ginseng to China. It was a very lucrative trade, Mr Clay was happy to tell them, and one which had helped in large part to finance the American Revolutionary Wars. Even today, it was America's greatest export to China. Mr Clay was based in Canton but was presently on his way back to America and doing a little travelling in the country. Spying, Nathanial thought, but said nothing. Charlotte had some difficulty understanding him. He came from a place called Kentucky.

Mr Ruschenberger was a ship's surgeon with the United States Medical Corps. American *bottoms* carried a large part of the coffee and sugar exports both to Europe and to America. The Dutch had found them useful during the English blockade, for the Royal Navy did not attack American ships. Currently the ships travelled constantly to China and all the countries of the South Seas and represented a commerce of at least ten million dollars. He regretted that the United States provided no naval support for such American fleets, which were constantly at risk from piracy. He had sailed to seek a treaty for the American government with the King of Siam in 1835 and had subsequently completed a journey around the world. He was currently chronicling this mission for publication. He had joined Captain Palmer to visit the famed Javanese courts, about which he had read in both Raffles's and Crawfurd's account of the archipelago.

In the rather stuffy atmosphere of a Java outstation, Charlotte was glad of their company, for they were easygoing and enjoyable. She sensed, however, that Nathanial was not of the same mind.

By and by, the evening grew cooler and everyone separated to prepare for what they all felt sure would be a remarkable encounter with royal Javanese life.

They gathered at the Residency. It was the occasion of the *Susunan*'s birthday. Charlotte and Takouhi had dressed very carefully in robes brought for this occasion. They were of the very finest materials which Tigran could buy. Charlotte had chosen a powder blue silk with dark blue velvet trim to wear with the ice blue diamonds Tigran had given her. Takouhi, too, was in European dress, pale green and gold.

Charlotte detected a certain ambivalence in this visit, as if her friend did not quite know where she belonged. Charlotte had always thought of Takouhi, in some manner, as straddling both sides of this extraordinary society with ease but, here in the princely dominions, that was clearly not so. It was as if she had suddenly to confront the truth of her origins and for the first time question her allegiances.

Whilst they waited for the arrival of the *Susunan*'s state carriage, which would, so they were told, lead them to the palace, Charlotte and Nathanial examined their fellow guests. The Duke was seated on a red velvet chair, dressed, they began to imagine, entirely for their amusement. The dark blue serge served as the basis for an alarming array of gold buttons, braid and cords which hung from his shoulders and arms. Every inch of his ample chest and protuberant belly was festooned with medals. A wide sash fell from shoulder to waist, from which dangled a long gold scabbard. His black cockade hat, frilled with gold feathers, hung in a great arc before his eyes and down to his shoulders. Charlotte and Nathanial were delighted to see that, even on this royal occasion, the Duke had not changed his footwear, and the same ragged velvet slippers peeped from under his uniform. The probability of his rising without difficulty was slim, and they both looked forward to it with eagerness.

The Resident was dressed in a rather muted version of the Duke's dress, though he was slimmer. Mevrouw Snijthoff, a plain woman with sallow skin, wore a splendid, if somewhat old-fashioned, gown of deep blue silk with pearls. The Americans wore dark tail coats and breeches with frilled undershirts. Nathanial had dressed as informally as he dared without risking ejection and occasionally threw glances at Charlotte, who, he thought, was tonight more lovely than Venus. Her colour had revived and her skin carried a glow. Her eyes were set off by the blue diamonds she wore. Her hair had been dressed with blue velvet ribbon and arranged becomingly high on her head. It was difficult to drag his eyes off her.

They were standing together in order to comment wittily on their companions, and she occasionally put her fan in front of her mouth, moving it gently, to muffle their conversation.

The fan was made of sandalwood and black japan lacquer and emitted a heady perfume at each movement. When he leaned forward to listen to her, he found himself befogged in this bewitching aroma, watching her pink lips, and suddenly found her presence desperately and uncomfortably arousing. Only when he saw Captain Palmer, Mr Clay and several others in the Duke's party ogling her in the same manner did he scowl and stop acting like a fool.

A flourish of gongs and trumpets brought all conversation to an end, for it announced the arrival of the *Susunan*'s carriage. It somewhat resembled an English post-chaise, what the French called a *diligence à l'anglaise*, large wheels at the back and smaller at the front, carved and gilt and somewhat worse for wear, Charlotte thought. The coachman wore a sarong with a scarlet coat and hat. Over the carriage floated two tiered, gold *payongs*, the umbrellas of state, which indicated the presence, even incorporeally, of the *Susunan*. Preceding the coach came several dozen nobles who formed a double line through which the carriage passed. The

Susunan's minister brought forward a gold salver. Upon it was a letter wrapped in yellow silk.

The Resident took it and, in its place, put the letters of introduction from his guests. The minister placed the salver inside the coach and with a flourish of trumpets marched out of the Resident's compound, leaving the Resident's party to follow the state coach to the palace.

Nathanial and Charlotte held their breath as the Duke roused himself. He made to rise, rocking slightly. The Resident looked straight ahead, then glanced down to the Duke. The rocking resumed more vigorously, this time with two servants holding him under the arms. The Resident continued to wait. Finally the Duke managed, with a loud grunt and several curses, to rise to his feet; the Resident gave him a stiff little smile and bowed slightly. He motioned for the Duke to go ahead of him down the steps of the verandah.

Although the Duke had managed to steady himself quite adequately, the long, dangling scabbard had not. As he took a step it swung, swiping the servant and causing him to drop his supporting arm. The Duke, suddenly deprived of one pillar of support stumbled; his cockade hat fell over his eyes and he grabbed at the first person to hand, which, unfortunately, was the Resident. At the same time, the scabbard made an arc and struck the Resident on the leg. All the prayers of heaven could not stop what happened next, and when it was over, both the Duke and the Resident were tangled in a mass of dusty gold braid and upturned swords at the foot of the steps.

As a crowd rushed forward to raise the two dignitaries from the ground, Charlotte and Nathanial retreated quickly, stifling their laughter. Fortunately, in all the fuss and bother their merriment went undetected.

Their departure was delayed whilst the men were led from sight and cleaned up. After a while, Captain Palmer came to find Charlotte and Nathanial, smiling, to tell them they had been asked to mount their carriages. Before Nathanial could move, Palmer took Charlotte's arm, and tucking it intimately into his own, led her back to the verandah before helping her, his hand on her waist, into the carriage. Before releasing her, he brought her hand to his lips, holding the kiss too long. Nathanial glowered, Takouhi frowned and Charlotte blushed. When the Resident returned, his face was red with repressed fury. The Duke, who had survived the fall surprisingly well, had been installed, with a flow of curses, in the coach, and the procession moved off to the sound of trumpets.

With flaming torches and lanterns aloft, they passed at a funeral pace around the high walls of the fort and entered the walled plain before the palace, where the imperial guard was drawn up under arms. They were somewhat shabbily dressed and armed with muskets. The royal flag was lowered as the carriages passed.

As they stopped at the principal entrance to the Palace, the *gamelan* burst forth in a wild flourish. The walls were ablaze with lanterns. Chiefs, lined up on either side, lowered their spears in salute as the visitors passed. Inside the gate, the entire party, preceded by a liveried guard of honour, made their way slowly through the maze of lamp-flickering courtyards and gateways. Here and there, half-shadowy figures appeared from the carved walls, the face of the Kala, with its grotesque teeth and tongue, smiling at them as they passed. In one courtyard, in a blaze of light, a band of Javanese musicians struck up an endearing if rather clumsy rendition of William of Nassau, the national air of the Netherlands. In others, they saw displays of French clocks, Venetian crystal, Spanish furniture, Dutch paintings. Relations between the Resident and the *Susunan*, Nathanial explained, involved a never-ending exchange of gifts, though whilst the Resident might present the king with a handmade Persian carpet, the king might return this largesse with the gift of two unusually shaped mangoes! This long transit on foot from carriage to throne room, he added, was calculated to aggravate and tire his often overdressed Dutch guests, a small revenge.

In the Duke's case it was successful, for he was dripping with sweat, tiring fast and the occasional *Kreuzmillionen! Donnerwetter!* reverberated around the corridors.

The Resident was finally greeted by two very old female attendants of the *Susunan*, who shook hands with him without speaking and led him into the royal presence. Finally, Charlotte thought, after this wearying, twilight journey, they would see the king, and she turned to Nathanial excitedly. He smiled but felt Palmer's eyes on Charlotte like some predatory reptile's. Really, he disliked this man.

18

His Majesty, the *Susunan* of Surakarta, was seated under the lofty square roof of the royal *pendopo*, which was resplendent with crystal chandeliers and Javanese lanterns. A carved wooden canopy of gilt and red hung from the roof above the throne. The throne was more like a large stool, in truth, but wrought entirely of silver. To one side stood two chairs, clearly set there for the principal guests, and on the other side was a table on which stood the royal regalia, the crown jewels, as it were, of Java. There were gold bowls and salvers, figurines of an elephant, a serpent, a bull, a deer, the royal betel box and spitting pot. Next to this were two more chairs, one occupied by a very small, fine-boned woman dressed in a shimmering bodice and sarong made of *songket*, a cloth of silk woven with silver and golden threads. Rows of chairs formed an aisle before the throne, one side occupied by royal princes, the other empty. Behind these chairs, on the ground, sat the rest of the court.

Guarding the king were rows of women, cross-legged and straight-backed, holding swords before them. They were beautiful, their brown skin covered with golden coats and pants, their dark hair crowned with golden headdresses and on their backs golden bows and arrows. Charlotte had never seen women warriors before, and her first view of the king was entirely eclipsed for her by these soldiers and by a group of dwarves and albinos crouching near the throne.

The king was clad in the jacket of a colonel in the Dutch army, complete with epaulettes and medals. Over his lower limbs he wore golden pantaloons and a sarong of brown and white. The Resident and, indeed, all the men had removed their hats as they went forward. The king rose to greet them. As he took his hand, the Resident bowed, and even the Duke removed his huge cockade hat. The Resident presented the letters of introduction from the golden tray, and the king passed them to his minister, who squatted at his side. The Duke and the Resident took their places on the dais; everyone else took their seats opposite the royal princes, who were dressed, rather indiscriminately, in the various ranks of the Dutch military. One, Nathanial pointed out quietly, wore a jacket designating him as an Admiral of the Fleet. Takouhi, Charlotte and Nathanial took up the last seats. Several princes ogled Charlotte with undisguised interest, some smiling at her with their pointed black teeth.

The Resident introduced his guests, while Mevrouw Snijthoff, seated next to the queen, spoke quietly to her. All seemed to be proceeding as decreed, when suddenly the Minister shuffled forward urgently and raised his hands in salute, waiting. After a short exchange the king rose and waved his hand towards Takouhi. Takouhi seemed unable to act until Nathanial whispered to her. The *Susunan* was now waggling his hand excitedly, giggling and saying something in Javanese.

"Go forward, Miss Manouk; he is calling for you."

Takouhi rose and with hesitant steps made her way towards the throne. The king and queen came forward to speak to her. A loud murmur went round the court. The Resident rose, taken aback at this sudden shift in protocol. With a flourish, all the guests were ordered to make way for Takouhi to sit in the chair nearest the throne, the king himself shifting them along like so many children at a garden party. The Duke stared at Takouhi as he might a prize specimen of onion.

"It is because they have found out she is a daughter of a royal princess of the palace," Nathanial said. "I'll stake my life on it. The king is delighted to find any reason at all to displace or annoy his Dutch guests."

The toasts began: "To the *Susunan*."

Charlotte almost dropped her glass as a cannon boomed, seemingly just behind her head.

"To the King of the Netherlands."

This time she was ready. And so it went, dozens of toasts, dozens of cannon volleys. "To the *Susunan*, to the Resident, the Resident's lady, the Queens of the court, the Princes, to the ladies of Java and, finally—to Java!"

The *gamelan* burst forth. The Resident rose, helping the Duke to his feet and into the arms of the servants. As the Duke teetered off, the Resident took leave of the *Susunan* and shook hands with all the princes as he passed down the line, put his hat on his head, held out his arm for his wife and promptly departed. The royal couple retired, accompanied by their female bodyguard, dwarves and albinos. With bewildering speed, the courtyard emptied. An old woman came forward and spoke to Takouhi.

"She wants us to go to meet the ladies of the court," Takouhi explained. Charlotte could come, but Nathanial must go. Already the lanterns and torches were being extinguished.

Takouhi and Charlotte followed the old woman down darkened passages until they passed, finally, into a large room where a dozen women were seated on a faded carpet.

They rose as one and came to Takouhi, their hands raised to their foreheads in salutation. When Takouhi addressed them in Javanese, the ice was broken and they all laughed and pulled her and Charlotte to sit with them, chattering and touching Charlotte's white skin. A very old lady entered and sat amongst them. She took Takouhi's hands and began to speak. Charlotte could make out nothing other than that this was an affecting tale, for Takouhi's eyes at one moment filled with tears.

"This old lady was friend of my mother's. They grew up together here in the palace. She was a *Srimpi* dancer, like my mother, a court dancer."

The old woman continued to relate her tale, her audience at moments letting out a sigh or a gasp.

"My mother was daughter of king and *selir*, secondary wife. *Selir* is not high rank. Daughter have more rank, but not high like child of main wife. She tell about what happened."

Two young princesses came next to Charlotte and took her hands to comfort her, perhaps not realising that Charlotte could not understand. The story had clearly reached a harrowing point, for several of the young girls were sobbing. Takouhi gripped the hands of the old woman, a tear rolling down her cheek. She turned to Charlotte.

"I cannot say like her, so sad, so terrible. She my mother's good friend.

When they sixteen, they called to dance for guests of my grandfather, the king. King like guests very much, spend all day eating and drinking with them. They are Resident and foreign guests, also my father. My father bring very good present for King. Two Spanish silver musket, Dutch lace, French sabre. They all drunk. *Srimpi* dancer is royal dancer, not *ronggeng* dancer, but all men drunk. All men and even king dance with girls. My mother very young, very pretty. My father want her and take her on his lap. She struggle and cry."

Takouhi choked and, seeing her distress, the young princesses surrounded her.

"King think is joke, but if man touch her how can she marry good husband? He say she is his daughter, offer her to my father for wife. Joke maybe, but already she is dirty, shamed. Other women watching this and send for Minister. Minister try to speak to king, but what can he do? King angry and order *imam* to come, marry them. Take them on his knee, give blessing, laughing, drinking. My mother must obey king."

Takouhi was calmer now, as she continued this tale. "Next day, big scandal. All palace shocked, but too late. My mother no more virgin girl. She married to my father and must go with him. She covered in dishonour. This old lady cry and cry for her friend but never see her again. This girl raised to be good girl, good wife. How can I tell you the shame of this?"

She looked more intently at Charlotte. "I think when my father wake up he cannot believe this. I think she is nothing for him. He want one drunken night with her, but she is a princess so he forced to take her. Poor child, poor my mother."

She gripped the old woman's hand and put her cheek against her cheek, reaching out, through this friend who had known her, to this ruined girl who had been ripped from her family and thrown upon an uncaring world.

"Mother body come back here. They bury her at old graveyard at Kartasura. We visit her."

Charlotte nodded, and they rose to make their way back, walking silently through the corridors of shadow and flame in the footsteps of a ghost.

19

"I have been observing," Nathanial said the next day, "the time-honoured and quaint ritual of the dinner plates."

He had strolled onto Charlotte's verandah, where she was taking tea and attempting to read a very old, yellowing Dutch newspaper. She put it down and smiled at him.

"Do pray tell," she said, pouring him a cup of tea.

Nathanial dropped into a chair, pushed back his sandy curls from his face and stretched out his legs, secretly enjoying for a brief moment the small fantasy that he and Charlotte were husband and wife enjoying a postcoital refreshment.

"Well, it seems that everyday protocol requires the Resident to send an array of cooked dishes—not less than four—to the palace for His Majesty's delectation. This, apparently, he must do come rain or shine. This morning the royal dinner consists of several fowls roasted and boiled, vegetables, pastries and three kinds of fish. In return, I am informed, the *Susunan* may, from time to time, send back under his royal gold umbrella perhaps one or, if fortunate, two oranges or other fruits of a particularly grotesque or interesting shape, as it may please the king. A fair trade, I think you will agree."

Nathanial tucked smugly into Charlotte's untouched breakfast, which consisted of an insipid broth, boiled tongue, calf's head, fricandel, fish, bread, a plate of rancid butter, cabinet pudding, stewed fruit, preserved ginger, a variety of unidentifiable dishes, a bowl of fruits and a jug of claret.

"We are invited to dinner at the Residency to meet the young

Pangeran, the prince from the rival court, who is visiting the Duke. Did you enjoy the little birthday party for the king last night?"

When Charlotte nodded, he added,

"Bear in mind that this ritual is carried out not once a year but every month, and one almost begins to feels sorry for Snijthoff."

Charlotte was about to reply when Captain Palmer turned the corner of the verandah and removed his hat. Nathanial scowled.

"Mrs Manouk, good morning. I have come to ask if you would like to accompany our party on a little stroll around the town."

He took her hand and put it to his lips in an almost possessive manner.

Nathanial spluttered and nearly choked on the fricandel. Palmer clapped him on the back so hard he almost sent him reeling from the chair.

"Is that better?" Palmer asked. "Saw a man choke to death once on a piece of bread. Ugly sight."

Nathanial ached to punch Palmer in the nose, insolent dog that he was, but, as he stood a full six inches shorter than the American, who was, to boot, well built, he knew he would come off the worse in any brawl. The risk of such humiliation in front of Charlotte resolved him to choose the better part of valour, and he sat and waved away her affectionate concern.

Charlotte was not sure what to do. She could see Nathanial's dislike of the Captain and was not fool enough to have missed his particular and pressing attentions. However, Takouhi was indisposed, and Nathanial was going to spend the day with a fellow naturalist. The prospect of a long morning on the verandah did not appeal, for she would only brood on this pregnancy. She was sure of it now, for the old feelings of nausea had struck her as she awoke. She therefore assented with a smile and rose to fetch her hat and parasol.

Nathanial's mind was in turmoil. Let her go with this blackguard? But he had made his arrangements and could not go back on them. He would be away until the afternoon. He could only watch as Palmer took Charlotte's arm in his, tipped his hat airily at Nathanial and left.

The three other Americans were waiting before the hotel. They paid their respects to Charlotte and were about to set off when Nathanial came racing around the corner with two of Tigran's men.

"Your husband would not forgive me if I were not to give you some bodyguards. After all, he has expressly sent them to care for you. They will follow to be sure you are safe."

Charlotte smiled at Nathanial, and he threw her a grin and turned. Palmer watched him retreat, his eyes narrow and his lips pursed.

They set off towards the river, the two guards following at a distance, passing through the small Chinese town until they reached a bridge. On the far side lay a grove of trees surrounding a Christian cemetery. Here, to her surprise, the three other men took their leave, and she realised that the Captain had intended to find himself alone with her in this isolated spot. She threw a glance at the escort behind and, reassured, went into the graveyard.

Charlotte disengaged her arm from Palmer's and they wandered about the mounds and headstones. Some of the inscriptions on the tombstones forced a smile. There were the usual records of human vanity. The epitaph of one former Resident declared him, "Gentilhomme de Mecklenburg". So that this should be understood by all, the words were repeated in Dutch and Malay. Another stone announced in letters of fading gold that the "Well-born Gentleman" who slept below had passed into a "Well-born Heaven."

Charlotte saw letters in English and made her way to a stone erected by the comrades of a Scotch soldier who had fallen in 1816. Palmer read the epitaph.

Gaily I lived as ease and nature taught,
And spent my short life without a thought,
I'm surpris'd at death, that tyrant grim,
Who thought of me, that never thought of him!

They smiled, and Charlotte turned to leave. She realised suddenly that they had arrived at the end of the graveyard by the low back wall and there was no sign of the bodyguards, who, being Mohammedans, must not have wanted to enter the grounds. Palmer, too, saw the situation and took Charlotte's hand in his and pressed it to his lips.

"How quickly death comes upon us. My dear Charlotte, you must allow me to tell you how much I admire you."

She felt his arm move around her waist and struggled to free herself. Her parasol flew from her hands.

"Captain Palmer, you jest surely. You do not know me, and in any event, I am married. Please stop at once."

For reply, she felt his lips on her neck. He was strong, and the arm at her back held her in a vise. He began to pull up her skirts.

She was suddenly afraid. She began to cry out, but he cut her off with his kiss, crushing her, grinding his teeth against her mouth. He tasted of tobacco and staleness, and she felt a wave of disgust. He had managed to raise her skirt, and she felt his hand on her thigh. He groaned loudly and suddenly picked her up and began to carry her into a thicket, pinning her arms to her sides. She was no longer in any doubt about his intentions and opened her mouth to scream but could emit nothing but a squeak. Then she heard voices raised. Palmer too heard and pulled his head away from the skin of her bosom. The two Sundanese bodyguards were standing outside the wall and drew their *krisses*, yelling at Palmer. One began to climb over the wall, and Palmer abruptly put her down and, in a trice, turned and walked quickly away.

Thank heaven, Charlotte thought, trembling uncontrollably. Her guards had followed from outside, skirting the wall. Recovering, she thanked them, but both men were clearly angry. She picked up her hat and parasol, but did not dare go back through the graveyard for she had no idea where Palmer might be lurking. His boldness and single-mindedness had caught her totally off guard.

She walked by the wall, the guards shadowing her, until she reached a pile of stones high enough for her to climb over. Her hands were still shaking, but with the help of the men, she escaped the confines of the burial ground and made her way back to the hotel.

There the guards gave a salaam and disappeared.

Still shaken, Charlotte decided that nevertheless she would rather do nothing about this. She intended now to stay well away from Palmer. If this were to come out, she feared not only what Nathanial would do but, more, what Tigran would do. She was not entirely sure that within Palmer's reckless nature there might not be a tendency to enjoy duelling.

Sweating and dizzy, Charlotte returned to her room and locked her door. The sonorous buzzing of the cicadas was piercing. A bath refreshed her, and by the time she saw Takouhi and Nathanial again she felt composed and ready for the evening ahead, which, she was sure, Palmer would not dare attend.

In this surmise she was quite wrong. Turning into the gate of the Residency she saw him standing on the verandah, entirely at ease, talking to his friends. As they approached, he looked directly at her and smiled. She felt herself tense. There was not one ounce of regret or shame on his face; rather, he wore an expression of pleased conspiracy, as if they were secret lovers, as if in some manner she had encouraged him.

They went up the verandah steps, merely nodding in the Americans' direction. To her amazement, Captain Palmer left his group and came towards them. Charlotte stared at him in disbelief. He bowed slightly.

"Good evening, Miss Manouk, Mrs Manouk—as usual, the most beautiful ladies here. Mr Fox, I hope you are well. It should be a pleasant evening."

He looked directly at Charlotte.

"I so much enjoyed our walk today, Mrs Manouk. Thank you."

She said nothing, trying to hold his gaze, but he was so filled with arrogant insolence that she lowered her eyes, immediately angry with herself. He knew she would say nothing. How, she did not know, but he knew. He was a man who preyed on women and relied on their shame. She looked up.

"Captain Palmer, I am afraid I did not enjoy the morning so well as you. I was just writing to my husband about it."

She paused and saw a flicker of doubt in his eyes.

"The oppressive heat, I mean, though of course the letter is not yet finished," she said and moved into the Residency without a backward glance.

To their surprise, the *Pangeran* turned out to be handsome boy of around nine, with large, intelligent eyes and a mop of unruly black hair escaping from his headdress, which was so unusual it caught the eye immediately. Above his kerchief was a high, round hat made of black velvet, with points resembling asses' ears on each side of the crown, a very large shade in front and a black tail hanging down behind. He wore a long, black velvet jacket with diamond buttons, a white *baju* and pantaloons with a loose sarong held by a girdle of gold and diamonds. His black silk stockings were filled with runs and holes. He slouched on his silver throne beside the Duke, a retinue clustered about his chair, quietly receiving introductions with not the slightest look of interest on his face.

As the drinks were served, he began to grow bored and pull at the gold braid on the Duke's uniform. The Duke had been half-slumbering when thus assaulted and woke jerkily. The *Pangeran* took a glass of wine and drank it down with one gulp. As the dinner was announced, he jumped to his feet, pulling at the Duke's arm and urging him to rise. At the long dinner table, Charlotte was glad to find herself far from Captain Palmer, next to Mevrouw Snitjhoff, who wanted to talk to these ladies from Batavia of things fashion-able, as she termed it.

No sooner was the *Pangeran* seated, once again with his entire retinue crouched behind him, than he attacked the food on the table as if this meal were the first he had encountered in a long month. He stuffed everything into his mouth at once—two plates piled high in front of him—without ceasing, occasionally lounging on the table or drawing up his legs to crouch on the silver throne which had accompanied him to the table. From time to time, he would climb up to reach a piece of fruit which caught his fancy, throwing the peels around him without troubling where they fell. Toasts were called, of which he took not the slightest notice.

Throughout this entire escapade, the Resident and his wife acted as if absolutely nothing untoward was happening, and Mevrouw Snitjhoff kept Charlotte engaged with questions about fashions in Batavia. Now sated, the young prince jumped from his chair and began running about the rooms, examining each object which caught his fancy. He jumped on the sofas to examine all the pictures on the wall, asking questions of the Resident, who was kept busy following His Majesty from place to place. A set of French table clocks drew his curiosity; he took off their glass covers, turning the hands round and round and making them strike the hours. A pair of porcelain vases next caught his fancy and, without consulting the Resident, he ordered them to be taken to his palace.

His curiosity and his appetite assuaged, the *Pangeran* promptly departed without taking leave of either the guests or the Resident.

Charlotte and Nathanial nearly wept with mirth, not only at these antics but at the face of the Duke, who, after all, had no reason to be appalled since he, in almost all but age and agility, resembled the young prince in every degree.

20

The trip to Kartasura, the ancient Mataram capital, proved both a failure and a success. The old palace had been a graveyard for many years, and it was here that Takouhi hoped to find her mother's tomb. They entered the massive, moss-encrusted brick walls and searched amongst the fragrant frangipani trees.

But their attempts to find the burial place proved fruitless. The tombs were old; many headstones had collapsed, and Takouhi admitted her written Javanese was poor. Eventually they gave up, sat on the mats the maids had spread and simply enjoyed the quiet peace of this shady and antique place, knowing her mother was here. Takouhi left a great garland of jasmine on one of the trees, lit incense among the tombs and watched the birds flitting from place to place. The graveyard was, ironically, filled with life: lizards, crickets, insects of all kinds and thick-striped wild cats made their home here too.

When they returned to the hotel, Charlotte was annoyed to see that the Americans were occupying the front verandah and were in heated conversation with Nathanial. Their guards, too, had seen Palmer and took up a position under the banyan tree. Takouhi wanted some tea, and Charlotte, against her will, joined her at a distant table. Not so distant, however, that they could not hear the conversation.

"For make no mistake, gentlemen," Nathanial was saying, "all the Javanese peasantry are Dutch subjects, the Dutch king is their king, the descendants of their ancient sovereigns are Dutch officials, promoted or demoted by the Governor-General in the name of the king. They live under laws made in Holland and pay taxes which benefit only the treasury and people of Holland."

Palmer blew out smoke from a cigar and eyed the men with the *krisses* who were watching him. "Naturally," he said. "If you Europeans must have your blasted colonies, it makes sense that they must exist for the benefit of the mother country."

This utterance was delivered in a low drawl, laconically, as if Nathanial were an idiot.

"No, sir, I disagree. You, an American, should know it better than I. It does not make sense to turn one of the richest and most productive countries in the world into a land of famine. I have seen the cadavers who walk the tracks of the provinces where forced labour and forced growth of export crops has reduced villagers to starvation, epidemics rife, illness and death everywhere. They try to flee this so-called Cultivation System, which is no system at all but merely slavery."

Roberts had looked on with surprise at Palmer's words. Violent objection to the idea that a colony existed only for the mother country was what had led to their own revolutionary war. Roberts was from the free state of Massachusetts. Slavery was a Southern disgrace and the subject of constant and emotional upheaval at home. He felt uneasy at such notions.

"Slavery, Mr Fox. Surely you go too far. The Javanese are not slaves."

"Why, sir, what do you call it when a people have no say in their own lives? The Dutch force the planting, fix the prices, tax the peasant. The Regent then taxes the rice again, and the omnivorous Chinese charge the peasant for transporting and selling goods and practise hideous usury, lending money they know can never be repaid, forcing the Javanese peasant into a yoke of unending debt. On top of this, the villager must give his corvée labour for free, making the roads and canals, walking hours from his village each day to work in indigo farms and sugar factories with no remuneration. Even the fruits of the forest, free to him since time immemorial, are forbidden. It is abominable. Only the Dutch demand this. Before they came, the regents demanded their share of the rice crop, the labours of their peasantry and a crawling obedience. The Dutch demand their whole lives—and for whom? For the civilians of Holland! If this hideous burden is not slavery, sir, then I do not know what is."

Nathanial drew breath, agitated.

"All this unending and unendurable labour means that the rice fields are neglected. There is famine in Java, sir, and it is a disgrace," he said more calmly.

Roberts frowned. Palmer, blowing smoke rings, looked as if he could not care less.

Mr Rauschenberger, who had until then remained discreetly silent, annoyed by Palmer's extraordinary and ungentlemanly behaviour and apparent ignorance, now spoke up.

"It appears that Great Britain made a great mistake in the Treaty of 1824 by ceding all these islands to the Dutch in return for obtaining Malacca, which had become useless to them in any case. Raffles did his best, but he was ignored. One can only wonder at the great lack of knowledge respecting the resources and geography of these islands. Not only was it prejudicial to the interests of Great Britain but entailed upon Borneo, Celebes, Banka and all the other islands, the extreme and benighted policy of Holland. Why, Banka is supposed to contain the richest tin mines in the world! The Dutch policy, as most men who have travelled here must agree, has had no beneficial effect. They have been in possession of these islands for nearly two hundred years, yet the natives are not to be found advanced in education, arts or sciences, nor are their comforts and conveniences of life in any degree improved by Dutch influence, though thousands of Europeans have grown rich upon their labours.

"Yes, sir, thank you," Nathanial said, grateful for a man of sense and experience. "Before the Dutch, the people of Java had for a millennium carried on a vast and lucrative commerce trading in the rich produce of these islands. Java was the natural emporium of insular Asia. Vessels from the Red Sea to Japan visited its ports. It is humiliating to the civilisation of Europe to see how completely the establishment of its influence in Java broke up this free and thriving commerce. The restrictions of the Dutch destroyed the native trade, turning former traders into pirates, to add to the vast number already marauding the seas. Having destroyed the sailors, they are now well on the way to destroying the peasant as well."

Roberts said nothing. Palmer thought Nathanial an ass and smirked and cast a glance in Charlotte's direction. Nathanial saw it and rose. He had had more than enough of Palmer's attitude and could feel his anger rising. He saluted Roberts cordially and bowed to Rauschenberger; then he joined Charlotte and Takouhi. In his pocket was a letter he had been handed for her, which Charlotte opened quickly.

"News", she said. "Tigran has heard from Billy Napier that George is returning. The house is awaiting him; it is definite. He is expected in November. Oh, Takouhi, what good news!"

Takouhi smiled, and Charlotte could tell she was pleased. This visit seemed to have been good for her, helped her in some small way to find peace of mind about her mother.

"Tigran has written to Billy not to renew the lease on Tir Uaidhne and given the tenant notice to quit."

Tigran's letter contained, as well, his passionate expressions of love, missing her, wanting her to come home. She, too, had had enough. Palmer had soured everything. She wanted to return to the safety and love of Tigran's care. It was time to go back to Batavia and plan the voyage to Singapore.

21

Charlotte and Takouhi were filled with happiness as the brig set its course.

Charlotte sensed a reticence in Tigran, but he was gracious, for news of the baby had filled him with joy, and he was glad for his sister in particular, hoping she could find contentment with George again. The weather held fine, the wind filled the sails and they skimmed over the shallow turquoise waters, the sleek *Queen of the South* pushing the sea aside, rolling on the waves as if she, too, was filled with the joys of the ocean.

The call of "Land ho!" brought them all to the rail, straining for the first glimpse, while gulls swooped and squawked overhead. As she caught sight of the distinctive red cliffs, Charlotte let out a whoop of pleasure. When they landed, finally, to be met by Robert and Billy Napier, Charlotte embraced this man she hardly knew as strongly as she had her brother. She looked over the Plain. Little had changed, other than an ugly steeple which had been added to St. Andrew's church. Her first thought was that George would be annoyed at such a hideous desecration. Tir Uaidhne welcomed them into its gracious charms and Charlotte left Takouhi and Tigran together to quietly rediscover Meda's home.

Meanwhile, Charlotte and Robert walked to the river, down High Street, slowly savouring the sounds and smells of the town, enjoying each other's company after so long, chatting, talking of past pleasures and future hopes. Charlotte leaned on her brother's arm, suffused with happiness at being with Robert. They passed the Court House, and Robert showed her the new police house next to the post office and the old fives court, a building of no distinction. Their home on the beachside was to be demolished to widen the rivermouth. Robert had moved to an old house on the corner of Beach Road and Middle Road. Their talk turned to Shilah, Robert's *nyai* of more than four years.

"I care for her still of course, but I cannot leave Teresa waiting much longer. And," he added in an afflicted tone, "Butterpot is not Bonham. It would not do to be seen to keep a mistress. He is the most appalling stickler for morals and etiquette and all that rot. Dreadful man."

Charlotte took Robert's hand. "Do you still ... visit Shilah, Robbie? You know what I mean."

Robert nodded, embarrassed. "I still care for Shilah in the way you mean. It is difficult to give her up. I would much rather not, you know. But I think ... she will not like any news of my marriage."

Charlotte shook her head. Robert was a brave man and a good policeman, but his knowledge of women was mystifyingly poor.

"No," she said, patting his hand. "She will not."

"I do love Teresa, Kitt, really. But I love Shilah too. It is a horrid muddle. I'd much rather do like the Chinese and have a wife and a concubine. They have the best ideas on this sort of thing. But I am quite certain Teresa would not like it either." He sighed. "Or Butterpot."

Charlotte smiled. "No," she said and for the very first time thought what life was like for Zhen's wife, what Chinese wives had to endure. Robert's words were utterly simple and true. Men, if they could, would rather have many women than one and, preferably, a system in place which kept them all quiet and obedient. Even dear, sweet Robert.

Sensing a change of mood, Robert dropped the subject. They gazed along the river. The familiar sights came flooding back: the river filled with boats, the constant industry of Boat Quay. Johnston's ancient house and godown at Tanjong Tangkap were still standing but, Robert told her, they were riddled with white ants.

Then Charlotte realised that something was missing. The river seemed bigger somehow. The bridge! Monkey Bridge, which had spanned the river linking North and South Bridge Road, was gone. She looked at Robert. "Heavens, Robbie, where is the bridge?"

"Oh, yes, I forgot to tell you. Knocked down, too dangerous. Two months ago, and the fuss over a new one is still going on. Butterpot, in his usual high style, says there will be no bridge; Coleman's will do very well. He has land to shift down there, we all know. One bridge is enough, and we might as well accept it. Pompous ass. Everyone's in high dudgeon, including all the Chinese, for the market gardens are this side and the market over there. They must take the long way round or pay the sampan."

Charlotte gazed at the Chinese town. Somewhere in there was Zhen.

Within a few days, they were invited to a reception given by Colonel Butterworth and his wife on Government Hill. Charlotte loved the ride, for gradually the view opened out and displayed the entire town below. From the verandah of Government House the eye was naturally led up the river, along the rows of houses and out into the harbour, with its tall-masted toy ships and junks and further, over the sea, now shot with the fiery sunset turning the water to gold.

The reception was in honour of Captain Keppel and James Brooke, whose ships were then berthed at Singapore, resting from pirate hunting in the waters of Borneo. Keppel was a small, stout man, prematurely balding, with a thick orange moustache. Colonel Butterworth introduced him as the son of the 4th Earl of Albermarle through marriage to the daughter of Lord de Clifford. A man who looked less like a romantic and dashing hunter of pirates it was hard to imagine.

James Brooke, however, was entirely different. He looked the very part: curly brown hair, tall and slim, dressed informally with a white shirt, short black naval jacket and a soft, loose cravat. He was around Tigran's age with tanned skin and brown eyes. It was impossible not to like him for he was easy of manner. Colonel Butterworth introduced him grandly as the Rajah of Sarawak and was clearly as much in awe of him as the rest of the room. Titles, she surmised, were rather a hobby of the Governor's.

In conversation with the Rajah later, she discovered, to her pleasure, that he adored Miss Jane Austen's novels and nurtured an ambition to meet Miss Austen's brother Charles, a naval officer. He was so unexpected that she found herself charmed. Nathanial's assessment of him she now dismissed as jealousy, for she could see how such an adventurer, a *successful* adventurer, could arouse strong feelings of envy in men. When Robert told her that it was Brooke who had dubbed the Governor *Butterpot the Great*, his place in her esteem was fixed.

The Rajah seemed to work the same magic on the other ladies in the room, who engaged him in constant conversation. Most of the gentry of Singapore were present, and she was happy to renew acquaintance. They would all meet again at Whampoa's, for he, too, was holding a lavish dinner party in honour of the Rajah and Captain Keppel.

Of her former acquaintance she was delighted to see Munshi Abdullah, who was accompanying the new Temmengong, Daeng Ibrahim. Abdullah had been her Malay teacher, a man for whom she had the greatest affection.

Of those she met for the first time, she immediately liked Miss Arabella Grant, who had come as agent for the Society for Promoting Female Education in the East and was assisting Mrs Dyer of the Missionary Society in running a boarding school on North Bridge Road for Chinese girls. Charlotte had met, through Takouhi, the Society's agent in Batavia, the rather valiant Miss Thornton.

To Charlotte's surprise, Mrs Butterworth turned out to be a pleasant and unusually informal woman. Charlotte wondered how her nature agreed with that of her haughty, snobbish and somewhat ridiculous husband. Mr Thomson, Singapore's new architect and surveyor, she liked instantly. He spoke in glowing terms of George's architecture, his work in building the town and his ready wit. He was looking forward to renewing his acquaintance with Mr Coleman. Charlotte wondered aloud then why on earth he had ruined the church with such an ugly addition, for she had discovered, upon mentioning it, that he was its creator. He begged forgiveness; it had been a commission from the Bishop of Calcutta who, during a visit to Singapore, had found the design of St. Andrew's to be "civic" and, worse, "popish", and had demanded a good English spire. Thomson shrugged, and she forgave him. No man could be blamed for the architectural vagaries of an English prelate.

She tried to remain patient, but after a few days felt she could wait no longer. Her natural curiosity and desires had begun to overwhelm her. She wanted to see Zhen. She waited until a time when Tigran was engaged in business in the town, for he was talking of taking leases on some properties. She took up her parasol and left the house, walking quickly up Coleman Street to Hill Street and turning towards the bridge. She had discovered that this bridge which he had built, formerly named New Bridge, had, on George's departure and in his honour, been renamed Coleman Bridge.

It was with pleasure then that she made her way across it to see all the new roads that had been laid out. Where before had been marshy swampland, now New Bridge Road stretched into the distance. She could have turned immediately into Upper Circular Road, but she wanted to savour this moment and continued, looking down the new streets on the left, Carpenter Street and Hong Kong Street; then she turned onto North Canal Road, one of the two roads which now framed the old creek. She thought of turning into Lorong Teluk but demurred, nervous suddenly, and walked as far as Philip Street.

She looked down Circular Road. A gentle curve in the road meant she could not see his shophouse. She gripped her parasol and began to walk. As the building came into view, she stopped and gazed. It had been improved: new tiling on the upper walls, the paint fresh on the shutters. There was now a shop on the ground floor, a medicine shop, she could see. It was painted outside in black and gold, a deep board across the door with four heavily carved gold characters. She wondered what they meant.

She just wanted to see inside this shop, she told herself. It would only take a minute. She walked to the door. The pungent and unmistakable aroma of Chinese herbs hit her as she stood looking inside.

It was sombre after the brightness of the street, and she could not make out its occupants. She lowered her parasol and went in, her heart beating wildly. As her eyes adjusted, she saw six or seven Chinese customers, who turned to stare at her. The herbalist looked up from his task. The clerk, seated at his high counter, stopped counting on his abacus and she felt utterly ill at ease.

She turned to look at the fragrant sacks of roots and herbs which stood to one side. The abacus began its clack again, to her relief, and several customers began chattering. She looked around his shop, admiring its clean and prosperous aspect. Dozens of shiny, tall glass jars of strange shaped roots, crabs, squids and what looked like preserved baby snakes and shelled sea creatures lined the walls. She wondered briefly what curative purpose the sweet little bodies of sea horses could serve. A tall, carved cabinet with a hundred drawers stood to one side of the shop, each drawer painted with gold characters. Before a shiny, black-tiled counter lay trays and sacks of black and brown fungus, seaweeds, dried fish, herbs, buds, pods, berries, preserved fruits and plants. The variety was overwhelming. The sun was slanting in through the open doorway, casting shadows on the gleaming tiled floor. She felt happy for him, for his prosperity.

Then, as she was about to turn, to leave, a shadow fell across the sun on the tiles, and she knew, instantly, that it was him. He did not move. She too could not move, her breath in her throat. The abacus had stopped again, and she sensed that everyone in the store was now staring at them. Somewhere there was a faint buzzing of an insect, and the ticking of the clock seemed to have assumed a cavernous sonority. Then the shadow changed. The sun returned to its position on the floor as he came in front of her. Her head lowered, she gazed at his high-soled Chinese shoes, felt his proximity like heat, could not look up.

Zhen stood motionless, gazed down at her, the wisps of black hair against her cheeks, the curve of her neck.

"Xia Lou," he whispered. She drew in her breath sharply, her heart beating so much she dared not move. The sound of his voice saying her name in his Chinese way—that was all it took for her to know she was still madly in love with him. The customers were staring at them even more intently.

She saw his hand move tentatively towards hers, then withdraw. He was shaking. Then he made a fist to calm his hand and bowed to her.

"I have not seen you for long time," he said in English, and she felt the effort he was making to keep calm.

Charlotte curtsied briefly to him. Then looked up.

"Yes, it has been ... a long time," she faltered as her eyes met his.

Zhen saw the tenderness in her eyes, saw the love she still had for him. These white people, he thought—he had found that for a long time now he could not think of her or her brother as an *ang moh*, a devil. These white people, so difficult to disguise their feelings. He smiled inside, glad of it, and she, knowing him, read his eyes, though his face had shown no emotion.

They stood unmoving, aware of the stares, wanting to touch. He felt a calm come over him.

"We cannot talk here. I want to meet you. Tonight, come here. Yes?" he said in a low tone.

Charlotte walked over to a tray of herbs and roots. Picking up a thick root shaped almost like a man, she said, "I cannot come here, Zhen."

Moving next to her, he took up a handful of small buds and herbs. Charlotte stared at his hands and felt a flush of heat, of desire for him so strong that she began to shake. He saw it and put down the herbs.

"Where? Tell me," he said quietly.

Charlotte tried to think, to calm down. "Whampoa is giving a dinner at his house. Can you come?"

Zhen's face remained impassive, but inside he smiled. He was already invited to this dinner, together with his father-in law. "Yes," I can come," he said. He bowed to her, knowing she must leave. The customers had relaxed a little, gone about their business, but one old woman was watching intently.

"Ever hard to meet, as hard to part," he said, very low, before rising from his bow and looking into her eyes.

It was a poem, she knew it because she knew him: a line from a Chinese poem which she did not know. He said it in the most perfect English. She sensed the effort he had taken to learn this strange language, to translate this poem from his own tongue into hers. She felt her lips tremble.

He went quickly with her to the door. As she left the shop, he stayed looking down the street. She left rapidly, not turning, not daring to turn.

22

Takouhi was adjusting her hat. She had taken special pains about her appearance. Today a brig, *Pantaloon*, would bring George to Singapore. She and Robert had smiled and wondered if George had chosen this brig specifically for its nominal connections to the miserly and libidinous character from the *commedia dell'arte*. The signal flag with *Pantaloon*'s colours had been hoisted; she had been sighted, and soon the ship would be in the harbour. Billy Napier had told them all when George was coming. A ship recently arrived from Calcutta had brought a short message.

Takouhi was dressed in pure European style today, autumn woodland colours, brown, green, dull gold: the colours of the legend of Tir Uaidhne. For her hat she had chosen a green which matched her dress, trimmed with black piping with two emerald feathers which emerged in a sweep from the side. The green of Ireland. Charlotte smiled at her friend, who looked so graceful and flushed with expectation of this meeting.

Billy Napier paced the hall, constantly adjusting his cravat. Billy was a small man, with small eyes, a small moustache and slightly crooked teeth. The only thing about him that was tall was his hair, which he wore brushed from the slightly balding crown into two waves half the height of his head. How he contrived to do it was the subject of much amused prattle. He had extremely small feet, and when he walked it was with a kind of bouncing movement which made him appear to swagger. Perhaps because of this peculiarity of gait he always carried his head high and this, added to his coiffure, gave him an air of cocky superiority.

George, and indeed almost everyone, called him Royal Billy. Charlotte joined him and, arm in arm with Takouhi, their parasols raised, they made their way to George's fine black-and-gold phaeton carriage, which stood outside the gates. Billy, who had charge of George's possessions in storage in Singapore, had agreed to allow it to be released for Takouhi's use. Even the parasol Takouhi had chosen was particular to George, a gift purchased from the cargo of a Spanish ship in port on its way to Manila. It was of black lace, its crown dense, the rim soft with intricate and exquisite edging which the wind rilled and fluttered, casting shadows like sprites along her dress.

The phaeton moved slowly down Coleman Street, around the Plain, past St. Andrew's Cathedral and towards the shore. Tigran followed on his horse at a slow trot. The day was warm on the treeless plain, but a wind from the sea cooled their faces. As they arrived on the edge of the seashore, Billy, who was carrying his spyglass, saw the ship and with a great bouncing and a cry of pleasure, jumped down and swaggered to the jetty. Takouhi gripped Charlotte's arm, and they smiled at each other. George would soon be here!

Robert joined them as the ship made its final approach, and they all heard the splash of the anchor. Billy looked up at the flagstaff on Government Hill. His joy at the imminent arrival of his great friend and companion was touching. Other friends were there. John Connolly arrived in his gig, greeting Charlotte, as always, with a mixture of pleasure and anguish. Billy let out a whoop, for the flag on the hill had been raised, giving permission for this ship to disembark.

They all watched, now, almost with bated breath, to catch a glimpse of George. The cutter was down. They could see men and women being lowered into it. Then Billy, his glass to his eye, suddenly caught sight of George and let out a great cry. He unfurled the flag he had carried and raised it, waving it madly to and fro. It was the standard of the Singapore Free Press, the newspaper he and George had founded many years ago. A small figure raised his arm, and a great cheer went up from the jetty. Takouhi drew in her breath, and Charlotte sensed she was on the verge of tears.

The cutter was full now, and the men began to row towards the shore. With each stroke Charlotte too felt her emotion rise. To see George again, this loving, amiable friend, after so long, was more than they could envisage with calm. The oars dipped and pulled three more times, and then Charlotte could see him. She got down from the carriage and moved forward next to Robert.

George raised his arm once again, but, Charlotte thought, rather stiffly. Her heart raced. Was he hurt? Had something happened to him after all this time away that they knew nothing about? It was hideous, this thought, that after all the expectations, George would be ill. She looked back at Takouhi, who had remained in the carriage on the higher ground, standing now, her eyes glued to the boat.

Robert called his name and waved again. This time George did not respond. He was staring, too, at the shore and Charlotte realised that he had seen Takouhi, recognised the carriage, the emerald feathers, her parasol. Of course, she was relieved to think, he is overcome with seeing her. Then with a loud bang, the cutter hit the jetty, driven forward by a wave, shaking its occupants. Billy moved quickly down the jetty to assist. Charlotte, too, made to go forward when Robert very suddenly took her arm. His eyes were on the boat, and she looked at him, not understanding. He bent and whispered into her ear, and her eyes flew to George, who was talking to a young woman sitting next to him in the boat, her arm through his.

George climbed onto the jetty and Billy bounced forward to take his hand, talking wildly, overcome with excitement. George embraced his old friend and raised his hand to the gathered throng. Then he turned and put his hand down to the young woman in the boat, helping her with solicitude onto the jetty. She had great difficulty rising and climbing for, Charlotte could see, she was heavily pregnant. How kind, was Charlotte's first thought, how like George to help a woman in such difficulty, even in this moment.

The young woman, pretty, delicate featured and pale-skinned with dark brown hair, adjusted her dress after this somewhat rough arrival and George looked beyond his friends to Takouhi, who had not moved. Charlotte glanced back and saw her smile, a smile of such loving radiance that she too smiled, as one cannot help but do in the presence of love.

Then the lady at George's side linked arms with him, she too smiling on him with adoration, and Charlotte frowned. George walked a few steps and stopped. He looked away from Takouhi, and Charlotte saw his look of frowning distress. In a flash, she understood. Robert and Tigran, quicker than she, had grasped the situation, for Billy, bustling over to greet the couple, had bowed graciously over the hand of the woman next to George and they had all seen the gold band on her finger.

Tigran moved back to the carriage and put his hand on Takouhi's arm. Robert arrived on the other side of her and they locked her between them. Takouhi shook her head, annoyed. Charlotte too, ran back to Takouhi, who looked at her friend's face and saw her deep distress.

She stopped struggling and stood again, looking at George. She saw the woman holding George tightly against her, leaning on him, her support, her eyes on his face in trust and love; she saw the enormous belly. Takouhi froze and understood. She sat down very gently.

George had seen Takouhi's reaction and now whispered something urgently to Billy and John, then turned and spoke to his wife, for by now all present understood that this woman was George's wife. She smiled and kissed George lovingly on his cheek and walked between John and Billy to the palky which stood ready to take her to their new home.

George moved forward. His friends rushed around him, slapping him on the back, shaking his hand. Charlotte thought him hardly changed; in fact, he looked younger, refreshed from this period spent away from the tropical heat. His hair was a little greyer round the temples, perhaps, but he had always been a good-looking man. He turned his green eyes on his friends. Tigran moved forward and shook his hand, Robert too and Charlotte, unable to stop herself, threw herself into his arms and hugged him, tears running down her cheeks.

"Oh George, how we missed you so," she wept.

George patted Charlotte and put his hand on her cheek. "Kitt, my sweet. Let me speak to Takouhi first." His eyes flew up to her. They were still separated by a crowd and he could not get through. Their eyes met, and for long seconds they both simply looked at each other. Then, before he could move to her, she called for the carriage to depart. He moved Charlotte away and made to go forward, but it was too late and he could only stand and watch the carriage move away around the Plain.

"I had no idea you would be here. No idea she would be here. My God, what have I done?" he said, running his hand through his hair.

"George," Charlotte said. "Are you married? Is that your

wife, really?"

George, distracted, was watching the two carriages, the small gig in front, the more poweful phaeton behind, make their way past all the places he had built. First they passed the Court House and then they turned to pass slowly in front of the three big houses on the Plain. He watched until he saw them turn into Coleman Street.

"Charlotte, he said. "I must speak to her. Make her speak to me."

"My God, George, what happened? Who is she? When did you meet her?" Charlotte was so filled with curiosity that she was not listening to him.

He took her by the hand, and she stopped talking. "Make her see me, Kitt, please," he repeated.

Charlotte nodded ... but she knew her friend. It would not be easy, given Takouhi's pride.

Tigran had seen to the luggage, which had arrived on the jetty, and with a brief word to Charlotte returned to Tir Uaidhne to be with his sister. George turned to all his acquaintance and now began to greet them. Finally, with promises to see them all within a few days, he got into John's gig, which had returned for him, and left for No.2 Coleman Street to rejoin his young wife.

Robert and Charlotte set out along the seashore to Robert's house on Beach Road, past the banyan tree which stood near the stone bridge over the freshwater stream, past the Institution, past the other big houses, discussing this extraordinary turn of events. They were filled with curiosity, glad to see George so well, and full of speculation.

Chattering, they turned into the gates and there, on the broad verandah, lay a table set for supper. Robert had planned this supper to be a revival of the camaraderie of his friends, the joyous reunion of George with Takouhi, a renewal, after so long, of their happy life in Singapore. As they gazed now at this table, the full import of the situation hit them both: Takouhi would be heartbroken.

When Charlotte returned to Tir Uaidhne, Takouhi was in her room. Charlotte knew it was pointless to try to speak to her at present. The shock was still too great. All the next day, too, though Takouhi appeared for lunch, she made it clear to Charlotte that she would not speak of it. Nor would she go to Whampoa's dinner, which she had fully expected to do with George on her arm.

Charlotte made no attempt to argue with Takouhi. She was, in any case, now filled with thoughts of the evening to come. She felt anxious, for this terrible blow of George's marriage had filled her with dark foreboding.

23

Charlotte's nerves were on edge as the carriage passed through the elaborate Chinese gate and into the courtyard of Whampoa's new and magnificent mansion in Serangoon Road. This road had improved vastly since her departure, with new dwellings lining either side. There was a racecourse nearby at Farrer Park, and new streets. Other acquaintances would be there, of course, for Whampoa's parties had, she learned, become famous for their lavish hospitality, as befitted one of the richest and most influential Chinese merchants in the town. Charlotte had to calm herself at the thought of meeting Zhen. Tigran would be by her side. She must contain herself. Also, she would not have Takouhi to lean on.

Charlotte worried for her friend. The shock of George's new wife had been a great blow, despite her cool demeanour. But for now, Charlotte could not turn her mind to this matter. She felt her agitation at the prospect of seeing Zhen as keenly as she had at their first meetings behind the hill in the old orchard. Thank heaven Robert was following closely behind.

Tigran helped her from the carriage, and they crossed the open garden and walked around a large pond filled with lotus and golden carp. Charlotte had dressed carefully, in ivory silk, her hair in a simple French twist. She was glad the pregnancy did not show much yet, but her dress was tight. Around her neck and in her ears were pure white diamonds, gifts from Tigran on their wedding day.

As they climbed the tiled staircase to the moon gate, Charlotte saw Whampoa. He was still handsome, though a little heavier, and he greeted her with a bow. As Charlotte rose from her curtsey, he held out his hands and smiled a broad welcome. He was dressed in dark blue silk, his long queue threaded with red silk ribbons, his dark eyes so like those of Zhen that Charlotte had to grip his hands to stop her own shaking. Whampoa looked at her for a moment as he felt this trembling, then released her and shook the hand of her husband. Robert came up almost immediately, taking his sister's hand, and Whampoa accompanied them inside the house.

Charlotte momentarily forgot her nervousness in the extraordinary aspect of the house and its Chinese decorations. Tigran, to her slight relief, left her with Robert to greet the Armenian merchants who had gathered in a side gallery, and Whampoa too went back to his guests. They were alone, and, taking up some refreshments, Robert took her on a tour.

The grounds of Whampoa's mansion were expansive. A Chinese garden lay to one side, with ponds and large, strange-shaped rocks, animal topiaries and curious dwarf trees. She was intrigued by these tiny trees and Robert, who had been many times to the gardens, explained that it was a practice from Japan called *bonsee* and a damnable mutilation as far as he could see.

Leaving the Chinese garden she discovered an animal sanctuary with small, tufted-eared ruddy bears and a family of monkeys. Robert showed her Whampoa's orange pet orang-utan, tonight confined and seemingly asleep. There were ponds with lotus, an aviary with peacocks. She found it impressive if somewhat overstuffed.

This perambulation, with its discoveries, steadied her nerves, and she was happy now to go inside the house and renew acquaintance with the charming Rajah Brooke. As the hall began to fill with people, Tigran was again whisked away by some merchants, and she sought a moment of quiet above the crowd and climbed the curved staircase to the balcony which overlooked the hall. Here a group of musicians were playing Chinese music. She did not care for its discordant tones. But it was soft and could, in any case, barely be heard above the roar of the crowd below. She fanned herself and gazed down.

Then she saw him, across the courtyard standing in the moon gate. He wore a long, loose, black silk coat and trousers and high-soled Chinese shoes. Charlotte moved almost involuntarily into the shadow of a pillar, for she was suddenly afraid. She could see Tigran talking to the Governor and Mr Church. Did she really want this renewal? Before the previous morning she had been sure of her composure, but now, she doubted her self-control. She watched as Zhen came into the room, his eyes scanning the crowd. Suddenly he moved forward, and she saw him approach Robert. Her heart lurched wildly; she knew he was seeking her.

She looked at him properly, from a distance, drinking him in with her eyes. He was scarcely changed—only more elegant, and still inexpressibly handsome. She watched as Robert greeted him, it was clear that they knew each other well. Zhen bent his head to talk into Robert's ear, and she saw her brother look around, shaking his head a little.

Charlotte jumped as voices squealed behind her. Isabel and Isobel da Souza now came up to her and, taking her by the hands, jumped and jiggled their delight at seeing her again. As she embraced these twins, friends from her previous time in Singapore, she looked down and realised that Robert and Zhen were looking up at her; the noise had gained their attention. Tigran, too, had raised his head at the noise and smiled at his wife. Her eyes met Zhen's. Then the two girls took her hands and dragged her away from the balcony and down the stairs to meet their family. Zhen followed her with his eyes as she descended.

A moment later his father-in-law came up to his side with several other Baba merchants, and Zhen lost sight of her. Now she was here in this house. He felt his heart return to normal.

Baba Tan eyed his son-in-law quietly. He was quite sure that this young man had had a relationship with Miss Mah Crow, now Mrs Mah Nuk, around the time Zhen had married his own daughter. Fortunately, that young lady had gone away, and nothing had interrupted the nuptials and subsequent good fortune of the birth of two children. No son, of course, but that would come. Zhen knew his duty.

Zhen did not live permanently under Tan's roof and only slept irregularly with his wife. Tan's new villa at River Valley was complete, and he had moved there with his old wife and two unmarried daughters, as well as his young concubine and their baby daughter. The mansion on Market Street was for Zhen and his wife and children. They shared it with his second daughter and her new husband.

Tan hoped that this might mean that Zhen would spend more time with his family, for he knew that Noan, Zhen's wife, was often unhappy at her husband's absences. On this matter, however, Tan would not interfere. Zhen was master of his own family, and despite Tan's love for his eldest daughter, he felt it was Zhen's right as a man to be free to pursue his own pleasures, just as Tan himself had done.

After a year, Tan had gradually come to the realisation that he loved Zhen like his own son, the two men sharing the pleasures of business; Zhen's Chinese was quite useful in negotiations with his native country. Zhen's medicine shop had proved very profitable, and Zhen had helped with the Tan family's occasional ailments. Both Baba Tan and son-in-law shared a considerable enjoyment in playing *wei qi*, which Zhen had learned from his own father and taught to his father-in-law.

Tan knew he indulged Zhen, but he could not help it. So long as Zhen was sensible and discreet, Tan would never object to his son-in-law's choices. He liked his company too much, his strength and resourcefulness, his good nature; Zhen was the son he wished he'd had.

Actually, he felt that this young man was truly his son. When the time came, Tan intended to leave the trading house and his businesses in Zhen's capable hands, and this thought was an enormous comfort to him. Zhen had taken the Tan name, and he knew that this young man would carry out the rites for him with diligence and affection, a knowledge that gave peace to his heart. So many other merchants had useless or profligate sons or greedy and stupid sons-in-law who would gamble or smoke away a fortune in no time. Tan felt blessed.

There was a vast difference, however, between taking a second or third wife or a string of concubines and carrying on with the white wife of one of the richest men in the South Seas. Baba Tan considered that difference now. Surely Zhen realised it as well.

Zhen took a drink of porter, one of the English things for which he had developed a taste. He would find her later. For now he wanted to meet the man who was her husband, and together, he and Baba Tan they made their way over to the Governor's side.

Tigran knew Baba Tan; they had had business dealings through one of the rich Chinese sugar merchants in Semarang. This was the first time he had met his son-in-law, though, a young Chinese who was introduced simply as such. There was something unaccountably familiar about him which he could not put his finger on. Had he met a merchant in Batavia who resembled him? Then he forgot it. Tigran congratulated them both on the recent birth of a new child, spoke of his own impending happiness, looked around for Charlotte but could not see her. As they talked, Baba Tan expressed his desire to renew his acquaintance with Mrs Mah Nouk and spoke briefly of his pleasure at her company when she had first arrived in Singapore. He did not mention that Charlotte had been the English teacher of his son-in-law, Zhen, and Zhen's best friend, Qian.

Zhen contemplated this man who was Charlotte's husband. She was pregnant: this "impending happiness" he understood—his English teacher had taught him these strange subtleties, as elusive as Taoist poetry.

It was unexpected and galling. He was annoyed that the man, though old, was good-looking and strong. He felt his fist curl as he thought of him lying with her, pleasing her perhaps, a small quiet fury in his chest. He knew he should not think of this. She had as little choice as him. But he could not stop himself. Fortunately, at this moment they were abruptly interrupted by a loud gong, and dinner was announced.

Dinner was a torment. Charlotte was seated, unaccountably, next to the Governor, who throughout the meal recounted anecdotes of all his famous acquaintance, particularly Lord Ellenborough, Governor of India, and Prince someone-or-other, from time to time stopping to enquire whether Charlotte knew them. At least his enquiries almost never required an answer. The occasional smile and nod of the head were sufficient encouragement for him to continue.

Tigran was seated half-way down the table next to, of all people, Lilian Aratoon, who had once been madly in love with Tigran and who, despite her recent fiançailles, clearly still felt some affection in that quarter. Lilian engaged his constant attention, and occasionally he sought Charlotte's eyes beseechingly. Charlotte, however, could not stop herself looking from beneath lowered eyes at Zhen, who was seated at a second long table. Only once did he look in her direction, and she felt her heart race as they locked eyes. He did not look away, impassive, and at last Charlotte, fearful that her face would reveal the violent emotion inhabiting her body, looked down and did not dare look at him again for the remainder of the meal.

Finally came the toasts and speeches, and the Chinese band began an oriental rendition of a polka. Zhen had disappeared. Charlotte sat with Isobel and Isabel da Souza, who chattered incessantly and asked her interminable questions about Batavia. To her relief, they were claimed by some young men for a dance, and she was joined by Robert.

"Kitt, I have misgivings about this."

Charlotte looked at her brother, frowning.

"What do you mean Robbie? About what?"

He handed her a note. She opened it and read: *Xia Lou, please meet me in the garden by the rocks.* Her hand went to her throat. She looked at Robert, who was looking rather grim.

"He wants to talk to me in the garden at the rockery. Will you take me, please?" She begged him with her eyes, and he sighed. She looked around for Tigran but could not see him over the press of dancers. Rising, she took Robert's hand and led him into the garden, its darkness punctuated here and there by pools of light from firebrands.

"Kitt," he said in the darkness, "I will not do this again, you understand. I cannot betray Tigran, much as I love you. Do not ask this of me ever again please."

Charlotte kissed Robert on the cheek and nodded. Yes, it was not fair to put Robert in this matter.

Robert took her to the bench at the edge of the rockery garden and waited. When he saw Zhen approach, he left quickly by a side path.

Zhen came up to her, and she rose. He stopped in front of her, and she looked up into his face. She could hardly make out his eyes in the flickering light, but she felt them on her. Charlotte wanted to cry, was barely in control of herself. His physical presence was so powerful she was trembling. Zhen took her hand and led her into the deep darkness of the rockery. Without a word, he took her into his arms and dropped his lips to hers. They were again in the old orchard, the magic of that first kiss as great now as then. She coiled her arms round his neck and head. He lifted her again as before and worked the same alchemy. Charlotte began to cry, pulling her lips from his, looking into his eyes, then, unable to bear even this tiny separation, kissing him again, tears running down her cheeks, sobbing against his lips. Zhen kissed and kissed her until he felt her tears and his own tremblings subside. Then he released her to the ground.

He led her to a seat where the light of a distant flame made grotesque shadows on the strange rocks. The high-pitched strains of the Chinese band came faintly from the house, and a querulous voice was raised in song.

"Zhen, I am married. I have no right ..." she began hoarsely.

Zhen put a finger to her lips, then took her hand.

"You live with another man, for the moment. When I think of this, my mind is like a raging wind. You understand, Xia Lou. Always I try not to think of this because must be this way now, at this time. But listen, *xiao baobei*. This is like a ... tree falling in the river, only others put this tree in the water, not us. The river flows on, quietly seeking ways around, under, but it cannot ever stop. Eventually the wood will move, or rot and the river will open out, free again. You are married to me."

Zhen put his hands in her hair and moved her face to his and kissed her again, murmuring against her cheek, her lips. "You understand, Xia Lou, you are married to me. You are the wife of my heart. Nothing can ever change that, I told you. I write this many times to you."

Charlotte sank against his shoulder. Why was he always so sure, so able to convince her with these extraordinarily jesuitical arguments? How she had missed him!

"Zhen, I have a son. Soon there will be another child. I have responsibilities," she protested feebly. Charlotte was not sure what he would do if he knew that Alexander was his own son. She did not dare tell him.

Then his words began to sink in. He had mentioned letters. More than one. "You wrote to me?" she said quietly. "I never received a letter. I waited so long. I would have given anything to receive a word from you."

He put a hand into his coat and drew out the paper, folded now and yellowing slightly. Charlotte looked at the letter in his hands, remembering that terrible morning, his anger and distress.

"The day you went away I thought I would die, but your letter saved me," he confessed. He opened the paper and read, not the Chinese, but a translation made long ago into English:

Journeying is hard,
Journeying is hard,
There are many turnings.
Which am I to follow?
I will mount a long wind some day and break the heavy waves
And set my cloudy sail straight and bridge the deep, deep sea.

Zhen folded the letter.

"This is poem by Li Bai, Chinese poet. I did not know how you knew this poem, but it saved my heart. Then I know I have to write to you. Words can save us from this awful thing. So I write a lot. I sent the letters to this Mah Nuk house through Chinese merchant. I write in Chinese at first, then later in English. My English very good now, no?"

He looked down at her, his pride boyish and charming. She smiled and brought his face down to hers again, kissing him, his soft full lips, his cheek, letting her tongue linger on the corner of his mouth. He smiled too, letting her love him, holding her tight against him, his hand in her hair.

Charlotte remembered now about the letter she had given him. She had gone to Qian, Zhen's greatest friend, and begged him to find some words which would give Zhen solace after she was gone. Nothing she could write in English would make any difference. Qian had tried to explain the poem he had copied for her, but she had not understood. Now she was grateful to him for his deep understanding of his friend. But more than this, she began to wonder about the many letters Zhen had written to her. Her face grew serious, and suspicions began to enter her mind.

Zhen put his cheek against her hair, filled with gratitude for this moment, remembering the day she had left; it still felt like a stab in his heart. When the brig had swung on the wind towards the south, he had raced along the beachside at Telok Ayer. The inhabitants had gaped at the extraordinary sight of a Chinese man running at full tilt.

He had passed the temple and the houses and the fishing boats pulled up along the shore. Sweating, he had climbed up the steep path to the top of Mount Wallich. Hot and wretched, he had pulled off his jacket, needing the high, cool air on his fevered body.

From here, the view opened out: the red-roofed town at his feet, the sapphire sea, the green islands. He saw the black brig and sank to his knees, watching until it disappeared. Groups of Malays who had been resting there gathered their belongings and fled. Then he had let his anguish and his anger show, pacing back and forth, punching the trees, hurling his misery to the wind. Zhen knew he must get this unbearable emotion out now, for soon he would have to return, impassive and calm, to his new family and his place in society. When he needed that release he had always come here.

> A gale goes ruffling down the stream
> The giants of the forest crack
> My thoughts are bitter—black as death—
> For she, my summer, comes not back.

He had been bitter and black, and he knew he had been cold to his wife. But there was nothing he could do about it. He had thrown himself into commerce and medicine, worked longer than anyone. He had slept in the house in Circular Road, in the bed where he had first made love to her, and waited to hear from her. He never went again to the old spice orchard at the foot of Bukit Larangan, so filled with memories of them. He was grateful for Qian, his true friend, to whom he talked of her, with whom he wrote the letters in English. Qian, he knew, wished he would try to forget for his peace of mind, but it was simply not possible.

"Charlotte, where are you?"

A voice came out of the darkness. It was Robert, calling her to go back. She looked at Zhen, her eyes wide. Zhen, too, stiffened.

"You stay in Singapore. Do not go away. I find you again," he commanded. He rose with her in his arms, kissing her again, wanting her promise. Charlotte nodded, breathing in the scent of him, feeling his hard body under his clothes, tasting him on her lips. The time without him might not have existed.

Zhen released her, turned and disappeared into the darkness of the garden. Charlotte called to Robert, and he shook his head at her mussed condition.

She sat on the bench, attempting to calm her pulse and the flutterings of tension in her stomach. Leaving him, even for this moment, even knowing they would meet again, was hard. She took a mirror and comb from her bag and tried to refashion her hair. Her hands were trembling so much she dropped her comb, and Robert, sighing, picked it up and sat with her until she had brought herself under control.

When she returned, she looked for Tigran and told him she felt very tired. Actually she *was* tired, with the pregnancy, but also with the emotion of this encounter, these last few days of upheaval.

Soon, they made their farewells and left. As she went to her room, she asked Tigran to excuse her: tonight she needed her rest and would like to be alone.

Tigran put his arms around her, wanting her kiss. She put her lips to his briefly and then turned. He frowned but made no objection. He knew she had not wanted this pregnancy, and he occasionally felt a little guilty at coming to her as he had at the river. As he turned to leave her for the night, her maid arrived, and she closed her door.

24

George went through the huge double doors of the house into the hall. He was in a very bad temper. He had written notes to Takouhi, and she had answered none. Three days with no reply, but he had been patient. He had wanted everyone to have a chance to get over the shock, to settle Maria into her new home. Now he had just been stopped as he crossed the threshold of this house he had built for Takouhi and asked to present his card. He pushed the servant away and walked inside. He stood in the middle of the hall and called her name loudly. "Takouhi!"

His voice reverberated around the circle of the hall, and he, momentarily and oddly, thought what a fine job he had done on this house. Sound rang out as in a concert hall. Then he called her again, louder, more angrily. "Takouhi, come out. I want to talk to you. If you hide, I will find you and I shall turn this house upside down to do it!"

He started towards the stairs, now in a small fury, but he stopped as the door to what had been their bedroom opened and she came out onto the landing and stood looking down at him.

His heart quieted; his anger dissipated. She had this effect on him. She radiated a calm beauty, like an aura, as if surrounded by light. He smiled up at her, an old thrill coursing. "Come down, my lovely. I must talk to you."

Takouhi did not move.

"Don't make me come up there, I warn you, Takouhi." He climbed two steps and saw her start. He smiled. "You are not safe on that floor, outside that room, for if I come there it will be to take what is mine, I assure you." He moved up two more steps, and she came forward and started to descend.

He moved back to the hall and waited as she swept past him, not looking at him, and went into the sitting room. He inhaled, with a sublime pleasure, the clean and heady scent of her, the perfume of jasmine which she always wore, on her skin, in her hair.

She turned to face him as he shut the door. "Take what is yours? Nothing to take in this house."

George could see her trembling. He had, perhaps, chosen the wrong words. He knew all of Takouhi's past, her treatment at the hands of the Dutch pig. Any suggestion of ownership made her sink into a deep stubbornness which even he could not move. Ah, but she was so lovely. She had aged a little; he could see it around her eyes, on her neck, but the difference in their ages had never meant anything to him. She had moved his heart, his body and his soul, and nothing had ever changed that. He wanted her now in his arms, but he stood, instead, behind a chair of green damask silk, leaving a space between them, giving her time to find her temper.

"You may not be angry at me any more. At first, I understand, there was a shock. I had no idea you had come back to Singapore. But now, that is enough. I had a full expectation that I would never see you again."

He moved round the chair, and she took a small step backwards, but he paid no attention. He took both her hands in his and put them to his lips. "Takouhi, how much I longed to see you. How far away you were."

Takouhi felt her heart soften, as it always did when George touched her. She looked at his face, his hair, unruly, falling to his shoulders, a little greyer now, but it looked well on him. He had never been conventionally handsome, but his face was that of a man, strong and well made, and his eyes, green eyes like she had never seen before, were filled with the spirit of a land far beyond her comprehension. These still had the power to shake her. The minute she had seen him on the shore, she noticed he had lost some weight, looked lean and strong—younger somehow. She had recently become aware of the passing years on her skin. She was always acutely aware of the difference in age, more than ten years, between herself and George. Now he had a wife half his age. Perhaps this contributed in some measure to his youthful appearance.

She pulled her hands from his and moved to the long, yellow silk sofa under the window. He watched her walk. She was dressed today in Javanese costume, gauzy and tight, outlining her body, the swish of her sarong sounding around her ankles. He liked to watch her walk, like a reed in water. He saw the outline of brown henna on her feet, vines and flowers rising around her ankles and disappearing under the sarong. She had anticipated his coming. He knew there would be henna too on her body, around her hips and waist, rising on her breasts. Making love to her was always like sipping at a spring filled with waving fronds or ravishing a nymph. In Europe, it was sometimes hard to remember the exquisite grace of Eastern women. All her exotic beauty was still as fresh for him as it had been twenty years before. The upward turn of her dark eyes, like an Egyptian queen, the full lips, so kissable, her supple slenderness. He walked over to her and made to put his hand round her waist. Suddenly, he could not wait to feel her against him. She sat so abruptly, though, that he found himself grasping at air.

He sat next to her and smiled. "Is it games you want to play, Takouhi?" He reached for her, putting his hand to her back, leaning her breasts against him, putting his face close to hers, waiting for her to close the tiny space between their lips. "Kiss me, my love."

Takouhi closed her eyes and moved her lips to his. She could not resist him; he was a force, like the wind. All the years flew away and they were once again in the garden of her house in Nordwijk, where he had kissed her for the first time.

There had been few men in her life after Pieter. She had taken lovers occasionally from amongst her servants. A Balinese, one of her guards, a Javanese musician from her *gamelan* orchestra. Others now and again. She had been courted by the English officers and the Dutch merchants for her beauty and wealth, but took little interest in them.

One day, George had looked up from some plans he was discussing with her father, looked up with his green eyes and stopped talking, abruptly, as if Aphrodite herself had stepped off a cloud and walked into the room, and he had stolen her breath and quickly her will. Without the least expectation she, who had been sure of her mind, her poise, had been thrown off balance by his devilish looks, his Irish charm, his total disregard of their differences in anything, his instant and overpowering passion for her. She had been sure there would never be children. What Pieter had done to her when she was very young had ruined her in some way inside, his evil infecting her from beyond the grave. She would not marry George, though he had asked her, but to not be with him had become instantly impossible.

Meeting Takouhi had ignited a deep ambition in him, an ambition for success and wealth. He wanted none of her money, he simply wanted her; she gave him peace and pleasure and the courage and space to be bold. When he had heard of Singapore, of the establishment of this new place where there was nothing and which offered opportunities beyond his dreams, he had sought out Raffles and built Maxwell's house, now the Court House, to impress him. Raffles had trusted him with the construction of the town, and George had done it all. He had built Singapore and turned her into the Queen of the British East. Takouhi had been at his side every step of the way.

He released her now from the kiss, and she put her head on his shoulder. All her shock and anger had evaporated. "I am sorry, George. I take Meda from you," she said.

He let her go suddenly and rose. This act, this death, stood between them like a wall. "Yes, it was a wicked thing to do to us both. Did she ask for me?" He stood, looking down at her. "No, don't tell me," he said. "I cannot bear it, to think of her wanting—"

He began to pace the room.

"I could not forgive you, Takouhi, for a very long time," he said, his voice hard.

Takouhi rose and put her hand on his arm, stopped the pacing. "She die very peacefully, George, in my arms. We talk of you and she say—" Takouhi's face crumpled, and tears fell on her cheeks. She could not continue, but in a moment drew a great breath as she saw George's face. She put her hand to her mouth and patted her lips, anxious. "She say, tell Daddy 'I love you,' and then she go to sleep."

George let out a cry from the bottom of his soul, a loud, heart-rending sound of anguish, like an animal's wounded cry. He pulled Takouhi into him, crushing her against him. "Dear Lord in heaven, I loved her, that darling girl. I could not hold her as she went. Ah, Takouhi, that was cruel indeed."

"I know. Oh, George, I am so sorry. I think that Jawa will cure her."

They both stopped talking and cried, holding each other, as they should have done at Meda's bedside. George ran his fingers into Takouhi's hair and she clung to him as to a rock in a stormy sea until gradually, slowly, their emotion subsided.

"I have carried that around inside me these years away from you." George pulled her head away from his shoulder and looked into her eyes. "You never talk to me of leaving again, you understand." He shook her head, his hands wound tightly in her hair. "You understand, Takouhi?"

She nodded, acknowledging her fault and the frightful culpability she had borne.

They sat, finally, side by side on the long yellow sofa and he began to tell her of his years in Europe: the pointless, driven travels from capital to capital, each more empty than the last. Hating her and missing her, thinking incessantly of Meda, breaking down at insane moments just when he thought he was recovered. He had gone back to Ireland and found it was cold and no longer a home. Then, when he had almost decided to come back to Singapore, he had called on a very old friend and met this girl, Maria, the old man's daughter. He had married the girl as a promise to a dying man and because he had been filled with anger and hopelessness.

He turned and took Takouhi's hand. He looked at the Claddagh ring which she had moved to her right hand in jealousy and anger, not yet quite resolute enough to remove it entirely. Tutting at her, he shook his head, looked up and smiled. Then he took the ring and put it back onto her left hand, the heart towards hers.

"She stopped the thoughts. She's young and filled with adoration for me. I admit it was a way to forget. She looked at me with fresh and tender eyes, and I suppose I basked in that. I am a man, after all, and a bit of an old Irish fool. I had no idea of ever seeing you again, even of wanting to see you again. A new kind of life, I thought—that's the very thing to chase out apathy, make me want to live again."

Takouhi had put her hand to his cheek. She understood everything. Every ounce of annoyance and jealousy had drained away. He had survived, and this young woman had helped him to survive. She kissed him gently and put her head on his shoulder, and he pulled her against him. "What's to become of this I don't know, darling girl, but you must stay here, that is all," he told her.

Takouhi nodded.

Takouhi had shown Charlotte the invitation days ago. Mr and Mrs Tigran Manouk and Miss Takouhi Manouk were cordially invited to dinner at the residence of Mr and Mrs George Coleman. Takouhi had shaken her head. George had left her arms and her bed only the evening before, for this discovery of each other had brought a renewal of passions which were as powerful as when they were much younger. Perhaps more so, tinged as they were with bitter-sweetness and intensity.

"I cannot go. Can George even know of it?"

Charlotte had taken the invitation and stared at it, hardly taking it in. A short hour ago, he had gone for a walk along Hill Street, over Coleman Bridge and onto Boat Quay and passed the Tan godown, hoping to see Zhen. Tigran was away, negotiating the leases on several properties in the town. He had recently talked to her of this, but she had hardly taken it in. Talks with Robert and the Armenian merchants had convinced him of the potential for growth here. The new steamers, he was certain, would only add to Singapore's prosperity. With Hong Kong established off the China coast, this port would be a vital coaling link in the chain of English trade which, he could see, was circling the world.

Zhen had sent a note to her by a young Chinese boy, asking her to come to him at his house at Circular Road. Since then, she had been in a state of emotional upheaval. Now this walk had calmed her, and when she saw him, she stopped to greet him and smile. He understood. They hardly exchanged two words, but she drank him in with her eyes, every inch of his body, in anticipation.

Now Charlotte put these thoughts aside and looked again at the card which Takouhi was shaking in agitation. Of course, Takouhi could not go to this dinner, but Tigran and Charlotte must attend. Charlotte paid attention now and nodded. She, too, was not sure if George liked this idea, but how could he refuse? After a week, it was natural that his friends should be invited to see his new wife.

Tigran had returned, pleased with his day's business. He went up to the bedroom and found Charlotte at her toilette. As the maid powdered and dressed her, he talked to her of the new houses he had bought on Queen Street. One, in particular, built after one of George's designs, was very fine. Perhaps Charlotte would like to furnish it, for it could be their house here in Singapore. Really, this was an interesting town, with such potential. The new law on land leases outside the town was encouraging. Now that perpetual land holdings had been granted, he had almost decided to buy a large property at Tanglin or Claymore, or perhaps out near Robert at Katong.

As he chatted, Charlotte's maid finished putting the final touches to her hair. Tigran stopped talking, signalled the maid to leave, and came to her, standing behind her chair and looking in the mirror. He thought she looked radiant, her skin a rose blush against her black hair, and he stooped and put his lips to her neck. They had not made love recently. She had been unwell with the pregnancy and tired since she had come to Singapore. As she rose, he turned her to face him.

"Tigran," she began, but he cut her off, putting his lips to hers. As he felt her respond, almost against her will, he wished they did not have to leave this room tonight. When he released her, she sank again to her chair, chiding him playfully for messing her. He smiled, for he could see that she was in good humour and hoped that the evening would end with them in each other's arms.

George owned three houses in Coleman Street. No. 1 was leased by the Reverend White, pastor of Saint Andrews. His former home, No. 3, was directly opposite Tir Uaidhne, a much larger, handsome building with bayed verandahs, standing in great grounds. When he had left, he had leased it to Gaston Dutronquoy, who had turned it into the Hotel London. Charlotte had asked George what he felt about No. 3 being turned into a commercial establishment with, of all things, a skittles alley. He had merely smiled and shrugged his shoulders.

"It is not important anymore," he had replied. "I plan to build a villa, a great villa in the Italianate style, out on Duxton Plain."

The house between, No. 2, was his new home. As they arrived, Charlotte could see that it had been completely refurbished, with many new additions. It seemed that Maria and George must have sought out the antiquities of England and Europe, for there were statues by John

226

Gibson and Giovanni Benzoni, alongside the items George had placed in storage. Charlotte always thought George's eclectic personality was amply and openly displayed in his choice of art. Statues of Psyche were his favourite: Psyche with Dove, with Cupid; then the Bacchante; but also busts of Augustus and Raphael. George had always been a generous man, and she could see, in the new vases and hangings, that he had indulged his wife. It spoke of a happiness which he must have found with her, at least until his arrival on these shores. Perhaps, thought Charlotte, with a small sense of unease, they should not have come back.

George was not in the hall when they arrived, but Maria came out, fanning herself. It was a humid night, and for a newly arrived young lady from England's temperate climes who was fully eight months pregnant at least, the climate, Charlotte could see, was a trial. She had a delicate lace handkerchief with which she attempted discreetly to dab her forehead and cheeks. Nevertheless, she put on a brave face and greeted her guests with smiles.

"Welcome, dear Charlotte and Tigran. I am so happy to meet you finally."

Charlotte embraced her, could feel her discomfort, and felt a great sympathy for her. Her first child, in such a heat! Charlotte's mind went immediately to the cool hills of Buitenzorg and Tigran's comforting and adoring attentions. After Tigran had bowed over Maria's hand, Charlotte put her hand in his and he looked down at her with a small, crooked smile of pleasure and they passed into the sitting room.

Several acquaintances were there, among them the Churches and the Whites, John and Billy, more than twenty couples. Charlotte thought of the work this young woman had had to do to put together such an event so soon after her arrival on these shores.

George was talking to a crowd gathered round him, and as she drew near, Charlotte realised to her consternation that he had been drinking. Generally when he had downed a few porters or whiskies, he became quite gay, and his Irish accent became even stronger, but that was usually when the evening was far advanced. Now Maria went and spoke to him. He turned as she came, and now looked up and came forward to greet Charlotte.

"My lovely Kitt," he said and bowed extravagantly over her hand.

Robert came up to his sister, greeting them all. George went back to the group, and Charlotte turned to Robert.

"What's going on, Robbie? George is half-drunk, and it is not yet half-past seven."

Robert shrugged, Tigran frowned, and Charlotte bit her lip.

At dinner, George poured wine, toasting and thanking his friends and recounting tall tales of the decadent European gentry. The meal was extravagant, with soups, meats, fowls, curried vegetables, puddings and fruits. At the end, George rose, taking Maria's hand and kissing it.

"A toast, ladies and gentlemen, to my lovely young wife."

Maria, Charlotte could see, was a little bewildered at his mildly sarcastic tone, and she flushed, but he put her hand to his lips in gallant manner and bowed to her. She flushed more deeply and gazed at him with eyes of such evident adoration that Charlotte had to look down, ashamed that at least half the guests in this room knew that George had renewed his acquaintance on one level or another with his former mistress.

After dinner, the band struck up, and the dancing began. Charlotte urged Tigran to waltz with some of the ladies, for she, too, was beginning to feel tired and a little short of breath. The pregnancy was beginning to take a toll on her in the night heat. She joined Maria on the verandah, where the *punkah* moved the air into some semblance of coolness.

Maria turned to Charlotte. "I am so very happy you have come. I hope we shall be friends."

Charlotte smiled at her, and Maria took her hand.

"You are George's friend. He told me about you and Robert. Now you are married to Mr Manouk. He is older than you—forgive me for being so forward—much as George is older than I. Are you happy, Charlotte?"

Charlotte was taken aback at this directness. "Yes, of course, Maria. Perfectly happy." And she was, wasn't she? Perfectly happy with Tigran? But for this one thing, this one man.

The conversation made her uncomfortable. She made to rise, but Maria held on to her hand.

"Forgive me. Sometimes I am too direct, my sisters have often told me. But you and I are the same age, almost. I am twenty-one. And Charlotte, oh forgive me again, but I am bursting to tell you, his friend, my soon-to-be friend, I hope. I love him so very much. He is every good thing."

Maria dropped Charlotte's hand and put hers to her belly with utmost tenderness. "I am to have his child. Nothing could be more wonderful. I long so for it to be a boy. To see his pleasure. When I first met him in Europe, he looked older, careworn. My father told me that the marriage had been arranged, but I was not sure if I could love him. But his life with me has rejuvenated him, I can see it. I have done that, and this child will do it even more."

Maria stood, smiling, and Charlotte rose with her, and they went back to the hall. Maria turned and kissed her suddenly on the cheek. Then she joined George, who was standing with Robert, and put her arm through his. He was tipsy, but happily so now, the mood of intensity passed.

Charlotte signalled to Tigran and said good night to them all. She was relieved to go: this little pantomime of deception was one which made her more than uncomfortable, since through it, her own duplicity was held up to her eyes as in a mirror.

That night she did not want to dream or think. They climbed the stairs, and Tigran took her hand to kiss it good night, for Charlotte, he thought, looked pale and worn out by the heat. But she opened the door and pulled him inside, and he smiled his crooked smile.

25

Two days later, Charlotte walked to the house in Circular Road. He was standing in the door next to the shop. As he saw her approach, he came to her and led her quickly inside, bolting the door. It was quiet and dark.

"There is no one here," he said. "We are alone."

She raised her arms and put them round his neck, and he kissed her—this time gently, without hurry, savouring her lips, lingering on her neck.

Then he took her hand, and they went up the stairs to the bedroom, the way they had three years before. In the bedroom, she sat on the stool looking around. The room was exactly as she remembered it: the black iron bed with its sensuous and delicate curves, the mirrored cupboard, the very stool on which he had sat, holding her, and put his lips to her skin for the first time.

Zhen lit some candles and put them before the mirror of the cupboard, and she smiled, recalling the cups and the red thread connecting them, the rice wine and the vows he had made, wedding them. He took out the same cups now. She took one in her hand. He poured them some rice wine. She kept her gaze on his dark eyes as they both drank. Then, standing, she took off her short cloak. Under this, concealed, lay the necklace of intricate red threads and the single pearl that he had given her.

When he saw it, he came to her, running his fingers through her hair, pulling her head back, dropping his lips to the soft hollow of her neck, taking the pearl into his mouth, kissing the skin where it lay. She sighed a deep sigh. His touch was possessive, brooked only surrender, and she was always aroused by it. She wanted her lips on his skin and quickly undid the toggles on his jacket, this time not slowly as she had done their first time together, but quickly, laying her lips onto the face of Guan Di, the Chinese god of war, red, black and blue, tattooed on his hard chest, kissing him there and running her hands up his perfect body, pulling him into her. Then, suddenly, neither could wait and he swept her onto the bed.

Charlotte lay back, letting her mind drift, letting him take charge of her body, do anything he wanted. He would take her to the place, that place they could only reach together.

Afterwards, as they lay naked, he ran his hand over her belly, the little bump of her child, which she was just beginning to show. Charlotte looked up at the circlet of metal which held the netting of the bed and listened to the distant sounds of the street.

"I would like this to be my child," he said quietly, kissing the bump and laying his cheek gently on her belly.

Charlotte closed her eyes. What should she say? What should she tell him? She ran her hands into his hair, which, in their wildness, had come loose from its plait. He moved his head into her arms against her breasts. She felt his breath against her skin.

"What would you do if it were? What would it change?" she said.

He looked up at her, putting his hand to her head and pulling her lips against his. Charlotte moved her head back, took his face in her hands.

"What would it change?"

"You would come here," he said, his eyes dark and narrowing slightly. "You would come here and be mine."

Charlotte moved out of his arms and sat against the head of the bed. He moved, too, straddling her legs.

"Come here and be mine," he said and brought her face to his, kissing her fiercely, then taking in his arms. She felt him grow erect against her belly, ready for her again. She pulled away. He rose to his knees, looking down at her and taking his penis in his hand.

"This is me, my body; this belongs to you. You belong to me."

She looked up and saw the look on his face, impassive, implacable, felt his will to rule her with desire. She stiffened.

231

"This changes nothing, Zhen. I cannot stay here. We cannot be together."

She shook his hand from her hair and moved off the bed. With a leap as quick as a panther he confronted her, took her by the arms.

"Then why come to me? If this changes nothing, why come? When you leave today, I shall be half mad again. Do nothing but wait for you again. How long can we do this?"

Charlotte felt her temper rise, angry at being constrained, at his hands hurting her. She tried to pull free, and he released her and fell to his knees, pulling her body against his face.

"I cannot be half mad again and again," he groaned.

Her anger fell away. "No, we cannot be half mad again and again. But this baby is my husband's child. What can I do? Shall I not come to you?" Even as she said it, it was unthinkable. What am I doing? she thought.

He tightened his arms, desperate now that she should not leave angry, fearful she would not come again. Then, rising, he lifted her once more to the bed.

When she returned, she found the house empty. Glad of the silence, she went to her room and slept. She wanted to dream of Zhen. When she woke, Tigran was at her bedside, and she started. She felt he had been sitting there for some time. He did that occasionally, watched her sleeping, she knew. She had chided him for it.

He moved onto the bed and took her hand. "You are tired, my darling Charlotte," he said, his voice full of concern. "I am sorry for it, but I must leave for home. Will you come or stay?"

"What is it, Tigran? What has happened?" she said, waking fully.

"Miriam's husband, Josef, is very sick, maybe dying. I must go back and help her. Takouhi will not come. Charlotte, I worry for her. She is adamant she must stay until George is ready. When that will be, the Lord only knows."

Charlotte moved into Tigran's arms. She felt his concern for both his sisters. She knew she should go with him, but she could not bring herself yet to leave Zhen. She looked down, ashamed of this feeling and, at the same time, flushed with excitement at the thought of this freedom. Just a few weeks with Zhen and then she would be stronger, able to be sensible; she was certain of it.

"I will stay, Tigran, for Takouhi may need me. George's child will be born in just a few weeks."

She did not look at him, spoke against his chest, in his arms. She felt them hold her more strongly. Then he made to release her, but she held on to him. Tigran put his hand to her hair.

"I love you, my darling. I will come back as soon as possible. Will you be well?"

Charlotte looked up and nodded. He put his lips to hers and pulled her into a deep, soft kiss. She returned it, guiltily grateful. He did not want to leave her, but it was his duty to Miriam. The letter he had received, he told her, spoke of Miriam's distress. She had begged him to come. Josef was succumbing to a grinding, painful illness. The doctors could not say what it was. Tigran must come: Nicolaus was far away, trading in the Moluccas, unreachable. Miriam was fragile, so long dominated by her husband, Tigran knew, that she could not cope. She needed a man, her brother. He had to go, though everything in his heart told him to stay.

The *Queen of the South* was being made ready, it would leave within the hour, he told her.

26

Charlotte would later recall the month of December 1843 as the strangest month of her life. Perhaps it was the rains of the monsoon, which thundered down for hours every afternoon, blotting all other sight and sound, muting reality. She felt as if she was moving under the water, dreamlike, amongst the swirling violence of the swollen river, the lashing boom of the sea and the boggy mud of the roads. Torrents gushed and growled off the roof tiles, closing the eyes of the windows in a stream, darkening the house like night.

She longed for the real night when she could meet Zhen under cover of darkness. It was always the same. They fell into each other's arms, impatient to touch. Then they would argue about where their actions were leading. Then one or other would be sorry, abject, fearful, and it would begin again—making love, kissing and kissing, dreading the separation that must take place. It was wonderful and a kind of hell, but above all, it was imperious.

George and Takouhi, too, had simply fallen under a spell. Unable to stay away, George came every afternoon to her at Tir Uaidhne, and they locked themselves away. Often, in the evening, when the rain had stopped and the stars shone with dewy brilliance, they went to the cupolas on the hill. What he said to his wife, Charlotte could not imagine. But she did not want to think about that, about anything, except making love to Zhen. This passion for him drove her, defined her day. When she left him, she fretted, watching the rain, until they were together again. When she found herself together with Takouhi, neither woman hardly spoke, so wrapped up in worlds of their own were they.

Christmas came and went. Charlotte and Takouhi went to lunch with the da Souza family at their mansion along the road at River Valley. Robert and Teresa seemed to have come to some arrangement, though Charlotte could not make it out. She had not spoken to Robert of Shilah since the day Tigran had left, but there was suddenly talk of an engagement. Charlotte looked at Robert and could simply not take it in. She was meeting Zhen the next day, and this interminable wait occupied her mind.

That morning, as Charlotte lay in her room, she heard a violent commotion downstairs. She went to the door, glancing along the landing to Takouhi's room. The door was shut, and Charlotte knew George was inside.

She looked over the banister and saw Billy Napier standing in the hallway, agitated, bouncing from foot to foot. He was red-faced and furious.

"By all that's holy, George Drumgold Coleman, you should be ashamed of yourself." He hurled the words ferociously up the stairs.

The door on the landing opened, and George emerged, half-dressed, throwing on a shirt. "What's all the commotion, Billy?" he said, looking down.

"Shame on you, mon, lying here with your—" Billy stopped, flustered. "Your sweet wee wife's in labour, for heaven's sake, George. Get yourself home."

George continued to look down at his friend's angry face as if he hardly recognised him. Then Takouhi came to his side, clad in a loose gown and whispered to him. As if brought to consciousness, he called down to Billy.

"Very well, Billy. I'm coming. Call Dr Oxley or Dr Little."

"All done, no thanks to you." Billy practically spat the words out, then turned on his heel and strutted from the house.

George looked along the landing at Charlotte.

"It seems I have offended Royal Billy." He put his hand to Takouhi's waist and pulled her tight against his chest. She melted into him, winding her arm round his neck, and he kissed her as if they were lovers of twenty, unashamed. Charlotte looked away, sure she too would want Zhen this way still when she was their age. Then George went down the stairs. His son was born the next day, December 27th. And everything began to change.

A week later, Charlotte and Robert went to see the little boy, George's little boy. The birth had been difficult, and Maria had taken some time to recover. George greeted them downstairs, diffident. Billy was seated in one of the armchairs, and it was clear that there had been a row. George accompanied them upstairs and opened the door to his wife's room. He went to her, telling her of her visitors, kissed her hand and left. Charlotte saw that he seemed utterly uninterested in this little baby, in his wife. She felt a pang of guilt, feeling somehow complicit in this indifference.

Maria lay, thin and pale, in the bed, the infant in her arms. This young girl had arrived young and very pregnant in this strange place and she, Charlotte, had left her utterly alone, though Maria was married to a man she loved dearly, though she had sought Charlotte's friendship. Charlotte realised she had no idea how this girl had coped for the last month and felt a flush of shame. She went up to Maria, kissed her cheek and looked at the tiny creature. He was still a little wrinkled and red, but she could see immediately that he looked like George.

She smiled at Maria. "Oh Maria, he is the very likeness of George."

Robert came forward to look too. He had seen more of Maria, for Teresa Crane had formed a friendship with her. Robert had tried to speak to Charlotte, but it was as if she was made of air; his words passed through her. He was concerned at her self-absorption, knew it was connected to Zhen, but his life involved a constant battle against the marauding gangs of Chinese which attacked the Kling moneylenders almost nightly or burgled the houses in Kampong Glam.

To the consternation of both brother and sister, a tear slipped down Maria's cheek, and she began to cry very softly.

"George does not come to see the baby, will not hold him," she said, so plaintively that Charlotte felt a lump in her throat. "What is wrong? Charlotte, you know him better than me. What is wrong?"

Charlotte had no idea how to respond. Robert was hanging back, looking uncomfortable. Before she could speak, Maria began again.

"I want to be a good wife, but since we have come to Singapore, it is as if I married a different man. I never see him. I thought, after the baby

236

is born, it will be well, but it is worse."

She began to sob and clutch the baby to her, and Charlotte, worried, rose and took the child, laying him in the crib at the bedside. He was fast asleep, his little lips pursing, and suddenly she remembered Alexander. She had not seen him for months, had not even thought of him. This passion for Zhen had taken over her life.

She motioned Robert to leave and, relieved, he said good-bye to Maria. Charlotte sat at Maria's bedside.

"I am sorry, Maria, that I have been so neglectful of you. I want us to be friends. I will speak to George. Perhaps it is the strangeness, the newness, of this situation. A new wife, a new child. He is an older man; it is a big change."

Maria was clutching her hand, but she had stopped crying and now, to Charlotte's embarrassment, threw her arms around her and hugged her. "Oh, yes, yes, please, Charlotte. I want to be friends. I thought you did not like me. I have seen so little of George's friends, so little of him. I have been so lonely. Please talk to him." Having said this, Maria sat back, releasing her and took up Charlotte's hand again.

"I love him so much, Charlotte. He is my life now. My family are dead or indifferent. I have no one else. We married quickly, I know. We hardly knew each other, but in the year after we married, he was wonderful to me, so kind."

Charlotte patted Maria's hand. "Take care of your baby, Maria, and yourself. I will speak to George. And I will come every day to see you."

Maria smiled a tired smile of such gratitude that it touched Charlotte's heart. She suddenly knew that this situation could not continue. Not for George and Takouhi, not for her and Zhen. Everything was wrong. What was right lay in the crib next to the bed. This was George's future. What was right lay across the Java Sea.

She rose, kissing Maria, and called for her maid. Then she went downstairs. She found Billy, Robert and George in the drawing room, and she went up to George and took him by the hand, pulling him into the deep verandah.

"George, this has to stop," she said urgently. "I have to stop, and you have to stop."

He dropped her hand and took a cigar from his pocket, dropping into a large cane chair, stretching out his legs. He lit the cigar and looked at the smoke curling around his hand. She began to grow annoyed.

"That is your son up there, and that poor woman is miserable," Charlotte insisted.

He took another puff and blew out some smoke. The silence lengthened. Finally he looked up.

"Sit down, Kitt, and let me explain something to you."

Charlotte sat at his side and watched him, wary now.

"You are saying nothing to me that I have not heard from Billy Napier, John Connolly, the good Reverend White, your brother, all my faithful friends." He smiled wryly. "You have been remarkably absent this last month and come a little late to the party. How is your love affair with the Chinese fellow progressing? Does Tigran know?"

Charlotte flushed, astounded at the coolness of his voice. He watched her, waiting.

"I ..." she hesitated, then found her courage. "Yes, George, I am guilty too. It took your little son's face to remind me of my own. I am not proud of this. I, too, have to make an end, find a way to go home."

She turned to him. "George, that boy looks just like you. Can you not love him?"

George sat, smoking.

"Of course I can, in time. Kitt, I married Maria as a favour to her dying father, an old and esteemed friend. His estate would pass to the son, of course. The poor girl was his last daughter, his favourite, unmarried, and though she had a small bequest, he feared leaving her to the rather cold charity of her sisters. I married her because it seemed the right thing to do. It set his heart at ease. She was pretty and agreeable, and what difference did it make with Meda gone and myself full of anger at Takouhi and no hope of seeing her again. You understand."

He crushed out the cigar.

"I know Maria thinks she loves me. She is young, and I like her. She has known no other man. If I thought at all, I suppose I thought we could have a pleasant life together. All this was very well until I saw Takouhi on the shore, the parasol, the hat with the emerald feathers. Ah, lovely girl, she'd made herself a vision for my eyes. It was like seeing her for the first time at her father's house in Batavia. The same firebolt. Nothing had changed."

He rose and faced her, looking down.

"We parted once, and it almost killed me. I lost my daughter; I lost Meda, and she is gone, I cannot have her back though I would give up my soul for it. But I can have Takouhi. Did you hear yourself? You said you have to find a way to go home. You know that this Chinese man is *pro tempore*, hard to give up, perhaps, but impermanent."

George stopped and looked at her more intently, his green eyes sombre, his voice quiet. "But, you see, dear Kitt, I *am* home. There is no other for me but her. If I lose her again, I will die."

He turned to walk away, then stopped and came back to her. "I will take care of Maria and the child. When Maria is recovered, I will tell her. If she wishes it, I will seek an annulment in the Ecclesiastical Court and petition Westminster for a parliamentary divorce. It's long, it's a mess, but it is not impossible."

He smiled slightly. "I do believe Billy would like Maria for himself. What a tangle we all get into, eh?"

Then he left, and Charlotte sat, not knowing anymore what to think.

27

Baba Tan was spending the evening with his young concubine. His little son had bowed to him and been taken to bed. He was very well pleased with the cool and elegant house that had been built from George Coleman's designs for Dr Oxley's mansion at Killiney. His wife had not been difficult about the matter of the second concubine, who was a beautiful, desirable creature. She was happy to entertain family and friends in this splendid country mansion which had been filled with her purchases: French clocks, Venetian mirrors and glass, Chinese porcelain. He had supplied a sumptuous carriage for her to visit the town and go to the temple. He had bought a gold *sireh* set which she could display to the envy of her companions. His younger daughters were approaching marriage age. His two granddaughters were healthy, and it only lacked a grandson for his world to be entirely pleasing.

But he was less pleased with the news that he had been given only this morning. His second daughter, Lilin, had come to visit her mother. The story she had related was troubling in several respects. First, Tan did not like the interference of his second daughter in Zhen's business. She took much too close an interest in her sister's marriage. Her own marriage seemed to interest her not at all. She had been married for almost three months, but was still not with child. Noan, by contrast, had been pregnant in the first month of her marriage. Really, he had made a good choice in Zhen. The man was like a younger version of himself, he reflected, full of sexual vitality. He knew his duty, and two children had been safely born within two years. A son was only a matter of time.

The interference, however, on this occasion seemed somewhat

justified. Lilin had told her mother that Zhen had not slept at the house in Market Street for many weeks. Noan, she said, was upset, the more so because there was talk that Zhen had been spending time at his shophouse with a white woman. Tan would not ordinarily have been bothered about these absences from the marital bed. He knew Zhen would be back to see Noan. The second child had only been born three months ago. It did not do to exhaust his wife. He knew his business, and a son was high on the list of his priorities. However, this news of a white woman was a concern, for Tan was entirely convinced that the woman was Mrs Mah Nuk. Why Zhen could simply not take a second wife or a pretty concubine was mystifying, but he suspected it was, unfortunately, not an affair of pleasure alone, but of love.

Tan sighed. He believed he had never known love. His wife he had learned to care for. The concubines were a pleasant diversion. But love? No, he could not say he had ever loved anyone.

Tan had known Miss Xia Lou Mah Crow when she first came to Singapore. He liked her a great deal. She was, surprisingly for an *ang moh* woman, very attractive, with a willowy figure and delicate features, skin like warm white jade, beautiful eyes and long black hair. She reminded him of a painting he had seen once of the ill-fated Yang Gui Fei, the beloved imperial concubine of Xuanzong, the Tang emperor, the most beautiful woman in China, who had turned the emperor from his duties and caused the downfall of a dynasty. She was a delightful girl. When she curtsied to him, the way the young English ladies did, with her eyes down in that submissive way, it was the most charming thing. Yes, he could see that she could turn a man's head and had long suspected that Zhen was utterly smitten. Time apart had clearly not changed his son-in-law's feelings.

Tan shook his head. What was he to do with this information? Such adultery would be a scandal; it would reflect badly on him and his relations with the English merchants and the government here in Singapore. He sighed. He would have to speak to Zhen.

The next day at the godown on Boat Quay, Tan called Zhen into his office. The two men worked happily together. Zhen's medicine shop had become a very profitable business and was ably managed by his herbalist partner, a man he trusted. Zhen was thinking of opening another shop in

Kampong Glam and taking leases on some new properties there.

Zhen had recently suggested investment in the tin mines on the mainland. A marriage perhaps between Tan's third daughter and the son of the Chinese Kapitan at Perak might be fortuitous. Or there was also the son of the Kapitan at Batavia, who was also of marriageable age and, he had heard, in need of capital to expand his sugar factories. The fourth daughter, both Zhen and Tan had destined to marry the son of Inchek Sang, the richest man in Singapore, who had died and left his vast fortune to his eleven-year-old adopted child. This child was, at present, in the care of Zhen's best friend, Qian, who had married Sang's second daughter and assumed control of the business.

Zhen wanted to talk to Tan of the new steamships which he had seen in the harbour, for he saw the future of the seas in these vessels. He had taken a lease on twenty-five acres at Bukit Jagoh, on the southern side of Telok Blangah Hill. The views from this property were spectacular, the eye tumbling from the trees down over the shore and out to the smudgy islands in the vast blue sea. Zhen had never thought of having such a place. A mere four years ago he had been a penniless youth in a grim and tumbledown village in China. Singapore had given him this, and *her*, and he never wanted to leave. Of this, he did not want to talk to Tan. Here he wanted to build a house like the rich white men's houses, designed by the foreign architect. One day, he was certain, he would need this house for Xia Lou. Both she and he were barely twenty-two years old. Her husband could not live forever; he was at least twenty years older than her. It was just a matter of time.

Tan motioned Zhen to sit, and Zhen bowed to his father-in-law, this man whose name he had taken, who was like a second father. Tan liked Zhen's old-fashioned Chinese manners. He always paid him the utmost respect. That made this conversation all the more difficult. They spoke in English, for Zhen's Baba Malay had never become really proficient and Tan's Hokkien was too rudimentary.

"Something has … come to my attention," Tan began.

Zhen knew exactly what was coming and sat, silently, waiting.

"It is the matter of a woman. I have heard you are seeing a white woman." Tan looked at Zhen and decided to be straightforward. "I think you are seeing Mrs Mah Nuk. Is that true?"

242

Zhen looked Tan directly in the eye. "Yes," he said.

Tan was a little taken aback and paused. He rather envied Zhen, but was not going to say so. He took on a severe tone. "It must stop. This kind of scandal will affect our business. You can see that."

"Yes. I do see that. It will stop. She will leave soon. She will return to Batavia to have her child. Her husband will come soon, I am sure of it. When her husband comes to take her away, it will stop."

Zhen paused and narrowed his eyes very slightly. "It will stop when she goes away."

Tan sighed. He could see Zhen was adamant. There was no point in arguing.

"This news has come from second daughter. She must have heard of it from somewhere. The women never stop gossiping. You must be more discreet. Don't forget who you are." Tan raised a hand.

Zhen rose and bowed to his father-in-law. The subject was at an end. Tan was right, of course. Just as before, this had to end before there was a scandal. The second daughter had gone to her father. Zhen reflected on this woman, this sister of his wife. She was a very pretty girl. Everyone called her Lilin, which meant "candle" in Malay. She had been called that because of her white complexion. She was a spoilt brat, Zhen could see that. She had been fussed over and indulged for her looks all her life. Everyone in the house but him was a little afraid of her, for she had a ferocious temper. From the moment he had entered the Tan household, she had been trouble. At fourteen, a few days after his marriage to Noan, she had come to him and lifted her sarong, revealing herself, wanting him to touch her. Since then, she found every opportunity to be alone with him, put her hand to his body, his hair. Zhen had pushed her away from him once, held her arms, and she had almost fainted, fallen to her knees and put her face into his groin.

He avoided her wherever possible. He had hoped all this would end with her marriage, but it had not. She took no notice of her husband. Zhen was not even sure if she allowed him to have sex with her. He was a thin, shy young man, extremely clever but unassertive. Zhen knew Lilin was jealous of Noan. It was a bad situation, made worse by Tan moving out. Now only the two sisters and his children were in the house at Market Street.

Now this. Zhen shook his head. Perhaps he should suggest to Tan that Lilin and her husband go and live with her father. The house was huge. But Tan would not welcome this suggestion, he knew. Lilin's toughness, the arguments with her mother, bothered him. He had been happy to have her married, hoping this would settle her. No, Tan would not like it at all. So something else had to be done.

And then, he thought, it would be hard on Noan. Despite Lilin's nature, Noan cared for her sister. He knew he had been neglecting Noan, this woman who loved him so much, who was gently and quietly a good wife. When Xia Lou had gone, he would lie with her more often. It was not good to have her frustrated. Giving a woman sexual joy was a central tenet of the Taoist art of the bedchamber. They would make more children, have a son. He would build the house on Bukit Jagoh, and he would wait for Xia Lou to be free. His love for her, he recognised, was inalterable.

That evening he went back to the house in Market Street for dinner. When she saw him, Lilin smiled. Zhen ignored her and went through to the living room. Lilin's husband, Ah Teo, was in the sitting room, reading the English newspaper. He was, like Zhen, from a village in Fujian province, and the two men shared a common language and often talked about their families back home. Zhen had noticed him working at the godown of Bousteads, one of the big English merchants. His English was already quite good, and he knew his business. He was older than Zhen, had been in Singapore for over four years. He had travelled the region on Chinese junks, keeping the accounts, learning Malay and English, for two years before that. He had a half-brother and nephews in Cochin-China and cousins in Manila and Bangkok. He brought *guanxi* to the Tan business network in many different countries, influence with family business partners whom Tan could trust. This *guanxiwang*, a clannish network of human relations, formed the backbone of all Chinese commerce, and a marriage was the glue which kept it together. Daughters were there for this sole purpose. When the prospect of marriage into the Tan family empire had been proposed, Ah Teo had agreed immediately. Ah Teo had met Zhen's wife several times before the wedding and been taken by her quiet nature and sweet charm. She treated Zhen as if he was a god, and Zhen's daughter was a pretty and loving child. Nothing at all had prepared him for Lilin.

She was lovely, the prettiest of Tan's daughters, and when he had lifted the veil on their wedding day, he could hardly believe his good luck. Their wedding night, however, had been a disaster. Lilin would simply not let him touch her, and he had not known how to react. His experiences with women were few and usually for money. When her mother had been presented with the sheet the next morning, and seen the virgin white perfection of it, she had taken Lilin aside and given her a good talking-to. The following night, Lilin had lain back on the pillow and, unmoving, allowed him to consummate the marriage. He had not the slightest idea of what to expect from a wife and presumed that this was an activity which women of good breeding simply did not enjoy.

Zhen suspected all this, though Ah Teo had, of course, said nothing. Something had to change. He did not like to interfere in the man's private life, but if things went on like this, Lilin would never get pregnant, and without a satisfying life in the bedroom, she would never leave him alone. Zhen knew that whilst this fellow was, in almost every other respect, a perfect addition to the Tan family, he was probably not the sort of strong hand Lilin needed. Zhen was fully aware of Lilin's feelings for him. Though Ah Teo was older than Zhen, as Tan's adopted son, husband of his first daughter and his heir, he had precedence, and it was part of his duties to the family to straighten this matter out.

"Brother, can we talk?" he began.

Ah Teo put down the paper, happy to chat to Zhen, whom he liked a great deal. Zhen came right to the point, knowing that no one in the house would understand what they were saying.

"This is not a subject that I would ordinarily raise, but I feel I must say something. Father-in-law," he lied, "is concerned that your wife is not yet pregnant. You understand your duty and hers?"

Ah Teo looked startled and stared at his hands. "I ..." he stumbled, "She ..."

"Yes, I understand. Some women take a little time, but you must take charge now. It has been three months. You are the man. You must insist she fulfill her wifely duties. That includes her duties in the bedchamber."

Ah Teo looked stricken, and Zhen softened his tone. "I do not mean you should hurt her, of course. But you must take charge of the situation. If she is refusing you, you cannot accept it. You must learn to tempt her, to give her joy. If you want the *er-hu* to make beautiful music, you must learn to play it well."

Ah Teo almost gagged with embarrassment. He could not believe his brother-in-law was saying these words. He blushed to the roots of his hair and rose, shaking. When he spoke, it was with a voice filled with horror.

"This cannot be a proper subject of conversation—"

Before he could finish, Zhen rose too. "I have said what I needed to. I did not mean to shock you. The subject of making children is a proper one for me to raise. Mencius said that of all the offences to filial piety, the most serious is depriving your family of posterity. You must speak to her of this, force her obedience. Lilin is strong-willed, but you must be stronger than her. There is no other way if you are her husband."

Zhen took a package from inside his coat and handed it to Ah Teo. "This may help," he said. Zhen knew well that he was the man to tame Lilin's violent passions. He had spent years learning these arts with the fourth concubine, who was adept beyond anything these women knew. He would have exacted her obedience in one minute—no, the second he stood in front of her. He was not sure Ah Teo was up to the task, but he had to try.

Ah Teo stared at the package, and Zhen went out of the room.

Noan was in the kitchen, directing the cooking. Lilin was there too, to scold the cooks. Both women looked up as Zhen came to the doorway. Ignoring Lilin, he motioned Noan to come to him.

"I will stay tonight," he said in Baba Malay. "Are you well?"

Noan nodded, knowing his meaning, and felt her heart flutter. Tonight they would share the bed if she was not menstruating. She was feeling desperate to be with him. During the pregnancy, sex had been forbidden, and her "sitting month" had lasted two. This part she hated: being confined to her room for forty days, unable to wash her hair or bathe properly in case she got cold and upset the *qi* balance. The smell of her unwashed body, the *sireh* leaves plastered on her forehead and her ears plugged with garlic. She was glad Zhen could not see her like this.

They had slept together for only a few weeks, and there had been a long period when he had stayed away. She was dejected and worried by it. Now, though, she brightened and set about finishing his meal with a light step. She did not worry about pregnancy. She was breast feeding and, in any case, Zhen most often used his hands and mouth with her, for he had explained that the main purpose of most Taoist sexual practice was to conserve and build the *qi*. The man should give the woman many orgasms whilst retaining his semen and absorbing her sexual fluids. In this way both man and woman would be healthy and live long lives. She had quickly learned his ways, wanting to please him as he ecstatically pleased her.

Childbirth had been relatively easy. Over some mild objections by her mother, Zhen had introduced a midwife who knew the art of *zhen jiu* and *zhi ya*, and the birth had been uncomplicated and the pain tolerable. She would have liked a thousand babies by him. Only the fact of him staying away gave her pause. But he controlled this aspect of their life together and had decided ideas on bodily health. When the baby was one year old, she knew they would make another. She wanted, more than any other thing, to give him a son. She went often to the shrine of Kuan Yin, Goddess of Compassion and Childbirth, to make offerings—for a son, for Zhen's health and affection, for her parents, for a happy life—for a son.

She had heard what Lilin had said about the *ang moh* woman. She did not believe what Lilin told her and asked her to stop such talk. Her husband had every right to do as he wished. He was a man who enjoyed sex for the health of his body. Over such a long period as pregnancy, it was natural for him to seek other outlets. She did not like to think about it, but she accepted it. In an uncharacteristic outburst of temper, she had told Lilin to pay attention to her own husband. Lilin had merely scowled.

But, in truth, other women ate at Noan's mind. Their own father had a new concubine who was barely seventeen. The prospect of Zhen taking a concubine terrified Noan. She would rather he was with some white woman than bring a concubine into the house and lie with her, make children with her, three rooms away. She was always very careful not to show any jealousy or give him cause to stay away.

Lilin, too, had heard. He would be with her sister tonight. She stopped smiling.

Ah Teo opened the package. It was a book. He turned the pages and read.

> *Among the skills possessed by men, a knowledge of women is indispensable.*
> *When one has a woman, only the skilful are equal to the task.*
> *Do not be too generous, or too controlling.*
> *Do not be too taxing, nor too apprehensive.*
> *One must be slow and patient; one must be gentle and sustained ...*

Ah Teo sat down hard on the chair, amazed. It was a pillow book. He had heard of such books but never seen one. He read on.

> *This is called the art of yin and yang; the principle of male and female.*
> *If one practises this without success, the fault lies in insufficient mastery of the art.*
> *The essence of dalliance is slowness.*
> *If one proceeds slowly and patiently, the woman will be exceedingly joyful.*
> *She will adore you like a brother and love you like a parent.*
> *One who has mastered this tao deserves to be called a heavenly gentleman.*

Ah Teo had never thought of such matters before. The book was filled with pages of Taoist sexual techniques. He turned the pages quickly. At the back were drawings of men and woman in positions he had never dreamed of. How he was to transfer such knowledge to the beautiful body of his rebellious wife was a mystery.

28

Charlotte read the letter again. Tigran would be coming to Singapore to take her home. He had been away for three months. Too long, but what else could he have done? Miriam had been in great need of him. Josef had died after a very long and distressing illness, and the burial had taken place at the Tanah Abang cemetery. Miriam had been distraught, but her spirits were gradually improving. She was staying at Brieswijk for the moment; it was healthier for her than her own home. Tigran was taking care of the official business which follows any death. Then he expected to be in Singapore at the beginning of March. She must prepare herself to come back to Batavia. He missed her and loved her.

She put the letter down and looked into the mirror. One week. He would certainly be here in one week. She felt the baby suddenly move violently, churning inside, and put her hand to her belly. She was seven months pregnant and was feeling unwell. She had not seen Zhen for two nights, but that was not what was preoccupying her mind. They had both accepted the fact of her departure. They were both much calmer now.

The concern was not Zhen. It was George.

For months, Takouhi had not wanted to see Maria or the child, but finally, on an impulse, she had called. As soon as she picked up this little boy who was the very image of George, she told Charlotte, she had known that she must leave. Memories of Meda's face flooded her mind.

She had told George he must reconcile himself to this new life and family. This little son needed him. George had forbidden it: this time Takouhi was not to leave him. Charlotte had heard his raised voice, his fury. He had slammed the door and left the house. Charlotte knew from

Billy Napier that he had told Maria of his plans for divorce. Maria was beside herself, Billy had said.

George had come to Takouhi last night, and this morning she had been too tearful to come to breakfast. Charlotte had taken a tray to her.

"I must leave. But George will not allow it. The worst is over, he said. Maria knows everything. He talk about building new house for us."

Takouhi took Charlotte's hand.

"I do some bad things in my life. Maybe I lose Meda because I do bad things. I think about this many times. Maybe I bring curse on my child."

Takouhi looked down, pain etched on her face. "This baby need a father for happy life. George is wonderful father."

She burst into tears. Takouhi rarely cried, and Charlotte knew she was thinking of Meda, of his love for their daughter, of her love for George, of giving him up, doing the right thing. All these thoughts and emotions were churning inside her.

Charlotte left her, took up her hat and walked across the road to George's home.

When Maria came into the sitting room, Charlotte was taken aback at her appearance. She was stick thin and ghostly pale. Charlotte rose from her chair and went up to Maria, putting her arms around her. "I am sorry, Maria."

Maria sat on the edge of a chair shaking her head, her hands twitching nervously. "It is so unfair. What have I done to deserve this? Oh, Charlotte, he was so cruel. Out of nowhere, he tells me he is going to petition for a divorce. He does not love me. The woman he loves is across the road. My God. It is Miss Manouk, Charlotte, he has loved her his whole life. This is what he said to me. Why did he marry me?"

She looked at Charlotte, anguished. "Why in the Lord's name did he marry me?"

Charlotte knew she owed Maria an explanation. "He did not expect ever to see her again," she said gently. We did not know he had married. She wanted to leave as soon as she saw you, but George would not allow it. It is all a dreadful mess."

Charlotte told Maria of George and Takouhi's years together until the death of their daughter, about Takouhi's departure for Java. George had not been at Meda's side when she died, and Takouhi had felt guilty. She had agreed to stay until he was ready to let her go. No one was to blame for this situation.

Maria rose suddenly and began to walk backwards and forwards across the room, twisting a handkerchief in her hands.

"No one is to blame, but I am to be punished. Me and that innocent baby. Divorced!" She spat the word out. "Do you know what it means? Billy has explained it to me. I must be at fault, not he. I must be the one cited as adulterer, for only the woman can be at fault, since I am his goods and have been defiled. No blame falls to him. Though I have done nothing, these are the slanderous grounds upon which I am to be a divorced woman, the scandalous butt of everyone's jokes, condemned to a life of spinsterhood. For who would marry a divorced woman, an adulteress? And his child must perforce be a bastard, for an annulment by the church would mean we had never married. I have never heard of such a thing. Is he demented to shame me so? To ruin me? In the meantime, I must simply put up with him living openly with his half-breed whore!"

Maria's face was suffused with fury, and Charlotte rose, alarmed.

"Get out!" snapped Maria. "You are her friend. You, and everyone, knew about this and no one told me. Not even Billy, whom I trusted. It is too much! How you must all have laughed when I professed my love for him. Stupid girl, stupid girl!" She came up to Charlotte and pushed her towards the door.

"Get out, and may the Lord strike you all!"

Charlotte left, shame-faced, for Maria was right. They were all complicit in this silence.

When George came that evening to Tir Uaidhne, Takouhi would not see him.

"George," Charlotte began. "Leave her for the moment. She needs some time alone. She is deeply ashamed of what has happened. She knows a divorce will ruin Maria and cannot think what will happen to your son."

George sat, his face in his hands. "I know. I have handled this very badly. When Takouhi talked of leaving, I just saw a red mist. Not again, I thought, and just went at it like a bull in a china shop."

"George, you cannot divorce Maria. It would ruin her. And what of the child? Where would he live? Maria could not stay in Singapore with the whole town talking about her. The child would have no father. Think of it."

George rose and went towards the door. "Yes, I have to think."

Charlotte, too, knew she had to think.

That evening she went to Zhen's house. When she could come to him, she sent him a note to the godown in the afternoon. Tonight, as soon as she entered, she moved into his arms.

"My husband will arrive soon," she told Zhen. "I will be going back with him."

Zhen nodded and held her tightly. Then they went to the kitchen, and he began to make her tea. Charlotte sat at the square table and watched him moving slowly, setting out the cups, rinsing the tiny brown pottery teapot he liked to use, with a monkey lid, taking the tea from the shelf next to the Kitchen God's altar, pouring the boiling water until it bubbled frothily over the side. She watched every simple gesture. He had a grace of movement in everything he did. Not just in lovemaking or when he practised the flowing movements of the *tai chi*, but even in these small domestic chores. This grace was inside him. For a big man, he had elegant hands, and she watched them as he poured the fragrant tea which smelled of jasmine blossom. When he concentrated, he opened his eyes wider, as if his almond eyes could not quite take in the whole scene.

I love you, she thought. He sensed her eyes on him and turned his head and smiled at her. She would always wonder at the effect he had on her. He was so solid, yet so like air, so simple, yet so complex. He was filled with richness. He made her fly. She rose and floated into his arms, pulling his lips to hers, stealing his kisses.

"It is fortunate that the Kitchen God is still out of house, or he would certainly report me for such things. I do like Zhang Dan. Kissing a woman not my wife!"

He smiled as he said it. She knew he was not in the slightest bit superstitious. In his life he adopted, for his health and his body, aspects of the *Tao-chiao*, the religious school, but for his mind he followed the *Tao-chia*, the philosophical school, and especially the writings of Master Chuang. In his bedroom he had a black-and-white brush painting of the

Seven Sages in the Bamboo Grove. It had an ethereal quality. The tiny figures were seated in a misty grove, drinking, playing instruments, under the towering bamboo trees. Charlotte did not think much about art, but she liked the peaceful, other-worldly effect the painter had made, so unlike anything she had ever seen in Scotland, where paintings favoured hunting scenes and dogs holding poor dead birds in their mouths. There was writing on this painting: a poem, he said, but he could not read the old Chinese. Between lovemaking, lying in each other's arms, he had explained something of these things to her, asked her about Western philosophies. He liked the sages' playful and irreverent attitude to life, the *qing tan*, a freedom of conversation and action, a love of nature, a harmony with the universe.

She looked up above the stove now and saw that the paper effigy of the Kitchen God had disappeared. He had long ago told Charlotte about Zao Jun, the master of the stove.

Zao Jun had once been a mortal man named Zhang Dan, who was married to a virtuous woman. However, Zhang Dan fell in love with a young girl and left his wife for her. From that day, he was plagued with bad luck. He was struck blind, the young girl left him, and he had to resort to begging.

One day, while begging for alms, he came across the house of his former wife. Being blind, he did not recognise her. Despite his shoddy treatment of her, she took pity on him and invited him in, gave him a sumptuous meal and tended him lovingly. He related his story to her and began to cry. As he did so, his eyesight was miraculously restored and he recognised this benefactress as his wife. Overcome with shame, he threw himself into the kitchen hearth. His wife tried to save him, but he was consumed by the fire, and all that was left of him was his leg.

His wife lovingly created a shrine to him over the fireplace where he had died. Heaven took pity on Zhang Dan's tragic story and instead of becoming an undead Jiang Shi, the usual fate of suicides, he was made the god of the kitchen and reunited with his wife.

Still today in China, Zhen had laughed, raising his eyebrows and brandishing the fire poker, we call this Zhang Dan's leg.

Ever since, Zao Jun went annually to heaven to report on the activities of the household to the Jade Emperor. To speed him on his way, offerings of sticky rice cakes and sweets were made and firecrackers lit. A little melted sugar had been put to his lips to sweeten his words and his paper image burned. He had left a few days ago and would stay away until New Year. Charlotte could see his shrine had been cleaned by Ah Pok, Zhen's servant.

As they sipped the tea, Zhen rose briefly and took a package from the shelf. He put it in front of her. It was a box covered in black silk, closed with a Chinese toggle of scarlet cords. She opened the case and inside there was a book, a Chinese paper book which unfolded like a concertina. It had a dark blue damask silk cover, and the stitched binding was of white silk cord. She opened it and read what was written there in Chinese and English.

Union is bliss, parting is woe,
Agony is boundless for a lovelorn soul.
Sweetheart, give me word,
Trails of clouds drifting by and mountains capped with snow
Whither shall my lonesome shadow go?

As he saw her reading it, he said the words in Chinese. She opened the pages of the book. Each of the ten pages contained a poem. He sat down next to her, his arm touching hers, her head against his shoulder, and read the verses to her in Chinese as she followed the text.

"*Wa ai lu,*" she said.

"Yes, Xia Lou, *wa ai lu,*" he repeated, correcting her tones and grinning.

Smiling, she finished her tea, entwined her fingers in Zhen's and led him up the stairs to the bedroom.

29

Charlotte stood on the steps of the old Police House which had been her home. The view from here was still breathtaking, especially now as the golden evening was drawing in. The rocks in the mouth of the river had changed shape. She had remembered them as long and pointed, one rising like a swordfish from the waters which swirled with eddies and whorls like green snakes. On the opposite bank, cleared of trees and growth, she could see the place where formerly a huge red stone covered in ancient text had stood like a sentinel. She had visited this stone with George. The rock had been hewn in two, the two sides facing each other, some distance apart, but leaning in towards each other as if to whisper some age-old secret.

Their inscriptions on the interior side were faded and worn. She had run her fingers over this antique script. He had told her that many had tried to decipher their meaning but none had succeeded. The stone had stood as a mute witness to an older time. She had watched it from this verandah, changing in aspect and colour as the sun moved around the sky, a massive shadowy presence in the moonlight. It had felt like an old friend.

There was a legend about this stone in the Malay Annals. She tried to recall it. It was about a man granted great strength by a ghost of some sort. What was his name? His fame spread to the Rajah of Singhapura where he became the king's champion. He had won a contest of strength for his lord against the champion of the Rajah of Kling by lifting a mighty stone and throwing it into the mouth of the river. When this Herculean hero finally died, he had been buried here, and the admiring Kling Raja had sent two stone pillars to mark his grave.

Now all of this was gone: the stone, the grave, the legend, and Charlotte felt a deep dismay. Abdullah had spoken of it to her, for he had been incensed at such destruction. The engineer of the settlement, Captain Stevenson, had ordered it blown up a year ago to widen the passage to the river and make space for an extension of Fort Fullerton. A piece, she had heard, had been taken to Govenment House and was being used as a seat for the sepoys. She shook her head and sighed. Now no one would ever know who had dwelt here. Shelley's "Ozymandias" entered her mind; it had been words only before she had seen the stone, but now so potent as she stared at this annihilated place.

"Nothing beside remains. Round the decay
Of that colossal Wreck, boundless and bare
The lone and level sands stretch far away."

She looked up to the flagstaff on the hill. It announced the arrival in Singapore waters of the *Queen of the South*, signalled from Pulau Blakan Mati to Government Hill. She had watched for days and finally seen Tigran's flag raised. The ship would not anchor in the harbour until after dark and would not disembark until morning.

Charlotte took a last walk around the old house, its rooms now standing empty. It had stood for almost the entire duration of the settlement, but now was to be demolished to widen the mouth of the river. A coal store was to be built. How hideous, thought Charlotte. A coal store in such a lovely place. But the new steamers, which appeared increasingly in the harbour, were hungry for this fuel. She thought it ironic that the coal for the steamers came in sailing ships! But she had been on one, the *Victoria*, a strange mixture of sail and steam. Tigran had booked cabins, out of curiosity and because he thought these ships might be the future and was considering adding some to his fleet. It had been the inaugural voyage to Penang, stopping in Malacca, an experiment to see if there was interest enough to establish a permanent steam line between the three ports of the Straits Settlements. It was enjoyable: the ship could travel in any direction, against the wind, against the tide; it was comfortable and reliable. But they were ugly things, and dirty, with their noisy engines and paddles and their squalid sooty noses. Nothing, she felt, equalled the beauty of sail.

Some old chairs and an ancient table stood forlornly on the verandah. Robert wanted to send the house off with a little celebration with his policemen. She watched the sunset falling rapidly.

Robert lived in a large old house on Beach Road. The really wealthy merchants now all owned estates in the surrounding countryside. Robert had done well for himself, investing wisely in land leases, a coconut plantation and a house on the beach at Katong, which he rented for holiday weekends and honeymoons. He wanted two or three more, for nothing matched the peaceful and pretty seclusion of this part of Singapore. He planned to marry Teresa before the year was out.

Charlotte had finally made sense of what was happening with him. Some other fellows had been paying court to Teresa, who was now seventeen and very pretty. He had, with the greatest trepidation, finally told Teresa about Shilah, for he had decided he could no longer submit to blackmail. Be damned! he'd said. If she was shocked and wouldn't have him, then so be it! Better to know right away.

And to his amazement, Teresa had told him it was all right. She was not as innocent as that. Most men had one of these women, and children and so on. You couldn't live in a family of scores of cousins and dozens of aunts and uncles and not know a thing or two. At least three of her cousins, to her knowledge, kept such a girl. She did not like it, though. It must stop, she had said. He had agreed. She was tired of waiting. They would get engaged immediately and marry as soon as possible. He had nodded vehemently. And she had kissed him passionately and told him she was very tired of being a virgin. He had dropped his jaw, and she had patted his hand.

Charlotte smiled. Teresa had set her sights on Robert, and now he was hers. They would be a good couple. Teresa was just right for Robert. Charlotte had vague forebodings about Shilah, however, for she knew that Shilah loved Robert and would very much resent this marriage and his subsequent withdrawal of affection. But she could not worry about that now.

She stood and looked along the river towards the Chinese town. It was not visible from here, for the river made a bend, but she could feel its bustling energy bursting over the waters. Throughout the Chinese New Year period she had not seen Zhen. He had been intensely involved in the celebrations with his family, his wife and children. It was impossible to ignore the festivities, for the deafening noise floated across the whole town. This, more than anything else, had reaffirmed the impossibility of a life, other than this transient life, with him. She could not share his world. For these months she had tried to justify it, reconcile it, write mental treatises about it, but there it was. She lived in one world and he in another and, like the cowherd and the weaver girl in the Chinese love story, they could only meet over the magpie bridge.

She had not yet said good-bye to Zhen; she was going to him now. Charlotte walked down onto the riverside and hailed a sampan to take her there, to his house.

He was waiting for her. She entered his house and took a look around. Love's last adieu, she thought. It was like a tormenting refrain. She put her hand to his cheek and, without a word, climbed the stairs. The last time. It bit into her brain. She did not want to speak to him. She disrobed, leaving only the pearl necklace, and started to climb up on the high bed awkwardly, her belly getting in the way. She wanted to watch him take off his clothes. Zhen smiled and teased her a little, patting her bottom, pretending she was too heavy for him to move, and she turned and scolded him. He laughed and picked her up easily in his strong arms and put his lips to hers and placed her on the bed. She lay back. The thought of robbing her eyes of his beauty caused her physical pain.

She was big now with her child, and he lay next to her and brought her head into his shoulder, moving her so she was nestled in his arm, her leg over his to rest her belly. He had bathed before she came, and his skin was cool and fragrant. He knew her husband had come to take her away, that this was farewell. He caressed her hair. Charlotte traced with her fingers the tattooed image of Guan Di on his chest, and they lay silently together for a long time.

He put his hand onto her belly and felt the movements of the child. With Noan's first pregnancy, he had been aloof, uncaring, he knew, trying to live somehow after Charlotte had left. With the second child, it had been different. He loved his pretty little black-eyed daughter more than he thought he would. He had found a pleasant affection for his wife. She adored him, and he had taken an interest in the growing belly. He had not made love to Noan during her pregnancy, for it was forbidden. It was with Charlotte he had learned how to give pleasure even as her physical abilities changed. Now that they could no longer make the extended and sometimes violent love of the last months, he wanted to pleasure Charlotte, maybe this one last time.

Cradling her, he turned her back to him, placing her bent leg on a porcelain pillow so that her belly was supported. He put a little oil on his fingers and rubbed her gently, moving on the lips and then onto the little bump which was already raised. Charlotte relaxed, knowing his touch, knowing his skill, revelling already, loose, in the almost unbearable sexual pleasure she knew he would give her. She no longer felt any guilt being with him. He had changed her. An aspect of their life together would be over soon. Perhaps they would not meet again this way. But the life force, this uncontainable vitality he had unlocked in her would always be there. It was outside of will, outside of thought. Magical, ecstatic, mysterious. Truly deep, truly loving. She would take it, if she could, and give it to Tigran.

A little squirt of wetness dripped from her, and Zhen kissed her neck, moved by her body's response to him. He turned so that his head was between her legs and opened her lips with his fingers, putting his tongue to her. She instinctively raised her leg onto his shoulder, allowing him more access to her, and let out a long sigh. The first orgasm came slowly with his tongue; then he put his fingers inside her whilst she was still in spasm, finding her place and bringing on the second orgasm, greater than the first, liquid gushing from her onto his hand, into his mouth still against her. He drank, sipping *the vast spring*, licking her, prolonging the climax with his fingers. He listened to her sounds as she lost herself. Then he quickly came behind her, gently putting his penis inside her, not deep, taking over where his fingers had left off. He felt her spasm again, the waves gripping him between her legs. Slippery and soft, he moved, bringing on his own pleasure, feeling her all tight from passion, absorbing her yin essence. He felt as if he could do this for hours, the feeling of her so delicious he did not want to stop, but he knew he would exhaust her. He brought her to the last climax, then moved deeply inside her, careful of the pregnancy, and released his *jing* essence, nourishing her.

He held her, unmoving, as she trembled in his arms, closed his eyes and buried his face in her hair.

30

Tigran turned the handle of the door and went into the bedroom. He saw her in the half-light, sleeping, and went up to the bed. He threw off his boots and coat, lifted the cotton cover. She had gotten so big; he had been away too long. He moved into the bed and laid his body next to hers.

Charlotte opened her eyes and turned. She knew it was him. She let him take her into his arms, touching her belly, waiting for the movement of his child. She let him kiss and nuzzle her neck. Then, as he moved his lips against hers, suddenly, she could not bear it and she sat up, pulling the sheet up her body.

"Are you well, Tigran? Was the journey a safe one? Is Alexander well?"

Tigran was surprised at her coolness, but he had been away a long time, and she was now advanced in the pregnancy. Much as he wanted it, he would not have proposed sex. She was too far along and he feared a mischief to the child. But he would have liked to hold her, the way he had with Alexander.

Give it a little time, he thought. Don't rush her. Pregnancy, he knew, could make women strange.

He got up, ringing the bell for some tea.

"All quite well," he told her. Alexander will want to see you, I think. It has been a long time. And you, my lovely Charlotte. Are you well?"

Charlotte nodded and rose, taking a gown and putting it around her, tying it over her belly. Soon the tea arrived, and he threw open the shutters onto the garden, which was fresh from rain. He looked out for a few moments, then turned and sat.

"It was a terrible time with Josef," he told Charlotte. "Thank the Lord, he has passed into greater hands. But he had a good deal of suffering. In the end, only laudanum kept him sane. It was horrible for Miriam. If I had not been there, I think she, too, would have died of distress."

Charlotte said nothing, and he frowned.

"Is everything well with you, Charlotte? Are you in pain?"

She looked across at him, saying nothing. Finally she spoke. "It is good that you are here, Tigran, for I fear that terrible things are about to happen with us."

Tigran took her hand, alarmed, and she gripped it. She was glad, of a sudden, that he was there. She had forgotten how reassuring his presence was and could see why Miriam had needed him in her moments of trial. This news of Josef was fearful.

"Last night we had word that George has taken very sick," she announced. She told him of the trouble with George and Maria. Takouhi had not seen George since he had announced this business of the divorce to her. Now she was distraught, for Maria would not let her into the house. Billy Napier had relayed news between the two houses, as upset as anyone. He had talked to Maria, but she was adamant that Takouhi would not cross the threshold. George could not leave his bed. Dr Oxley attended him.

"Fever, he says, but then that is the response for every possible ailment that they know nothing about. What if it should be like Josef? Oh no; it is unbearable!" said Charlotte. She stared at Tigran and rose, distressed, and he rose with her and put his arms around her. She leaned against him.

"I have never believed there is a God, and now I am sure of it," she said in an agitated voice. "Such lives of sorrow and misery we mortals lead. But if I thought it would help George, I would pray for a hundred days to any God of any creed on earth."

At that moment, there was a commotion downstairs, and Tigran went to the door and opened it.

Billy was in the hall, and Tigran went quickly down to him. Charlotte, her heart in her throat, stayed on the landing, and Takouhi opened her door. Charlotte was shocked: Takouhi looked like a wraith. She appeared to have aged a hundred years in one night. She went down the stairs like a ghostly spirit, and the two men turned. Tigran let out a cry of alarm at the sight of her and took her into his arms, but she only looked at Billy. He, too, was shocked. It was written on his face.

"George?" she asked, and it was like a tiny voice carried on the wind. Charlotte burst into tears.

Tigran did not know who to attend to, but his sister felt so frail in his arms that he stood still, holding on to her. They looked at Billy.

"He is still sick, a return of the swamp fever, brought on, Dr Oxley thinks, by a neglect of his health and too much sun. He went several days without eating or drinking and then went into the jungle. He has been given *chinchona*, and Oxley hopes that with careful nursing and more fluids he will recover."

Takouhi let out a cry of anguish and slumped into her brother's arms.

"Billy, you must tell her to let us see him. Look at my sister, for God's sake. Look at my wife," Tigran commanded.

Billy looked up at Charlotte, who was slowly descending the staircase. His face wore an expression of gaunt and sorrowful misery. "He is my best friend. I am fearful …" Billy could not finish his words, and he too looked on the verge of collapse.

Charlotte went up to him. She had stopped crying and found some resolution. "Get John, John Connolly," she said firmly. "Maria likes him. He is a religious man. Though he is Catholic, she will listen to him. He will convince her. Seeing Takouhi will revive George's spirits. If you love him, she must see him."

Billy nodded and left the house

"Tigran, take Takouhi to her bedroom. I will give her something to calm her," Charlotte said.

Charlotte had learned from Zhen something about Chinese medicine, and he had given her some herbs when she had, on occasion, been distressed. The brew had calmed her a great deal, and she had found sleep and solace. She went to the kitchen to brew some of these herbs for Takouhi.

When John Connolly arrived, Takouhi was asleep. He had seen

George, who, though still feverish, was calm. He had talked to Maria, but she was adamant. Tomorrow he would return in the morning with Father Baudrel, for his influence was very great.

John looked at Charlotte. He still loved her. He still remembered the gash on his heart when she had refused him, the misery of her departure. He wished that this child she was carrying was his. He could not forget her and feared that now he would not marry. If he could do her this service, for her sake and George's, he would try.

Charlotte put her hand on John's arm and smiled her thanks.

That evening, dinner was gloomy. Charlotte had made Takouhi rise to bathe. She had been taken soup up to her friend, but Takouhi had refused to eat and had gone back to bed. Charlotte could see her friend was on the brink of an abyss. She paced the floor of the sitting room nervously. Tigran sat by the window, staring out. They were waiting for news of George.

Tigran rose and put his arm around Charlotte. "Rest, please. Think of your health, the baby."

Charlotte stopped pacing and sat down, but when she heard Billy's voice in the hall, she ran to the door.

Billy simply looked at her and shook his head.

Charlotte let out a great wail and sank to the floor. Tigran lifted her into his arms, filled with horror.

"Billy," Tigran said, his voice tense, "What is the news? Is George—" He stopped, unable to utter the words in front of Charlotte. She leaned against him like a rag doll, sobbing.

"No, no." Billy realised suddenly the awful effect of his actions. He came up to Charlotte and took her hand.

"No, Charlotte, no. He is alive. But he is very sick. Tomorrow may be too late."

Charlotte put her hand to her mouth.

"John and all his friends have been to see him. Oxley and Edward White have been there for an hour. White has given George extreme unction. He seems peaceful. I will join them. After she was with him, I told Maria to keep to her room. She cannot refuse to let his friends see him *in extremis*."

Billy squeezed Charlotte's hand.

"George is my friend too, Charlotte, but we cannot collapse. He has given me his will. He knows Takouhi has no need of his money. He leaves everything to Maria and the baby. He has asked me to bring Takouhi. I cannot ..." Billy's voice broke, "refuse this last wish."

Billy looked at Tigran. "It has been very sudden. He seemed to revive—well enough to speak to me. He asked Maria for her pardon. He has done everything a good man should. I am sorry I was angry with him. I will not deprive him of anything he wants. He has been my boon companion these many years."

A tear slid down Billy's cheek. "Please get Takouhi," he said.

Tigran lowered Charlotte into a chair and went upstairs. Within a few minutes, Takouhi appeared on the landing, with such a frightful demeanour that Charlotte pulled herself together, rose quickly and went to her.

"We will go to George, Takouhi. Let's get ready."

She guided her friend to the dressing table, and they sat. Charlotte had never seen Takouhi look so beaten. Within a few days, her skin had become sallow, her eyes sunken and lifeless. Her bones protruded from her shoulders. She blamed herself for his illness, and nothing would give her solace.

"Takouhi, you must be beautiful to see George."

Charlotte poured a glass of water and made her drink. Then she called the Javanese maids, who set about restoring their mistress to some semblance of beauty. Her hair, at least, had not lost all its lustre. As they began to apply *kohl* to her eyes, Charlotte went to the wardrobe and selected a plain white embroidered *kebaya* and an emerald green sarong. When she came back to the mirror, Takouhi took her hand.

"This is good-bye, eh, Charlotte? Good-bye to George."

Charlotte sat next to her friend, and their eyes met in the mirror. She breathed deeply and spoke to herself words that helped her find a deep, calm place. She would need great strength and calm to see Takouhi through this trial.

"Yes, this is good-bye. We must be *alus*, Takouhi. We must not create *isin*. He is on his journey. Let him go."

Takouhi looked back at Charlotte, nodded and closed her eyes. When she opened them again, Charlotte could see that she had found the natural resignation which so characterised the Javanese and which had carried her through the death of her only child.

Now she rose and dressed carefully. The maids put jasmine flowers in her hair, and then she turned and went out of the room.

George was awake, sitting up, waiting, when Charlotte went to him. She told him Takouhi was there, and a look of warmth and joy came into his eyes. Charlotte gasped at his appearance, for the illness seemed to have ravaged him in such a short time. But she could not believe he was dying. He looked sick and thin, sweating, the fever had eaten at him, it was clear, but his face showed a deep calm. She knew it was because Takouhi was coming.

Charlotte kissed him on his cheek and, despite all her admonitions to Takouhi, could not hold back tears. George raised his hand and touched her face.

"Do not stand at my grave and weep,
I am not there; I do not sleep.
Remember."

Charlotte did remember. It was the poem, a strange American Indian poem from a captain on a clipper ship in port at the time. It had given him solace when Meda had died.

Charlotte smiled at him, and he took up a glass of porter which stood on a table to one side and raised it.

"Here's to me and here's to you;
And here's to love and laughter;
I'll be true as long as you
and not one moment after."

Charlotte laughed, spontaneously, a jerking, crying laugh. It was one of his favourite drinking ditties. He drank a little and licked his lips.

"Ah! Not quite so tasty as quinine, but beggars can't be choosers! I'd like a glass of porter every now and again after I've joined my Maker. Are there inns in heaven? I must ask the Reverend. Surely yes, for Jesus was born in one. Eh? Why does this important question not come up in theological discussion?"

He had begun to shake and sweat profusely. He smiled wanly. "Say God speed, Kitt, and let me see her."

Her face crumpled into tears, and she held on to him. Robert came, put his hand in George's for a moment. George squeezed it gently and nodded at him with a smile, and then Robert, trying so hard to keep a strong heart, turned quickly and took Charlotte. He called Takouhi.

Charotte watched as Takouhi went up to him, standing next to the bed, letting him see her. She saw his rapturous smile. Takouhi knelt down at his bedside in one graceful and beautiful movement and leaned forward, taking up his hand. She put her lips against his ear and whispered. He closed his eyes. Robert shut the door.

31

Zhen walked along Circular Road, crossed South Bridge Road and turned towards the bridge. He knew that Charlotte was today going to her temple and then to the graveyard of the Christians on the hillside. She had sent him a letter, telling him a friend she dearly loved had died, that she would leave in a few days. She had sent him an English poem, and he had liked it. It was a Taoist poem, he thought, filled with the eternal duality of yin and yang, written by a man called Sher Li. He had not known that English people also had this philosophy, but why should they not? Everywhere men had thoughts and wisdom.

> *The fountains mingle with the river,*
> *And the rivers with the ocean,*
> *The winds of heaven mix for ever,*
> *With a sweet emotion,*
> *Nothing in the world is single;*
> *All things by a law divine*
> *In one another's being mingle—*
> *Why not I with thine?*

He knew he could not see her intimately again, but that was not important. It would torture him later, possibly, but not now. Now he simply wanted to see her, watch her from a distance, remember the time she had floated into his life on the pretty English ship the very night he had arrived in Singapore. He did not believe in fate, but it felt as if they had met, from two ends of the earth, like the loop in a thread pulled into a tiny knot. It seemed as if this loop had been slowly closing from the day they were both born until that moment in the moonlight, in the harbour.

There were tracks all over Government Hill. He would watch her arriving with the catafalque onto the road which led to the burial ground. He turned after the bridge onto River Valley Road and made his way slowly up and around the hill to sit below Government House, at the rim of the trees.

He heard the bell of the white man's church begin to sound in the distance. She would be coming soon. He trembled slightly. He could sometimes not believe how he felt about this woman.

Charlotte held Takouhi's hand. They rose as the bell began to toll and the coffin was raised. All George's friends were his pallbearers. The Reverend White made his way down the aisle, carrying the cross aloft, leading this man to God. Behind him, Robert and John at the front, the eight bearers shouldered his mortal remains and began the slow walk to the cemetery. Billy was not amongst them for, try as they might, his height could not be reconciled with the burden of the pall. A hearse had been suggested, but none of the men had agreed. They would carry George. It would be an honour.

A wreath made of fresh green leaves entwined in the shape of an elaborate Celtic knot lay on top of the coffin. Billy had been accorded the duty of accompanying Maria and, together with Mrs White, she followed, a thin figure in black, her head covered in a veil. The Governor and Mrs Butterworth and the Churches were behind her, the Colonel and officers of the regiment, the government.

George's coffin passed out of the portal of the church that he had built. As it passed, Takouhi gripped Charlotte's hand a little tighter. With Tigran, the two women waited until the procession had passed.

Takouhi did not want to see him put into the ground. She had held him, her lips against his as he drew his last breath. She wanted to go to his grave when no one was there. Many people knew about George and herself. Their union, their daughter: these things were common knowledge to the old-timers in Singapore. Let Maria bury him. It did not matter.

The regimental band had struck up Chopin's funeral march, which had become vastly popular in recent years. Charlotte and Takouhi thought it gloomy, but knew George would rather have liked this pomp and a splendid dirge. *Dirige, Domine, Deus meus, in conspectu tuo viam meam.*

They joined the end of the procession. The entire length of Coleman Street, from the church gate to Hill Street, was strewn with leaves and flowers. The door of the house where he had died was covered in black. But Tir Uaidhne, the house he had built for her, was festooned with flowers. The doors stood wide open under the porte-cochère, urns of incense burning throughout the garden, the length of the surrounding walls decorated with jasmine, lotus, Buddha's hand, orchids, yellow meranti; a myriad of species tumbling from pots and vases, a wild and fragrant offering to this man she loved.

Tigran took Takouhi into the house, and Charlotte fell in next to Teresa Crane, her future sister, who had waited for her. As the coffin arrived on Hill Street, it halted. The Armenian community had gathered in the grounds of the church. The priest intoned a prayer, and suddenly a great peal of bells rang out to honour the man who had constructed it. As Charlotte trod on the leaves and blooms under her feet, she reflected on the fact that, from the church to the graveyard, everything was George's. He had built all the roads, the houses, the churches, the very gates of the cemetery through which they passed, and, of course, the two pretty cupolas, standing white and pure against the green of the entwined banyan and tamelan trees. These he had built for Meda and Takouhi. The two he loved would be watching in spirit. The coffin was placed on the stand, and Reverend White stepped up.

Zhen had searched the crowd of people following this man's coffin. Others were joining the procession from the Chinese town as it arrived at the little church on Hill Street. To his astonishment, he spotted his father-in-law. It had not occurred to him before, but he realised now that these two men had known each other most of their lives. Chinese, Indian, Arab and Malay mourners joined the crowd. George had built the Chinese godowns, their palaces of trade; the Indians had been his allies and partners in this enterprise. The Malays were his friends, and he had built the Sultan's new palace at Kampong Glam and many of their houses.

269

Suddenly, he saw her in the crowd. So lovely, so sad. Then she passed from his sight, and he rose, moving quickly around the hill to a point above the cemetery. A vast crowd filled the grounds; there was hardly room to move, and he could not see her. The music had stopped, and he could hear words intoned.

A myna bird alighted on a branch nearby and put its head on one side. He smiled. This fearless little black bird, with its yellow legs and beak, had been a companion when he had practised the *tai chi* in the orchard years before, hopping around him, eyeing him curiously. He knew it could mimic human sounds. Now it gave a little click and whistle. He put out his hand, and the bird rose, flew down into the grounds of the cemetery and hovered briefly. Zhen saw her. It was as if the bird had directed his gaze, and he shook his head, mystified.

Charlotte too had seen the bird as it hovered strangely over her head and looked up as it flew into the trees on the hill. An immediate sensation of presence told her Zhen was there. She searched but could see nothing.

They had said good-bye the last time they had met. He had told her he would watch her ship from Mount Wallich as he had done before. She should look there; he would be there, even though she might not see him. He would not be half-mad as he had been before, nor must she be half-mad. They would accept the unavoidable. They would hold to the middle. They would preserve their well-being. They would adopt the *wu wei*, the letting-be of the Tao, not scratch and fight and wear themselves out.

She thought of these words and searched for him. She could not see George's coffin—the crowd was too great—but somehow that was no longer important. She had a sudden realisation that it did not matter that George's body was gone. His spirit was here, right here in these woods. She felt him all around, and the feeling of comfort was like warmth after cold.

Robert moved back to join her. He was upset, more than she was now, remembering, she was sure, his long and close acquaintance with George as he had matured from a callow youth, a mere clerk in the godown of Johnston and Co., through the difficulties and insecurities of his new role to his place now of respect and confidence. Through it all, George had been his ever-constant companion, a whimsical and amusing friend.

She put her hand on Robert's arm, and he looked down, tears in his eyes. Suddenly unable to contain himself, he pulled her against him and began to sob. She moved away, further back against the wall of the cemetery, near the cupolas. She remembered how she had sat here with George, lighting incense for his daughter. He had loomed large in all their lives. She held on to Robert, and he became calm.

She looked up again at the trees on the hill and saw him. He stood, seeing her too. She raised her arm, her hand, reaching out to him, and he too held out his hand. The band unexpectedly struck up again, and she turned her head. When she looked again at the hill, he was gone.

Zhen had pulled back into the darkness of the trees. He had seen Ro Bett, Xia Lou's brother, observed his profound grief. It was not right for him to interrupt this ceremony. The music began again, and the coffin was being lowered into the grave.

Zhen sat. He would have liked to tell them that this death was not important, a mere transformation. George's matter had changed, become one again with the void. Death was just another part of life's infinite changes.

> Like a water-wheel awhirl,
> Like the rolling of a pearl;
> Yet these but illustrate,
> To fools, the final state.
> The earth's great axis spinning on,
> The never-resting pole of sky --
> Let us resolve their Whence and Why,
> And blend with all things into One;
> Circling the void as spheres
> Whose orbits round a thousand years:
> Beyond the bounds of thought and dream,
> Behold the Key that fits my theme.

As the coffin was laid in the grave, Zhen took up a stick and drew the Zen circle in the ground in one smooth stroke, welcoming this man into eternity.

32

The day of their departure dawned, and with it came the rain. Takouhi and Charlotte nevertheless left Tir Uaidhne and walked, under their umbrellas, towards the cemetery. Since the funeral, Takouhi had come every day to light incense and place flowers. She and Charlotte put candles under the cupolas to cast a flickering beam into the night. Charlotte, in their long conversations, had begun to learn something of Zhen's philosophy. She knew they did this for themselves, for their own comfort, not for George. He had passed into the raindrops, *the diamond glints on snow*.

Takouhi had asked Tigran to stay until the seven-day *slametan* for George.

Yesterday, the house had been thrown open to all the town who wished to come to eat, drink and be merry. Half the town had passed through at some point or other. It had lasted until the night. A proper Irish wake, John Connolly had said. Maria had not come.

Now they entered the Armenian church and sat, breathing in the moist air, waiting for the rain to stop beating down, enjoying the building wrought by George's hand. They talked of departure. The luggage had been sent to the brig, along with all the items that Takouhi wanted from the house. When she was ready, she would sell Tir Uaidhne and everything in it and leave Singapore.

She was not ready yet. She had kept the bed in which she and George had conceived Meda, in which Meda had been born, in which such final happiness had been found. Charlotte said nothing, but she was sure that Alexander, too, had been conceived in this bed the day Zhen had surprised her at the empty house. This would be the last thing to go back to Batavia with her.

They talked quietly, and Takouhi prayed. Charlotte and Tigran would leave on the afternoon tide.

The rain suddenly stopped, and, as it does in the tropics, the sunlight burst out like a furnace, throwing steamy shadows on the floor. They rose and made their way up the hill. George's grave stood in the corner, with a simple white wooden cross. The workmen, who had been sheltering, had begun again to lay the foundation of the tomb into which his coffin would be moved.

Charlotte had seen the design which Billy had shown them. She was not sure George would have approved, but doubtless he would have laughed. Billy Napier's tastes ran to dabbling in the new Gothic. It would have amused George to know he would spend his eternal rest under a monumental, spurious Gothic tomb designed by a Scottish lawyer. Still, none of them doubted Billy's sincerity and the depth of his affection for his lost friend.

Or, it seemed, for his lost friend's wife. Billy spent all of his spare time in consoling Maria, advising Maria, acting for Maria, looking after the probate, sorting out her affairs. Maria had not set foot inside the cemetery since the funeral. Charlotte and Takouhi had not dared call on her. From Robert, though, they learned of her grief. She had loved George, there could be no doubt; her deep disappointment merely concealed this fact. Charlotte would have liked to talk to her, console her, but it would have been unwelcome. Only once had they seen the baby, when the nurse had been rocking him in the front garden. They had stopped and looked, and there was little George's face, for the son had been baptised with his father's name. Takouhi had touched the tiny hand and smiled. Whilst she and this little boy lived, George could not die.

They walked home in rain, but, by the time of their departure, the sun shone. On the old jetty, Charlotte hugged Robert tightly. She embraced her friends: Evangeline, Teresa and her family, and finally Takouhi. She knew her friend would come back when she was ready.

Tigran helped Charlotte into the cutter, and with shouts and cries, the men began to pull away from shore. She watched as, once again with sadness, she left these shores. The tide was up, and the brig stood close in. It took them only a few minutes to reach the ship. Charlotte stood as she had before and looked over the town. It had changed; it had grown, but she loved it still. Her eyes went to Mount Wallich and the long ridge which bordered the bay. She could see only the luxuriant growth of the hill. It was impossible to see the Chinese town in Telok Ayer Bay, for it lay beyond the headland.

Then, suddenly, she saw him. He was standing on one of the piers which gave out from the back of the godowns on Commercial Square. She stood looking at him. He did not move, watching the ship. Tigran turned from giving some orders and saw her, leaning forward, looking to shore with an unconscious intensity. He saw her smile quietly. He went forward and stood next to her.

She dropped her eyes, but he had seen who she was staring at. Tigran said nothing; he, too, now stared at the man, frowning, trying to think. And then he saw, knew. This was the son-in-law of Baba Tan. This man was the father of Alexander. He knew now why the man's face had been so familiar to him. The eyes, the curve of the jaw, the now unmistakable signs of blood and bone written into Alexander's face. Charlotte had been seeing this man whilst he had been away, he felt certain. He did not even have to ask her. She had not moved, had not looked at him. Her gaze had returned to the man on shore, who turned and quickly disappeared behind the godown. She knew he had gone to Mount Wallich.

She faced Tigran. He stared at her, for the first time ever, with anger. He took her arm, moved her off the deck, into their cabin and shut the door.

"So, madam, I see I am to be deceived, cuckolded, if ever you are in Singapore. Whilst I have been struggling with death and misery, writing you letters of love and constancy, you have been playing your adulterous game behind my back."

Charlotte looked him straight in the eye. She gave no thought for her words. They simply came rushing out.

"I do not wish to hurt you, Tigran. It was in this very cabin that I told you of my love for him. I thought those feelings had changed, but they have not. *Love dwells not in our will.* It is now over. I am returning to Batavia with you."

"To think of him, to dream of him. Again, like it was before? No, it is too much."

Chrlotte felt her temper rise. "How dare you! You destroyed his letters to me, which would have given me comfort in misery!" She stared at Tigran, her fists clenched. "What I dream, what I think, neither you nor even I can control."

The ship lurched slightly as the winch began to weigh the anchor. The noise of barked orders and shouting came from deck as the sails were set, and the deep thrumming of the wind began in the rigging.

Tigran was lost for words. He wanted to strike her, tell her to stop loving this man. To go back was intolerable. It had taken too long for her to come to him, and now this. He had been her support, her friend, her lover, and she had betrayed him. Something like hatred entered his mind.

"Stay here in this cabin. I do not wish to see you for this entire voyage. You will take your meals here. Do not come on deck. Your maids will attend to you." He turned and left the cabin.

Charlotte sat on the edge of the bed, shocked. He had flung these words at her with contempt. She felt the wind's hand on the ship, turning it away from shore. He would not allow her even to wave good-bye to Robert, to Takouhi. She went to the door and opened it. A man had been stationed outside! She could not believe it. She asked him to bring her husband. The man, obviously confused about his orders, hesitated. The mistress was with child. But he had been ordered not to leave the door. He called a ship's boy to send for the master.

Whilst she waited for Tigran, she found her composure. When he opened the door, he stood waiting, coldly.

"Tigran, this is intolerable. Please, may I wave good-bye to Robert and Takouhi?" she said.

Tigran motioned her to come and let her pass onto the deck. She went to the side and waved, and they all raised their hands. Safe voyage, they called. She looked up to Mount Wallich. When the ship had caught the wind, the sails cracking with air, it moved rapidly away from shore. Soon the figures were a blur. Tigran came up to her, grasped her by the arm and once again took her to the cabin. This time he took the key from inside the door and went outside. She heard it turn in the lock.

She gasped. A prisoner! Had he gone mad? She had not meant to provoke him. She had had every intention of returning to him a loving wife, giving birth to his child, sharing this joy together. This very evening in this very bed, she would have welcomed him into her arms. She could put Zhen quietly in her heart now. She had learned to accept this, he had taught her how.

And now, in the blink of an eye, everything had turned hideously sour. She went to the line of windows and opened one, letting the air rush in. She watched as the shoreline of Singapore receded, keeping her eyes on Mount Wallich. But now she was not sure which hill was which. And as they left the harbour, the sea became rough. She shut the window and lay on the bed. The baby had begun its churning. Surely Tigran would calm down, surely he would forgive her. She closed her eyes.

33

Charlotte awoke as the light began to filter into the room. The oblivion of sleep left her and the day, and her thoughts rushed in. She remembered. Tigran would not speak to her. She lay and watched the passage of the early morning pass across the floor.

For four days she had been confined in the cabin, but the journey had taken much longer than expected. For days they had lain windless, floating on the shallow blue sea of the Straits of Carimata, which joined the South China Sea to the Java Sea. The main island in the passage rose, a lofty, barren height of grey and yellow; another lay like the backbone of a stooping creature. Further off, a smattering of insignificant and indistinct islets curved into the haze. The ship floated motionless, chained to its mirror image on the glassy sea. This becalming seemed, to her fevered mind, the very symbol of her plight: stuck immobile between Singapore and Batavia, between two men, utterly incapable of action, just as the wind had seemingly deserted the earth.

Sometimes there would be an inexplicable long, heavy swell, as if the sea had inhaled a deep breath, and this would cause the ship to move forward, raising spirits. Charlotte could hear it in the animation and chatter of the Malay and Javanese sailors. It would give only brief hope, however, for soon, again, they lay unmoving. Then would come only what sailors called the baffling winds, the shifting, varying breeze which caused the idle sails to flap. There was surely no more hideous sound at sea than the monotonous and never-ending flap, flap, flap of the idle sails against the masts and yards.

Charlotte thought they might never leave these regions of the doldrums. When the sun was at its zenith, the breeze would die altogether and the sun beat down, scorching the ship, heating them like a furnace and reducing them all to dripping, exhausted wraiths.

The food was adequate, for rice was plentiful and the men fished and shot seabirds. The water, though, ran low and the men took the cutters and went to Caramata Island for fresh supplies, to look for firewood, fruits and whatever else they could gather. The water party returned, but the second boat was attacked by a small group of natives, with one man killed and two wounded.

Now the fear of pirate attack added to their woes. After two days, both wounded men died, and the captain held a burial at sea. Charlotte could not bear to watch, hearing from the cabin the splash of their bodies.

On the fifth day, Tigran, seeing the prospect of a long voyage, allowed Charlotte to come on deck, though he remained unremittingly cold to her. He responded when she spoke, but otherwise he addressed not a word to her. Charlotte was certain she would go into labour on this mirrored sea and die in hideous agony in the relentless heat. She would stare down into the waters, watching the sunlight move on beds of coral and dark indistinct shapes and imagine her body floating there: she and her child still joined by the cord.

The captain could not help but notice the tension; he could not make out what had so suddenly turned this loving couple against each other. Mrs Manouk looked sickly, so heavy with the child, but her husband seemed indifferent.

To raise her spirits, he talked to her of the sea and of the ship. He told her that the word "brig" came from "brigand", for some believed that pirates lay at the origin of this two-masted vessel. The *Queen* was an old-fashioned lady, over twenty years old and much modified. She had been an English privateer which Tigran's father had bought because he liked her English name. The upper cabins behind the wheel, which the captain and the ship's master occupied, had been added so that the roomy main cabin was reserved for the owner or his guests.

The *Queen* was a good sailor, quick to respond and courageous in all weathers, he told her, and she felt his affection for this sleek craft. They talked of the stars and navigation. Captain Elliott showed her how to use a sextant and found her quick to grasp the concepts. They discussed the merits of steam and both agreed that it was in seas like this when every sailor would be glad of it to confound the capricious spirits of the air.

Charlotte was comforted by the captain's little mongrel dog, Tasty, which lay in the day, panting, at her side in the rigged shade of an old sail and in the evening shared her lonely cabin. Elliott told her he had named him this when he had saved him, as a pup, from the jaws of a crocodile during some village foraging. When Tigran saw them talking together, he turned away.

Charlotte could not reach him. She had been angry at this confinement, determined to make him pay for it, but as it extended, she had become bored, agitated. When she had been allowed on deck, initially she had been happy to be free, still annoyed with him. After a week, however, she had become anxious. The voyage which should have taken four days had, finally, taken sixteen. It had been hideous, long, hot and tedious. She had been sick and frightened, filled with visions of madness. Only the Captain's kindness and the presence of the young Javanese maid had kept her mind in order, for this young girl was more terrified than she. Charlotte longed for Brieswijk.

Now she was here, but nothing had changed. Tigran left in the early hours for the Kota. He returned in the afternoon, but then, after bathing and changing, he went to the Harmonie Club or the Concordia Club or the Hotel de Provence or the Masonic Lodge or heaven knows where. He slept not in the room next to hers, but in apartments at the other end of the house.

They were invited to dine, but he refused everything on grounds of her health. She felt, now, that what had been wounds of love had festered into hatred of her. She longed for Takouhi to come home, but her friend wrote that she could not. She wanted to see George's tomb built. She wasn't ready to leave him.

Nathanial was absent, on another expedition to the East. Louis was away too, travelling with part of the troupe to Semarang and Surabaya. She spent her days with Alexander, who barely recognised her, in her room, or in the library and at the river. The river gave her some comfort. The maids were charming and attentive, but they chatted in a language she could not understand.

Once she went at sunrise to the river and watched quietly as the villagers bathed in the green and golden waters. The men, half-naked, ran and leapt into the water, diving under and emerging, their copper bodies gleaming wet. The women, sedate, pulled their sarongs over their bosoms, leaving their shoulders bare. At the edge of the water they paused and lifted their arms to twist their heavy hair into knots. Young mothers coaxed their little ones into the stream. Crowds of small boys and girls plunged and splashed noisily. Half-hidden in clumps of reeds, the young girls poured water from palm leaves over each other's heads until their sleek black hair melded with their garments in flowing, clinging folds, moulding their lithe figures into those of nymphs. She turned away. She took her meals alone. She did not know how long Tigran meant to punish her.

Now, today, she did not want to get up. It was too much effort. It was so much easier just to go back to sleep. She half-awoke when the maid came with tea, but then returned to slumber. In the evening she awoke, surprised to find she had slept all day. She rose, needing relief from the sticky heat and went to the verandah, where she felt a waft of cool evening air and sat looking out into the darkness. Her maid, anxious, appeared instantly at her side, with tea and some food. Charlotte smiled at her and resumed her vigil over the darkness.

Charlotte's maids liked her a great deal. She never bullied them, was always gentle and kind. They could not speak her language, could only watch as she fell into this despond. Madi should come, but without the master's permission it was impossible to send for her. When she heard, the housekeeper informed Janszen, the major-domo, who ran everything in the house.

Tigran failed to return that night, and Janszen became concerned. The mistress slept all the time. She had taken a little water but had eaten nothing now for two days. The maid feared for the master's child.

When Tigran finally came back, Janszen made his report. Tigran frowned and went to her room. Charlotte lay naked on the bed. She had lost weight, and her skin was sallow and sweaty; her hair stuck to her.

He went to the bed and touched her, tried to wake her, but she did not move. She was all belly, so thin it protruded like a barrel. Had he done this? He had not seen her for two weeks. Had he done this?

He saw the movement of the child, raking an elbow or kicking a foot against her inside, rolling under her skin like some huge parasite. Her skin was almost translucent, her belly a map of blue veins. He saw she had marks where the skin had stretched, and they looked red and raw. She looked neglected, abandoned, and he felt a terrible remorse.

Tigran tried to rouse her again. She opened her eyes and looked around a moment, her eyes rolling, then closed them again. He rose in alarm. She had not seen him. She did not know where she was. She had suffered on the voyage, and now she had drunk nothing for two days. He called a servant to fetch the civil surgeon. Then he returned, tried to raise her, give her some water. Again, she opened her eyes. She seemed to recognise him, but it was if she was looking at him from across a vast space. He called the maids and lifted her into his arms. Despite the weight of the baby, she felt like air, and he shook his head at his own folly.

He carried her to the bathing room and put her in the cool, scented bath. The water revived her so that she was half-awake as they washed her hair and body. Tigran saw that she no longer wore her wedding ring and shook his head. How had it come to this? He sat by the bath, and she took some water from him.

But they could not rouse her more than this. He carried her back to her bed, now remade with fresh sheets. She fell again into a deep sleep. Now Tigran was frantic. He sent another servant urgently to the civil surgeon. Then he remembered Madi. In his anger at Charlotte, he had not called Madi to care for her in this late stage of her pregnancy. Furious at himself, he sent for her.

Tigran took up Charlotte's hand, kissing the white mark where her wedding band should be. He opened the drawer at her bedside and it lay there, forlornly, shorn of its power and meaning. She had simply removed it one day when he had not been there, perhaps because she could not bear to see it any longer on her finger, this symbol of their union, now destroyed. He loved her so much, yet he had caused this suffering.

He had a horrible premonition suddenly that she might die, like Surya, from melancholy and misery. And this time, he would be the cause. The thought was unbearable.

He rose, putting his lips against hers, kissing her, again and again, her lips, her cheeks, her eyes. Touch: she had loved his touch before, longed for it. Lovely Charlotte, his sensual, beautiful wife. Wake up, my love, he murmured, kissing her neck, running his hands through her hair, running her fingers into his plaits, over the beads which he knew she loved to touch. But she did not move, and he rose, letting out a roar of anguish, pacing the floor.

Madi arrived. He went to her, his eyes filled with tears, and she looked at Charlotte, went to the bed, felt her face, then turned. She had delivered him and all his children safely, gotten rid of others, ministered constantly to the needs of his women. She said nothing, but he felt her anger and sat on a chair like a child. She turned to Charlotte and took out a bottle of liquid from her bag. In a small glass of water she put three drops. She raised Charlotte's head, and with a bamboo straw she sucked up some of the liquid then put the straw between Charlotte's lips and blew the liquid into her mouth. Charlotte swallowed, involuntarily, and within a few minutes opened her eyes. Madi put the rest of the liquid to her mouth, chanting quietly, and Charlotte drank.

Madi called the maid, who was hovering anxiously, to prepare some herbs. She felt Charlotte's belly, assessing the child. It seemed to be well, but it had drained its mother of everything. More than this, though, Madi knew there was some problem in the mind.

The herbal brew revived Charlotte, and she looked around her. She felt a raging thirst and asked for more to drink. She was so happy to see Madi and kissed her hand. Madi smiled a black-toothed grin, poured more of the brew and ordered the maid to make a honey, ginger and ginseng drink. For a few hours, Charlotte would do nothing but drink and excrete her liquids, bringing back balance to her body.

The civil surgeon arrived, and Madi retreated in the presence of this *tuan*. After examining Charlotte, he pronounced her somewhat debilitated and advised bloodletting and purging. Madi's brew had relaxed Charlotte, and she had begun to feel pleasantly well. Now she looked at Tigran, terrified.

"I feel better Tigran, please don't ..." She spoke in a frightened little voice, cowed, and he realised that she feared him.

He went up to her, and she flinched. He was filled with anguish. "Oh, no, no, Charlotte. It's all right."

He turned to the doctor. "I am sorry to have bothered you, Willem.

I was concerned, but Charlotte is much better."

Tigran propelled the doctor firmly towards the door. "Send me your invoice and add something extra for your trouble. Let's dine in a week or so at the Harmonie?" They left the room, Tigran taking him to his carriage.

Madi went immediately to the bed and helped Charlotte to drink. She stroked her hair and clucked softly, crooning a Javanese lullaby. When Tigran returned, Madi put up a warning hand, not letting him touch her. Charlotte looked at him. She had no idea what she felt for this man anymore. She could not imagine him holding her, touching her during labour as he had with Alexander, when she had sunk into his strong arms and felt his comforting power. Now, wherever the fault lay, she was wary of him. She was in his power, and she did not like it. He could isolate her, trap her. She remembered Takouhi's story. He was not like that; it was not fair, but he had exacted an obedience nevertheless.

He saw it in her eyes, this guarded assessment. He was relieved that she would be well now, the panic of the past few hours over. He had to think what to do next. If she could not ever love him … His paralysing anger had receded, and the thought drained him of all vitality.

They looked at each other silently until she lowered her eyes.

He turned and left the room.

34

Tigran paced the library floor. He felt utterly drained of imagination, unable to act. Over the past few days, Charlotte's health had improved. She had begun to eat; her colour had returned. This morning he had joined her at breakfast, thankful that she had come to the table, could take some food. He poured her some tea. She thanked him very quietly, but would not look at him. Everything in her attitude told him she wished he were not there.

He wanted to apologise for his treatment of her. Everything had got out of hand so quickly, for he had been uncontrollably angry. On the ship, when he looked at her he had seen her betrayal, his head full of savage and unbearable visions of her lying with this man, making love with him even whilst she was carrying his child. It made blood come to his eyes. He supposed he had intended to punish her, make her change her ways, forget her lover. He had not intended to break her spirit or ruin her health, though. He couldn't remember now why he had let it all drag on.

He had started to speak, but as he began, she rose abruptly.

"Excuse me, please. I feel unwell," she said.

She stood, waiting, and he realised she was waiting for his permission to go. He couldn't believe it. She had no right to make him feel like a monster. She stood there, thin and frail, with this huge belly, unmoving. His anger evaporated. He felt a flood of sympathy and love for her. He wanted to put out his hand, touch hers, but he knew she would pull away.

He rose quietly. "Please finish your meal, Charlotte. You need your strength."

He left, and Charlotte sat down, frozen with misery. She knew he wanted to talk to her, to try to end this, but she just could not forget how ill she had become at his hands, how he had imprisoned her. Now they were both stuck in this emotional mire. She did nothing but think and think how to change this, how to get out, but all ways seemed closed. She tried to follow Zhen's advice and find the middle way, stop these swings in mood to which she had become horribly prone. But it was hard. Sometimes a black gloom simply enveloped her. Madi had made her body well, but she feared, sometimes, for the balance of her mind.

Then, a few days later, finally, Louis came to see her. She was so happy to see him that she burst into tears and hugged him. He made her laugh with stories of the troupe and the good burghers of Semarang. They sat on the verandah at Brieswijck, and she told him everything.

"Oh, Louis, I would give anything to stop feeling this way, just to stop thinking."

Louis put his hand in his pocket and took out a pretty silver box. He opened it and held it towards her. She looked at him quizzically.

"L'opium, ma belle. Le cadeau precieux du coquelicot." He took out a small pill and put it in her hand.

"It will give you rest. Take it this evening and you will forget every trouble; it will take you in its arms and embrace you. It will dim the light, and when you wake, you will be refreshed and revitalised. It is the panacea for all ills. It is the secret of happiness."

Charlotte stared at this pill. Opium. She had seen it, smelt it, in Singapore; its sweetish odour poured out of dozens of doors in Chinatown from behind grimy, tattered curtains. The smell was not disagreeable, something like roasted nuts.

"Do you take it, Louis?" She looked up at him.

"My dear Charlotte, of course. Everyone takes it. The Pharaohs, the Romans, the Greeks, all of antiquity knew of its divine powers. It is God's gift to mankind, a recompense for our mortal sufferings, nôtre miserable existence."

Charlotte frowned. Did Tigran take opium? Did Zhen? She looked again at the pill.

"Charlotte, ma chère, n'hésite pas. It is regenerative. You will find again rest, a peaceful nature.

> *"When I build castles in the air*
> *Void of sorrow, void of fear*
> *Pleasing myself with phantasms sweet*
> *Methinks the time runs very fleet."*

He grinned his infectious grin and flopped back in his chair.

When he left, she looked out over the lawns. Two peacocks moved with slow elegance from the shadow of a tree, and one, suddenly, spread its tail into a magnificent fan, the eyelets shuddering and shaking. The baby moved violently, and she put her hand to her side, feeling a pain shoot around her and into her hip. She was so heartily sick of this pregnancy. She had become anxious about the pains of labour. More now even than before, when she had Tigran at her side. Yet she longed for it to come on, so she could be rid of it, this parasite that was eating her alive.

Just as she was thinking this, Madi arrived with a tonic drink for her and a tray of tiny dishes.

That evening she went downstairs and found Tigran waiting. He had sent a note to her asking her to please come to dinner on the terrace. She had toyed with refusing, but what did it matter? The pill Louis had given her was in her room. Somehow he had reassured her. Tonight she would be at rest.

Tigran rose as he saw her. He had dressed carefully for her. The perfect gentleman, the Arjuna she had known. He took her hand and bowed over it. Honouring her, moving her chair, helping her sit. She looked at him and could find nothing.

The servants came with some dishes: a stew of tender beef and potatoes; some vegetables from the hills, where spinach and peas grew; a dish of soft, pink peaches, ripe plums and raspberries, too, from the farm at the plantation. All the fruits and vegetables of Europe grew happily in the upper reaches of the hills, where the air was temperate. From the coastal plains to the jungles and high mountain plateaux, with all its climates, there was no gift this island could not bestow in abundance and beauty. Java truly was the home of the gods.

There was something she tried to remember. Something Nathanial had said about hunger, but she could not quite remember. How could there be hunger in Java?

They ate in silence for a while. Then Tigran spoke. "Charlotte, are you feeling better? Can I get anything for you?

She shook her head and toyed with her stew. She heard him breathe a sigh and put down his fork.

"I know you are angry with me," he said quietly, "but we must talk about the birth of the baby. Our feelings are something we cannot help for the moment. I am so heartily sorry for my treatment of you."

He wanted to add that she might have respected him more, not betrayed him, but he did not. "It is your well-being and that of the child which concern me. Would you rather go to Buitenzorg or stay here?"

Charlotte looked at him. In the candlelight she remembered how much she had cared for him, yet something, something, stopped her from caring any more. It was not Zhen. She had not thought of him for a long time. He had faded. She lay down her fork. She wanted to go away from them all. They all wanted too much.

"It is of no matter where I give birth to this child. Just so long as I can rid myself of it. Here is well enough," she said. She looked over at him dispassionately.

"Must you be present? At the birth?"

He did not know how to respond.

After she left, he rose and walked out onto the grass in the dark, towards the dimly lit path to the church. From the balcony, Charlotte watched him, then returned to her room. She took a glass of water and looked at the little pill in her hand.

35

The pains began at midnight. She was awakened from her befogged slumber. At first she thought they were in her dreams. She had taken a pill after dinner and lain back on the bed, letting the delicious sensation flow down her body, warming her, tingling, insulating her from pain, fear and sadness. Truly, Louis was right. It was as if she were lying in her mother's arms, all the comfort of maternal love washing over her. She had misty visions of her mother, her lovely face, her long black curls, and she, Charlotte, rested in her arms.

The contractions must have been proceeding for some time unknown to her, for, she realised, they were strong and close together. Her waters had broken, and this was what had awakened her. Here was bliss. This birth, under the beneficial effects of opium, would be put speedily behind her.

One of her maids, seeing her mistress awake, rose from the mat on the floor. Madi had made sure that two maids slept with Charlotte every night for the past two weeks, waiting for the labour to begin. Madi knew Charlotte had begun taking opium. She was not averse to this, for it calmed her and eased her mind. Since she had begun opium, her brightness had returned, and she ate well and had a pleasant demeanour even with Tigran, who had, Madi knew, begun to despair.

This was good for her and the child. Charlotte did not know it, but Madi had given her a brew of crushed poppy heads during her last labour. Had she not somehow come to this on her own, certainly Madi would have made her a mild potion from a recipe that her mother had passed down to her—a potion which soothed the worries of the world.

Madi liked to smoke opium with tobacco in the evening, after her work was done, for it eased the joint pain in her hands. She knew that though she might continue to chant to keep the jealous spirits at bay, her days as a birthing *dukun bayi* would be soon over. Perhaps this would be the last child she would deliver.

Madi was called and Tigran informed. Next they helped Charlotte to the downstairs bathroom, where the water was being prepared. Charlotte was given a strong brew to help the labour, which she took down in small gulps. She was still under the influence of the drug, Madi could tell, and this caused her to frown a little. Usually she gave a mild poppy brew to ease pain when the labour was well underway and the time to push arrived. She was not sure what would happen in this circumstance, and this uncertainty made her nervous.

Madi's assistants, her apprentices, helped Charlotte into the water, after Madi had taken oil and checked the dilation. She was pleased, relieved that the dilation was good. Tigran had sent for the doctor, to stand by in case of complications. The doctor was not well pleased that they only called for him *in extremis*, but Tigran paid him very well for his troubles, and he knew that many families in Batavia preferred these old methods of birthing amongst women.

The contractions continued, and Tigran relaxed. He had changed into a clean white sarong and was happy that Charlotte had settled into his arms to wait. He massaged her belly with warm oil. He had ordered the *gamelan* to play outside the window quietly, for it was a relaxing and hypnotic sound.

He had been surprised at Charlotte's change of heart when he had seen her next. He had gone to the church in utter despair and kneeled in front of the altar, where a single candle burned. He did not pray often, but he felt at the end of all thought. And, it seemed, God had answered.

She had returned to a semblance of liveliness. They took their meals together, and she seemed to find some enjoyment in his company. She was a little strange, perhaps, occasionally other-worldly and speaking little, on other occasions full of vitality. He was so relieved at her improved health and her newfound calm that he was happy to just let everything go.

Now, though, he was a little troubled at her lack of movement, her seeming lethargy in the midst of this labour. Then, as he massaged her belly, he realised that the strong contraction he had felt before had weakened. Charlotte, too, had become restless. She realised suddenly what was happening. She began to feel the pain of the contraction and moved back against Tigran. Madi felt the belly. There had been a sudden dropping-off in the strength of the spasm, yet pain had returned. The opium was wearing off, but the contraction had not strengthened but weakened. She could not make it out. It was outside of all her experience.

Charlotte grasped Tigran's hand. "I need more opium, Tigran, for the pain."

His eyes opened wide. Opium? Now he understood. Certainly Louis had given her opium, for he was the only person who came every day to see her. He must be a foolish man not to have seen the evidence of his own eyes. The evidence which lay everywhere he went in Java, from the opium dens of Chinatown and the *warungs* in the countryside to the great houses of Batavia, everyone, more or less, took opium. Occasionally, he took a grain in wine for pain.

He looked at Madi. "Does she take opium every day?"

Madi nodded. "It has relieved her, but perhaps she has taken a little too much."

Charlotte gripped Tigran's hand again as a contraction began. This one was stronger, and Madi showed her black teeth in a smile. Charlotte groaned and writhed in pain. She had gone from ease and comfort to this grinding torture.

"Opium, Madi, I need it."

"I will give her the poppy drink, but first we must watch the spasms," Madi said.

They lifted Charlotte, and Madi felt the dilation. It had moved on very slightly. Charlotte again moaned as a contraction came, faster now. Too fast, thought Madi. Everything was a little strange, the contractions changing in strength and timing. Charlotte looked up at Tigran in a fury. She spoke through clenched teeth.

"Tigran, by all that's right, give me something. Have you not punished me enough?"

Tigran looked at Madi with anguish, but Madi shook her head. She spoke quietly to Charlotte, stroking her hair. "Ssh, ssh. Not yet, the pains are not regular—you are not open enough. All is well, but we must wait. I will give you a drink to dull the pain, but not the poppy, not yet."

For two hours they waited. The contractions became more regular, close and hard. Charlotte gasped and groaned, sweat pouring off her. She had forgotten this hideous pain, like hot knives twisted in your back, between your legs. The wrenching, torturous feeling of being torn in two. As she felt the wave rise and squeeze, she cried out and gritted her teeth. Tigran lifted her onto her knees. He was desperate, feeling useless as she sank into this sea of agony. It gave some respite, as walking had done for a while, but below her waist she was now just one vast and excruciating wall of pain.

Finally, the urge to push came, and Charlotte cried with relief. Madi felt the dilation, felt the head of the baby engaged. Now Madi gave Charlotte the poppy brew, and she gulped it down. Within a minute, a sweet ease came over her—not so great as with Louis's pills, but the pain had diminished to the bearable. Charlotte was thankful and gripped Madi's hand. She threw a look of dislike at Tigran, so strong that he left her side to wait in the shadows at the edge of the room.

The birth attendants helped Charlotte, pushing down on her belly, helping each contraction. She was getting exhausted, Madi could tell. She had been too thin and weak, and despite all Madi's ministrations had had too little time to regather her strength. The baby was ready to be born, but Charlotte could not bear down strongly enough. Charlotte's head fell onto her chest, and she seemed to swoon. Tigran moved forward, frantic. Madi whispered to a maid, who was starting to cry out of fear for the mistress, and she ran away. Within a few minutes, she came back.

Madi took some finely ground pepper in her hand, waiting to feel the contraction rise, and put it under Charlotte's nose. Charlotte looked at her, eyes wide with consternation, but within a few seconds, she gave a great sneeze, followed by three more and the baby slipped quickly out into Madi's waiting hands and gave an angry cry.

It was over. The baby was cleaned and, when the pulsations had ceased, Tigran tied the cord with woollen threads and severed it. He had done this so many times. Now here was his child, a boy, his son by this woman he loved so much. Charlotte leant back on the cushions of the cot to which she had been moved, waiting for the final contraction to expel the placenta. The brew had done its work and she felt pain free but alert. She looked at Tigran holding his child. Thank God, she thought, it is over. He has his new boy. Never again. I never want another child.

Within thirty minutes, she was cleaned and wrapped and resting on her bed. Tigran brought the baby and she looked at him. He was red and squashed, as newborns are. She felt absolutely nothing for this child, just a deep relief that this trial was finished.

"Thank you, Charlotte, my darling. Thank you for this little boy." He took her hand and kissed it. "Can you forgive me?"

Charlotte looked at him and smiled, shrugged slightly. "I don't want to feed it. You must get a wet nurse." With that, she lay back and closed her eyes, sinking back into the visions of endless clouds and peace.

He frowned and took the child to Madi.

36

The carriage turned into the gates of Brieswijk and rounded the final curve, past the trees. Home, Takouhi thought, at last.

She was content. She had spent every day at the graveyard, sitting near the cupolas on a bench which she had caused to be placed under the shade of the tamelan trees, watching the workmen build George's tomb. During this time she had taken up embroidery, which she had done as a child with her stepmother. She would no longer dance, as she once had, the Javanese dances of the court. She had begun to feel age creep on her, knew it was because George was gone and there would never be another man, but she did not mind. To have had George's unswerving love for so long. To have loved him and found together a late, youthful passion with him. It was more than enough.

She had spent a great deal of time with Teresa Crane and her sisters and cousins. The da Silva family was one of great generosity and hospitality—too much, sometimes, when she simply wanted to be left alone with memories. She had gone more often to the Armenian church and found that prayer, especially in this place, gave her solace, for she was as close to George here as she could be. She had felt enclosed in his hands, his mind, remembering the building of this beautiful offering to the glory of God and the continuation, in faith, of a dispossessed people.

She had been part of a sewing circle, which good-hearted Evangeline had started when she discovered Takouhi's new pastime, to beguile her friend from sorrow. There were ten to fifteen women who had come after supper several times in the week. Some embroidered, some sewed children's garments and christening gowns. Evangeline made lace, the most exquisite lace: needle lace, bobbin lace. Her family came from Calais and had been lace-makers for generations. There were machines now, of course, but Evangeline still enjoyed the pleasures of *la dentellerie*, which she sold to raise money for the new church. Her lace and crochet work were so exquisite that she could command almost any price. The Arab and Chinese ladies, she had found, liked to wear lace under their garments as much as the European ladies did.

Robert and Teresa had dined once a week. She had had news of the birth of Tigran's second son, Adam, though strangely, Charlotte had not written to her for a long time.

Billy Napier, John Connolly and several of George's friends had come every Sunday to take tea and talk about old times and George. They had all promised George this: not to abandon Takouhi, no matter what.

Billy had proposed to Maria, and she had accepted him. He would adopt George's boy after the wedding. Takouhi had been glad, though she felt, in some measure, sorry for Maria. To pass from the arms of George to those of Billy ... but women often had few choices. George's son would have a good father, who would love him as he had loved his friend.

She rarely saw Maria, despite the proximity of their houses. If their carriages passed sometimes or they met, shopping, in the Chinese town, Maria would turn away. She had come, once, to the cemetery and seen Takouhi and turned back. Takouhi had been sorry and through Billy had told Maria the times when she would be there so that Maria could come to George's grave if she wished. She had realised that she needed to leave soon so she would stop haunting this young woman's life.

Finally the day had come when George moved residences and the ceremony had been completed with a memorial service at the church. She had laid great garlands of white perfumed jasmine flowers on his tomb and in the cupolas and written to Tigran and asked him to send *Queen of the South* for her and her things. She had left instructions with Billy to sell the house and everything in it. There were memories here, and for months she had walked the rooms and the garden, basking in them.

Then it was time. From the sitting room of Tir Uaidhne, she had heard the church bells ring out for Billy and Maria's wedding and knew little George would be safe.

And now she was home. She had heard little from Batavia for these many months. Tigran wrote of the children and work and some of their acquaintance. Charlotte he mentioned as "well." She had written not at all, and now, as Takouhi got down from the carriage, she had a sudden sense of foreboding.

She stepped inside the hall, and Jantzen came forward to greet her, his hands raised to his forehead. She was very happy to see him so well. She smiled at him and asked where the master was, the mistress. A slight shadow seemed to pass across his face.

She had known this man most of her life. He had come when she was sixteen, living back in Brieswijk, her vicious husband gone to Macassar. He had been a small slave boy who had grown up in Brieswijk. When Takouhi made Tigran free all the slaves, he had become Tigran's servant and took the name of the *mestizo* cook who adopted him and taught him the ways of the house. Within a few years, he had taken over the duties of the whole household. He now received a generous salary, and his wife made exquisite batik cloth which Takouhi bought at above-market price, for it was the finest in Batavia, and kept for herself or gave as gifts. They had five children. He knew he owed his freedom and much of his small fortune to this woman, and she knew he was a good, kind and irreplaceable man.

"What is it? Is something wrong?" Takouhi asked urgently

He bowed. "Mistress, the master said he will come soon from the Kota. The mistress is at the river. The children are with their *babus* in the garden."

Takouhi frowned. Something was going on here. She asked Jantzen to send some tea to the verandah and went out to look for the children. She found them under a tree to one side of the house. Alexander had grown tall. He was almost three, she calculated. She went up and looked at him, then sat on the grass, and he came up to her and sat in her lap. He remembered her, she could see, and she hugged him and kissed his cheeks and neck. He showed her the straw elephant which the *babu* had made for him, talking to her in Javanese, calling her *bibi*, auntie, and they chatted amiably. Then he got up and chased some birds from the grass, running fast, screaming, his *babu* in pursuit, calling to him frantically. She smiled. He was beautiful and strong. She could see his Chinese blood, but it would not be obvious to most people, for his eyes had something of Charlotte's, a lightness. She had seen Zhen in the town sometimes. Now she could see his height, his build, the strength of his face, in his son.

She went over to the hammock which Adam's *babu* was swinging gently and looked inside. The baby was fast asleep. She could not make out who he resembled, but he looked something like Meda when she had been a baby, his hair dark and unruly. She told the *babu* to stop and picked him up. He lay in her arms, and she rocked him and kissed him. It was wonderful, this constancy that nature gave. George had died, but his son lived. Meda had died, but somehow here she was reflected in this child's face. She put him back into the hammock. It was good to be back. She never wanted to go away from these children again.

Returning to the verandah, Takouhi sat, pouring tea and looking out over the grounds. She took from her bag a cardboard picture wrapped in silk. It was a daguerreotype which Gaston Dutronquoy had made of her and George.

She remembered with what excitement and almost trepidation they had set foot in his studio, which was in George's house at No. 3. George had taken a look around his old house and declared it quite splendid. There was a small theatre for amateur theatricals, and a production of the farce *The Spectre Bridegroom* was that night, the 14th of March. She would never forget that date. Robert and Billy had appeared, and it was hilarious, as such a play can be in a small settlement where everyone knows each other. Charlotte had laughed to tears, she remembered, at the sight of her brother in make-up. George had loved the idea of his house as a place of ribald humour.

There had been a taproom stocked with barrels of beer and wine where his inner hall had once been, and he liked it very well. They had giggled like children. They had posed for a brief time, and then, miraculously, they had this image of them both. Thirteen days later, he was dead.

Now she gazed at the picture, touched his hair, ran her finger down his cheek. It was, she thought, the most beautiful thing, better than any painting. It was the finest invention of mankind. With this miraculous machine, you could keep the ones you loved with you always. She desperately wished she had a picture of Meda. Faces faded, no matter how you strove to hold on to them. Now Adam would remind her of Meda, blessedly. And with this picture, she could see George's face at any time. It gave her the greatest comfort. Later she would take it to show Meda.

Finally she heard footsteps and raised her head. Tigran came out onto the verandah and she stood at his entrance, shocked. He looked gaunt. She took him in her arms.

Tigran held on to his sister, glad she had come. When he had received her letter to send the brig, he had closed his eyes in relief. He loved her. She understood everything about him, about Charlotte. Surely she would know what to do.

They sat down, and she poured him some tea. "What is happening here, Tiga?" she demanded.

Tigran took off his coat, trying to think how to explain this, where to start. He told her of his discovery of Charlotte's affair with the Chinese man. Takouhi looked down. She had known about this and had not told her brother. She was as complicit as Charlotte; she had been heedless of everything but George. It had been as if no one else existed.

She kept silent as he related the whole story: his punishment of her, the terrible voyage, the hard birth, the opium. On the third day after the birth, she had lapsed into a fever. Madi had given her *jamu* drinks, cleansing baths. It had lasted five days, and when it finished, she was very weak. But she had recovered. Tigran had determined then to put an end to their estrangement. She had nearly died. He had horrible dreams of Surya. Charlotte asked for the opium, and he wanted to give her what she wanted. With it she rested; he could see that, and she was in good humour when they were together; she ate well.

Louis brought her supplies and spent days at her side. She took no interest in either Alexander or Adam, however, and he had grown concerned. She had recovered her health and a degree of vitality. He wanted her to come back to him, to his bed, but when he had said this, she had simply looked at him as if he were demented. "Come to your bed!" she had said and laughed. "Make another child, so you can finally kill me."

He had been struck as if by a thunderbolt. Everything had gone terribly wrong. Once, Charlotte had even disappeared into Chinatown with Louis, to smoke opium, like the Chinese do. The damn stuff had taken over her life. He wanted to confine her, to stop this, but he did not dare. Once before he had done it, and he felt ashamed. It had turned her against him.

Takouhi took Tigran's hand. "I know opium. It is good for pain and for sadness. I took this when was I young and had trouble. Usually it is good. I sometimes make poppy tea. After George died, it was helpful for me to rest my mind. Maybe she is taking too much?"

"Taki, I don't know, but something ... we must do something. Charlotte and I have no life, no wedded life, no family life, no social life."

Takouhi rose and looked down towards the river. She could see the carriage pulling away, bringing Charlotte back to the house.

The moment she saw Takouhi, Charlotte ran into her arms, thrilled to see her friend. She had had such a lovely day at the river. The colours and shadows blended into phantasmal shapes, and even the wind could speak.

That night, in her room, Takouhi brushed Charlotte's hair. "Charlotte, Tigran is worried about you." she said.

Charlotte turned to face her. "Tigran is worried about everything. He worries too much." She laughed and turned back to the mirror.

Takouhi thought a moment. "Alexander and Adam look well. Do you think? Alex so big now."

Charlotte frowned. She was starting to feel agitated. She had taken her last pill before lunch, and now it was time for sleep. She wished Takouhi would go away so she could get into bed. She yawned.

Takoui stopped brushing, kissed Charlotte on the cheek and said goodnight. She went to Tigran, who was sitting disconsolately on the terrace.

"It seems that she has come to need opium to sleep. She became anxious when she was ready to take the next pill. Tiga, you and I take opium. Many people we know use opium from time to time. Why can we stop and ignore it, and she cannot?"

"I don't know." He looked at his sister. "Is it because she is so very unhappy? Do you think? You can die from unhappiness. Surya did."

He put his head in his hands. "It began on the ship," he said. "She was so pregnant and so distressed and, no matter what the reason, I made everything unbearable for her and Louis came and gave her something which made her feel well. Then the birth, which was hard ..." He raised his head as if something had suddenly occurred to him.

"I am responsible. She sees me and remembers misery. God help me. That is the truth."

He looked at Takouhi. "Should I bring happiness to her? Should I ask this Chinese man to come?

Brother and sister stared at each other. Neither spoke for a long time.

"You and I have not had easy lives," Tigran said finally. "We lost our mothers young. You had a vicious marriage. But we both had happiness too. I had Surya for a while. You had George and Meda a long time. These are blessings. And Charlotte, I wanted her. She did not want me."

He stopped.

"But she learned to care for me, give herself to me, because I was generous and patient. I don't know, Taki, but I think I have to ask him to come."

The memory of the first time he saw Charlotte came flooding back. He had been complacent, his wealth assured, his children grown, a man who strove for nothing more than a peaceful life, and she had walked into the room. She had been dressed in a robe the colour of her eyes; she was like a scent made corporeal, a whisper of lavender turned to woman. He had been lost to her from that moment. Now he had half-killed her.

He made up his mind.

He rose and went to his sister, leaned down and kissed her cheek. "Good night, Taki, thank you for coming home."

In his room, he took up his pen. He wrote to Robert, telling him of Charlotte's state of health, how for one reason or another she had come to depend on opium. He asked him, confidentially, to speak to the man who was Baba Tan's son-in-law, ask him to come to Batavia. He knew that Charlotte cared for this man; Robert must understand that this was all that was important now. Zhen was Chinese; they knew about opium, and he was also a man who knew about Chinese medicines. Tigran knew Madi used some of the remedies from the Chinese herbalists in Glodok, but he could not trust her with this. He had gone beyond pride or righteous anger. Perhaps if she saw a face of one she loved and trusted, as clearly she no longer did him, this would help. He was at the end of his tether, and for Charlotte' sake, he wrote... .

Tigran could hardly believe he was inviting this man into his house. He put down his pen, stretched his neck and stared at the candle.

37

Tigran had rarely been to the Gong Guan, the offices of the Kapitan Cina and the Chinese Council in Batavia.

He had met Tan Eng Guan on several occasions at his compound on Molenvliet West, however, for the leader of the Chinese community entertained his wealthy compatriots and the Dutch community frequently and lavishly.

Long before the Portuguese and Dutch had come to Jayakarta, a Chinese community had existed here. They were indispensable to all the colonial cities in the East. Colonists were invariably a small group of men, dependent on the large communities of peaceful and industrious Chinese for almost everything. In the Dutch Indies, every possible consumable item was made or supplied by the Chinese: they ran the sugar plantations and factories; through the farm system, they controlled the tolls, the markets, the river transport, the *wayang*, the arrak trade, the opium farm, the gambling farm, money-lending. For the organisation of all this, they paid the Dutch government valuable concessionary taxes and relieved the Dutch bureaucrats of a heavy administrative burden. The colonial government might be the artery of trade and the Javanese peasant the agricultural heart, but the Chinese were the veins linking the two in an efficient web of networks which profited themselves and the Javanese Regents and, most importantly, the Dutch rulers.

The massacre of 1740 had taught them this lesson very starkly. Tigran was not amongst those who resented the Chinese. He knew the charges laid against them. They were the *bloedzuigers* of the Javanese peasant through money lending, which year upon year mounted drastically. They charged too much for the road and market tolls. But Tigran found them courteous, industrious and clever. A certain ruthlessness in business was not unusual, and he sometimes found it strange that the Dutch, who were hardly gentlemen in the world of closed and monopolistic commerce, should criticise them. All the laws they worked under were those made by the Dutch and could be improved at any time to the benefit of the peasantry. The Dutch chose not to do so, for the status quo suited them very well.

He knew of the massacres, occasioned by suspicions and resentments, which had led to the indiscriminate killings of 8,000 Chinese.

On the wall of the Chinese Council hung a large board carved with red characters. Tigran had been told that it read:

Since the appointment of the first Chinese headman, eleven kapitan had already served for a hundred peaceful seasons until in 1740, when weapons were suddenly taken up. Creatures grow and wither away, that is how the ultimate embracing of life and its negation, good and bad, were destroyed alike; the excellent and depraved befell the same misfortune. How can this be expressed in words? But by the spring of Ren-wu (1742,) the disturbances came to rest. The great King Banxinmu promoted Wei Hanlin to serve as kapitan; then the Gong Guan council was established. Their virtuous hearts assist the people; with civilising teachings, all reach the path of virtue!

Tigran knew that Banxinmu was Governor-General Van Imhoff, who had swiftly recognised how much the Dutch needed the indefatigable industry and intelligence of the Chinese. They had been moved outside the old city walls, to Glodok, to separate them from the Dutch, but the Council had quickly been established and renewed Chinese immigration encouraged. The Dutch government charged a head tax on them, which accounted for a quarter of the revenues of Batavia. For their own people, the Council ran orphanages, schools and a hospital, the temples and cemeteries, settled grievances and disputes, gathered taxes, registered births, marriages and deaths.

The Kapitan Cina's private residence was an extensive series of compounds of curved-roof buildings, surrounded on all sides by high walls. He had sometimes wondered why the Chinese houses were so contained—secret worlds within themselves. They had an ancient, quiet charm, these courtyards over which a veil of incense always hung. The entertaining areas, which in general were all anyone was permitted to enter, were highly decorated in carved wood, red and gold, covered in symbols which were particularly auspicious: fish, cranes, peaches, ducks and lotus pods. Huge, six-sided glass lanterns etched with characters lit the rooms. Along one wall stood a massive four-part screen decorated with precious stones, mother-of-pearl and jade, depicting the four seasons. Beyond lay a world unseen and unseeable.

Like the Dutch women in Holland, Chinese women were banned from leaving China, and Tigran knew the Chinese men also took mainly Balinese wives or married within their own community. They preferred the Balinese above all others—for their looks, of course, but also because the Balinese had no religious objection to the preparation of pork, as the Mohammedan women did. Tigran understood that Tan had many wives and consorts. As rich as he was, Tigran knew his wealth paled in comparison to the wealth of many Chinese merchants.

Tigran stepped up to the plain red door. He had walked from his offices on the Kali Besar to this unprepossessing Chinese building in Jalan Tiang Bendera. At his approach, the door swung open, and he was ushered inside. Immediately from one of the rooms at the side, Tan came out to greet him. Tan knew Tigran quite well from social occasions and because Tigran had once offered him a very comfortable berth on his brig to travel to Semarang when no junk could carry him. The Manouk household employed many Indies-born Chinese—in their offices in Batavia, in the plantation as scribes and comptrollers, and especially in their sugar factories at Semarang. Tan had been surprised by this rather strange request to facilitate a meeting of these two men who seemingly had little in common: a wealthy Armenian merchant in Batavia and the son-in-law of Tan Seng, whose mission in coming to Batavia was to talk to him of a marriage between their two houses, a proposition which had certain attractions.

Shaking hands, the two men went into a room where there were a thick, marble-topped table and some hard Chinese chairs. Once tea was served, Tan raised a long-nailed finger to a man nearby and spoke to him quietly.

Tan's Dutch was good, and they chatted for a moment before the man returned. Behind him stood Zhen, who bowed to the Kapitan and Tigran. His face was completely impassive. You could never tell what they were thinking, mused Tigran.

Tigran stood, turned to Tan and said in Dutch, "Thank you for making this meeting possible. It is an entirely personal matter, and I am grateful for your discretion."

Tan inclined his head. One of his most important duties as Kapitan Cina in this town was to make affairs run smoothly between the Europeans and the Chinese. He left the two men alone.

Tigran sat and motioned Zhen to a seat. "Do you prefer to speak English or Malay? I cannot, I'm afraid, speak any Chinese," he said.

Zhen sat and looked at this man. He had understood it was about Xia Lou. Something was wrong. She had got involved with opium. He had been horrified to learn this, for Zhen had seen the effect that opium had had on his own family. His father had become its ruinous slave, and still was. Zhen sent money back to China every month to keep his family from penury. He planned to bring his younger brother to Singapore, but as yet it was impossible, for he was charged with helping the eldest brother with their father and with the small business Zhen had financed in Fujian. The quantity of opium his father required never ceased growing, and Zhen paid for all this without demur: it was his duty. But he had seen how, gradually, this drug had eaten his father alive, and he could not believe this was happening to Xia Lou.

"I speak English. You want me to help Xia Lou? She is sick?"

Tigran was glad the man had come straight to the point. He would like this done with quickly. It was bad enough to have to call on this adulterous swine whose child he was raising. Tigran had no intention of having him meet Alexander, whose features he could see on this man's face.

"Charlotte is, I think, deeply unhappy," Tigran said. "The birth of our second son was difficult, and she became ill. I think it would be helpful for her to see you." He looked Zhen in the eyes. "I do not want you, I assure you, in my wife's life. I am aware that you are not an honourable person."

Zhen's eyes narrowed slightly but he said nothing, and Tigran became annoyed at the man's silence.

"You lay with my wife? You have a wife. Did you think of this, that Charlotte is *my* wife?"

"She is my wife first. I married her long ago."

Tigran stared at him and rose. "What are you talking about?"

Zhen rose too and the two men stood facing each other, hard-eyed. Tigran felt his hand trembling, aware of the *kris* at his back, wanting to strike this insolent beast, kill him for the mockery he had made of his marriage, for crushing Charlotte's love for him.

Zhen too felt a fury which he was attempting to keep under control. He moved away, putting space between them. "Not in your white man church, but before Chinese gods, before Heaven and Earth, she is my wife. That is all I will say. I want to help her."

Tigran tried to calm himself. The fellow imagined himself wed to Charlotte in some appalling pagan rite, justified in every vile thing he did. God in heaven! He shook his head and waited until his voice was steady.

"Yes, I want to help her too. That is the only reason I do not kill you this very minute."

Zhen smiled inside. The man had guts, for though he was sure the fellow could use the *kris* he doubtless had on his body somewhere, he, too, carried a weapon and was, in addition, quick on his feet. He had been the *hong gun*, the enforcer, of the secret society for years. This old man held no terrors. The threat came from his insecurities. Xia Lou was more important.

"Thank you." He bowed very slightly. "Take her away, far from here where she cannot find opium, where she has no one to turn to for opium. Is there such a place?"

Tigran felt rather than heard the insolence in his voice, but he calmed down. After all, he himself had asked the man to come. "Yes, in the hills," he replied.

"Take her there. Leave message how to go there here at the Gong Guan, and I will join you in two days. Let her have opium until then. Do not tell her about me. Let her be calm."

He bowed again and left the room. Tigran stood, stunned at the man's swiftness, and shook his head. What on earth was he getting them into?

305

When Tigran returned to Brieswijk, Charlotte was on the verandah with Takouhi. She smiled at him as he came to the table and let him kiss her cheek. She looked well. What was this stuff which she could not give up but which made her so sweet-natured? It was not her true nature, of course. It was a different kind of sweetness. On opium, she took little interest in her children, did not care about her life here, did not care about anything. She only cared about the opium, her new lover.

That evening he spoke to Takouhi. The children would stay at Brieswijk. They themselves would go to Buitenzorg tomorrow and wait for Zhen. Takouhi put her hand in Tigran's.

"You are remarkable man, Tiga, to bring this man you dislike to your home."

He smiled at her, ruefully. "I do not like it, but the alternative is worse. To take a little opium is very well, good for her health. But she takes it to cloak her misery, and I fear it will turn her into a wraith. She married me because she trusted me, not because she loved me, and I have killed that trust. I must restore her mind."

He gazed out into the darkness, and Takouhi was not sure what visions he saw there.

"When she is well, I will think what to do."

38

Charlotte turned from the terrace wall. The mountains and the tea plants looked wonderful in this light. She could sit for hours watching the shifting play of sunlight and cloud making formations against the sky. She had begun to write poetry.

Takouhi came to her side and they walked arm in arm back up the hill to the house. As they crested the last small hillock, the house came into view. She looked at the two men standing there like shadowy figures. Then, suddenly, there was a startling clarity. It was Tigran and Zhen. She frowned and moved forward. Zhen took her hand.

"Hello, Xia Lou," he said. Charlotte, with a smile of pure joy, went up to him. He touched her cheek, looking into her eyes. He could see the contracted pupils. She moved into his arms, laying her head against his chest.

"Thank you for coming," she said quite formally. Zhen dropped into a chair, bringing her onto his lap, and held her face on his shoulder. Soon, he knew, she would wish he had not come at all. She would want him gone. But now she curled up into him.

Tigran stood watching as this man tenderly wrapped his arms around her. He could sense the waves of love emanating from them and turned on his heel. He went to the stables, mounted his horse and galloped out into the hills.

Zhen moved Charlotte onto a chair. He bowed to Takouhi. "I know it is very difficult for you and your brother. I am sorry for this. I am grateful that your brother has such courage. I will make her well."

Takouhi nodded her head. She, too, had seen how much this couple loved each other and was inescapably reminded of George.

They talked a little while Charlotte held his hand. Charlotte, she knew, had taken opium after lunch. Between waking and lunchtime, Charlotte seemed to have no need of it. It was as if she simply scheduled it into her day, like bathing, or writing letters. "Very well," he said. "Tonight I will make her some herbs, which will make her sleep deeply."

When Tigran returned, he found Takouhi and Charlotte together. Zhen was not present. Walking, Takouhi said. In the hills. She had sent one of the men with him to guide him. He had made a brew for Charlotte after dinner, before she had time to go to her room. What the startled natives would make of a large Chinese man striding through their villages she was not sure.

Zhen did not return until the evening had begun to draw in. Charlotte went up to him without a backward glance and took his hand. Tigran and Takouhi left them to eat alone. Zhen hardly touched his food, which, in any case, he did not much care for, but Charlotte ate heartily. Tigran could hardly bear watching her with him. They saw him pour her the drink and give it to her. She took it and drank without a thought. Tigran knew she did this only because she trusted him absolutely.

In fifteen minutes, Zhen took her into his arms, half-asleep, and carried her to the bedroom, kissing her until she fell asleep. Tigran did not want to think what had occurred in the bedroom, overcome with doubt at letting this man into his house, yet somehow succumbing to the inevitability of this decision.

"What will happen?" Takouhi asked.

Zhen had come to say good night, but now he sat. The brother was, understandably, aloof, but the sister seemed very kind. He suddenly remembered that he had made love to Charlotte in this woman's magnificent house in Singapore and felt somewhat uncharacteristically abashed.

"Tomorrow morning she will wake, and she will not feel good. I will be there. I will sleep in her room." He threw a glance at Tigran. "On the floor. Just a mattress and some bedclothes in front of the fire. It is cold here. The mountains are beautiful, remind me of Fujian, my home. But I am not used to it."

Takouhi smiled, liking him, and called a servant.

"Her stomach will ache and her bowels will go loose," Zhen said. Opium always ... mmm ... stop the bowel. She will feel sick and feverish, eyes, nose, lots of liquid, trembling. It will be at least fifteen hours since her last pill. I will give her medicine to help these feelings. The fire must be kept all night and in the day in the house. She will feel very cold."

Zhen had made a calculation of how many grams Charlotte had been taking. He was not sure how she had started or how much she had taken, but he knew she had recently progressed to two pills a day. He had seen them. This was not good over such a short period, only six months. Some people, he knew, accustomed themselves quickly. But she was eating opium, not smoking it, for which he was grateful. It was infinitely harder to cure a smoker, for some reason he did not understand. He guessed it was the effect of smoke on the *qi* breath, but thought no further.

"She will ask me for opium, she will ask you. She will be angry at all of us. It is we, not her, who have made this decision," Zhen warned them.

Overnight, Zhen dozed a little. It was strange to be here in front of a fire with her sleeping nearby. He rose, drawing a blanket round his shoulders, and looked at her. The herbs were powerful; he knew she would not wake for hours. Every night he would give them to her so she could rest. In the day, he would give others, for the cramping, the spasms, the terrible aching limbs. He hoped it would be quick, perhaps ten days before all the symptoms went away. It was tempting to undress and lie with her all night, holding her, for perhaps tomorrow she would begin to dislike him.

"Not forever, Xia Lou. You will not dislike me forever," he murmured. He bent over and kissed her soft lips and went back to the fire.

When she woke, it was because of a churning ache in her bowels. She sat up, alarmed, and Zhen rose from the chair where he had sat watching her for the past hour. The servant was building the fire. He went to the door and called her maid. Together they went to the commode. Zhen took up the drink he had made for her, and when she came out, he helped her back to the bed and put the glass to her lips.

"Zhen." Charlotte looked perplexed; she trembled and pushed away the glass. Her nose was running and her eyes liquid; she felt feverish. She leaned over to the drawer and opened it for the pillbox, but it was gone.

He looked at her. "Drink this, Xia Lou, you will feel better."

She frowned. "Feel better, Zhen? If you give me my pillbox, I will feel better immediately."

Another wave of nausea struck her; her legs ached, and a deep wrenching pain in her stomach doubled her up. She looked at him.

"Zhen, please. What are you doing?

He put the glass to her lips. "Drink, *xiao baobei*, quickly, for me."

She shook her head but took the drink, which was bitter and sweet, and swallowed it, shuddering. Within a minute, the nausea passed and the ache in her stomach lessened. She started to panic with the sudden realisation of what was happening. Only now did she wonder why on earth Zhen was here.

"You! You do this. You and Tigran. I want to see Takouhi."

He took her hand. She tried to pull away, but he held her. He needed to make a diagnosis. He felt her pulse, which was rapid and thready on right and left. She was shivering but sweating, her muscles were in spasm. The kidney and liver were yin deficient in heat; the weakness and looseness of the bowel were a spleen *qi* deficiency; her agitation and anxiety showed liver *qi* stagnation. He knew what to do. The mixtures of medicines and acupuncture would relieve the symptoms, allowing her time to find balance.

He sat on the bed and took her in his arms. She struggled, but he would not let her go. "Xia Lou, all will be well, *xiao boabei*." He sang his mother's lullaby to her and rocked her and she relaxed.

"Xia Lou, you trust me, yes?

The drink he had given her had eased her ache. Being in his arms had eased her panic.

"Yes, Zhen," she said, head against his chest.

"Good, my heart. You have to stop the opium." He felt her tense and began rocking her again. "You have to stop the opium. I will make it easy for you."

He took up a thin needle from the bedside table and showed it to her. "This is China way to ease pain and feel better. Does not hurt."

He put the needle in his hand and let her touch it; then he took another and inserted it gently into her hand. She felt the slightest feeling, not pain, and as he moved the needle gently, her hand grew warm. He stopped and took it out.

"I am going to put these needles in your ear." He lifted her head and kissed her, softly, deeply, willing her surrender. "Sounds strange but works very well. Yes?"

Charlotte nodded, obeying him. His kiss was like honey, almost better than opium.

"First kiss me more," she said, and he smiled at her.

"Later, after the needles, I will kiss you until you say stop." He took up the hair-thin needles he had placed on the bedside table. Holding her head gently, he put them into her ear, manipulating them. Her ear began to tingle, and a feeling of warmth and relaxation spread down her body. He lay her back on the bed, covered her and moved beside her, holding her hand. He began to tell her of his father's addiction, what it had done to him and their family, how he hated it. An hour later, he took out the needles and gave Charlotte another drink. He explained what she could expect over the next few days.

She turned into his body, snuggling into his arm, still trembling. It would take time but he knew, now, it would be well. The addiction was of short duration. She would obey him, and the cravings would go. In four or five days the worst would be over. Then he would talk to Tigran. This situation had a remedy for this moment, but not for the years ahead.

When he came down with her in the afternoon, Tigran could see that whatever Zhen had said or done, she had surrendered to him. He had been right to bring this man. His love and his knowledge would get her over this. Even as he thought it, a feeling of leaden resentment filled his veins.

At dinner, Charlotte ate little, shivering, her nose and eyes streaming. When she became agitated, Zhen gave her the drink, which she gulped down. He carried out the acupuncture five times a day.

On the fifth day, he found Tigran when Charlotte had gone to sleep. Soon she would be well. It was time to deal with the cause.

"I must speak to you" Zhen said.

Tigran nodded. He had found a certain annoying respect for this fellow.

"Xia Lou will soon be well enough. I have explained the medicine to your woman. She knows herbs, she understands the treatment must continue many months. In three days, I will leave. This is problem I think. When I leave."

Tigran nodded again.

"Yes, that will be a problem. What do you propose?"

Zhen went up to Tigran, stood near, wanting to speak man to man.

"You are good man I think. I am not bad man. You love Xia Lou. I love Xia Lou. She is woman, Yin, tender, like flower, not strong like man. Sometimes when woman lose love, she can be very sad, more sad than man."

Zhen shook his head slightly. He could not quite explain his thoughts in English. Tigran knew very well his meaning. His thoughts had flown to Surya. But he was not going to help the man out.

"I think she love me, want to be with me. I want to take her back to Singapore with me. I am not rich like you, but I can give her a house, always love her," Zhen said.

"As your concubine, you mean? And what of our children?"

Zhen frowned. "Yes, children, this is big problem." It was a hideous, insurmountable problem. Zhen was Confucian enough to respect the bonds of family.

"Yes," said Tigran, the thought that Alexander was this man's child filling his mind. He turned away.

One thing was certain. When she was well, Charlotte must choose.

39

One morning Charlotte awoke and realised that she had no pain, no ache. She felt refreshed—not necessarily better than when she took opium, but somehow more aware of herself. The memories of what had driven her to this had surfaced, bright, without the dulling edge of the drug, but seeing Tigran and Zhen together had reassured her. The feeling of utter hopelessness had evaporated. She knew she must take the medicine for a long time, but it did not matter. She wanted, now, to see her children. Poor baby, little Adam, that she knew not at all. She could not even recall his face.

Zhen, too, had risen when he heard her. He went to her bedside, and she put up her arms and drew him to her. Ah! Lovely, lovely, to be in his arms. She still didn't know whether to tell him about Alexander. This admission seemed too shattering to utter. She knew the way the Chinese men felt about their sons. Knew, too, the way Tigran felt about Alexander.

Zhen sat beside her. She moved her hand under his soft jacket and ran it over the silkiness of his skin. She felt her desire for him return. She sat and put her lips to his.

He rose, for the first time pulling away from her. She felt his tension.

"Tomorrow I will leave. Xia Lou, you must talk to him."

She nodded, and he left the room.

She went to *la seraille* and took a long warm bath, inhaling the scent of the petals and fragrant oils. Ah! Java, she thought, so sensuous and rich. Why couldn't they just all stay here? Tigran and Zhen. She could love them both. As the thought strayed across her mind, she knew today she must make a choice.

She dressed, enjoying every simple gesture. Brushing her hair, looking at herself in the mirror, things she had forgotten she liked. She looked good; she had gained weight, and her skin was plumper and prettier. She had been too thin.

She went to breakfast. Zhen was not there, and a momentary flare of anxiety hit her.

Tigran saw her eyes. "He is walking, in the hills. They remind him of his home. He is a good man. You owe him a great deal, Charlotte," Tigran said honestly.

She sat, poured coffee. Did she owe him a great deal? Perhaps Tigran owed him a great deal. They had both conspired to rid her of her "habit", which she had rather enjoyed. But she had heard Zhen's story of his father, the overwhelming outpouring of the anxiety and resentment towards the sufferings opium had brought on him and his family, the hatred and contempt he had for it. Fiercely, imperiously, he had made her swear she would not go back, and she had understood and made him this promise.

"Since you like him so much, perhaps I should depart the scene and leave you two together," Charlotte teased.

Tigran smiled. She had found her nature again. No matter what, he was glad.

"Charlotte," he began, "I see you have found your wits. In that case, it is time for us to talk. I cannot bear ever to go through this again, and doubtless neither can you. We are not children, and we must find a solution."

He looked her in the eyes. His throat became dry, for he had absolutely no wish for what he was about to propose. He took a drink of coffee and steeled himself. "If you want a divorce, I will give you one."

He looked down and took a breath to calm his feelings.

"Dutch law requires a five-year separation before any official divorce. In the meantime, you need have no fear about money. The house in Singapore, a settlement, all can be arranged. You will be independent; you may choose your own way. I love you and our children. I would never see you in financial difficulty, of this you can be sure."

He felt drained. He had poured out these sentences as quickly as he could, before he could think any more about what he was saying. Charlotte made a *moue* and looked out over the hazy purple hills.

"The children, where would they live?"

"In Brieswijk. You cannot expect me to give up the children to a life of uncertainty. Alexander is my son, Charlotte, as much as Adam." He softened his tone. "But you could stay and be with them as much as you liked. I am offering you your freedom. The freedom to be with him."

Charlotte looked at Tigran. He would not give up the children; she saw it in his face. She had wanted him to love Zan, and he did; she could not reproach him for it now. All the reasons she had needed him before were still there. She loved Zhen, with an insane, desperate love. But she needed Tigran, though this love was of a different kind. She sighed.

When Zhen returned, she took his hand and they walked to the terrace wall, down to where the mountains kissed the valley, and asked him what their life would be together. He told her of the land on the hill, his plans to build a house. It would not be a conventional life for her, he could not offer that. But he would be hers forever; they would be together. Even as he heard himself say these words, he knew it was hopeless. But he had to ask her and hear the response from her lips.

She stood looking down over the shifting shades of endless cloud which wrapped this place and told him what he feared, although he understood as well as any sensible man could. Ties were here. He could not offer her marriage, social respectability, a proper home for her children. These things were important, he knew. He was Chinese.

He left the next day. He was angry, expressing in his manner a silent, hardly discernible sullenness. Angry at her or himself she was not sure. Again they would part in anguish.

Well, so, he said, she had made her choice. He faced her and took her by the arms, and she felt the force of his fingers gripping her. But, he said, do not come to me again unless it is forever. He dropped his hands and stood looking down at her.

"Unless you can accept this way, do not see me again. You understand, Xia Lou."

Her heart had contracted at these words, so firmly spoken, and she had felt a heaviness in her limbs, as if the blood in her veins had turned to molten lead. He meant it. He never said anything he did not mean. She bowed her head in sorrow, for what else was there to do? He stood silently looking at her. The fierceness dropped away like a discarded cloth, and he put his hand to her cheek. She felt doubt surface like bubbles. She nestled her head in his hand for a moment, and he held it still, as if to imprint the shape of her face on his palm. Then he turned and mounted the carriage, and in a second he was gone.

40

Tigran watched from the bedroom window as the carriage pulled away. It was over. She had made her choice. He dropped into a chair, half-drained, grateful she had chosen him. Tomorrow they would go back to the children in Batavia.

When she came upstairs and opened the door, he held out his arms. She sank onto his lap. She would never love him as she loved Zhen. It was unrealistic of him to ask it. Theirs was the love of first love, of youthful fire. She would be sad for a while, but not like before. He was glad he had given her a choice, glad she had chosen their family. Now it was time to be happy again.

When they arrived in Brieswijk, he knew that happiness was now a possibility. To his *babu*'s annoyance, she picked up Adam and spent hours with him. Alexander, who had forgotten her, gradually came to know his mother, though he adored his father more than anyone.

One night she came to Tigran's room and climbed into his bed. He had been half-asleep, but as he felt her hand move around his waist and onto his chest, he had turned to her. She showed him the wedding band, which she had put back on her finger.

"Yes," he said. "Yes," she answered, putting her hands into his hair, and they smiled at each other.

Miriam became a regular visitor to Brieswijk, and Charlotte found a different side to her character. Without her overbearing husband, she had a gaiety and lightness which was charming. Takouhi and Charlotte convinced her to change her hair, dress more in fashion, and now they were all friends. Captain Palmer had leased an estate at Meester Cornelis to install his harem, and Miriam and Takouhi decided to turn the house at Nordwijk into a school for girls.

Nathanial had returned from the East, filled with anger for what he saw there. Famine was threatening in Cirebon. Villagers were fleeing the harsh constraints of this endless and, for them, profitless production. They were rounded up for punishment before being forced back to the regions they had fled. The Dutch, Nathanial fulminated, were turning the richest land on earth into a place of starvation and misery.

Nathanial and Charlotte began a tour of Brieswijk. Here, at least, he hoped to have some influence. The private estates had self-interest at heart; the needs of the Dutch state did not concern them. He engaged Charlotte and Tigran in talk of the policies of liberalisation which the Dutch government could not find, though they made the soundest economic sense. Indigo headed Nathanial's list of abhorrent manufactures. There had never been such a noxious and crushing agriculture as this was for the Javanese peasant. To prove it, he took her to see the blue people.

For the first time, Charlotte crossed the Japanese bridge to the other side of the river. She could hardly believe that she had never done this before. The path led past the rice fields, some yellowing and ready for harvest, some springing fresh and green. The villagers planted the fields at different times to ensure a constant supply of new rice, and she found this chequered carpet of green and yellow a reassuring promise of abundance. After *sawah*, the wet rice fields, came the *tegal*, the dry fields where cucumbers, long beans, luffa vines and amaranth grew. Between were the big fish ponds, with beds of floating, leafy *kangkong*, the indispensible green vegetable of Asia. Nestled into a grove of long-leaved banana trees was a *madrassah*, a simple hut of bamboo posts and an *atap* roof; from inside came the boys' voices, raised like the sleepy droning of bumble bees, in recitation of the Koran.

They walked on. Rising above the rice paddies was a vast field of head-high green plants covered in masses of pink and violet blossoms.

"Indigo," said Nathanial. "The natives hate it because it is planted on the *tegal* fields where their vegetables and dry rice are usually grown. This crop here, on Tigran's land, is two years old and still close to the village. After it has been harvested, the field will be useless for years to come, for the plant exhausts the soil quickly. Nothing else will grow here.

In the Eastern provinces, this means the villagers must move constantly, opening up new fields further and further from their homes, walking hours each day. Even on Brieswijk, next year's crop must be sown on the other side of the forest, and this land must be left to recuperate."

Charlotte nodded. The field looked beautiful as they walked through it, but then, suddenly, she smelled an odour floating on the air, an odour so revolting that Charlotte could not breathe.

"The effluvia of the process," said Nathanial, putting a hand to his nose. He had warned Charlotte, and she took out a perfumed handkerchief. The stench grew stronger as they arrived at the factory, a series of three-stepped vats and drying and pressing moulds set inside a fenced area by a small stream.

The putrid smell rose from the first vat, where the plants were steeped in water, rotting and bubbling. The ground around the vats was bright blue. Charlotte had never seen anything like it, as if they had wandered into a deep lake. The stream, too, was streaked with the dye. A mountain of rotting stalks stood behind the factory, steaming in the sun, swarming with flies. Men, their arms and chests stained blue, blue splashes on their faces, sat disconsolately taking the final product from the moulds, cutting it into small, hard, dry cakes of iridescent dark blue. They did not look up even as this white woman came into the grounds.

"When the fermentation is complete, the plant is drawn down into the beater vat, where the detritus is picked out of the liquid by hand, and it is churned continuously with paddles for two hours to add oxygen until it turns green and then violet-blue. Then the indigo turns into specks and flakes and sinks to the bottom like mud," Nathanial explained.

Charlotte was feeling quite sick, but she felt she must see this through, for the men on the ground had haunted faces of abject misery.

"The clear water is drained from the second vat, and the mud is spooned into bags to drain overnight," said Nathanial. "The next day it goes into those moulds with holes, for pressing and drying."

Charlotte could stay no more, and Nathanial walked quickly away with her, back to the village, speaking quickly as they went.

"The men who enter into this noxious manufacture, I have ascertained, do not live beyond seven years and must endure this hideous staining, which causes them humiliating miseries. The production befouls the air and the streams."

Nathanial turned to Charlotte. "Charlotte, imagine this life. For this gruelling and disgusting manufacture, they receive no remuneration at all. It is part of the corvée. It is slavery, Charlotte, you can see. It must stop."

Charlotte put her hand on Nathanial's arm. She would speak to Tigran tonight, but, she added, Nathanial would have to talk to him, convince him perhaps to turn the fields to tobacco or some other equally profitable crop. He would have to give Tigran good reason to do it. Though he would want to heed her wishes, he would need an accounting.

Nathanial nodded in agreement, impressed by Charlotte's sound judgement.

It was not just to help Nathanial that Charlotte proposed to Tigran a voyage together, but she knew he was pleased and agreed, for her sake, to read a report by Nathanial on alternatives to the indigo production. She asked Tigran to show her the Spice Islands, for she wanted to go away with him in their brig, to cleanse it of bad memory. So, for a time, they left Nathanial to make his report and took *Queen of the South* and two other ships on a trading voyage to Surabaya and on into the Moluccas. She wanted to learn Tigran's commerce, and they both loved the sea. This ship had been a place of such misery to them both, but, now, standing in his arms, looking out over the night sea with its moonbeam trails, she saw that this contentment was love too.

As the months passed, she became Tigran's enthusiastic student, learning the business of Brieswijk and Buitenzorg, finding she was clever and quick, enjoying the evenings spent at his side discussing, to her amazement, crops, trade and liberal economics.

One day, Charlotte was attending to some papers at the desk in the bedroom at Buitenzorg. Tigran had been showing her the accounts for the plantation. Today they would tour the tea factory together. The fire was burning fiercely in the big fireplace, for it was early, and the day was chill. She looked up as she heard a distant clamour in the mountain silence. She rose and went to the landing and called to the housekeeper, but there was no answer.

Frowning, she went downstairs, worried for the children. She went immediately to the playroom and saw the *babus* together with Alexander and Adam before the fire. It was so cold that she had told them to play in the house until the mist went off the hill a little and the day warmed. Seeing her, Zander came to her side and took her hand. He so rarely did this that she was arrested by the gesture, and she heard him say, very quietly, "Papa." He wanted Tigran. She picked him up in her arms. "Papa is riding. He will come soon."

She smiled, but he pushed against her. He was so strong that she was forced to put him down, and he looked at her with his dark almond eyes and, without a word, ran towards the door. He was so fast and sometimes so reckless that she followed him, alarmed, calling the *babu*.

As she passed through the hall, which, even with two fires burning at either end was still cold, the noise of the commotion grew greater. The big teak doors stood ajar, and Alexander slipped through. She ran after him, calling his name. As she passed outside, she saw the reason for the commotion. The syce was trying to calm Tigran's horse, which was clattering its hooves against the flint of the courtyard, its eyes wild, panicked, sweaty. Charlotte stopped, her breath in her throat. She looked frantically back and forth, seeking Tigran. The *babu*, running and crying, grabbed Alexander. Servants gathered round, chattering and they all stood as the horse was calmed.

The gravity of the situation hit her. Tigran was not here! The two big black dogs which always ran by his side were not here. She let out a blood-curdling scream and fell to her knees. The syce was now shouting to the men, and the *mandoor* came forward, shouting orders. A search party: the master must have fallen. A man hoisted himself quickly onto Tigran's mare and calmly began to urge her forward.

Charlotte rose, aided by the housekeeper and her maids.

"No, no, no!" She felt a hideous premonition. She went to her room and sat before the fire, staring. This was to be her punishment. Not the children; it would not be the children, nor her. Whatever it was that needed to be appeased, it would take Tigran, the very best thing, the most worthy one, the white prince. This is what the dark world did. Charlotte fell to her knees, and for the first time in her life, she began to pray. She said his name over and over again like a mantra, sending out a protective mantle.

It was dusk when they found him. He had been thrown from his horse, which had been frightened, they thought, by a snake: nearby was evidence of a nest. The dogs had lain by him like sentinels. It was their whining and keening that had led the party to him. They had put him in the study on a bed. His neck had been broken. Charlotte had known he was dead the minute she had seen his horse without him. Alexander, too, had known. He had spurned her comfort and buried himself in the arms of his *babu*.

She rose, finally, wrapped herself in a woollen shawl and went slowly down the stairs to the study. It had been cleared of everything but the bed upon which he lay. The door stood open, and candles were laid about his bier and throughout the room. Villagers and servants sat silently around him. The estate manager was present, the housekeepers, the maids, as well as Madi, who had brought him into the world, all keeping vigil over him throughout this long night. His body had been prepared, she could see, cleansed and dressed in white, his arms by his side, a white cloth covering him from his waist to the floor.

The room was cold, the yellow flames of the candles merely the colour of warmth, without its substance. Her breath faltered on the frosty air. The breaths of those around him, too, rose in a brumal tapestry, floated fleetingly and was consumed by the darkness. In the midst of this ghostly host, Tigran lay, as if asleep, yet no breath came from him.

She stood transfixed. Raindrops spattered against the windowpanes beyond the thick curtains, like muffled tears. She could not see where he was broken and for a moment thought they had made a mistake. Then Madi begin to chant, quietly, a haunting Javanese song, and the sound was like a sorrowful sacrament. She stepped haltingly up to him and touched his cheek. It was glacial, like ice on the moors, and she recoiled in horror.

But he looked still so like himself that she went up again and put her warm hand to his cheek, looking on his face, so late beloved, and all repulsion disappeared. She leaned over him, the warmth of her breath swirling about his face like a dewy mist, and put her lips to his. She took her shawl and covered his body carefully, pulling it to his neck. Then she put her fingers into his hair and rested her head against his chest. He had left her this morning, left their warm bed and dressed quickly for his ride. He had come to her for a kiss, nuzzling her neck like a puppy, and she had pushed him away playfully because his nose, his cheeks were cold. She had not kissed him good-bye because he had felt cold. Suddenly she began to shiver, her body trembling at this terrible thing.

41

Charlotte and Nathanial left the chapel grounds. She felt bludgeoned by remorse, bruised with guilt. This man who had loved her beyond reason haunted her. For months after his funeral, in the midst of some activity, she would suddenly drift into misery. Every time she thought about it, she thought of her fault, his love and kindness which she had not even repaid that morning with one small kiss. This kiss grew in her mind until it took on enormous importance. She could not shake the idea that it was this that had separated Tigran from life and death: if she had taken him into her arms that morning, he would be alive now.

Charlotte plucked a gardenia flower and placed it carefully on the Balinese shrine. Tigran's grave lay nearby. Perhaps he would find Surya again, and his baby daughters. She felt in her heart that he had never truly recovered from that first love, that in some way she had been Surya's shadow. She shook her head. Delusion—delusion and guilt. She just wished it to be so, to assuage her own feelings. Nathanial, the man of science, of reason, had tried desperately to rationalise the events of that day, but he knew he was trying to help her fight a battle she had to fight alone.

They walked out into the park and looked down towards the distant silver gleam of the river. The pony trap was waiting, drawn by the same two gentle black-and-white ponies which had taken her on her first tour of these grounds. She moved between them, remembering, her hands caressing their soft noses, their big liquid eyes gazing at her. Nathanial helped her into the carriage. Charlotte took the reins and set the ponies at a clip down along the drive. She contemplated the vast grounds, now bathed in late afternoon light.

Tigran had appointed her legal guardian of their children and left everything to her: Brieswijk, the trading house, the plantations, the Singapore properties, all his vast fortune. She was now, undoubtedly, one of the richest women in the East Indies. This thought, too, left her exhausted with guilt. The oblivion of opium had tempted her, like a loving friend, to take him again into her arms, but her promise to Zhen and the thought of what humiliations and torments Tigran had endured to rid her of it gave her pause. Finally it was Nicolaus, who came with his own two children, with Alexander by his side and Adam in his arms, who gave her comfort, talking of his father, these little boys, of Tigran's legacy. Resolve took the place of withering, guilt-laden inaction.

Nathanial had given her Alexander Pope's *Essay on Man*, for he lived by Pope's words that "the proper study of mankind is man," and she found, within this book, an inspiration.

Such is the world's great harmony, that springs
From order, union, full consent of things;
Where small and great, where weak and mighty made
To serve, not suffer, strengthen, not invade;
More powerful each as needful to the rest,
And, in proportion as it blesses, blest;
Draw to one point, and to one centre bring
Beast, man, or angel, servant, lord, or king.
For forms of government let fools contest;
Whate'er is best administer'd is best:
For modes of faith let graceless zealots fight;
His can't be wrong whose life is in the right.
In Faith and Hope the world will disagree,
But all mankind's concern is Charity:
All must be false that thwart this one great end,
And all of God, that bless mankind or mend.

Charlotte had recently completed the papers to divide the trading house into equal shares between all of Tigran's children by both herself and his *nyai*. She had set out with absolute determination to find out if he had other children in the villages at Brieswijk, but none had been found. She had arranged a fund invested at the Javische Bank to help former slaves and to provide funds where need be to compensate those owners of slaves who agreed to manumission.

She ordered that the plantations at Buitenzorg and elsewhere should be managed as to increase the benefit to the native population, all taxes on rice land to be one fifth of the revenue and paid labour to replace the corvée duty. She knew from her new Dutch-English *mandoor* at Brieswijk that this produced far greater productivity than the corvée. She had appointed *mestizo* overseers, vetted by Nathanial, to all the estates and factories and enjoined them to propriety and good offices. The indigo farms were closed. The native villages were empowered to grow crops which could bring them profit and reject those which were unprofitable and caused harm, leaving this decision to consultation and their enterprise.

She had devoted herself to reading at the library of the Society and had come to believe in the liberal policies of Adam Smith, Von Horgendorp, Raffles and Muntinghe. Above them all was Nicolaus, Tigran's eldest son, responsible for all the business of the Manouk house, in whom she had absolute trust. She had given the shipping fleet to him, drawing a percentage of its revenues and keeping only *Queen of the South* as her ship, at her command.

She had made a generous bequest to Valentijna and a donation of sufficient largesse to the coffers of the Orphan's Chamber to ensure, finally, with the backing of Pieter Merkus, her husband's promotion to the position of Resident somewhere. She had kept to herself and her two sons absolutely Brieswijk and its revenues and the properties in Singapore. Takouhi and Miriam would live at Brieswijk, where their children and beloved brother reposed. Charlotte had made an annuity to Takouhi and Miriam's school and a grant of funds for the Armenian Church of the Holy Resurrection. It had taken more than a year, but she had learned a great deal, and the constant activity had helped her through her grief.

Now she contemplated her future. She knew she must go back to Singapore. She wanted to see Robert, take her sons to him. They could not stay here and be raised by Javanese maids. There were no proper schools in Batavia. They needed an English education if they were to take their place in society. She wanted them in the Institution at Singapore, learning Chinese and Malay perhaps, these little children of the East. She had already written to ask Aunt Jeannie to come to Singapore, to visit at least, perhaps to stay. And she wanted to sit by George's grave and talk to him. She wanted ... she was no longer sure what she wanted, or would even receive, from Zhen.

The pony trap arrived at the river. The sun was sinking slowly behind the great trees along the bank. A flock of white birds wheeled suddenly in the sky and swept in an elegant arc down to the water. She thought they must crash, for the river here at its very centre was shallow and ran clear and bright over the shingly bottom. At the last instant, though, they swung into a perfect formation, their white breasts and underwings flashing green and blue, reflecting the colours of the water in the light as they raced past. The luxuriant trees hung over the river, bamboo and wild sago, with leaves like ostrich feathers. In the forks of trees were tufts of lush green leaves living off the watery bark of their hosts and creepers spread long, flowering arms from branch to branch. The beauty of the ancient Javanese countryside suddenly overwhelmed her with its passionate wildness, its riotous and abandoned growth. Charlotte saw it as if for the first time, as if a veil had lifted. A rustling breeze brushed its fingers over the green rice stalks in the village paddies.

Nathanial turned to Charlotte. "You will go to Singapore?"

Charlotte looked at him. How she loved him, this perfect friend. She shrugged and took his hand. He did not know it yet, but she had also arranged a large sum to be paid to Nathanial after she left—for his studies, for his independence. She knew she was divesting herself of this money to pay back, to give back, to lessen her constant feelings of blame. This money, which was simply the material manifestation of Tigran's love for her, she was determined should be used only for whatever good she could do.

"I must," she said.

Nathanial nodded and fell silent. Now was not the time, but one day he would like to tell her how much he loved her.

She looked along the river, to the bathing pavilion. Slowly, she stepped down from the carriage and went into the Arjuna grove. The trees were in flower: masses of tiny white buds hanging like snowy tresses amidst the green. She stepped between the deep buttressed roots of a tree which surrounded her like loving arms and put her hands and cheek gently against the trunk. This was his grove, planted for him.

The wind moved quietly through the leaves and sent a shower of petals floating down, carpeting the ground. She pulled off a little of the white, stringy bark and wound it around her finger. Opening the silver and pearl locket which contained the miniature drawings Nathanial had made of Tigran and her sons, she placed the coil of bark next to a lock of Tigran's hair. She looked at his face, put his image to her lips, climbed into the carriage and sat. Waiting, waiting for something. For a sign, of forgiveness, she supposed, of peace. But all was silent, as silent as the jungle ever got, a calling of creatures, an incessant rustle. The river's rush above all.

She took up the reins with a sigh, remembering the day Tigran had taught her to drive the carriage.

Then, without warning, a ray of late, brilliant sunlight pierced the grove and shot a gleaming arrow along the river, down, down to the sea. It was like a lava flow, turning the waters to gold. They both gasped and looked at each other.

Charlotte enclosed Tigran carefully in her heart. To the last, he had been Arjuna, the perfect knight. Whatever awaited, it was time to walk into this golden stream. Time to sail back across the warm, shallow seas to Singapore and see if she could find again Arcadia.